ΛSTRONEER®

COUNTDOWN

SYSTEM ERA

TITAN
COMICS

ASTRONEER®

COUNTDOWN

GROUP EDITOR
JAKE DEVINE

DESIGNER
DAN BURA

ASSISTANT EDITOR
CALUM COLLINS

SENIOR CREATIVE EDITOR
DAVID MANLEY-LEACH

EDITOR
PHOEBE HEDGES

PRODUCTION MANAGER
JACKIE FLOOK

PRODUCTION CONTROLLERS
CATERINA FALQUI & KELLY FENLON

ART DIRECTOR
OZ BROWNE

SALES & CIRCULATION MANAGER
STEVE TOTHILL

MARKETING COORDINATOR
LAUREN NODING

PUBLICITY MANAGER
WILL O'MULLANE

PUBLICITY & SALES COORDINATOR
ALEXANDRA ICIEK

HEAD OF RIGHTS
JENNY BOYCE

ACQUISITIONS EDITOR
DUNCAN BAIZLEY

PUBLISHING DIRECTOR
JOHN DZIEWIATKOWSKI

PUBLISHING DIRECTOR
RICKY CLAYDON

GROUP OPERATIONS DIRECTOR
ALEX RUTHEN

EXECUTIVE VICE PRESIDENT
ANDREW SUMNER

PUBLISHERS
VIVIAN CHEUNG & NICK LANDAU

Astroneer: Countdown Volume 1, first published in March 2023, by Titan Comics, a division of Titan Publishing Group, Ltd, 144 Southwark Street, London SE1 0UP, UK. Titan Comics is a registered trademark of Titan Publishing Group Ltd.

10 9 8 7 6 5 4 3 2 1
First edition: March 2023
Printed in Spain
ISBN: 9781787739901

A CIP catalogue record for this title is available from the British Library.

ASTRONEER®

COUNTDOWN

WRITER
DAVE DWONCH

STORY & EDITING
MIA GOODWIN

ARTIST
XENIA PAMFIL

OUT OF BOUNDS

STORY & ART
JEREMY LAWSON

DECAF NOIR

WRITER
DAVID PEPOSE

ARTIST
ERYK DONOVAN

LETTERS
MIA GOODWIN

HAVE WE MET?

STORY & ART
MIA GOODWIN

SYSTEM ERA

TITAN COMICS

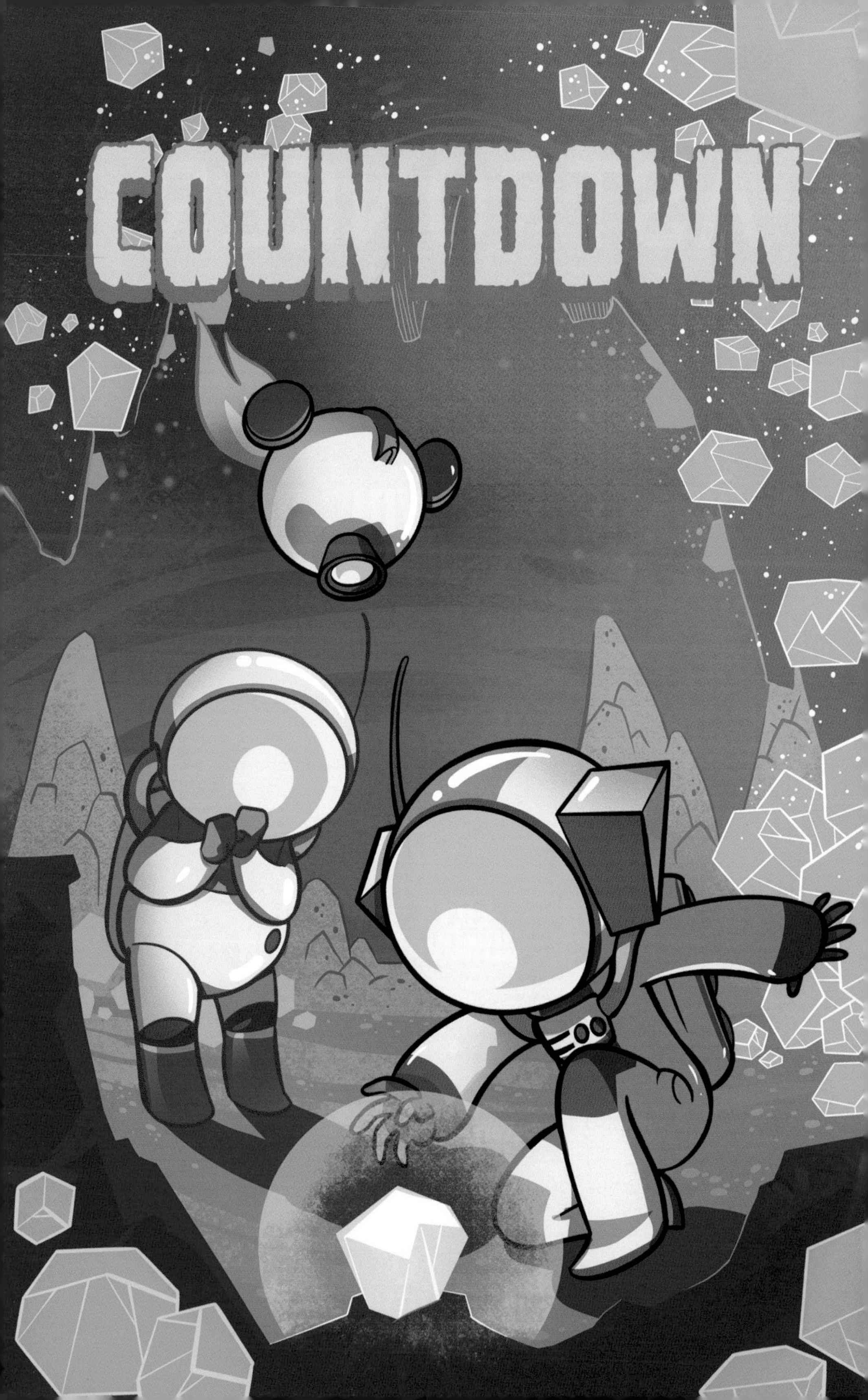
COUNTDOWN

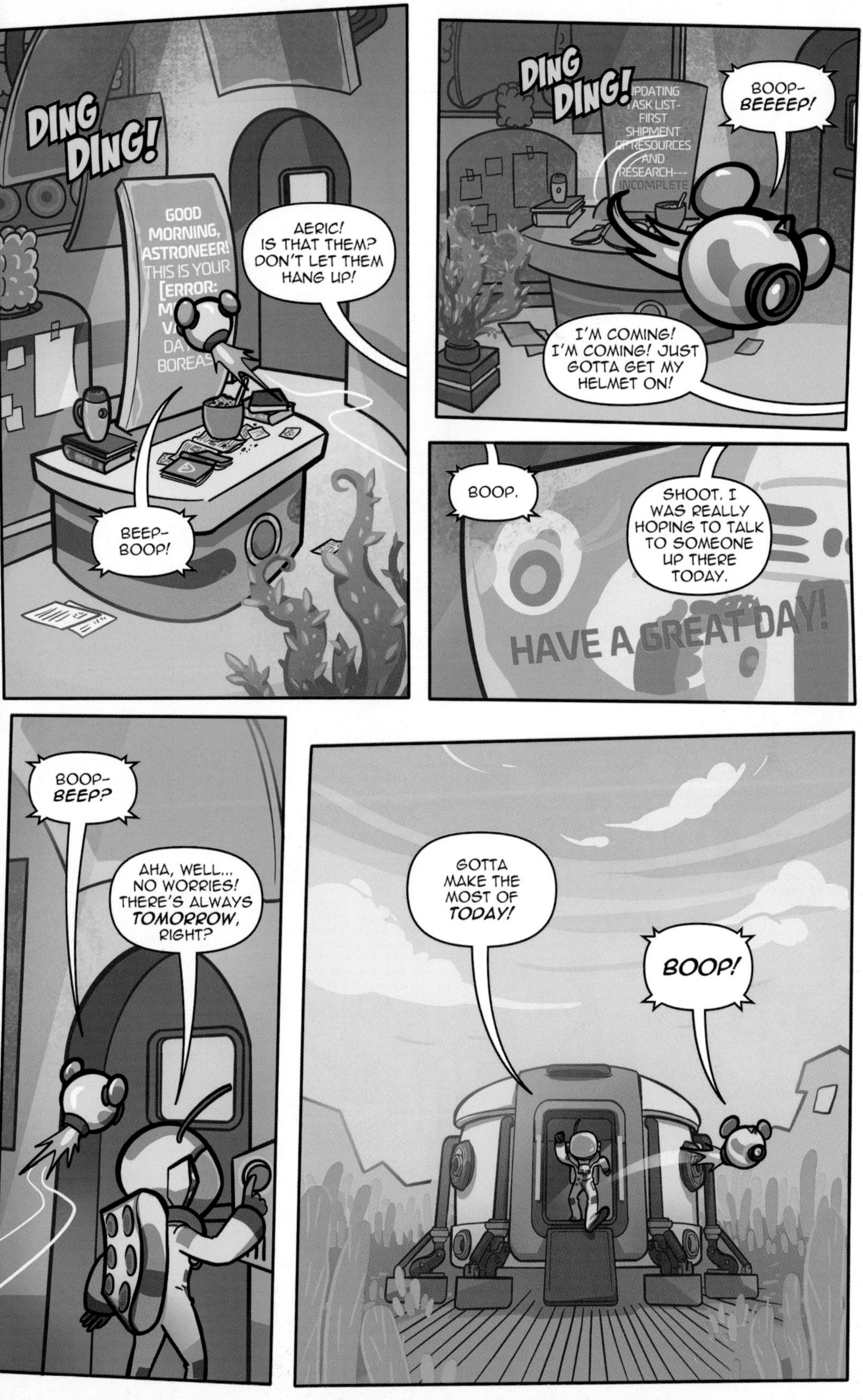
DING DING!
GOOD MORNING, ASTRONEER! THIS IS YOUR [ERROR:
AERIC! IS THAT THEM? DON'T LET THEM HANG UP!
BEEP-BOOP!
DING DING!
UPDATING TASK LIST- FIRST SHIPMENT OF RESOURCES AND RESEARCH--- INCOMPLETE
BOOP-BEEEEP!
I'M COMING! I'M COMING! JUST GOTTA GET MY HELMET ON!
BOOP.
SHOOT. I WAS REALLY HOPING TO TALK TO SOMEONE UP THERE TODAY.
HAVE A GREAT DAY!
BOOP-BEEP?
AHA, WELL... NO WORRIES! THERE'S ALWAYS TOMORROW, RIGHT?
GOTTA MAKE THE MOST OF TODAY!
BOOP!

ASTRONEER®
COUNTDOWN

Written by
DAVE DWONCH

Story and Editing by
MIA GOODWIN

Art by
XENIA PAMFIL

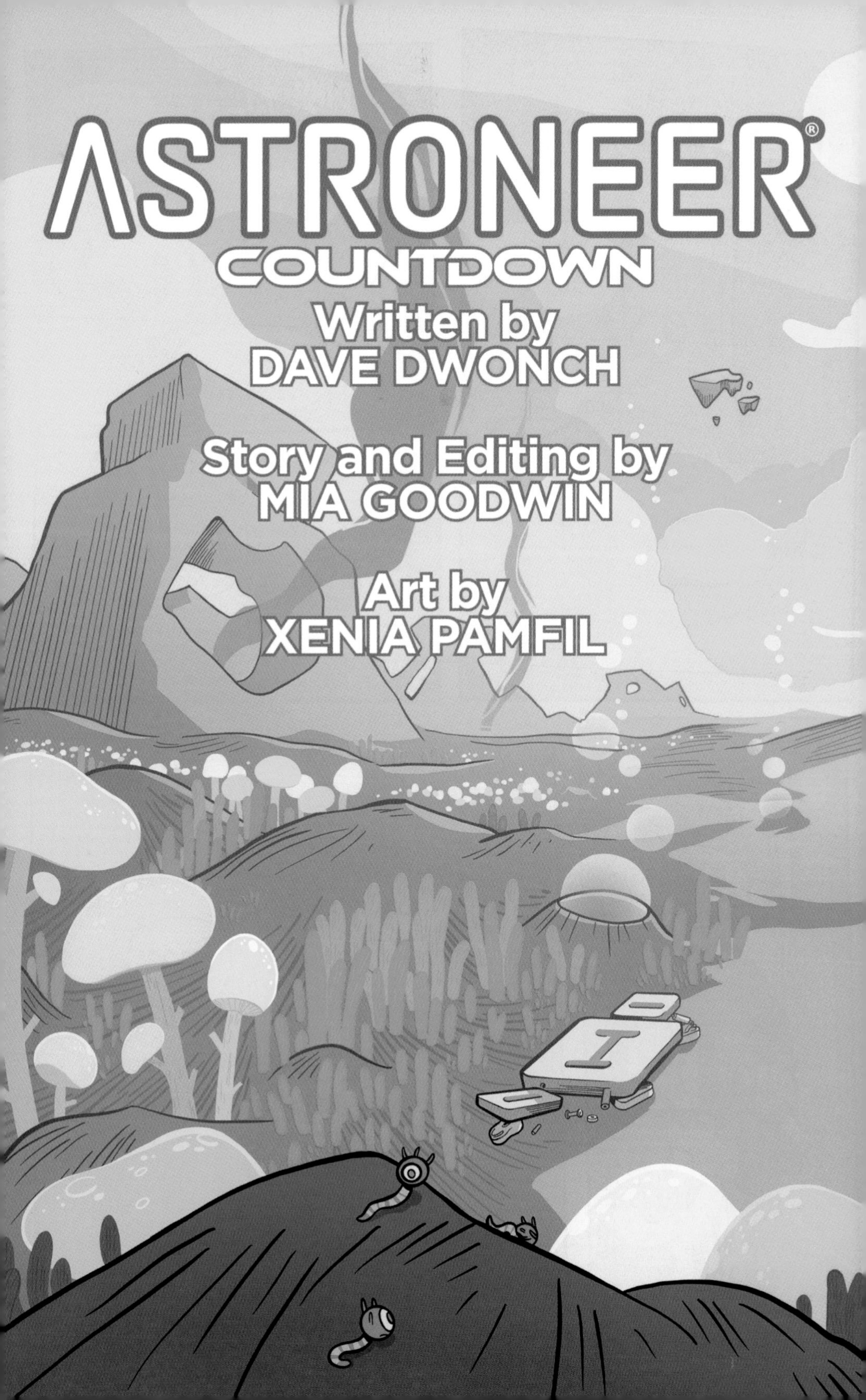

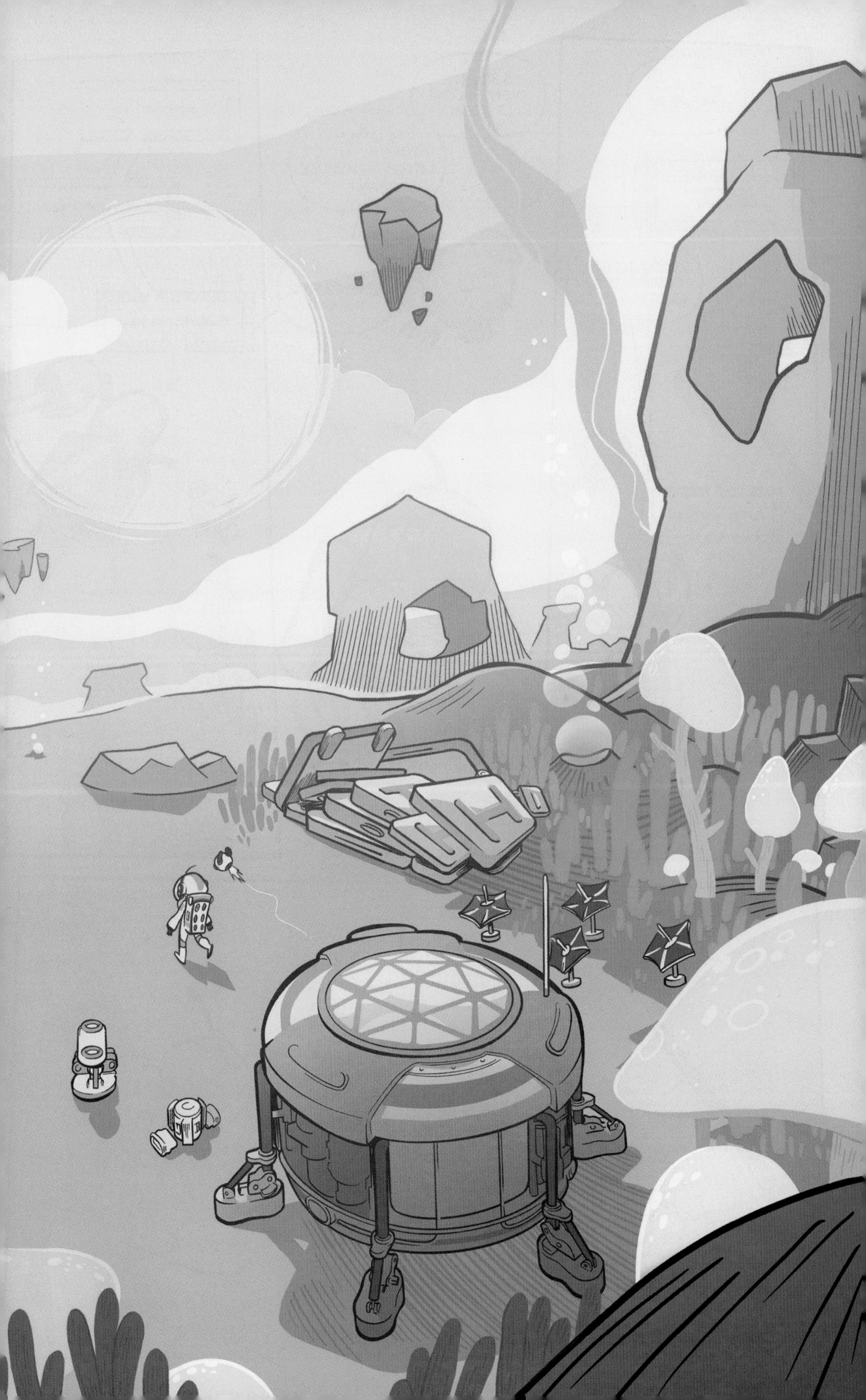

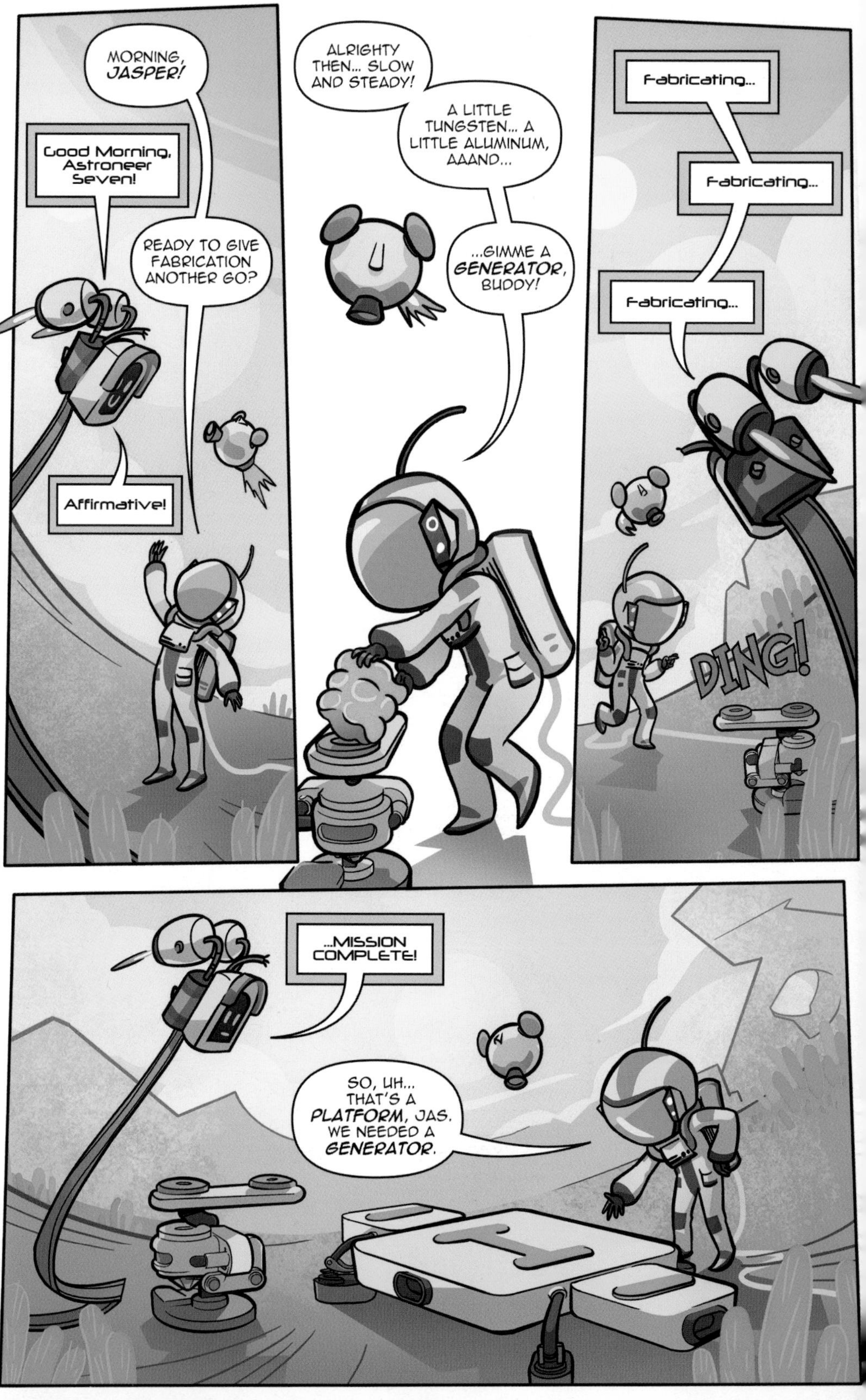

MORNING, JASPER!
Good Morning, Astroneer Seven!
READY TO GIVE FABRICATION ANOTHER GO?
Affirmative!
ALRIGHTY THEN... SLOW AND STEADY!
A LITTLE TUNGSTEN... A LITTLE ALUMINUM, AAAND...
...GIMME A GENERATOR, BUDDY!
Fabricating...
Fabricating...
Fabricating...
DING!
...MISSION COMPLETE!
SO, UH... THAT'S A PLATFORM, JAS. WE NEEDED A GENERATOR.

Affirmative!
One medium platform-- as requested!
PRAISE ME.
-SIGH- YOU... YOU DID GOOD, BUDDY. NICE WORK.
I'LL JUST... PUT IT WITH THE OTHERS FOR NOW.
Your blood pressure is elevated. Are you in distress?
I'M FINE, JAS. EVERYTHING'S -HRK- FINE!
I'm sorry, Seven, but your vital signs say otherwise.
Shall we initiate Emergency Calming Exercises?

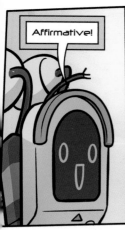

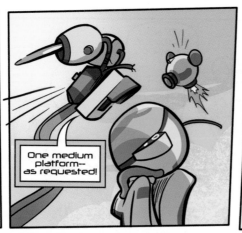

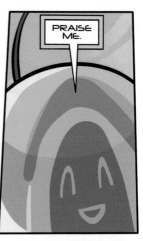

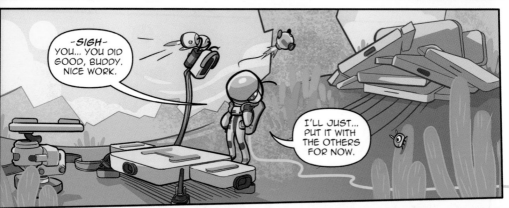

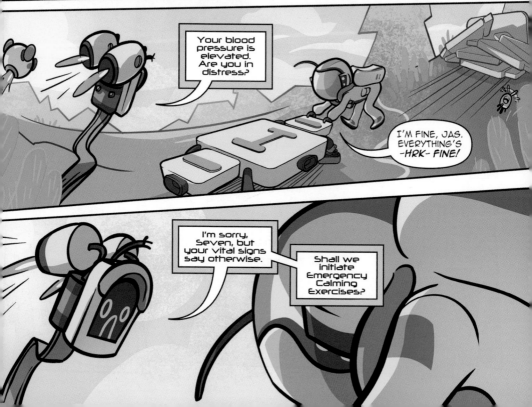

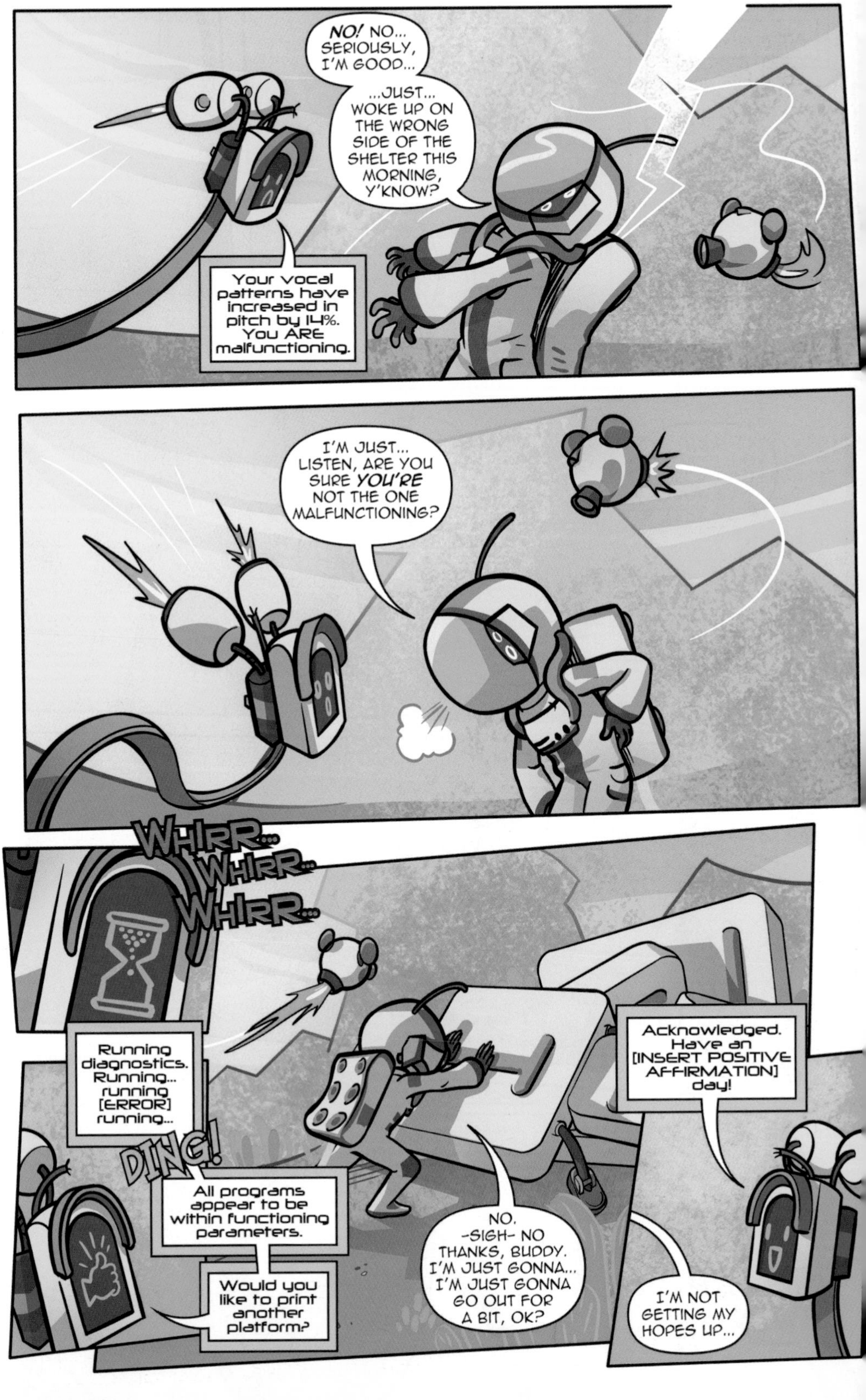
NO! NO... SERIOUSLY, I'M GOOD...
...JUST... WOKE UP ON THE WRONG SIDE OF THE SHELTER THIS MORNING, Y'KNOW?
Your vocal patterns have increased in pitch by 14%. You ARE malfunctioning.
I'M JUST... LISTEN, ARE YOU SURE YOU'RE NOT THE ONE MALFUNCTIONING?
WHIRR... WHIRR... WHIRR...
Running diagnostics. Running... running [ERROR] running...
DING!
All programs appear to be within functioning parameters.
Would you like to print another platform?
NO. -SIGH- NO THANKS, BUDDY. I'M JUST GONNA... I'M JUST GONNA GO OUT FOR A BIT, OK?
Acknowledged. Have an [INSERT POSITIVE AFFIRMATION] day!
I'M NOT GETTING MY HOPES UP...

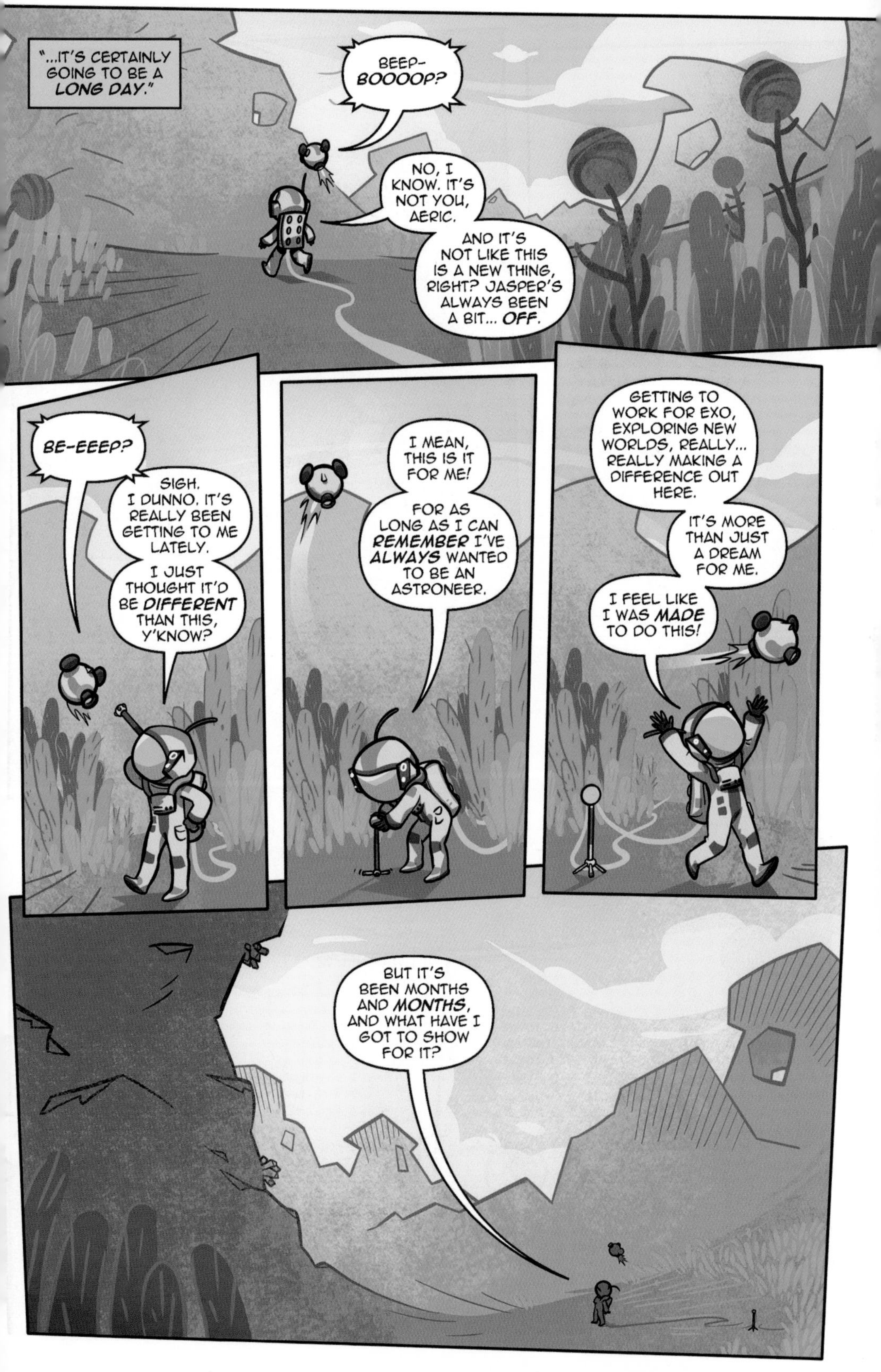
"...IT'S CERTAINLY GOING TO BE A *LONG DAY*."
BEEP- *BOOOOP?*
NO, I KNOW. IT'S NOT YOU, AERIC.
AND IT'S NOT LIKE THIS IS A NEW THING, RIGHT? JASPER'S ALWAYS BEEN A BIT... *OFF*.
BE-EEEP?
SIGH. I DUNNO. IT'S REALLY BEEN GETTING TO ME LATELY.
I JUST THOUGHT IT'D BE *DIFFERENT* THAN THIS, Y'KNOW?
I MEAN, THIS IS IT FOR ME!
FOR AS LONG AS I CAN *REMEMBER* I'VE *ALWAYS* WANTED TO BE AN ASTRONEER.
GETTING TO WORK FOR EXO, EXPLORING NEW WORLDS, REALLY... REALLY MAKING A DIFFERENCE OUT HERE.
IT'S MORE THAN JUST A DREAM FOR ME.
I FEEL LIKE I WAS *MADE* TO DO THIS!
BUT IT'S BEEN MONTHS AND *MONTHS*, AND WHAT HAVE I GOT TO SHOW FOR IT?

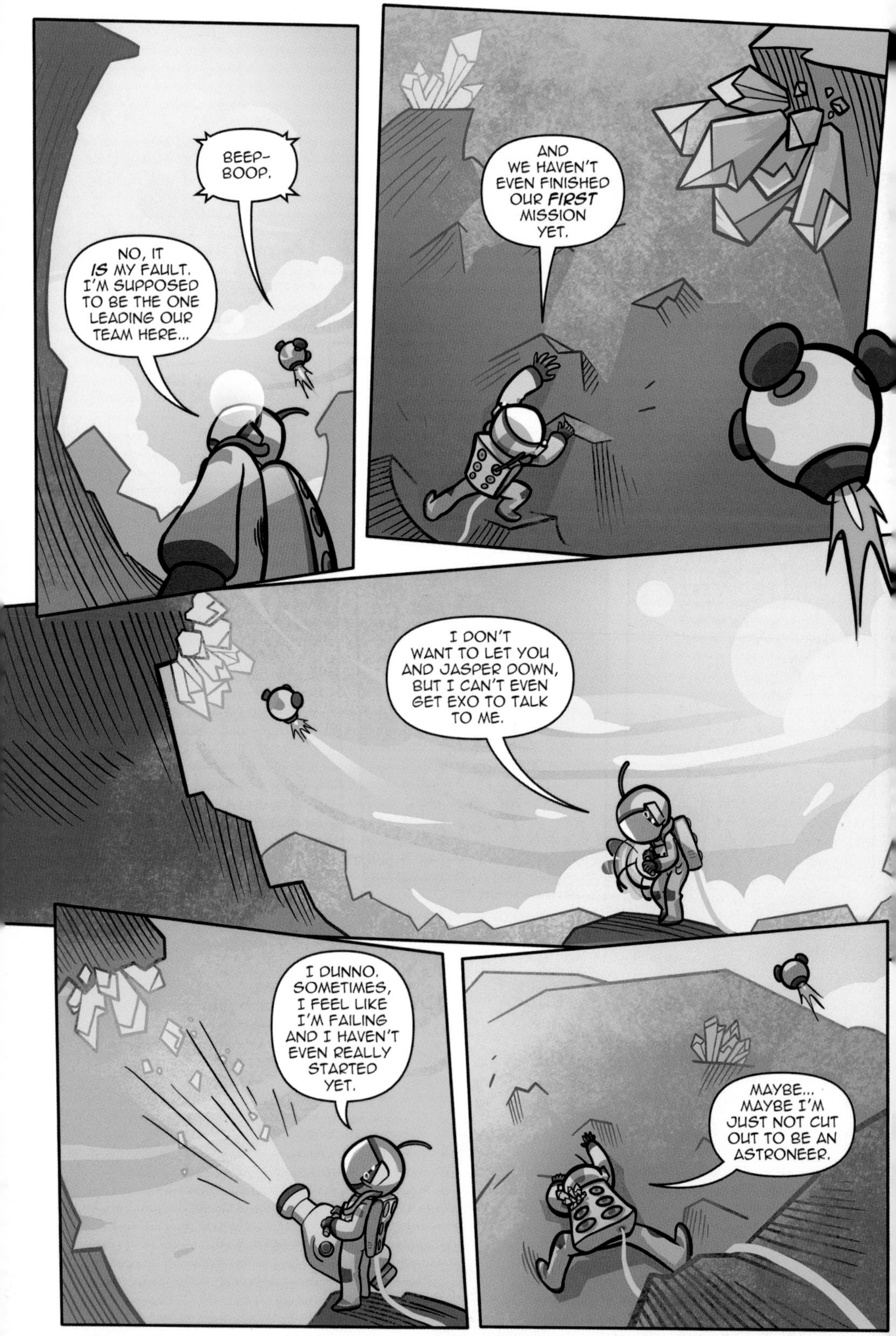
BEEP-BOOP.
NO, IT IS MY FAULT. I'M SUPPOSED TO BE THE ONE LEADING OUR TEAM HERE...
AND WE HAVEN'T EVEN FINISHED OUR FIRST MISSION YET.
I DON'T WANT TO LET YOU AND JASPER DOWN, BUT I CAN'T EVEN GET EXO TO TALK TO ME.
I DUNNO. SOMETIMES, I FEEL LIKE I'M FAILING AND I HAVEN'T EVEN REALLY STARTED YET.
MAYBE... MAYBE I'M JUST NOT CUT OUT TO BE AN ASTRONEER.

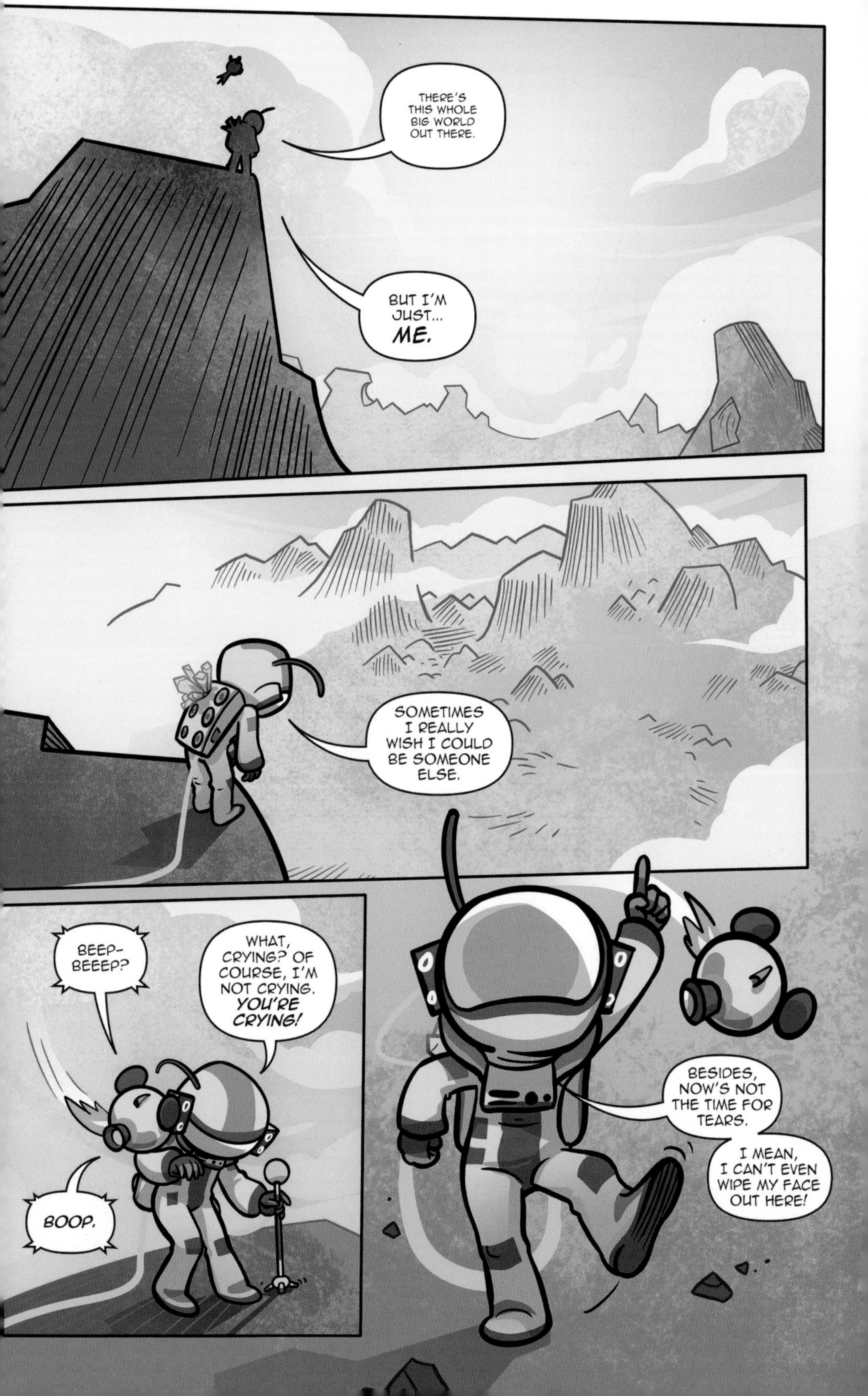
THERE'S THIS WHOLE BIG WORLD OUT THERE.
BUT I'M JUST... ME.
SOMETIMES I REALLY WISH I COULD BE SOMEONE ELSE.
BEEP-BEEEP?
WHAT, CRYING? OF COURSE, I'M NOT CRYING. YOU'RE CRYING!
BOOP.
BESIDES, NOW'S NOT THE TIME FOR TEARS.
I MEAN, I CAN'T EVEN WIPE MY FACE OUT HERE!

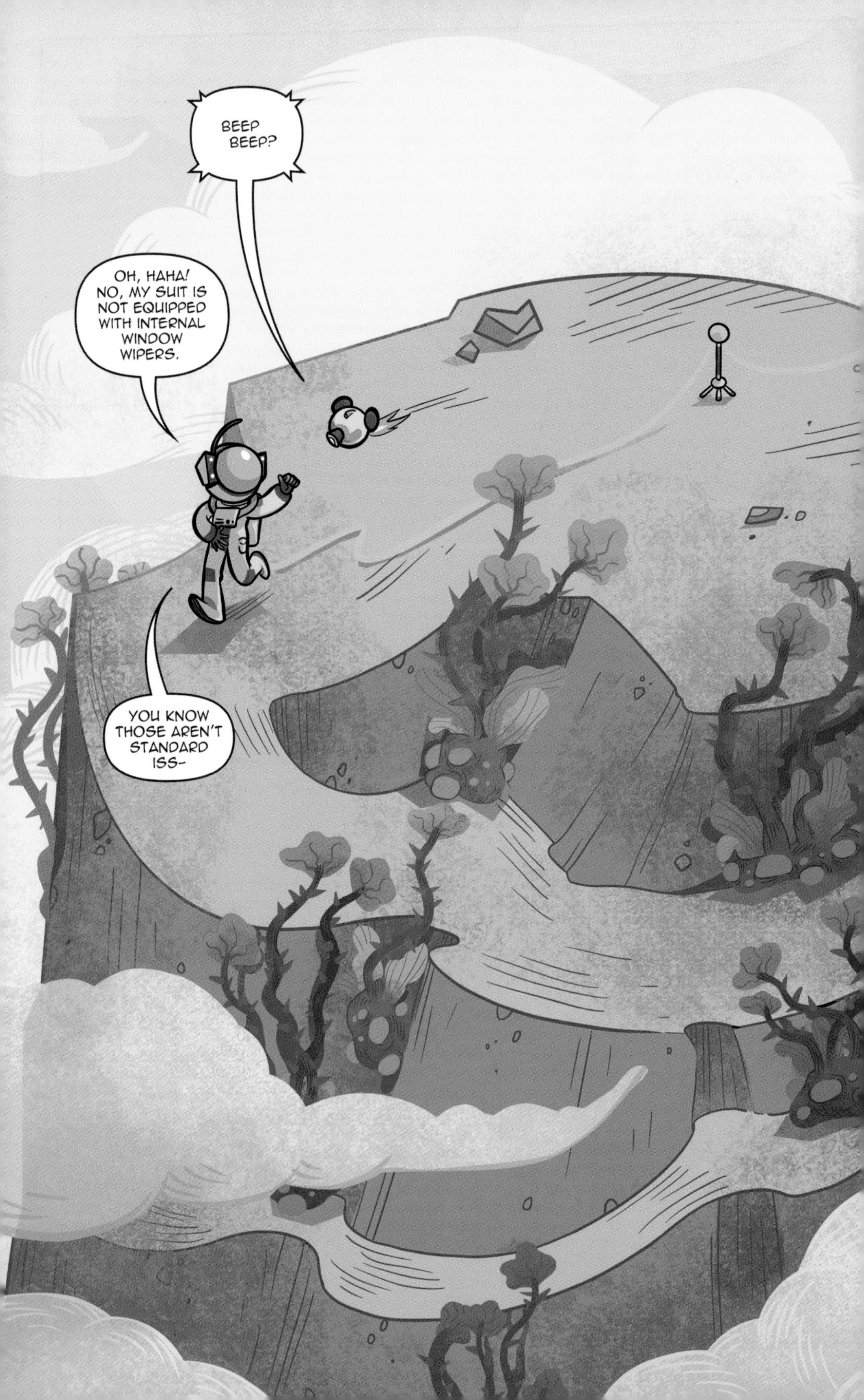

BEEP BEEP?
OH, HAHA! NO, MY SUIT IS NOT EQUIPPED WITH INTERNAL WINDOW WIPERS.
YOU KNOW THOSE AREN'T STANDARD ISS-

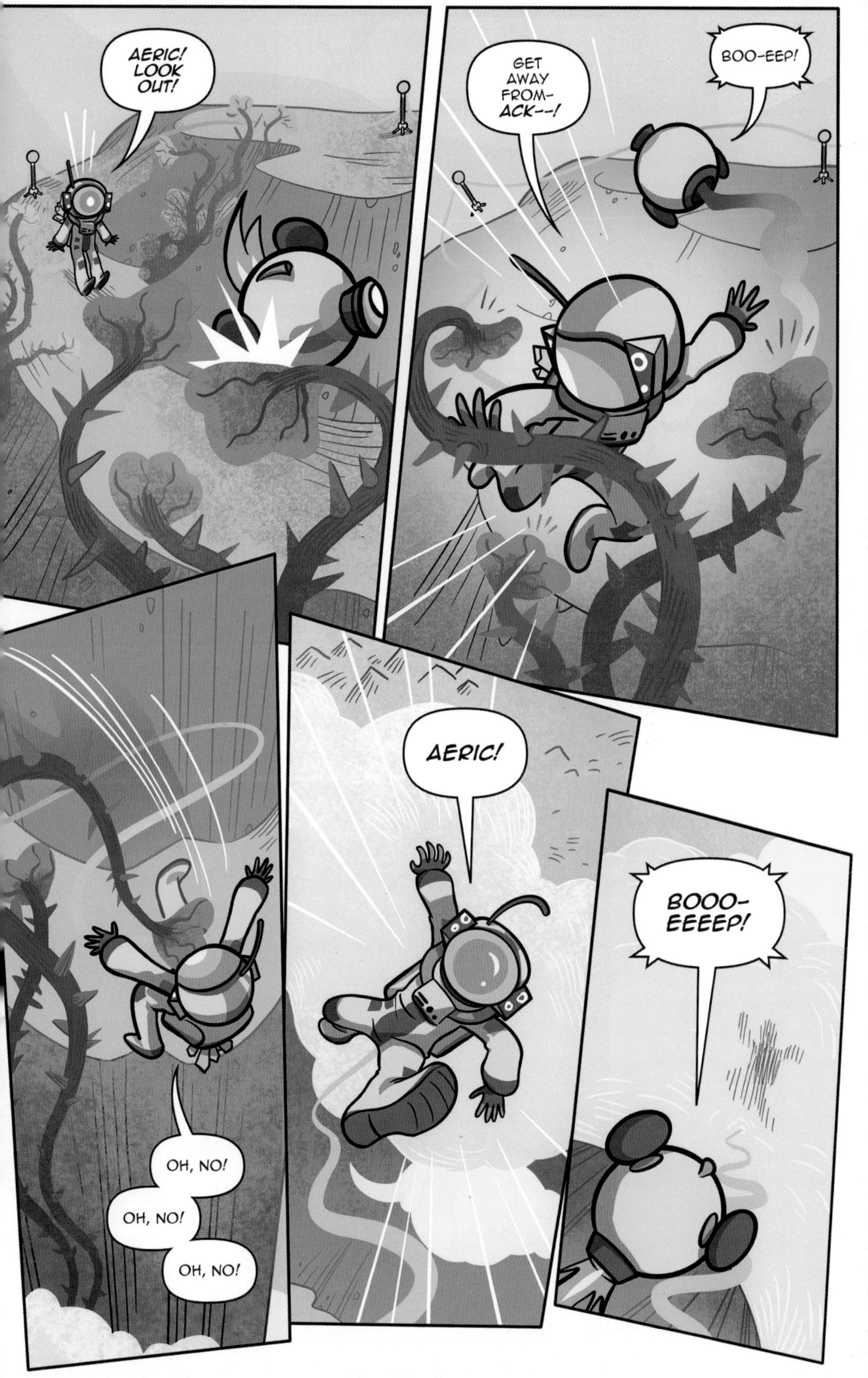
AERIC! LOOK OUT!
GET AWAY FROM-ACK--!
BOO-EEP!
OH, NO!
OH, NO!
OH, NO!
AERIC!
BOOO-EEEEP!

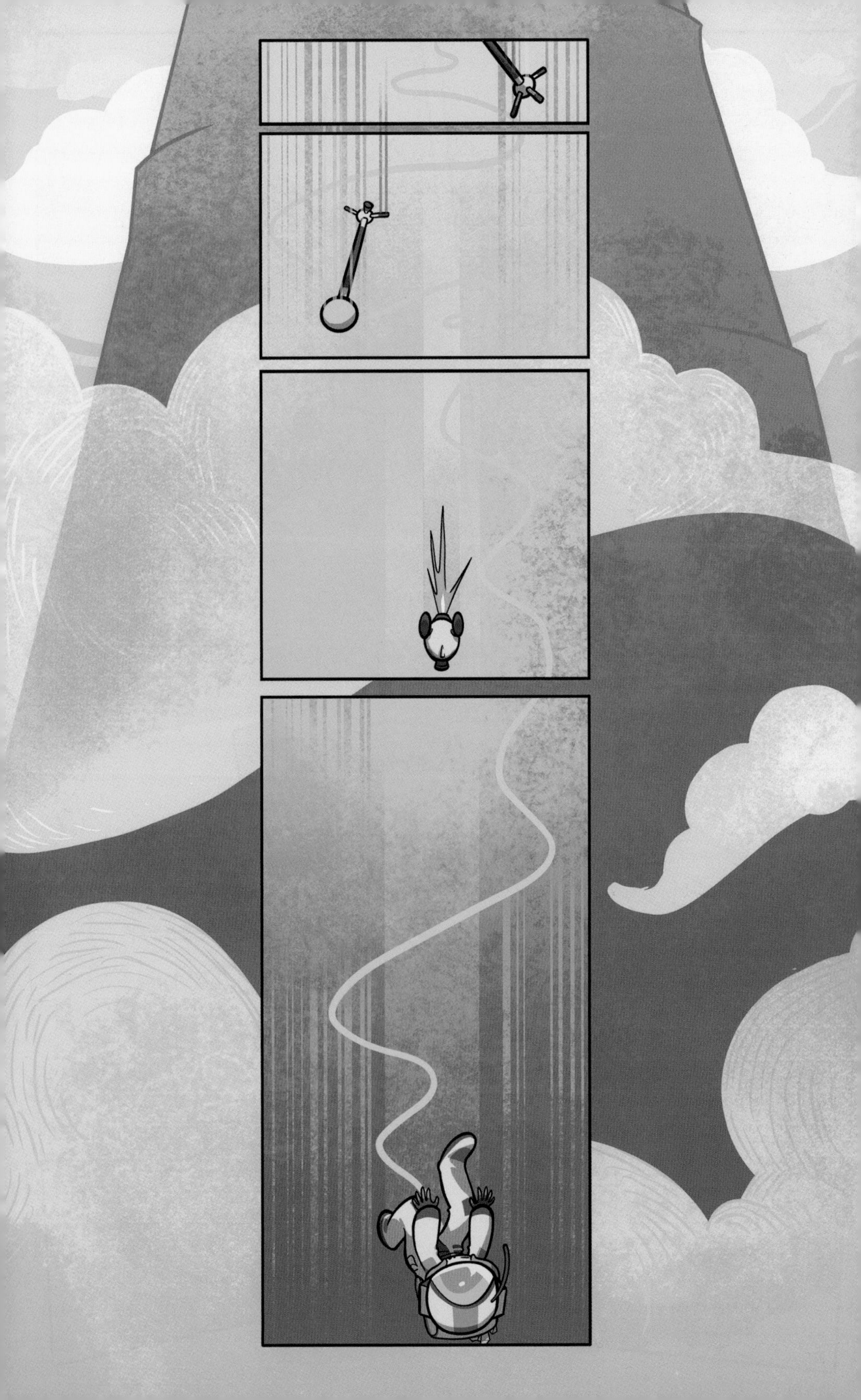

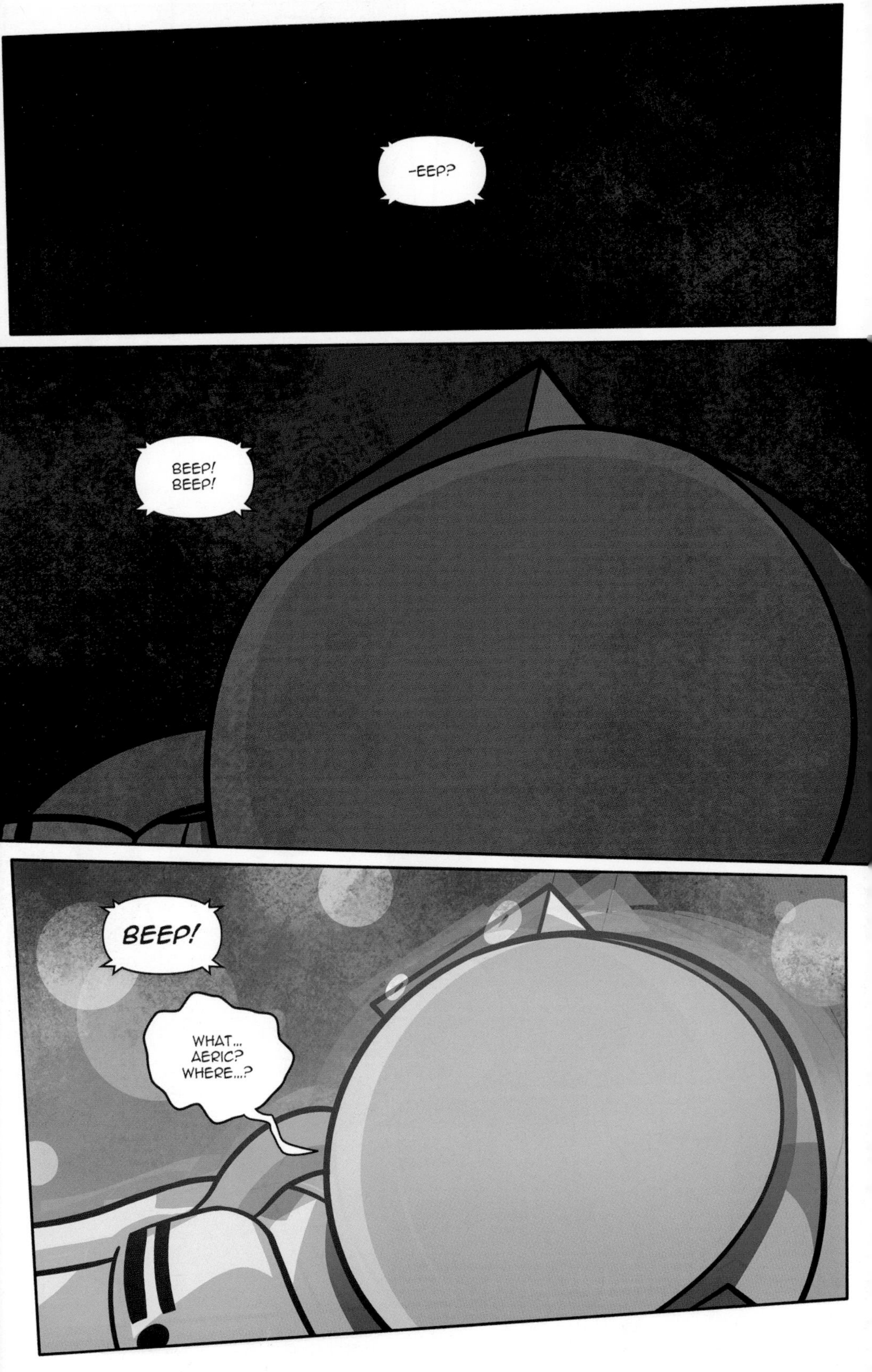
-EEP?
BEEP! BEEP!
BEEP!
WHAT... AERIC? WHERE...?

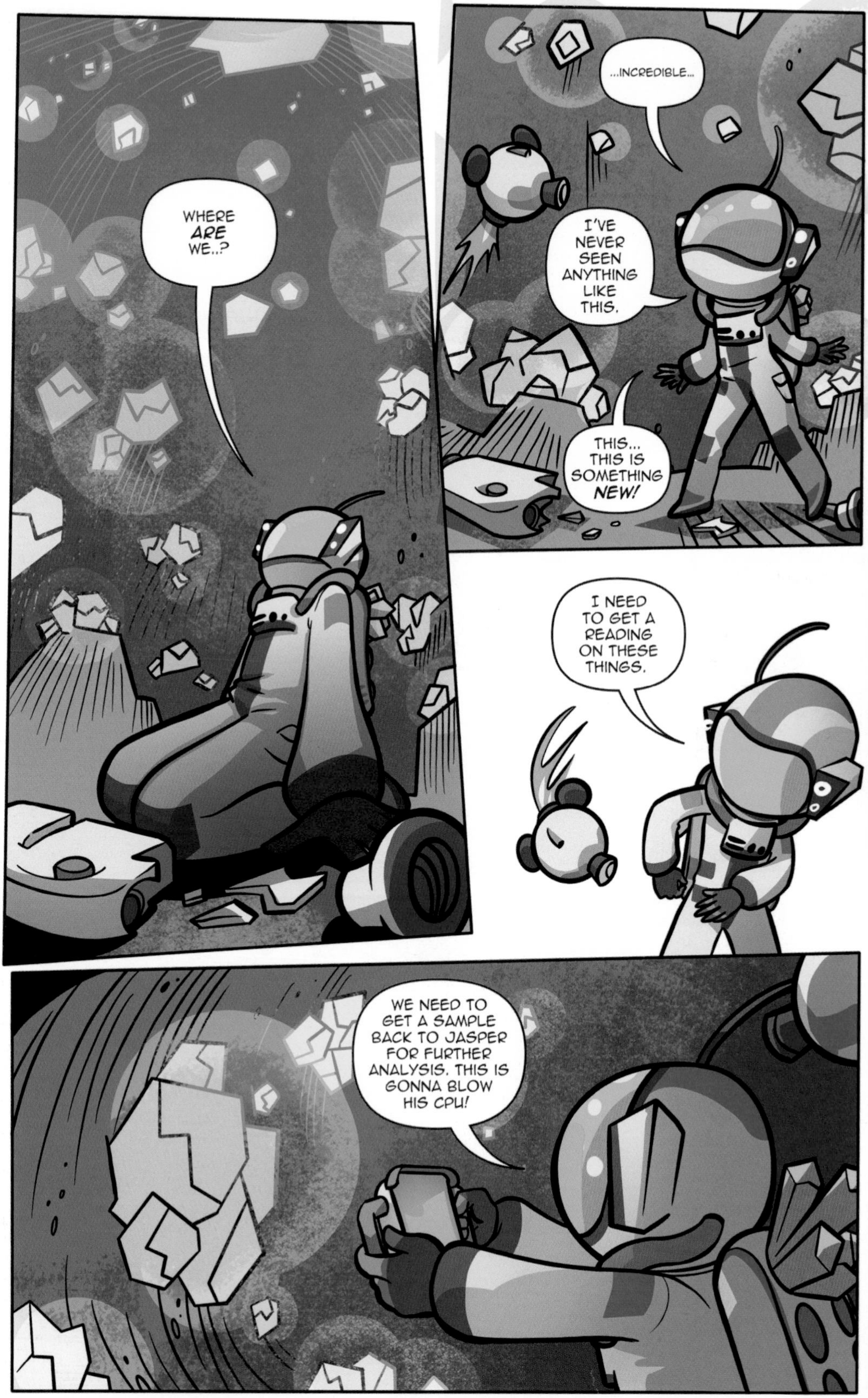
WHERE *ARE* WE..?
...INCREDIBLE...
I'VE NEVER SEEN ANYTHING LIKE THIS.
THIS... THIS IS SOMETHING *NEW!*
I NEED TO GET A READING ON THESE THINGS.
WE NEED TO GET A SAMPLE BACK TO JASPER FOR FURTHER ANALYSIS. THIS IS GONNA BLOW HIS CPU!

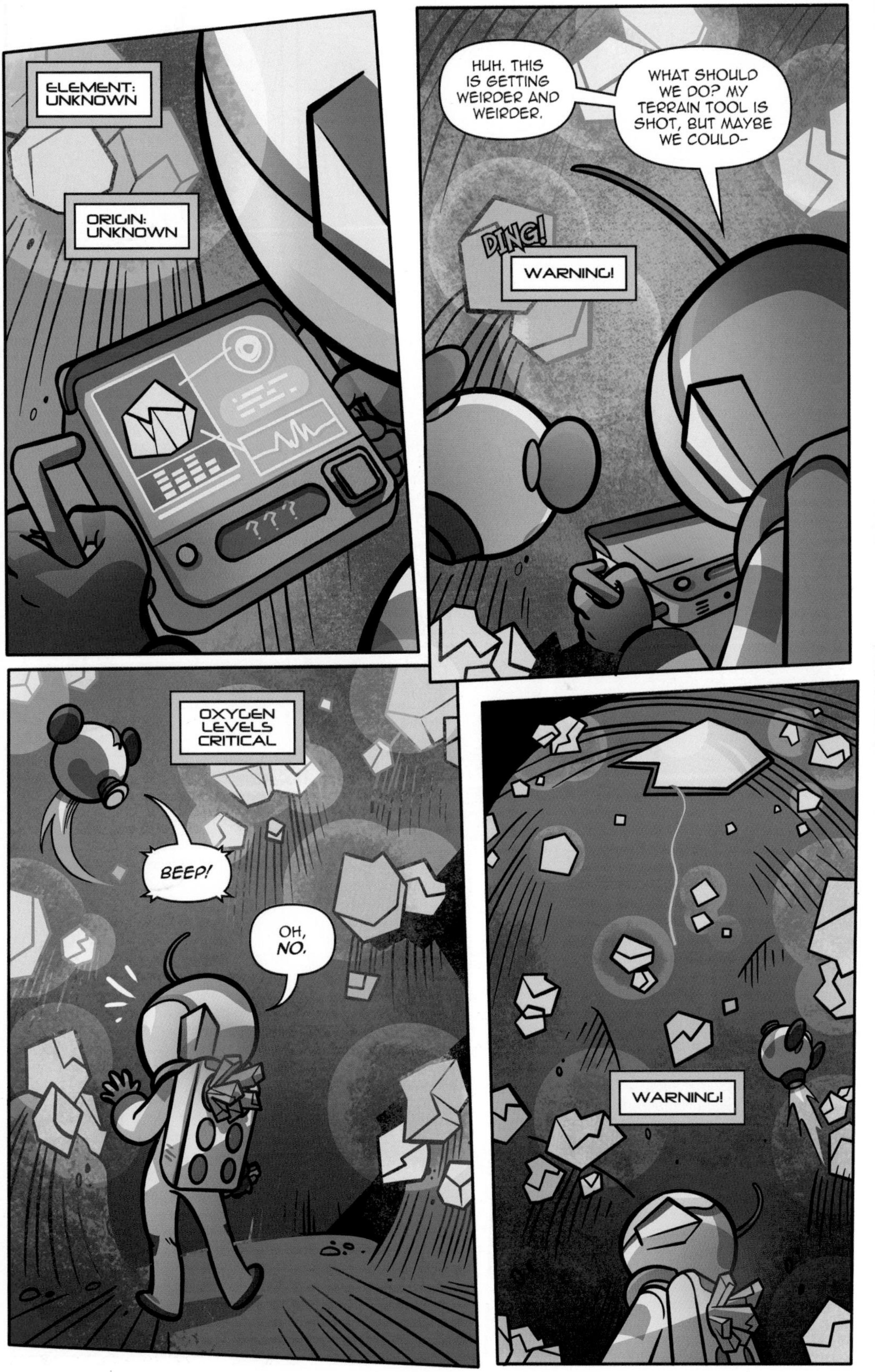
ELEMENT: UNKNOWN
ORIGIN: UNKNOWN
???
HUH. THIS IS GETTING WEIRDER AND WEIRDER.
WHAT SHOULD WE DO? MY TERRAIN TOOL IS SHOT, BUT MAYBE WE COULD-
DING!
WARNING!
OXYGEN LEVELS CRITICAL
BEEP!
OH, NO.
WARNING!

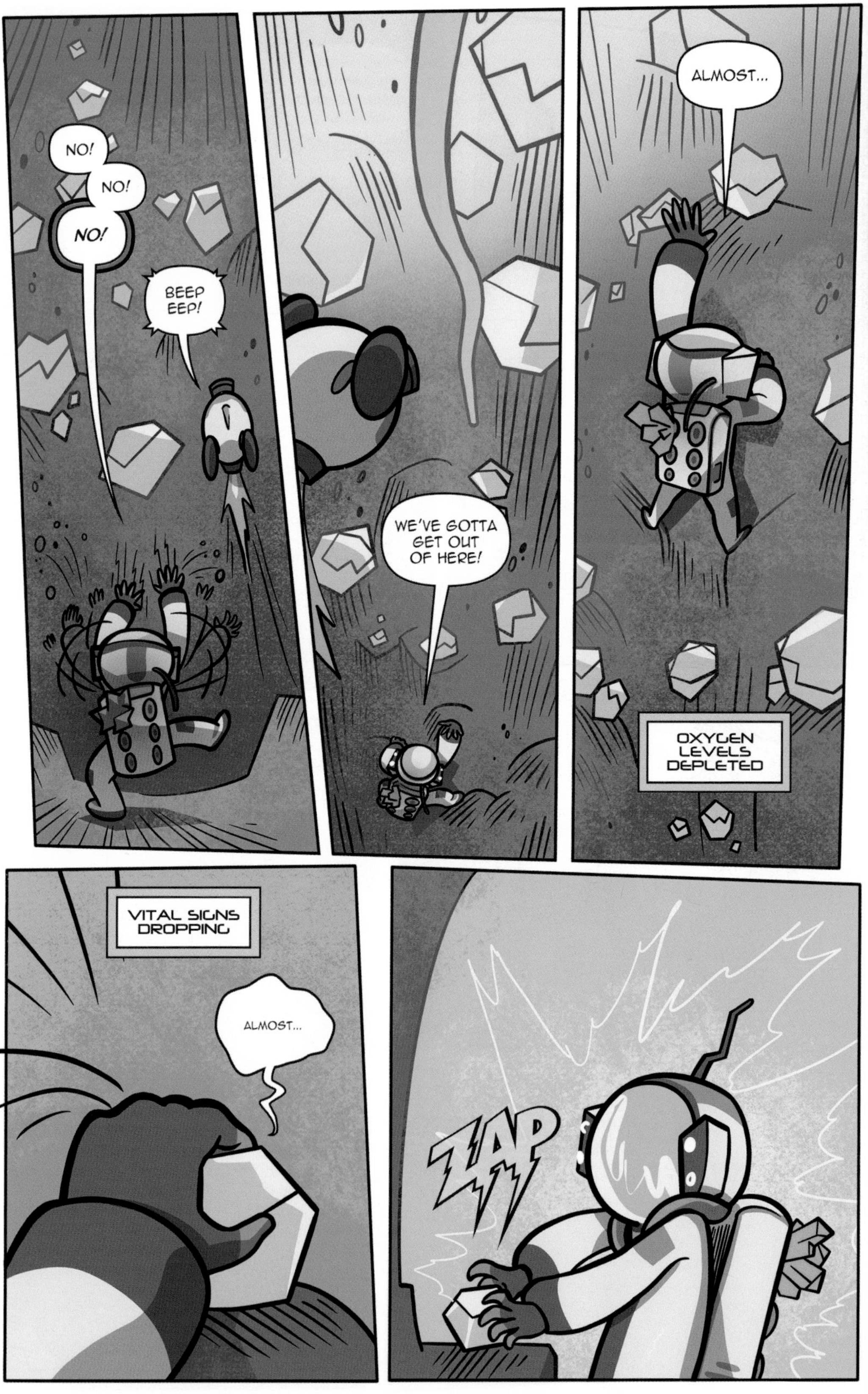
NO!
NO!
NO!
BEEP EEP!
WE'VE GOTTA GET OUT OF HERE!
ALMOST...
OXYGEN LEVELS DEPLETED
VITAL SIGNS DROPPING
ALMOST...
ZAP

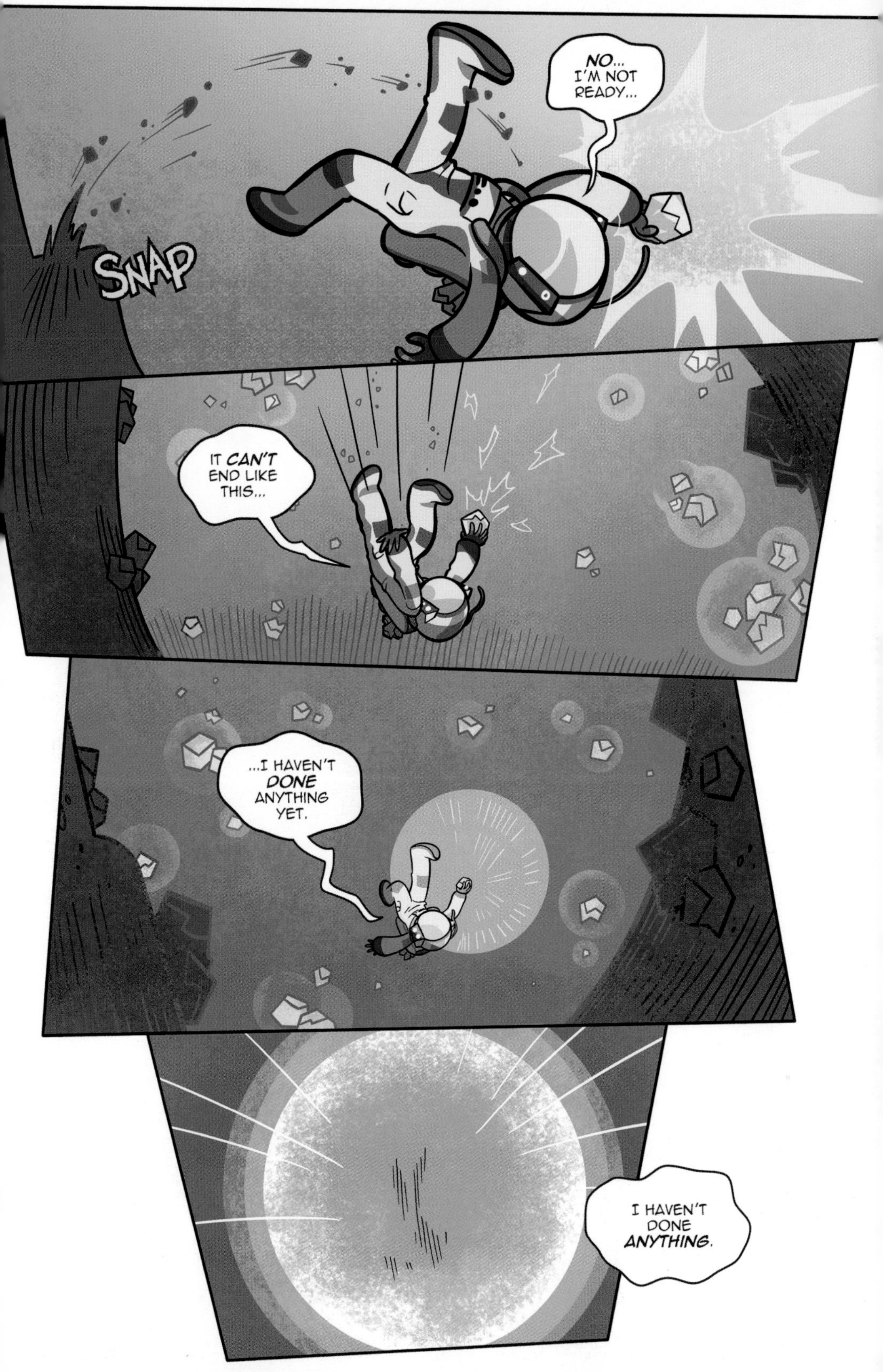
SNAP
NO... I'M NOT READY...
IT CAN'T END LIKE THIS...
...I HAVEN'T DONE ANYTHING YET.
I HAVEN'T DONE ANYTHING.

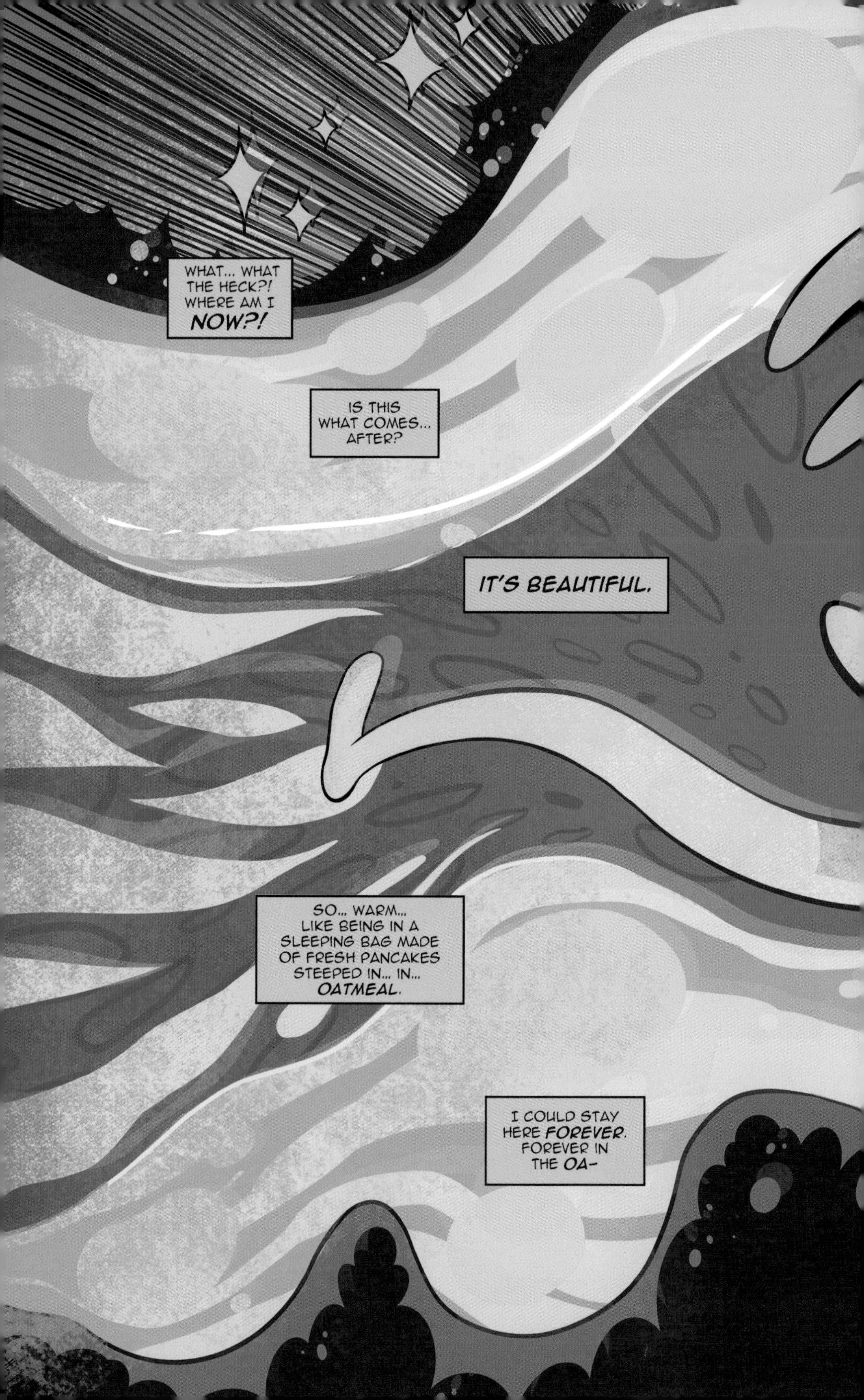
WHAT... WHAT THE HECK?! WHERE AM I NOW?!
IS THIS WHAT COMES... AFTER?
IT'S BEAUTIFUL.
SO... WARM... LIKE BEING IN A SLEEPING BAG MADE OF FRESH PANCAKES STEEPED IN... IN... OATMEAL.
I COULD STAY HERE FOREVER. FOREVER IN THE OA-

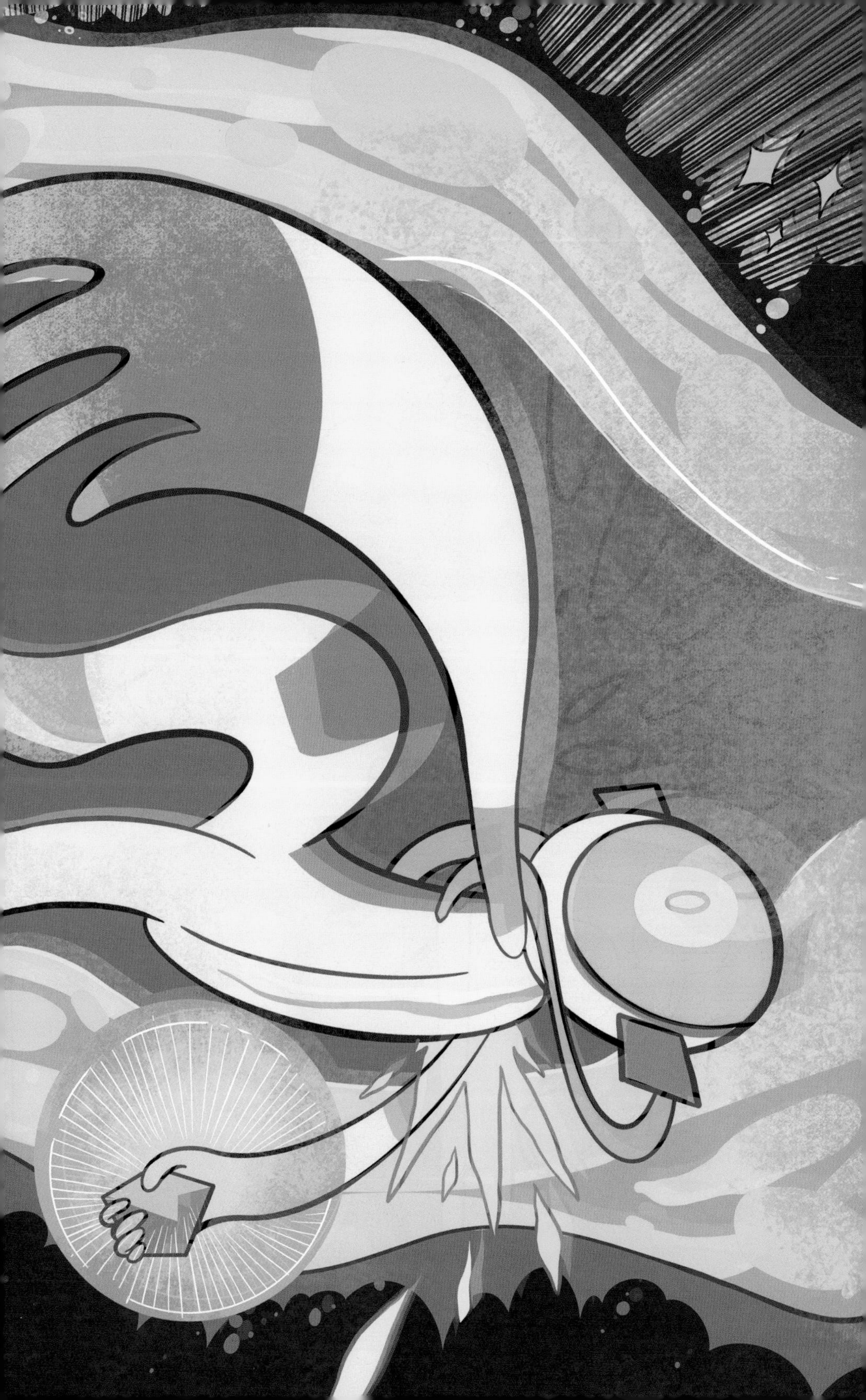

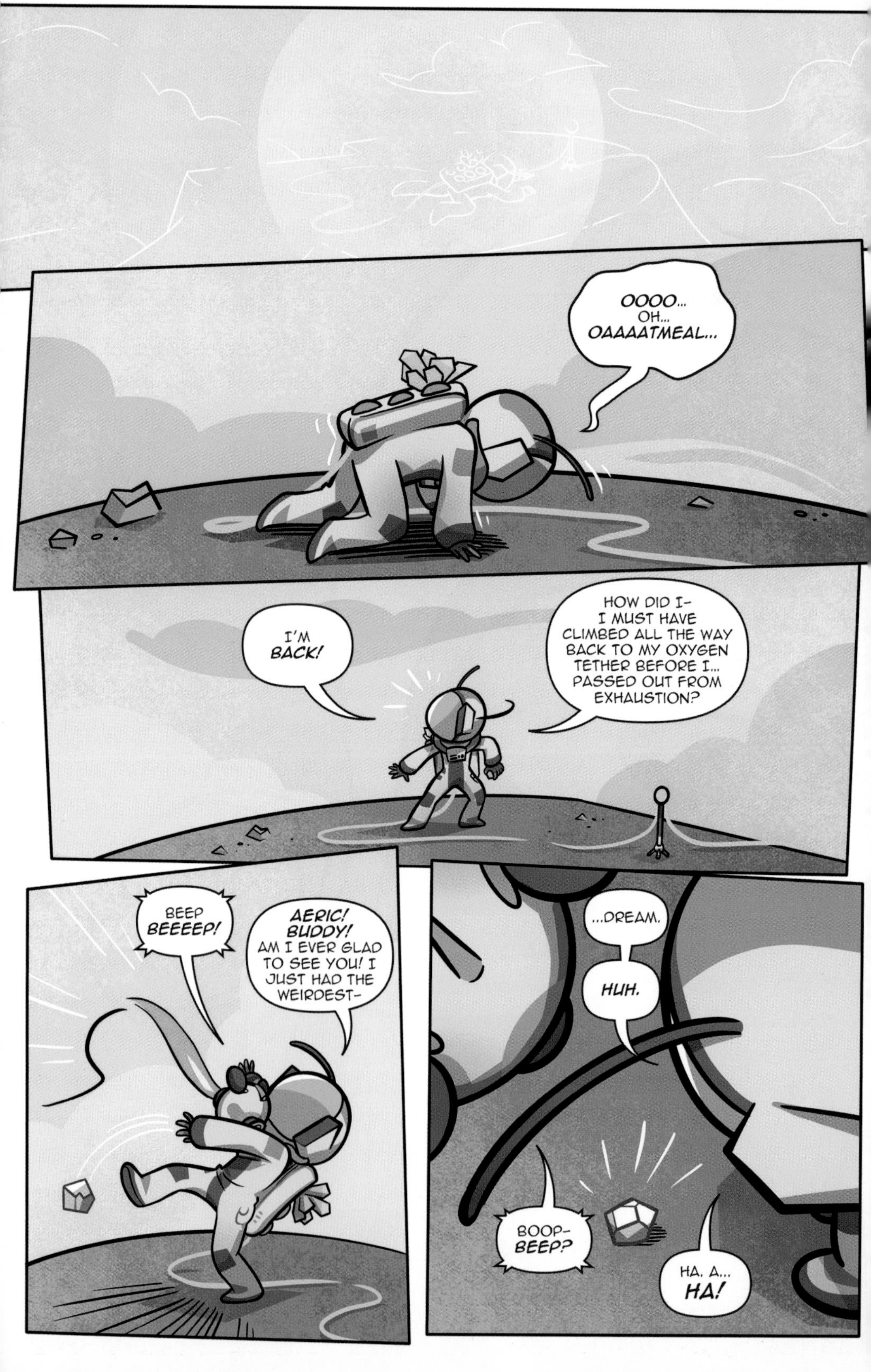
OOOO... OH... OAAAATMEAL...
I'M BACK!
HOW DID I- I MUST HAVE CLIMBED ALL THE WAY BACK TO MY OXYGEN TETHER BEFORE I... PASSED OUT FROM EXHAUSTION?
BEEP BEEEEP!
AERIC! BUDDY! AM I EVER GLAD TO SEE YOU! I JUST HAD THE WEIRDEST-
...DREAM.
HUH.
BOOP-BEEP?
HA, A... HA!

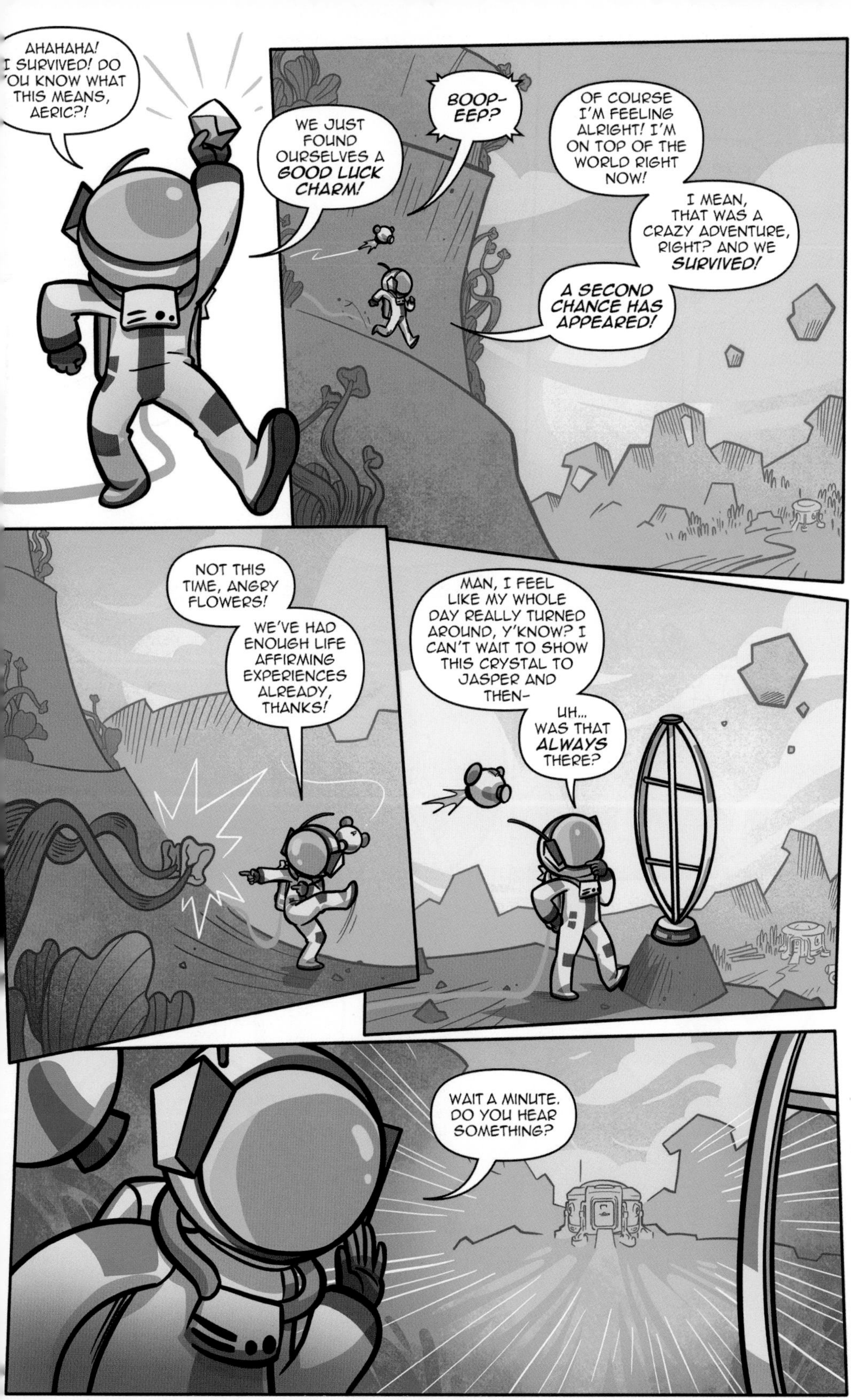
AHAHAHA! I SURVIVED! DO YOU KNOW WHAT THIS MEANS, AERIC?!
WE JUST FOUND OURSELVES A GOOD LUCK CHARM!
BOOP-EEP?
OF COURSE I'M FEELING ALRIGHT! I'M ON TOP OF THE WORLD RIGHT NOW!
I MEAN, THAT WAS A CRAZY ADVENTURE, RIGHT? AND WE SURVIVED!
A SECOND CHANCE HAS APPEARED!
NOT THIS TIME, ANGRY FLOWERS!
WE'VE HAD ENOUGH LIFE AFFIRMING EXPERIENCES ALREADY, THANKS!
MAN, I FEEL LIKE MY WHOLE DAY REALLY TURNED AROUND, Y'KNOW? I CAN'T WAIT TO SHOW THIS CRYSTAL TO JASPER AND THEN-
UH... WAS THAT ALWAYS THERE?
WAIT A MINUTE. DO YOU HEAR SOMETHING?

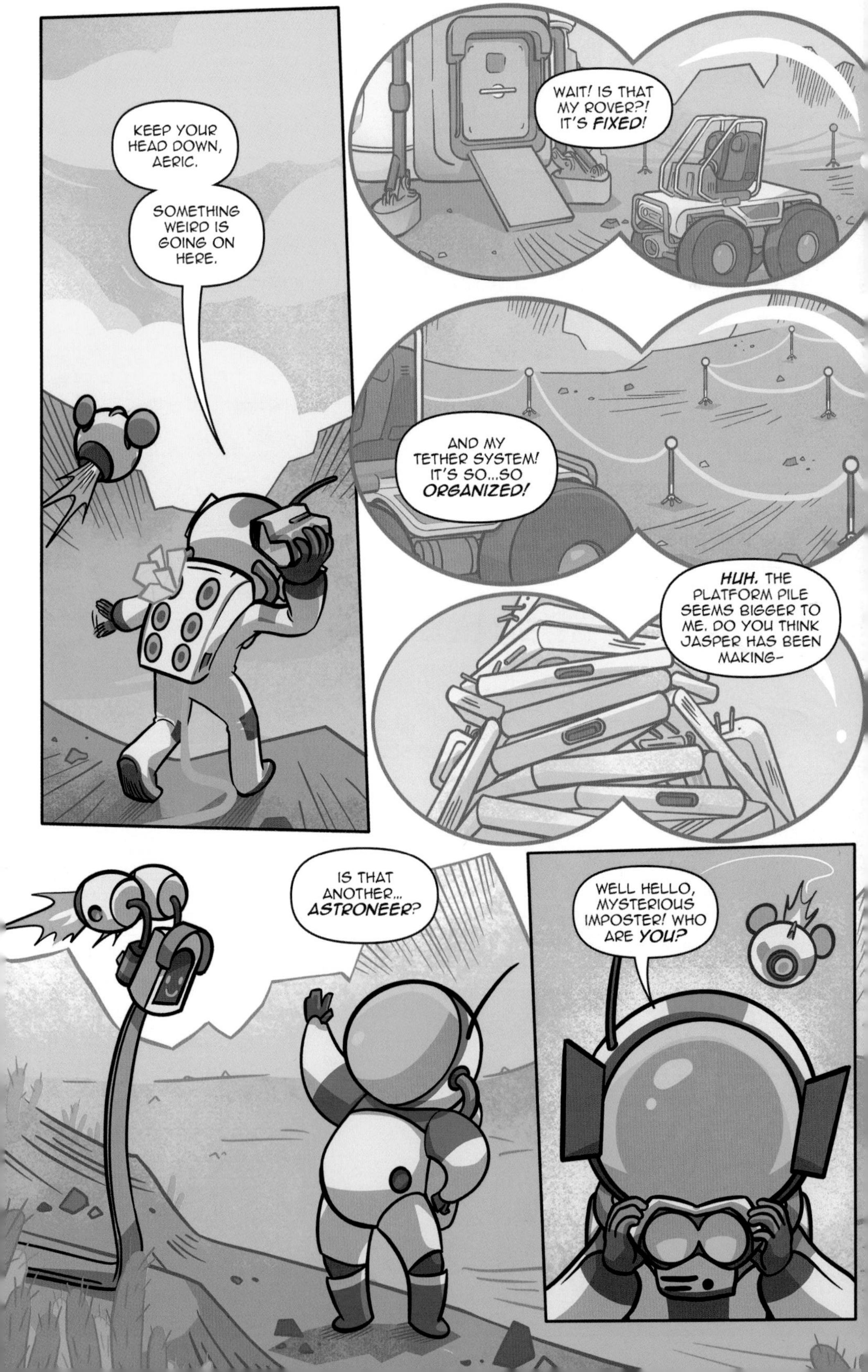
KEEP YOUR HEAD DOWN, AERIC.
SOMETHING WEIRD IS GOING ON HERE.
WAIT! IS THAT MY ROVER?! IT'S FIXED!
AND MY TETHER SYSTEM! IT'S SO...SO ORGANIZED!
HUH. THE PLATFORM PILE SEEMS BIGGER TO ME. DO YOU THINK JASPER HAS BEEN MAKING-
IS THAT ANOTHER... ASTRONEER?
WELL HELLO, MYSTERIOUS IMPOSTER! WHO ARE YOU?

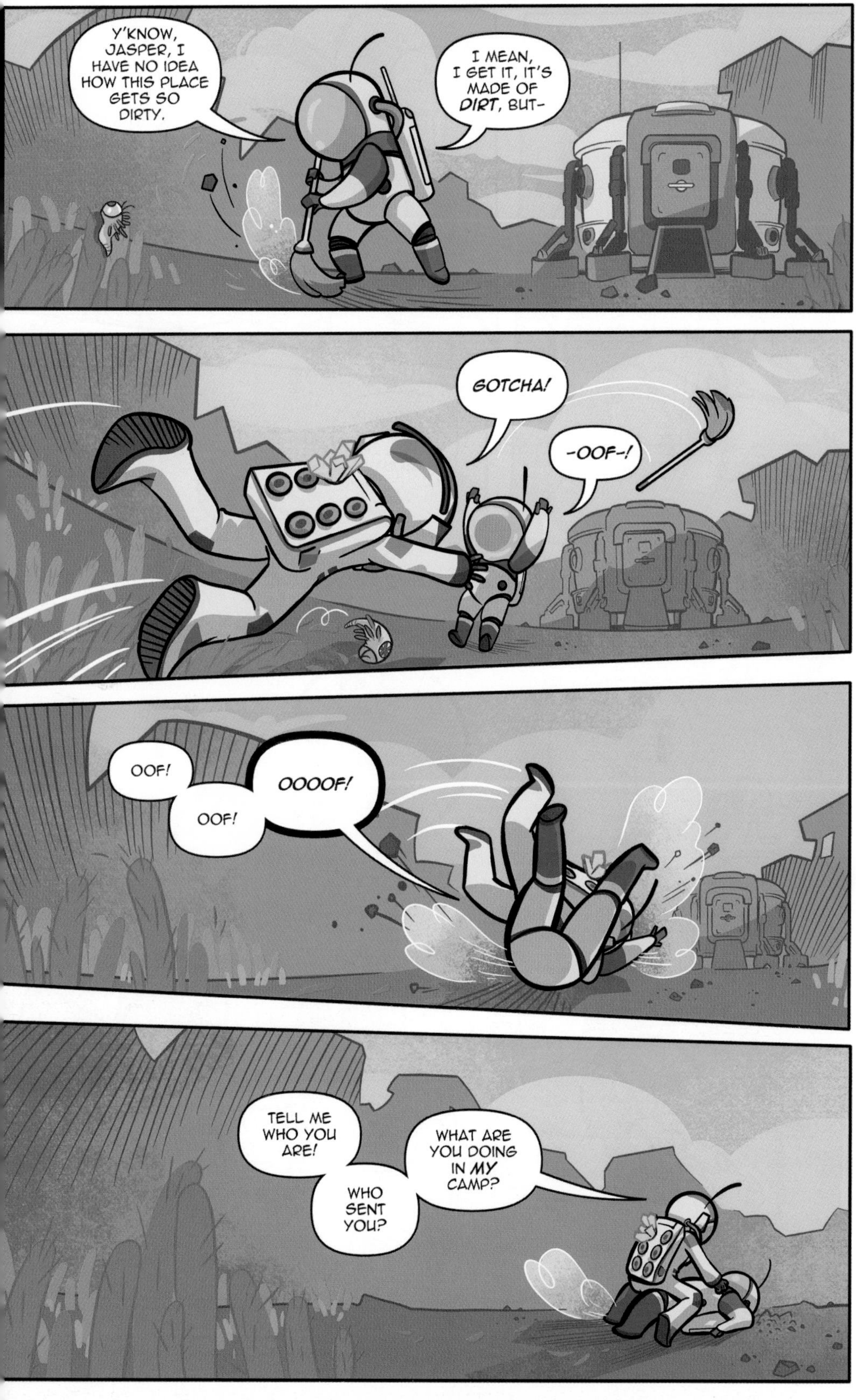
Y'KNOW, JASPER, I HAVE NO IDEA HOW THIS PLACE GETS SO DIRTY.
I MEAN, I GET IT, IT'S MADE OF DIRT, BUT-
GOTCHA!
-OOF-!
OOF!
OOF!
OOOOF!
TELL ME WHO YOU ARE!
WHO SENT YOU?
WHAT ARE YOU DOING IN MY CAMP?

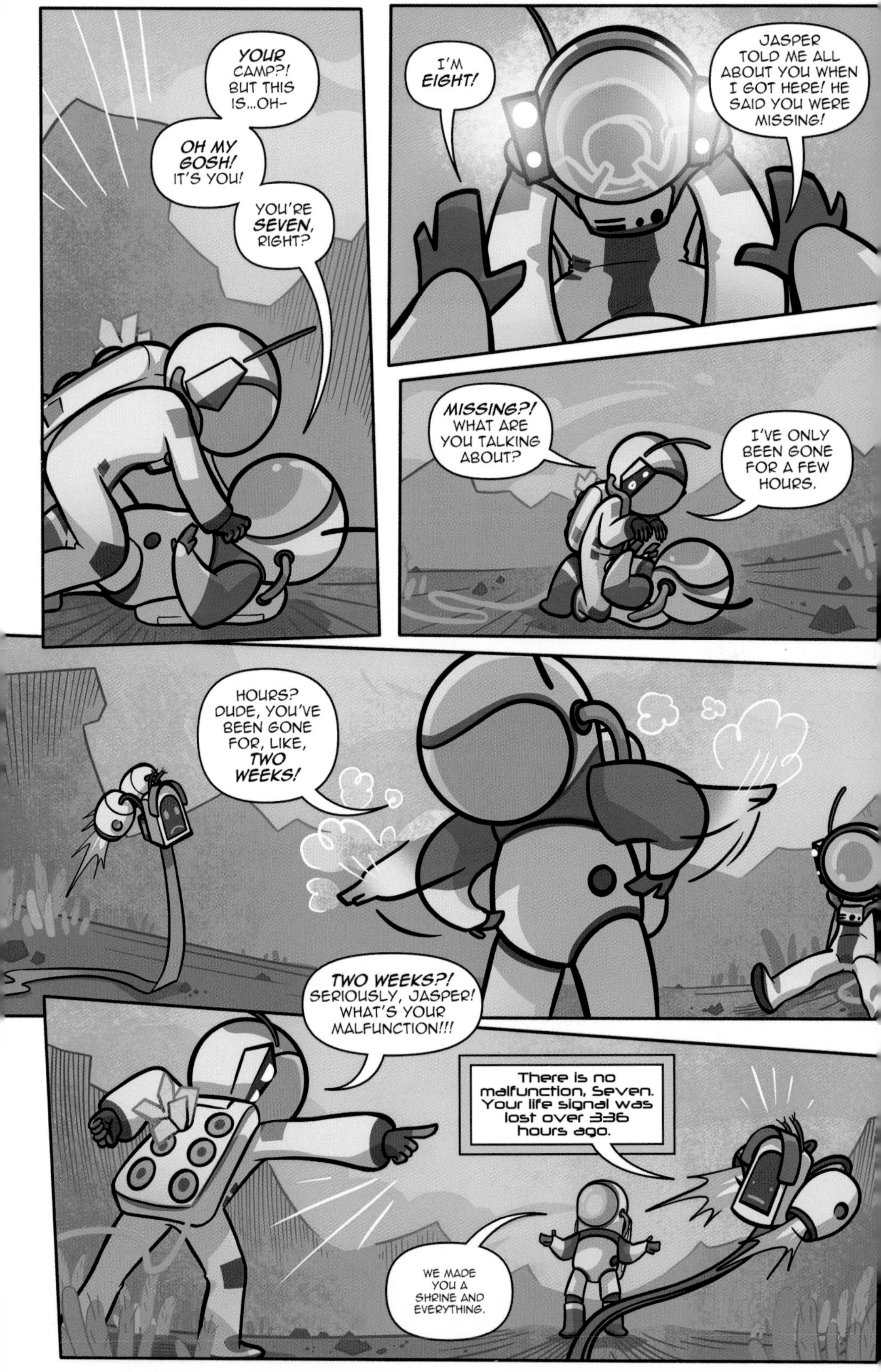
YOUR CAMP?! BUT THIS IS...OH-
OH MY GOSH! IT'S YOU!
YOU'RE SEVEN, RIGHT?
I'M EIGHT!
JASPER TOLD ME ALL ABOUT YOU WHEN I GOT HERE! HE SAID YOU WERE MISSING!
MISSING?! WHAT ARE YOU TALKING ABOUT?
I'VE ONLY BEEN GONE FOR A FEW HOURS.
HOURS? DUDE, YOU'VE BEEN GONE FOR, LIKE, TWO WEEKS!
TWO WEEKS?! SERIOUSLY, JASPER! WHAT'S YOUR MALFUNCTION!!!
There is no malfunction, Seven. Your life signal was lost over 336 hours ago.
WE MADE YOU A SHRINE AND EVERYTHING.

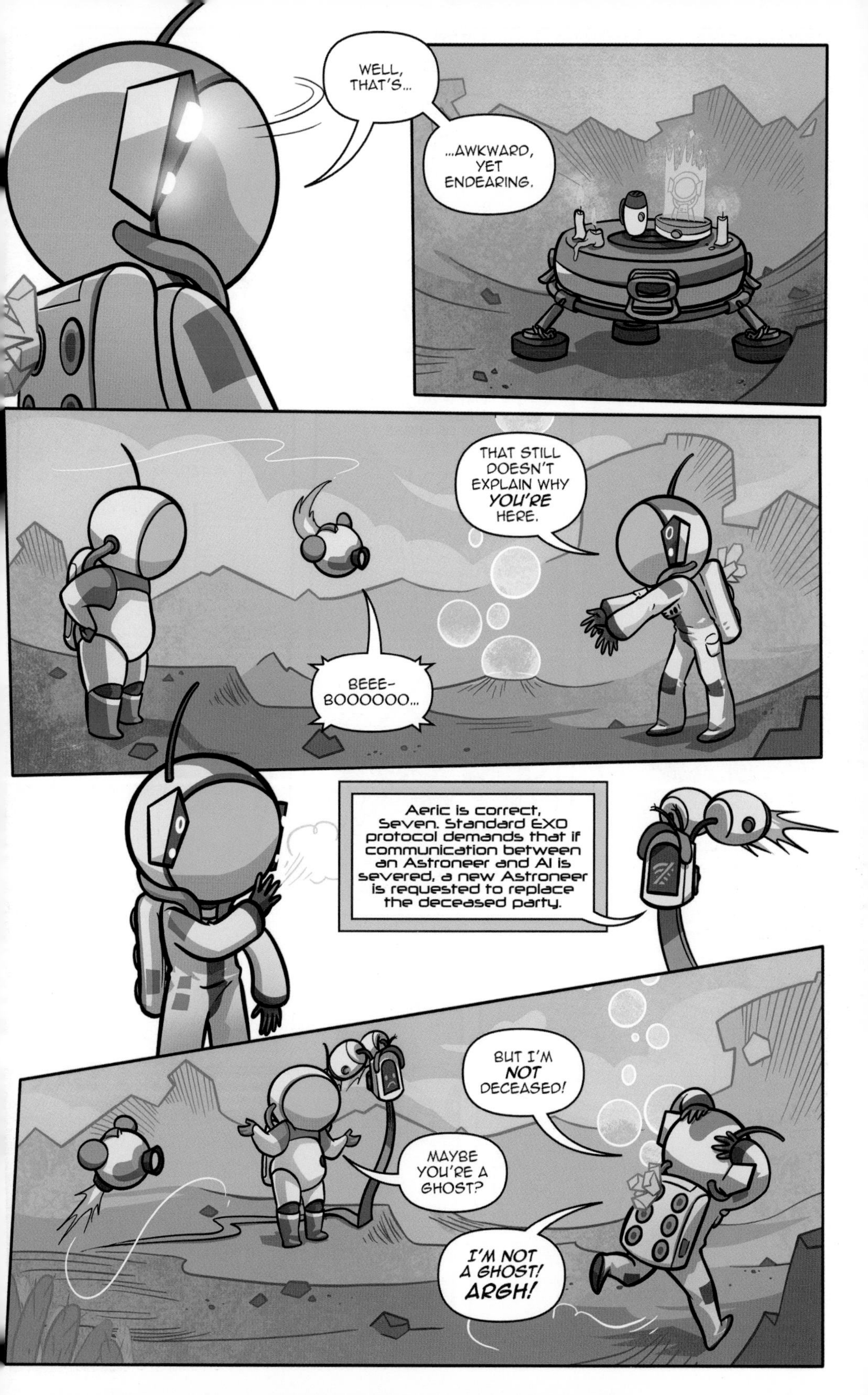

WELL, THAT'S...
...AWKWARD, YET ENDEARING.
THAT STILL DOESN'T EXPLAIN WHY *YOU'RE* HERE.
BEEE-BOOOOOO...
Aeric is correct, Seven. Standard EXO protocol demands that if communication between an Astroneer and AI is severed, a new Astroneer is requested to replace the deceased party.
BUT I'M **NOT** DECEASED!
MAYBE YOU'RE A GHOST?
I'M NOT A GHOST! ***ARGH!***

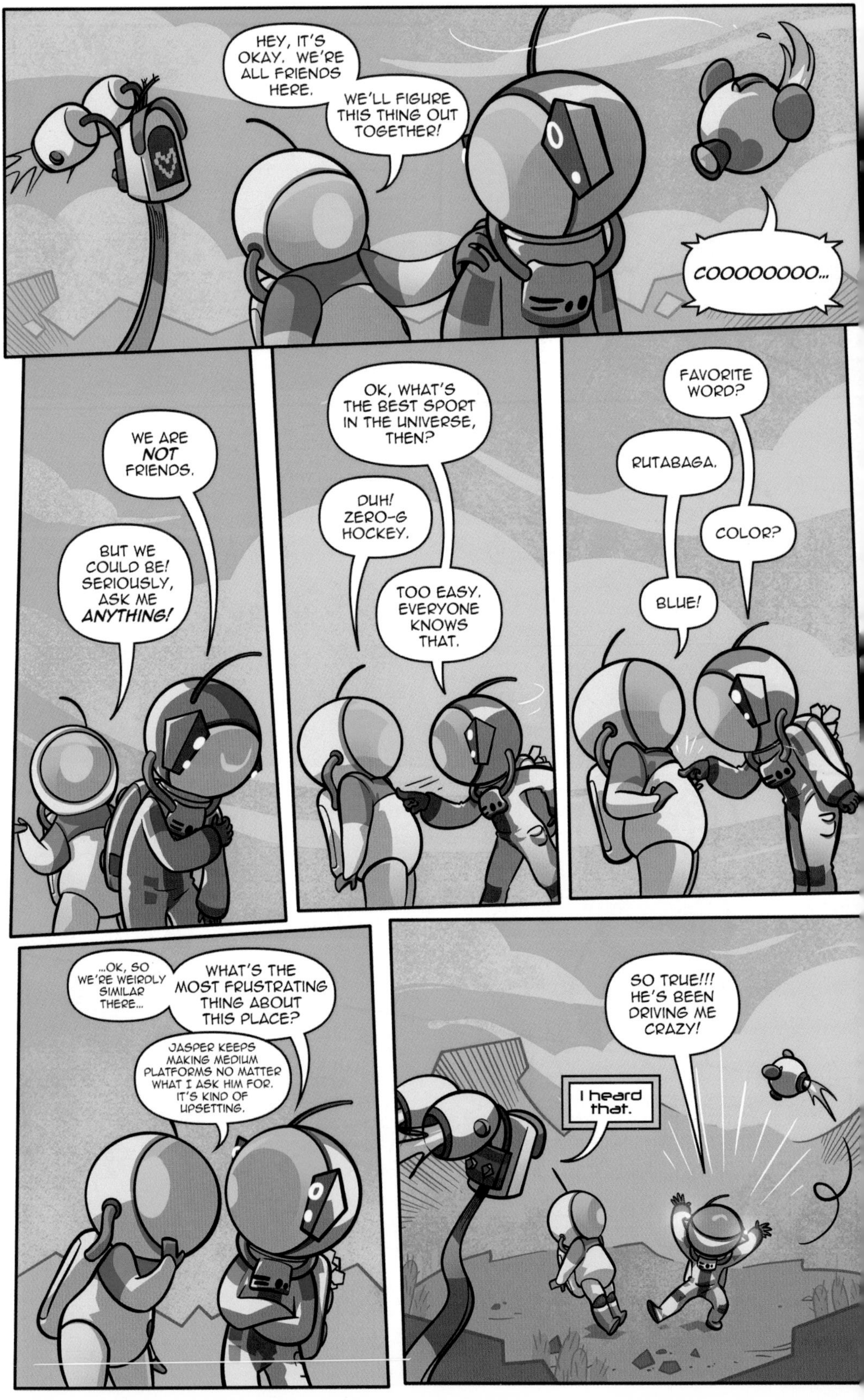
HEY, IT'S OKAY. WE'RE ALL FRIENDS HERE.
WE'LL FIGURE THIS THING OUT TOGETHER!
COOOOOOOO...
WE ARE NOT FRIENDS.
BUT WE COULD BE! SERIOUSLY, ASK ME ANYTHING!
OK, WHAT'S THE BEST SPORT IN THE UNIVERSE, THEN?
DUH! ZERO-G HOCKEY.
TOO EASY. EVERYONE KNOWS THAT.
FAVORITE WORD?
RUTABAGA.
COLOR?
BLUE!
...OK, SO WE'RE WEIRDLY SIMILAR THERE...
WHAT'S THE MOST FRUSTRATING THING ABOUT THIS PLACE?
JASPER KEEPS MAKING MEDIUM PLATFORMS NO MATTER WHAT I ASK HIM FOR. IT'S KIND OF UPSETTING.
SO TRUE!!! HE'S BEEN DRIVING ME CRAZY!
I heard that.

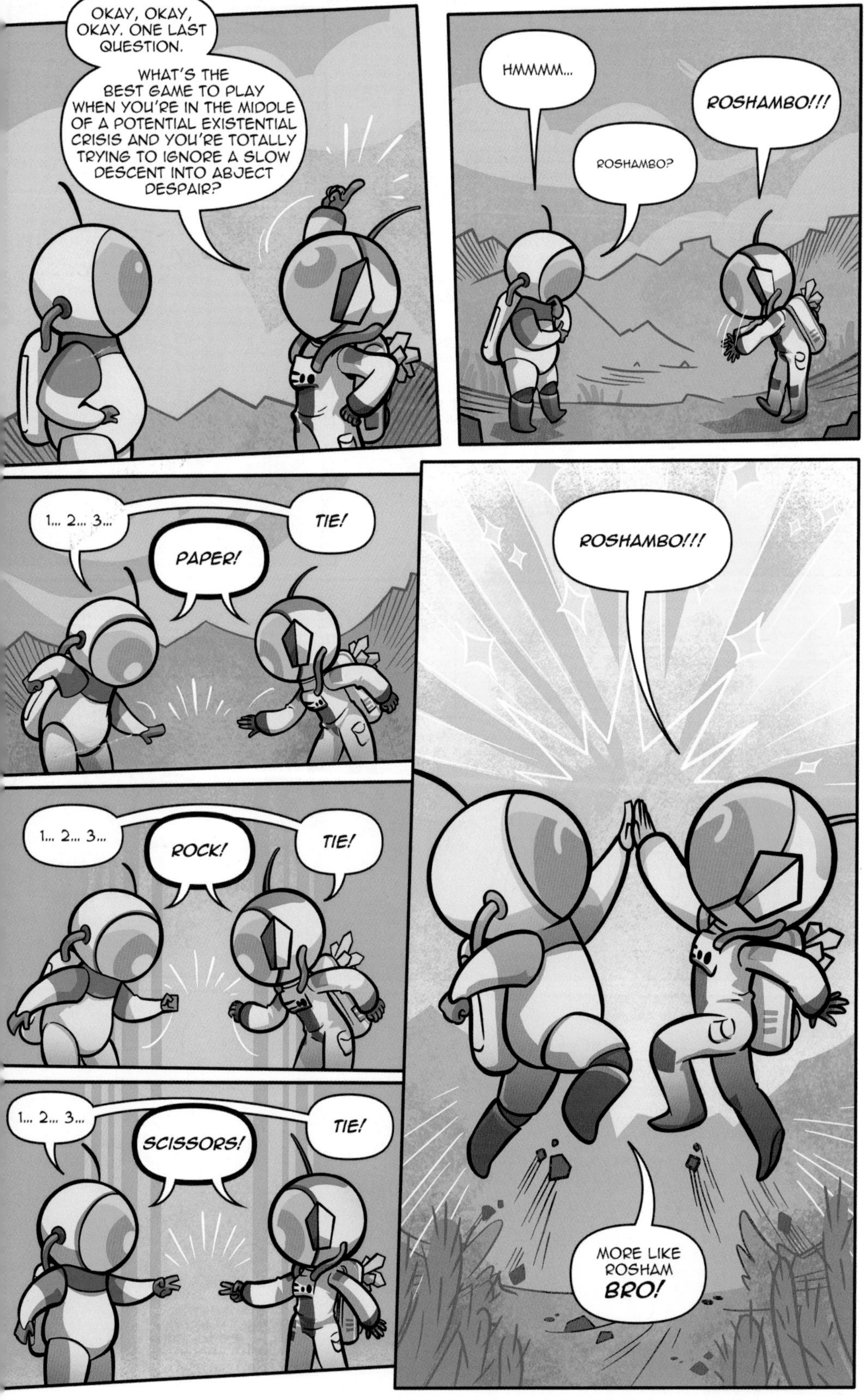
OKAY, OKAY, OKAY. ONE LAST QUESTION.
WHAT'S THE BEST GAME TO PLAY WHEN YOU'RE IN THE MIDDLE OF A POTENTIAL EXISTENTIAL CRISIS AND YOU'RE TOTALLY TRYING TO IGNORE A SLOW DESCENT INTO ABJECT DESPAIR?
HMMMM...
ROSHAMBO?
ROSHAMBO!!!
1... 2... 3...
PAPER!
TIE!
1... 2... 3...
ROCK!
TIE!
1... 2... 3...
SCISSORS!
TIE!
ROSHAMBO!!!
MORE LIKE ROSHAM BRO!

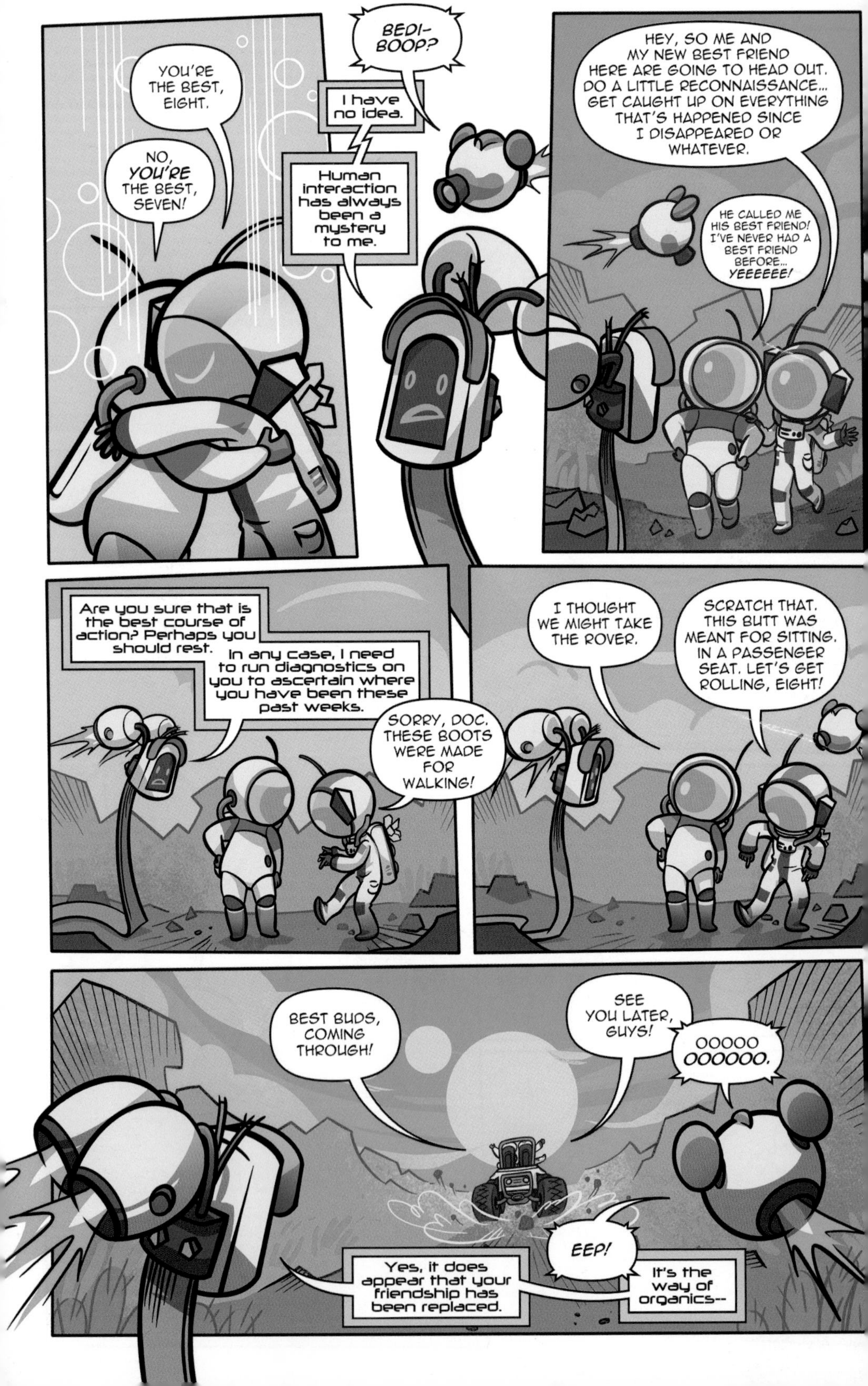

YOU'RE THE BEST, EIGHT.
NO, *YOU'RE* THE BEST, SEVEN!
BEDI-BOOP?
I have no idea.
Human interaction has always been a mystery to me.
HEY, SO ME AND MY NEW BEST FRIEND HERE ARE GOING TO HEAD OUT. DO A LITTLE RECONNAISSANCE... GET CAUGHT UP ON EVERYTHING THAT'S HAPPENED SINCE I DISAPPEARED OR WHATEVER.
HE CALLED ME HIS BEST FRIEND! I'VE NEVER HAD A BEST FRIEND BEFORE... *YEEEEEE!*
Are you sure that is the best course of action? Perhaps you should rest.
In any case, I need to run diagnostics on you to ascertain where you have been these past weeks.
SORRY, DOC. THESE BOOTS WERE MADE FOR WALKING!
I THOUGHT WE MIGHT TAKE THE ROVER.
SCRATCH THAT. THIS BUTT WAS MEANT FOR SITTING. IN A PASSENGER SEAT. LET'S GET ROLLING, EIGHT!
BEST BUDS, COMING THROUGH!
SEE YOU LATER, GUYS!
OOOOO *OOOOOO.*
EEP!
Yes, it does appear that your friendship has been replaced.
It's the way of organics--

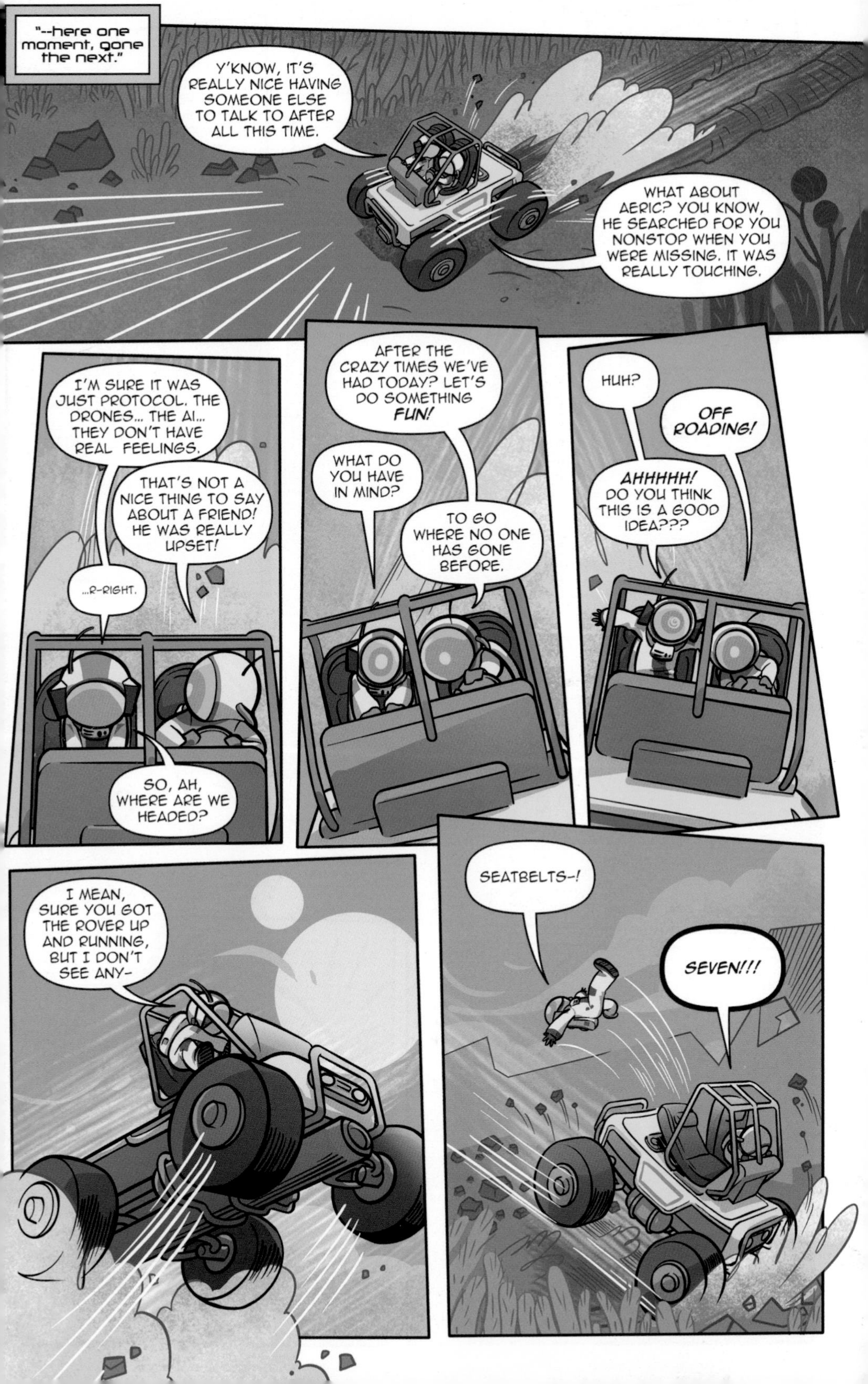
"--here one moment, gone the next."
Y'KNOW, IT'S REALLY NICE HAVING SOMEONE ELSE TO TALK TO AFTER ALL THIS TIME.
WHAT ABOUT AERIC? YOU KNOW, HE SEARCHED FOR YOU NONSTOP WHEN YOU WERE MISSING. IT WAS REALLY TOUCHING.
I'M SURE IT WAS JUST PROTOCOL. THE DRONES... THE AI... THEY DON'T HAVE REAL FEELINGS.
THAT'S NOT A NICE THING TO SAY ABOUT A FRIEND! HE WAS REALLY UPSET!
...R-RIGHT.
SO, AH, WHERE ARE WE HEADED?
AFTER THE CRAZY TIMES WE'VE HAD TODAY? LET'S DO SOMETHING FUN!
WHAT DO YOU HAVE IN MIND?
TO GO WHERE NO ONE HAS GONE BEFORE.
HUH?
OFF ROADING!
AHHHHH! DO YOU THINK THIS IS A GOOD IDEA???
I MEAN, SURE YOU GOT THE ROVER UP AND RUNNING, BUT I DON'T SEE ANY-
SEATBELTS-!
SEVEN!!!

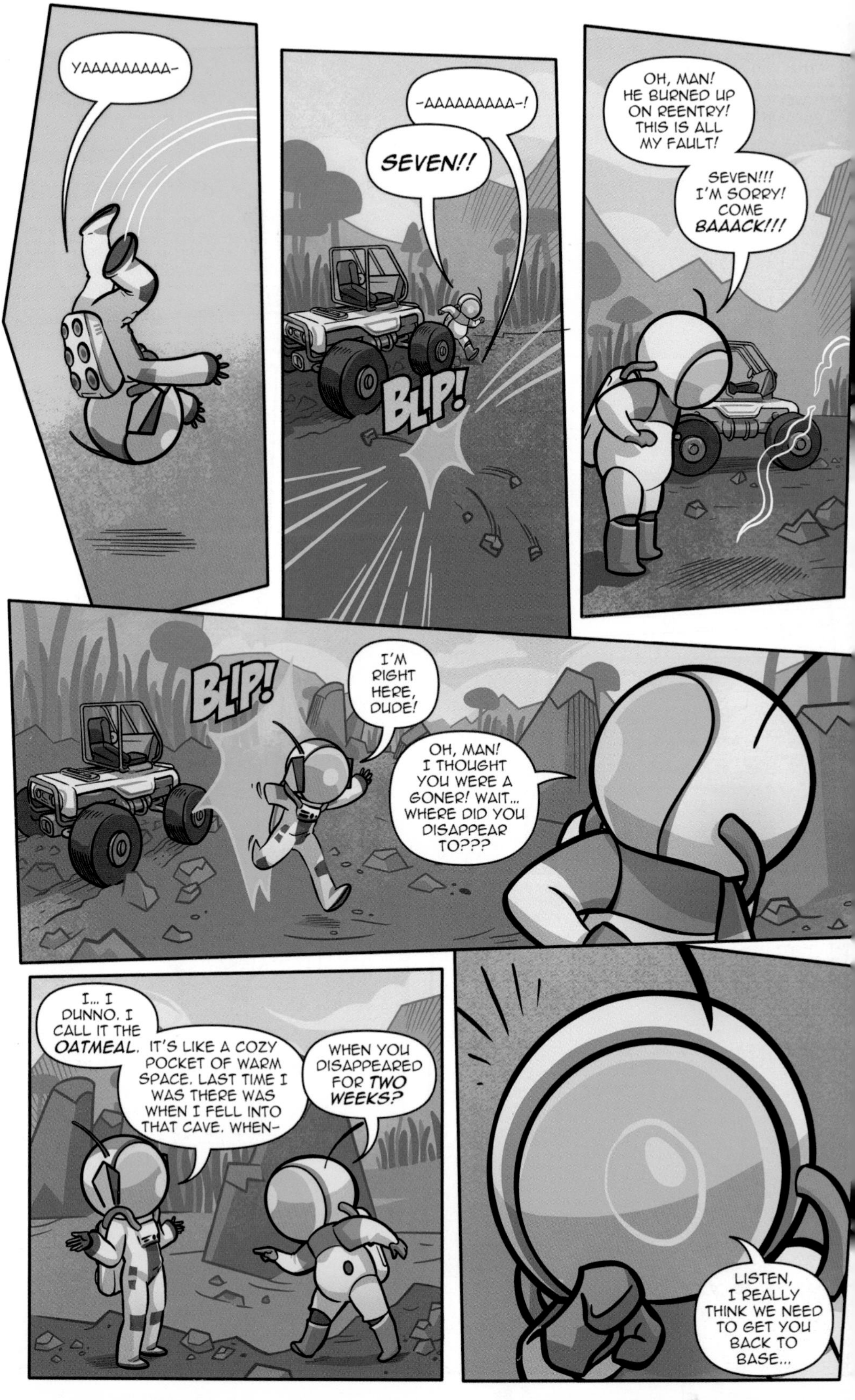
YAAAAAAAAA-
-AAAAAAAAA-!
SEVEN!!
BLIP!
OH, MAN! HE BURNED UP ON REENTRY! THIS IS ALL MY FAULT!
SEVEN!!! I'M SORRY! COME BAAACK!!!
BLIP!
I'M RIGHT HERE, DUDE!
OH, MAN! I THOUGHT YOU WERE A GONER! WAIT... WHERE DID YOU DISAPPEAR TO???
I... I DUNNO. I CALL IT THE OATMEAL.
IT'S LIKE A COZY POCKET OF WARM SPACE. LAST TIME I WAS THERE WAS WHEN I FELL INTO THAT CAVE. WHEN-
WHEN YOU DISAPPEARED FOR TWO WEEKS?
LISTEN, I REALLY THINK WE NEED TO GET YOU BACK TO BASE...

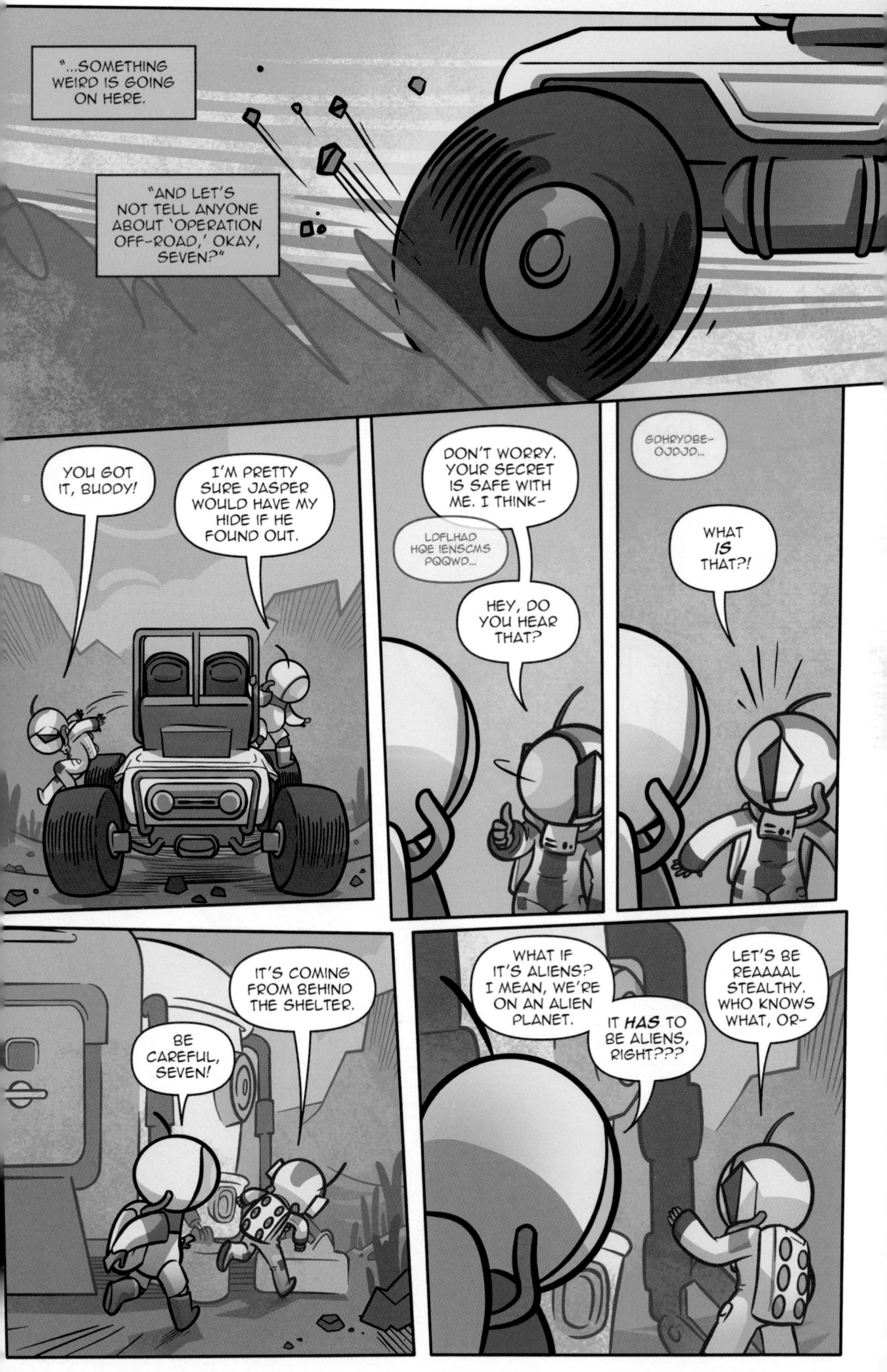
"...SOMETHING WEIRD IS GOING ON HERE.
"AND LET'S NOT TELL ANYONE ABOUT 'OPERATION OFF-ROAD,' OKAY, SEVEN?"
YOU GOT IT, BUDDY!
I'M PRETTY SURE JASPER WOULD HAVE MY HIDE IF HE FOUND OUT.
DON'T WORRY. YOUR SECRET IS SAFE WITH ME. I THINK-
LDFLHAD HQE IENSCMS PQQWD...
HEY, DO YOU HEAR THAT?
GDHRYDBE-OJDJD...
WHAT IS THAT?!
BE CAREFUL, SEVEN!
IT'S COMING FROM BEHIND THE SHELTER.
WHAT IF IT'S ALIENS? I MEAN, WE'RE ON AN ALIEN PLANET.
IT HAS TO BE ALIENS, RIGHT???
LET'S BE REAAAAL STEALTHY. WHO KNOWS WHAT, OR-

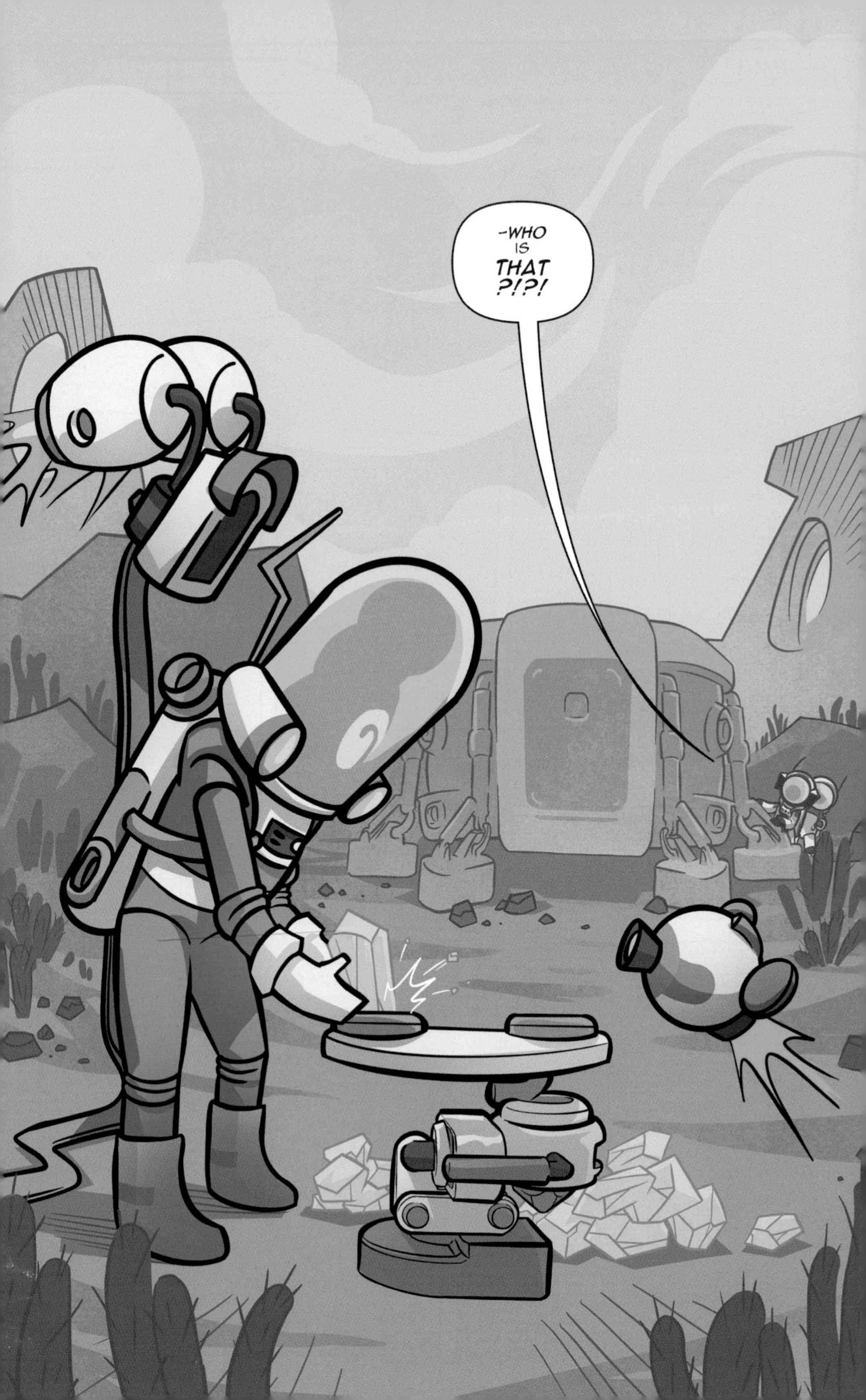
-WHO IS THAT ?!?!

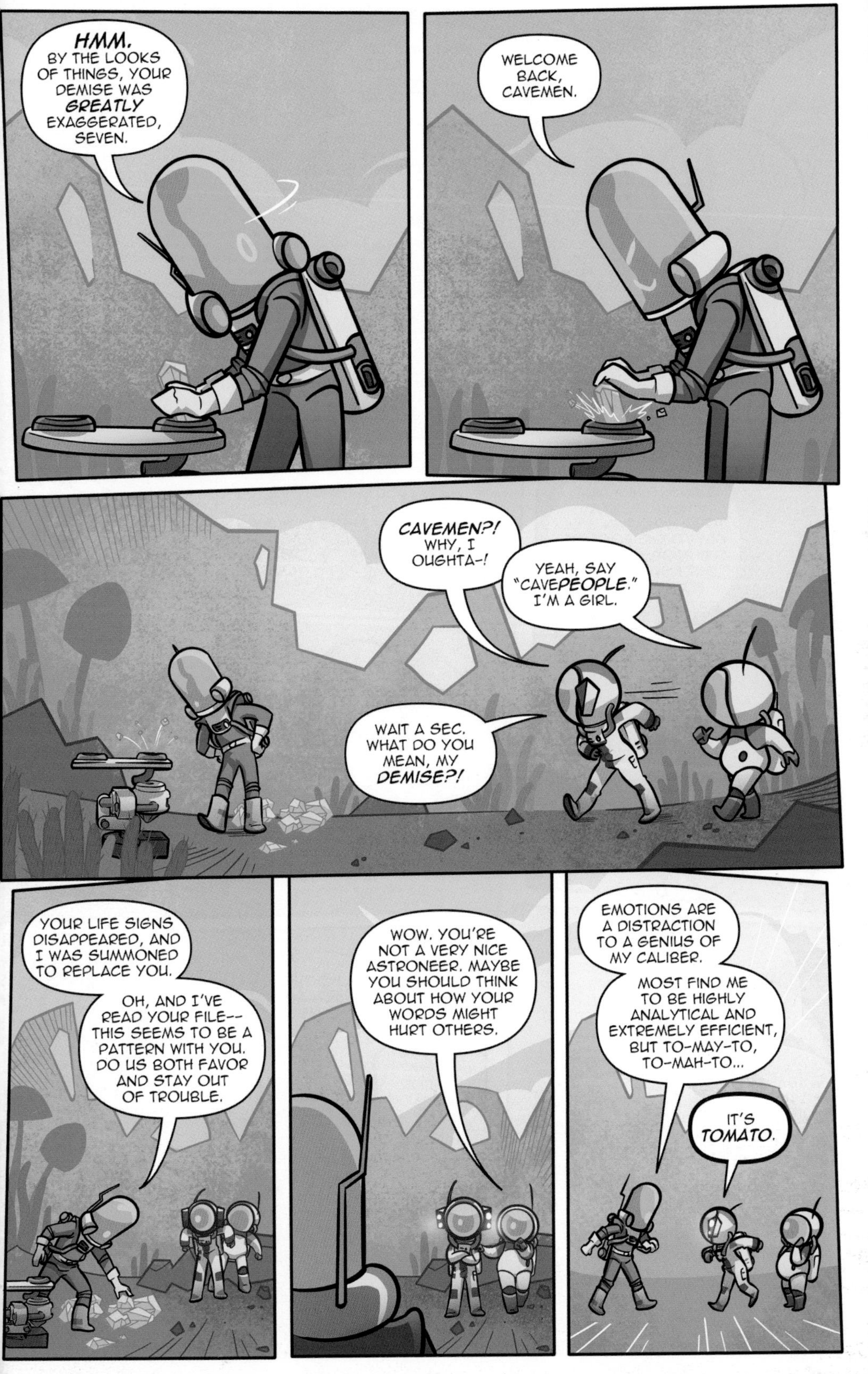
HMM. BY THE LOOKS OF THINGS, YOUR DEMISE WAS GREATLY EXAGGERATED, SEVEN.
WELCOME BACK, CAVEMEN.
CAVEMEN?! WHY, I OUGHTA-!
YEAH, SAY "CAVEPEOPLE." I'M A GIRL.
WAIT A SEC. WHAT DO YOU MEAN, MY DEMISE?!
YOUR LIFE SIGNS DISAPPEARED, AND I WAS SUMMONED TO REPLACE YOU.
OH, AND I'VE READ YOUR FILE-- THIS SEEMS TO BE A PATTERN WITH YOU. DO US BOTH FAVOR AND STAY OUT OF TROUBLE.
WOW. YOU'RE NOT A VERY NICE ASTRONEER. MAYBE YOU SHOULD THINK ABOUT HOW YOUR WORDS MIGHT HURT OTHERS.
EMOTIONS ARE A DISTRACTION TO A GENIUS OF MY CALIBER.
MOST FIND ME TO BE HIGHLY ANALYTICAL AND EXTREMELY EFFICIENT, BUT TO-MAY-TO, TO-MAH-TO...
IT'S TOMATO.

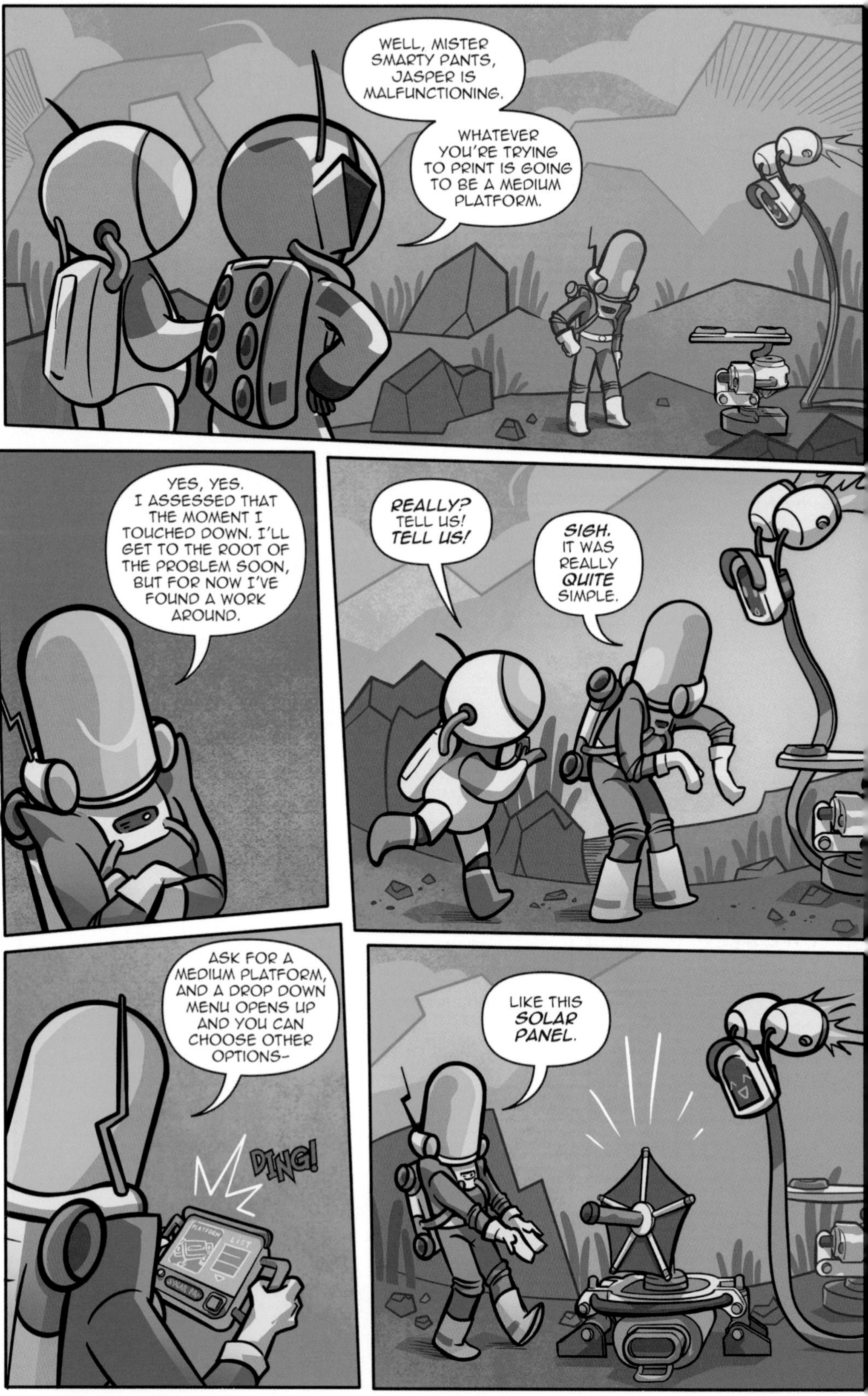
WELL, MISTER SMARTY PANTS, JASPER IS MALFUNCTIONING.
WHATEVER YOU'RE TRYING TO PRINT IS GOING TO BE A MEDIUM PLATFORM.
YES, YES. I ASSESSED THAT THE MOMENT I TOUCHED DOWN. I'LL GET TO THE ROOT OF THE PROBLEM SOON, BUT FOR NOW I'VE FOUND A WORK AROUND.
REALLY? TELL US! TELL US!
SIGH. IT WAS REALLY QUITE SIMPLE.
ASK FOR A MEDIUM PLATFORM, AND A DROP DOWN MENU OPENS UP AND YOU CAN CHOOSE OTHER OPTIONS-
DING!
PLATFORM
LIST
LIKE THIS SOLAR PANEL.

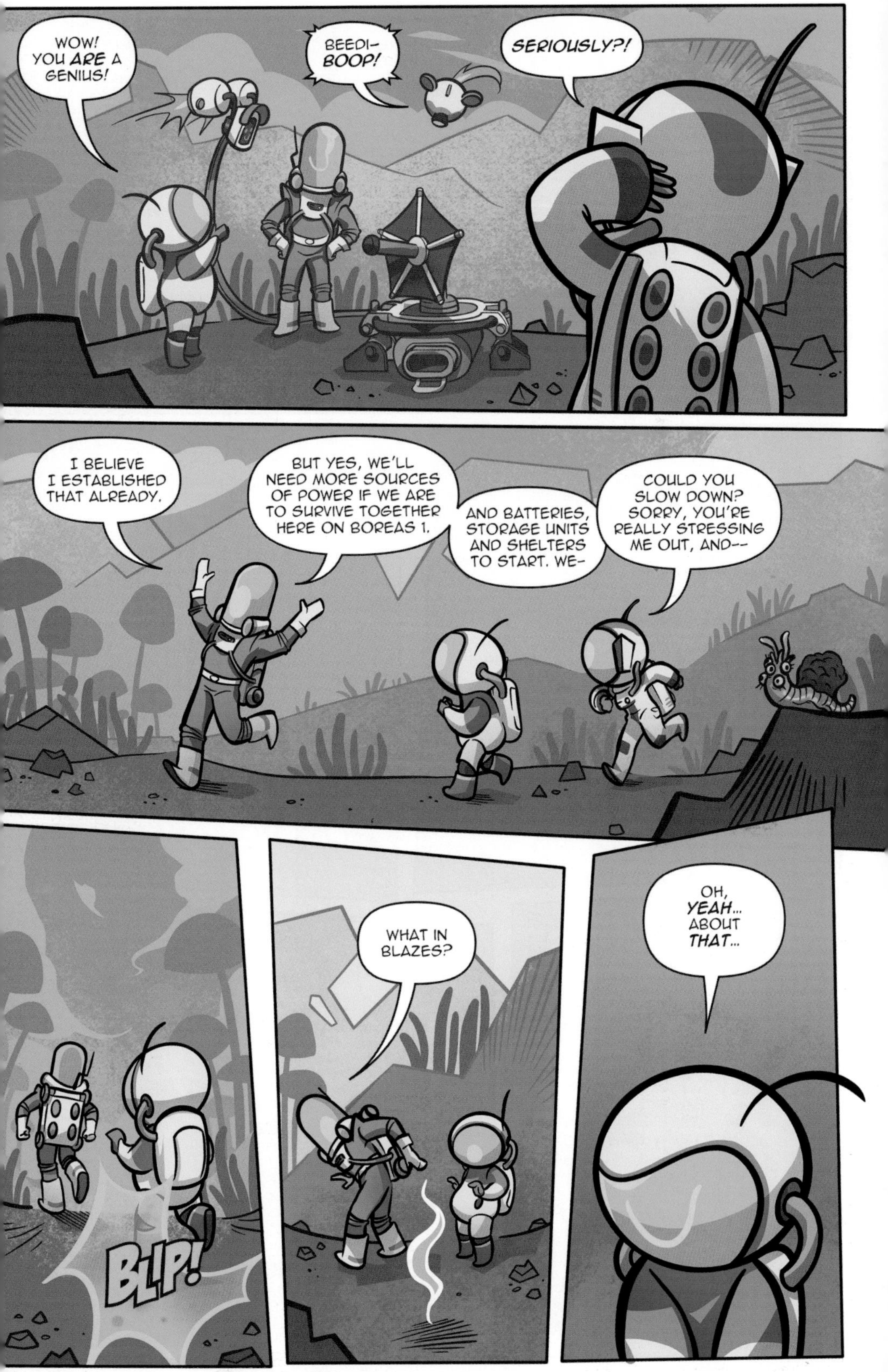
WOW! YOU ARE A GENIUS!
BEEDI-BOOP!
SERIOUSLY?!
I BELIEVE I ESTABLISHED THAT ALREADY.
BUT YES, WE'LL NEED MORE SOURCES OF POWER IF WE ARE TO SURVIVE TOGETHER HERE ON BOREAS 1.
AND BATTERIES, STORAGE UNITS AND SHELTERS TO START. WE-
COULD YOU SLOW DOWN? SORRY, YOU'RE REALLY STRESSING ME OUT, AND--
BLIP!
WHAT IN BLAZES?
OH, YEAH... ABOUT THAT...

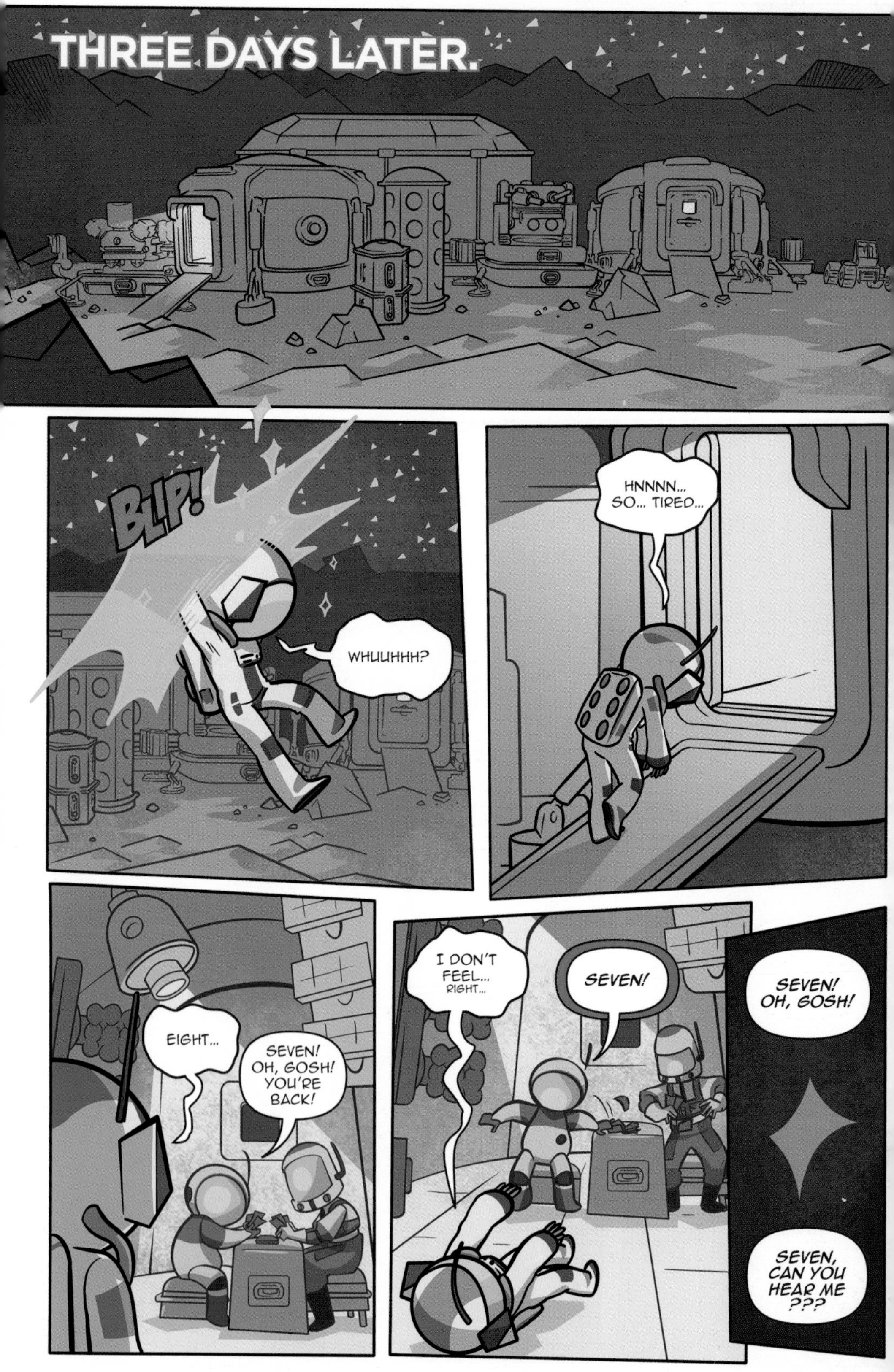
THREE DAYS LATER.
BLIP!
WHUUHHH?
HNNNN... SO... TIRED...
EIGHT...
SEVEN! OH, GOSH! YOU'RE BACK!
I DON'T FEEL... RIGHT...
SEVEN!
SEVEN! OH, GOSH!
SEVEN, CAN YOU HEAR ME ???

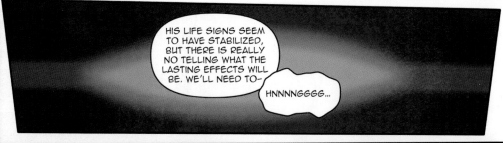

HIS LIFE SIGNS SEEM TO HAVE STABILIZED, BUT THERE IS REALLY NO TELLING WHAT THE LASTING EFFECTS WILL BE. WE'LL NEED TO—

HNNNNGGGG...

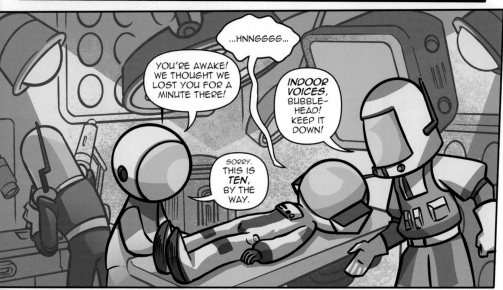

...HNNGGGG...

YOU'RE AWAKE! WE THOUGHT WE LOST YOU FOR A MINUTE THERE!

INDOOR VOICES, BUBBLE-HEAD! KEEP IT DOWN!

SORRY. THIS IS TEN, BY THE WAY.

EIGHT... AND... COMPLETE STRANGER, AH, TEN... WHAT... WHAT'S GOING ON?

I'LL TELL YOU WHAT'S GOING ON, MY LITTLE CAVEMAN.

TOO... WEAK... TO... ARGUE...

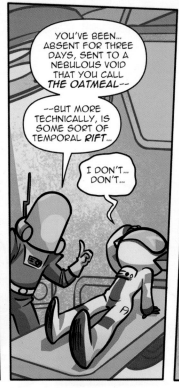

YOU'VE BEEN... ABSENT FOR THREE DAYS, SENT TO A NEBULOUS VOID THAT YOU CALL THE OATMEAL—

—BUT MORE TECHNICALLY, IS SOME SORT OF TEMPORAL RIFT...

I DON'T... DON'T...

I'M IN THE MIDDLE OF A MONOLOGUE HERE. HOLD ALL QUESTIONS UNTIL THE END, PLEASE.

SUFFICE TO SAY— THIS IS THE REASON BEHIND IT ALL.

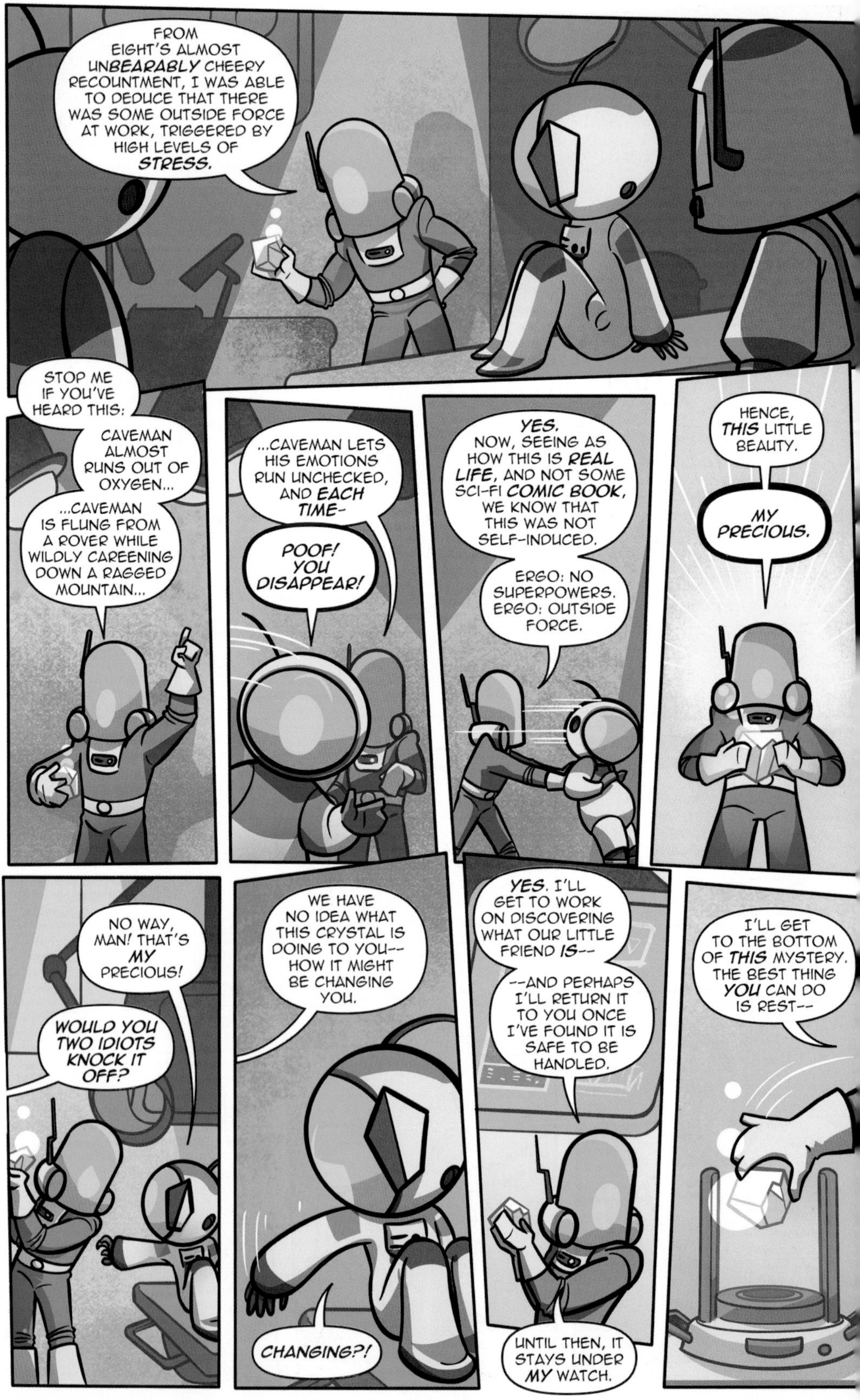
FROM EIGHT'S ALMOST UNBEARABLY CHEERY RECOUNTMENT, I WAS ABLE TO DEDUCE THAT THERE WAS SOME OUTSIDE FORCE AT WORK, TRIGGERED BY HIGH LEVELS OF STRESS.
STOP ME IF YOU'VE HEARD THIS:
CAVEMAN ALMOST RUNS OUT OF OXYGEN...
...CAVEMAN IS FLUNG FROM A ROVER WHILE WILDLY CAREENING DOWN A RAGGED MOUNTAIN...
...CAVEMAN LETS HIS EMOTIONS RUN UNCHECKED, AND EACH TIME-
POOF! YOU DISAPPEAR!
YES. NOW, SEEING AS HOW THIS IS REAL LIFE, AND NOT SOME SCI-FI COMIC BOOK, WE KNOW THAT THIS WAS NOT SELF-INDUCED.
ERGO: NO SUPERPOWERS. ERGO: OUTSIDE FORCE.
HENCE, THIS LITTLE BEAUTY.
MY PRECIOUS.
NO WAY, MAN! THAT'S MY PRECIOUS!
WOULD YOU TWO IDIOTS KNOCK IT OFF?
WE HAVE NO IDEA WHAT THIS CRYSTAL IS DOING TO YOU-- HOW IT MIGHT BE CHANGING YOU.
CHANGING?!
YES. I'LL GET TO WORK ON DISCOVERING WHAT OUR LITTLE FRIEND IS--
--AND PERHAPS I'LL RETURN IT TO YOU ONCE I'VE FOUND IT IS SAFE TO BE HANDLED.
UNTIL THEN, IT STAYS UNDER MY WATCH.
I'LL GET TO THE BOTTOM OF THIS MYSTERY. THE BEST THING YOU CAN DO IS REST--

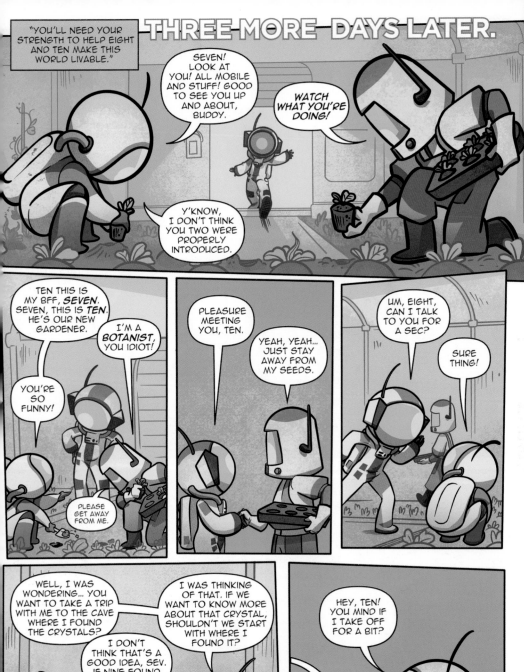

"YOU'LL NEED YOUR STRENGTH TO HELP EIGHT AND TEN MAKE THIS WORLD LIVABLE."

SEVEN! LOOK AT YOU! ALL MOBILE AND STUFF! GOOD TO SEE YOU UP AND ABOUT, BUDDY.

WATCH WHAT YOU'RE DOING!

Y'KNOW, I DON'T THINK YOU TWO WERE PROPERLY INTRODUCED.

TEN THIS IS MY BFF, *SEVEN*. SEVEN, THIS IS *TEN*. HE'S OUR NEW GARDENER.

I'M A *BOTANIST*, YOU IDIOT!

YOU'RE SO FUNNY!

PLEASE GET AWAY FROM ME.

PLEASURE MEETING YOU, TEN.

YEAH, YEAH... JUST STAY AWAY FROM MY SEEDS.

UM, EIGHT, CAN I TALK TO YOU FOR A SEC?

SURE THING!

WELL, I WAS WONDERING... YOU WANT TO TAKE A TRIP WITH ME TO THE CAVE WHERE I FOUND THE CRYSTALS?

I DON'T THINK THAT'S A GOOD IDEA, SEV. IF NINE FOUND OUT, WE'D–

I WAS THINKING OF THAT. IF WE WANT TO KNOW MORE ABOUT THAT CRYSTAL, SHOULDN'T WE START WITH WHERE I FOUND IT?

YOU MAKE A GOOD POINT.

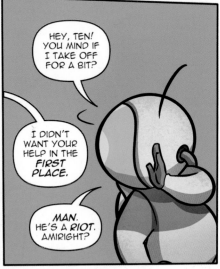

HEY, TEN! YOU MIND IF I TAKE OFF FOR A BIT?

I DIDN'T WANT YOUR HELP IN THE *FIRST PLACE*.

MAN. HE'S A *RIOT.* AMIRIGHT?

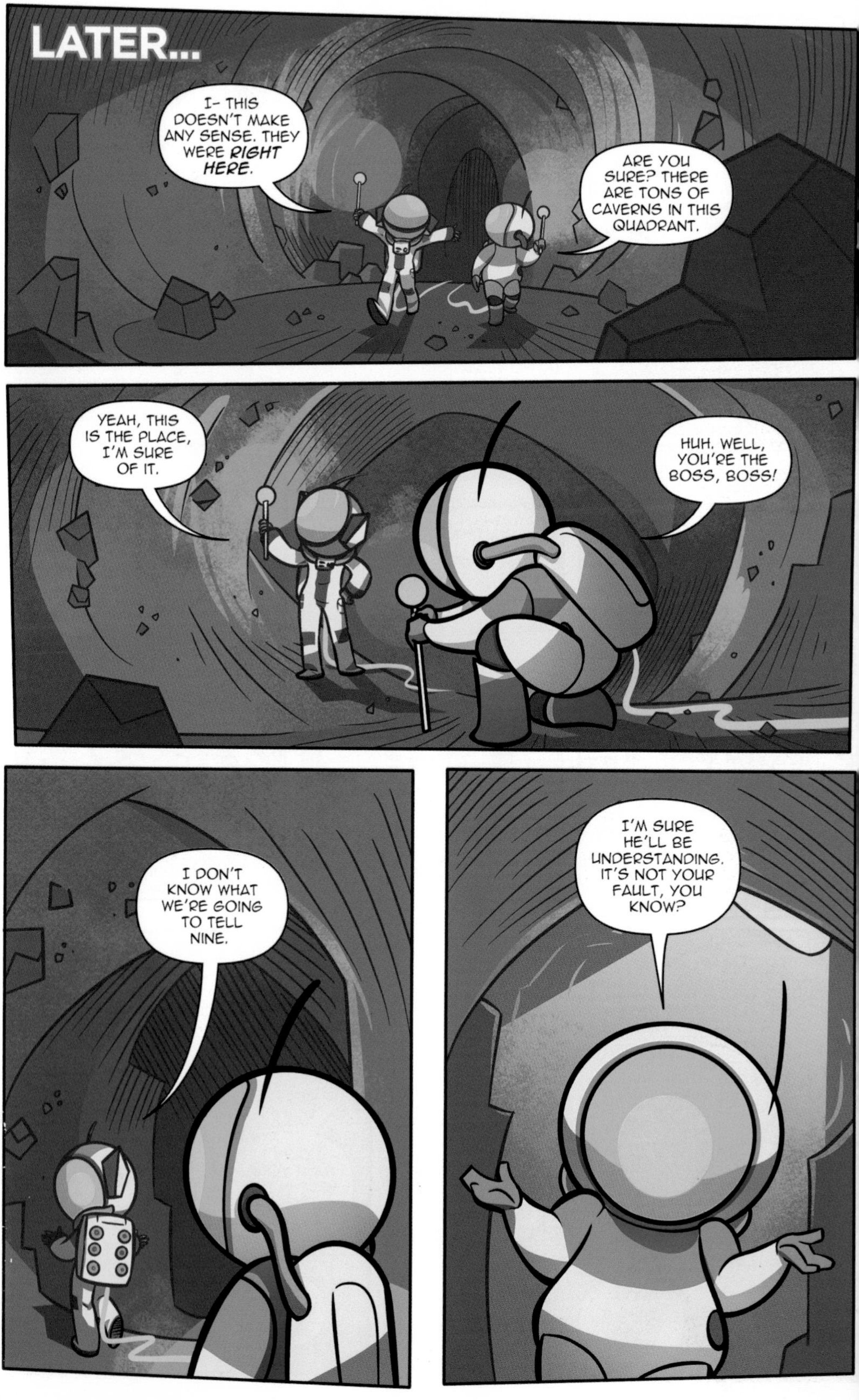
LATER...
I- THIS DOESN'T MAKE ANY SENSE. THEY WERE *RIGHT HERE*.
ARE YOU SURE? THERE ARE TONS OF CAVERNS IN THIS QUADRANT.
YEAH, THIS IS THE PLACE, I'M SURE OF IT.
HUH. WELL, YOU'RE THE BOSS, BOSS!
I DON'T KNOW WHAT WE'RE GOING TO TELL NINE.
I'M SURE HE'LL BE UNDERSTANDING. IT'S NOT YOUR FAULT, YOU KNOW?

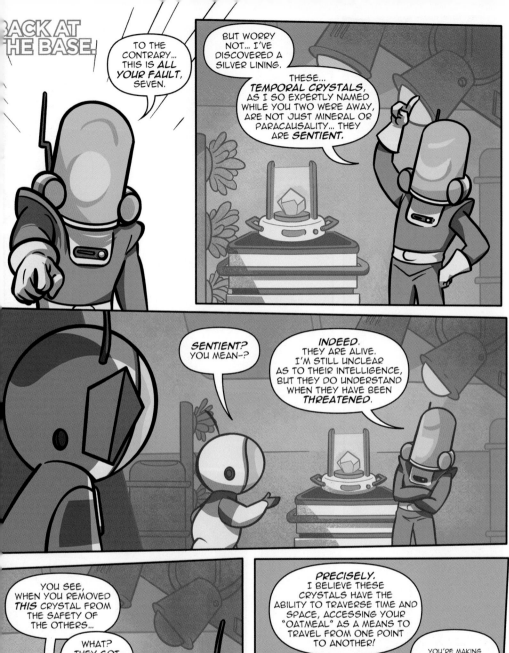

TO THE CONTRARY... THIS IS *ALL YOUR FAULT*, SEVEN.

BUT WORRY NOT... I'VE DISCOVERED A SILVER LINING.

THESE... *TEMPORAL CRYSTALS*, AS I SO EXPERTLY NAMED WHILE YOU TWO WERE AWAY, ARE NOT JUST MINERAL OR PARACAUSALITY... THEY ARE *SENTIENT*.

SENTIENT? YOU MEAN–?

INDEED. THEY ARE ALIVE. I'M STILL UNCLEAR AS TO THEIR INTELLIGENCE, BUT THEY DO UNDERSTAND WHEN THEY HAVE BEEN *THREATENED*.

YOU SEE, WHEN YOU REMOVED *THIS* CRYSTAL FROM THE SAFETY OF THE OTHERS...

WHAT? THEY GOT SCARED? WENT INTO HIDING?

PRECISELY. I BELIEVE THESE CRYSTALS HAVE THE ABILITY TO TRAVERSE TIME AND SPACE, ACCESSING YOUR "OATMEAL" AS A MEANS TO TRAVEL FROM ONE POINT TO ANOTHER!

YOU'RE MAKING ME VERY UNCOMFORTABLE.

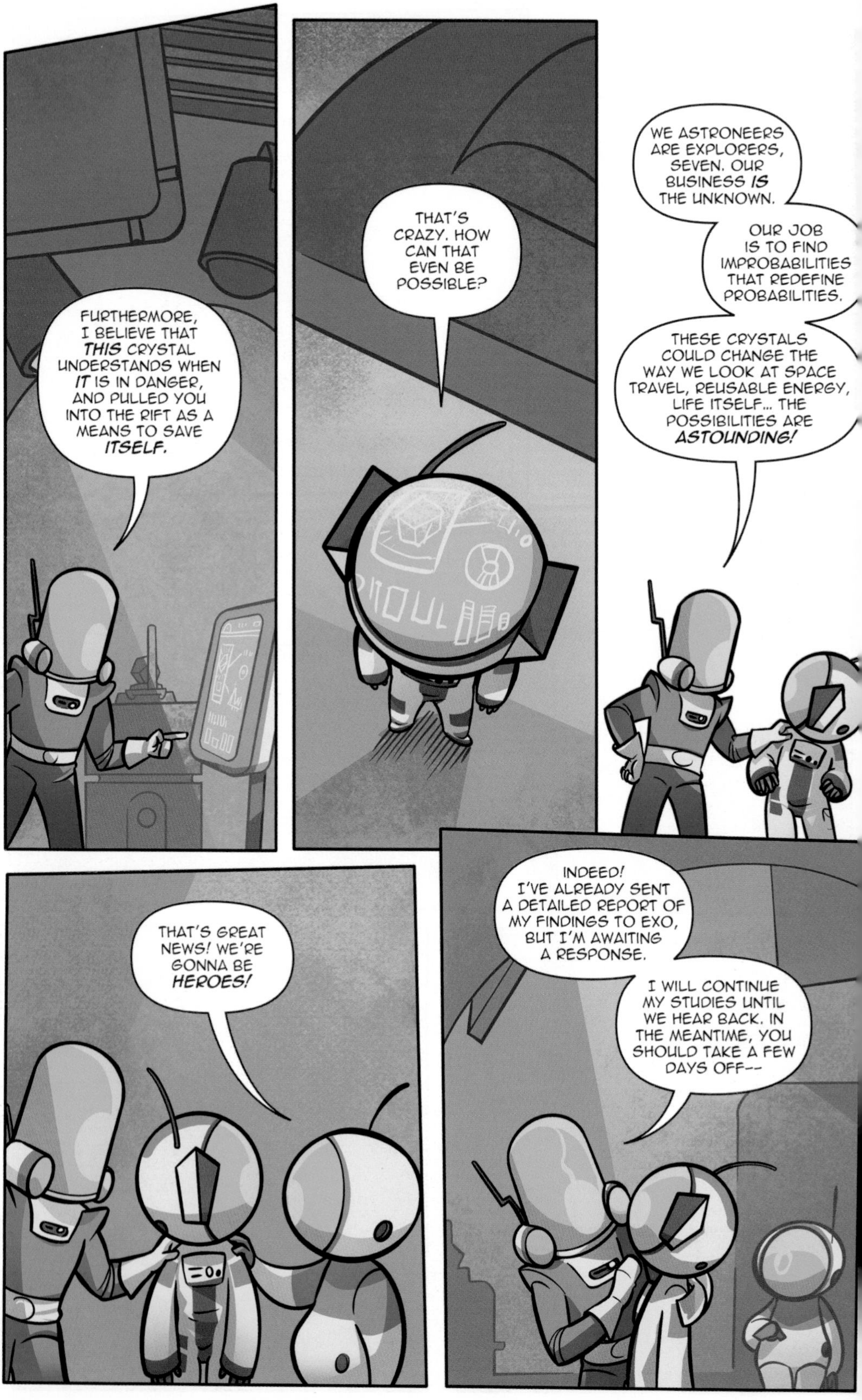
FURTHERMORE, I BELIEVE THAT THIS CRYSTAL UNDERSTANDS WHEN IT IS IN DANGER, AND PULLED YOU INTO THE RIFT AS A MEANS TO SAVE ITSELF.
THAT'S CRAZY. HOW CAN THAT EVEN BE POSSIBLE?
WE ASTRONEERS ARE EXPLORERS, SEVEN. OUR BUSINESS IS THE UNKNOWN.
OUR JOB IS TO FIND IMPROBABILITIES THAT REDEFINE PROBABILITIES.
THESE CRYSTALS COULD CHANGE THE WAY WE LOOK AT SPACE TRAVEL, REUSABLE ENERGY, LIFE ITSELF... THE POSSIBILITIES ARE ASTOUNDING!
THAT'S GREAT NEWS! WE'RE GONNA BE HEROES!
INDEED! I'VE ALREADY SENT A DETAILED REPORT OF MY FINDINGS TO EXO, BUT I'M AWAITING A RESPONSE.
I WILL CONTINUE MY STUDIES UNTIL WE HEAR BACK. IN THE MEANTIME, YOU SHOULD TAKE A FEW DAYS OFF--

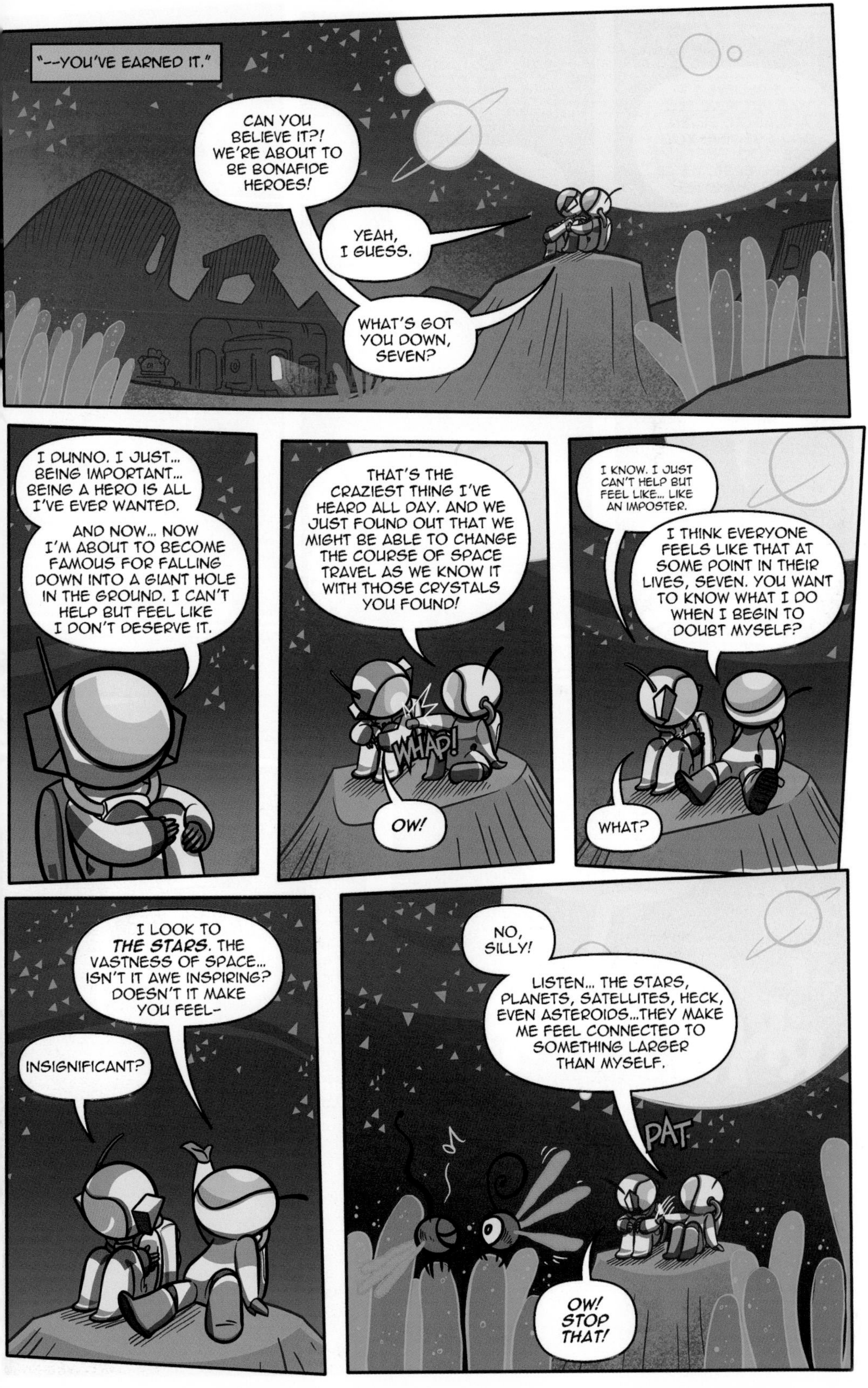
"--YOU'VE EARNED IT."
CAN YOU BELIEVE IT?! WE'RE ABOUT TO BE BONAFIDE HEROES!
YEAH, I GUESS.
WHAT'S GOT YOU DOWN, SEVEN?
I DUNNO. I JUST... BEING IMPORTANT... BEING A HERO IS ALL I'VE EVER WANTED.
AND NOW... NOW I'M ABOUT TO BECOME FAMOUS FOR FALLING DOWN INTO A GIANT HOLE IN THE GROUND. I CAN'T HELP BUT FEEL LIKE I DON'T DESERVE IT.
THAT'S THE CRAZIEST THING I'VE HEARD ALL DAY. AND WE JUST FOUND OUT THAT WE MIGHT BE ABLE TO CHANGE THE COURSE OF SPACE TRAVEL AS WE KNOW IT WITH THOSE CRYSTALS YOU FOUND!
WHAP!
OW!
I KNOW. I JUST CAN'T HELP BUT FEEL LIKE... LIKE AN IMPOSTER.
I THINK EVERYONE FEELS LIKE THAT AT SOME POINT IN THEIR LIVES, SEVEN. YOU WANT TO KNOW WHAT I DO WHEN I BEGIN TO DOUBT MYSELF?
WHAT?
I LOOK TO THE STARS. THE VASTNESS OF SPACE... ISN'T IT AWE INSPIRING? DOESN'T IT MAKE YOU FEEL-
INSIGNIFICANT?
NO, SILLY!
LISTEN... THE STARS, PLANETS, SATELLITES, HECK, EVEN ASTEROIDS...THEY MAKE ME FEEL CONNECTED TO SOMETHING LARGER THAN MYSELF.
PAT
OW! STOP THAT!

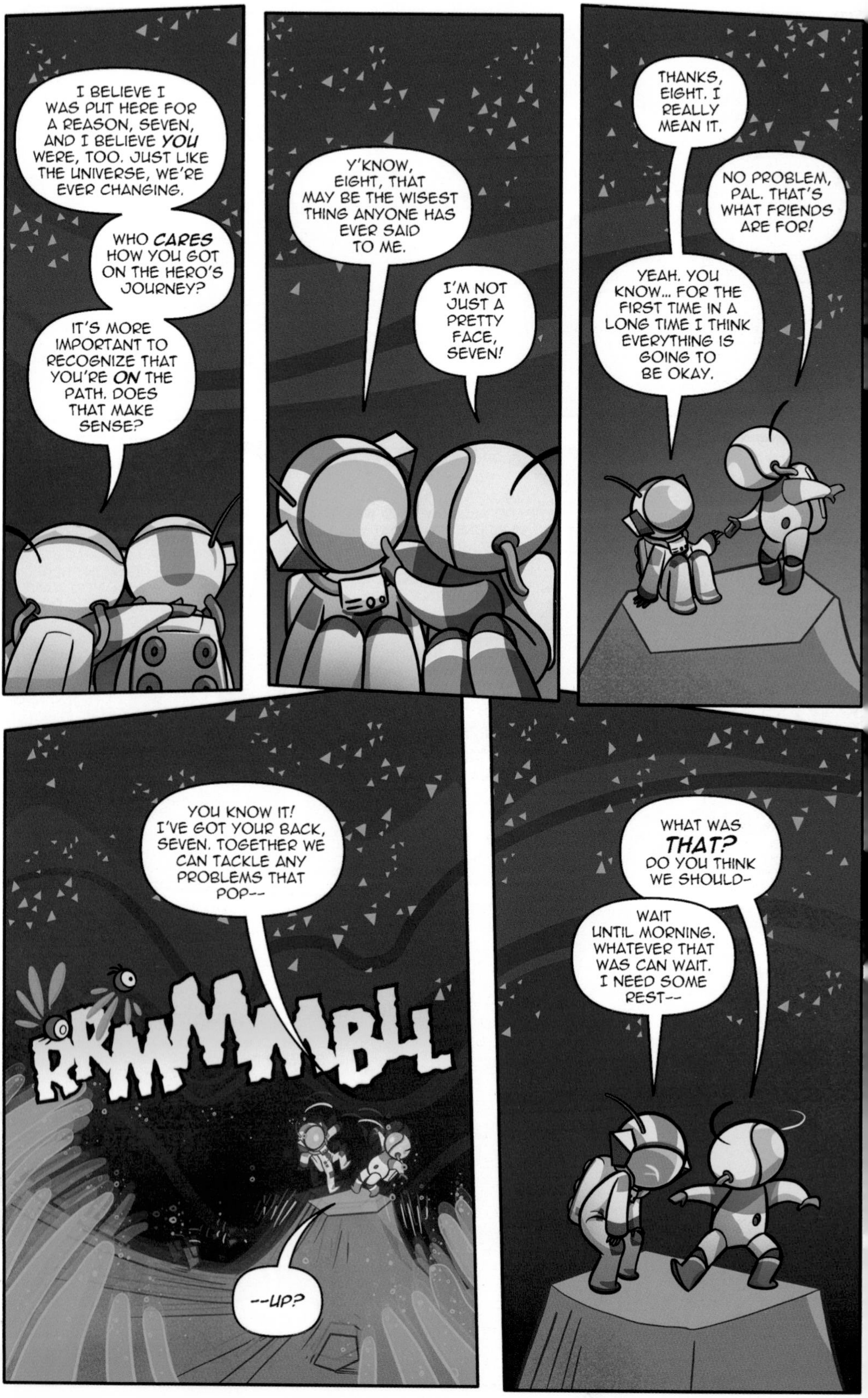
I BELIEVE I WAS PUT HERE FOR A REASON, SEVEN, AND I BELIEVE *YOU* WERE, TOO. JUST LIKE THE UNIVERSE, WE'RE EVER CHANGING.
WHO *CARES* HOW YOU GOT ON THE HERO'S JOURNEY?
IT'S MORE IMPORTANT TO RECOGNIZE THAT YOU'RE *ON* THE PATH. DOES THAT MAKE SENSE?
Y'KNOW, EIGHT, THAT MAY BE THE WISEST THING ANYONE HAS EVER SAID TO ME.
I'M NOT JUST A PRETTY FACE, SEVEN!
THANKS, EIGHT. I REALLY MEAN IT.
NO PROBLEM, PAL. THAT'S WHAT FRIENDS ARE FOR!
YEAH. YOU KNOW... FOR THE FIRST TIME IN A LONG TIME I THINK EVERYTHING IS GOING TO BE OKAY.
YOU KNOW IT! I'VE GOT YOUR BACK, SEVEN. TOGETHER WE CAN TACKLE ANY PROBLEMS THAT POP--
RRMMMBLL
--UP?
WHAT WAS *THAT?* DO YOU THINK WE SHOULD-
WAIT UNTIL MORNING. WHATEVER THAT WAS CAN WAIT. I NEED SOME REST--

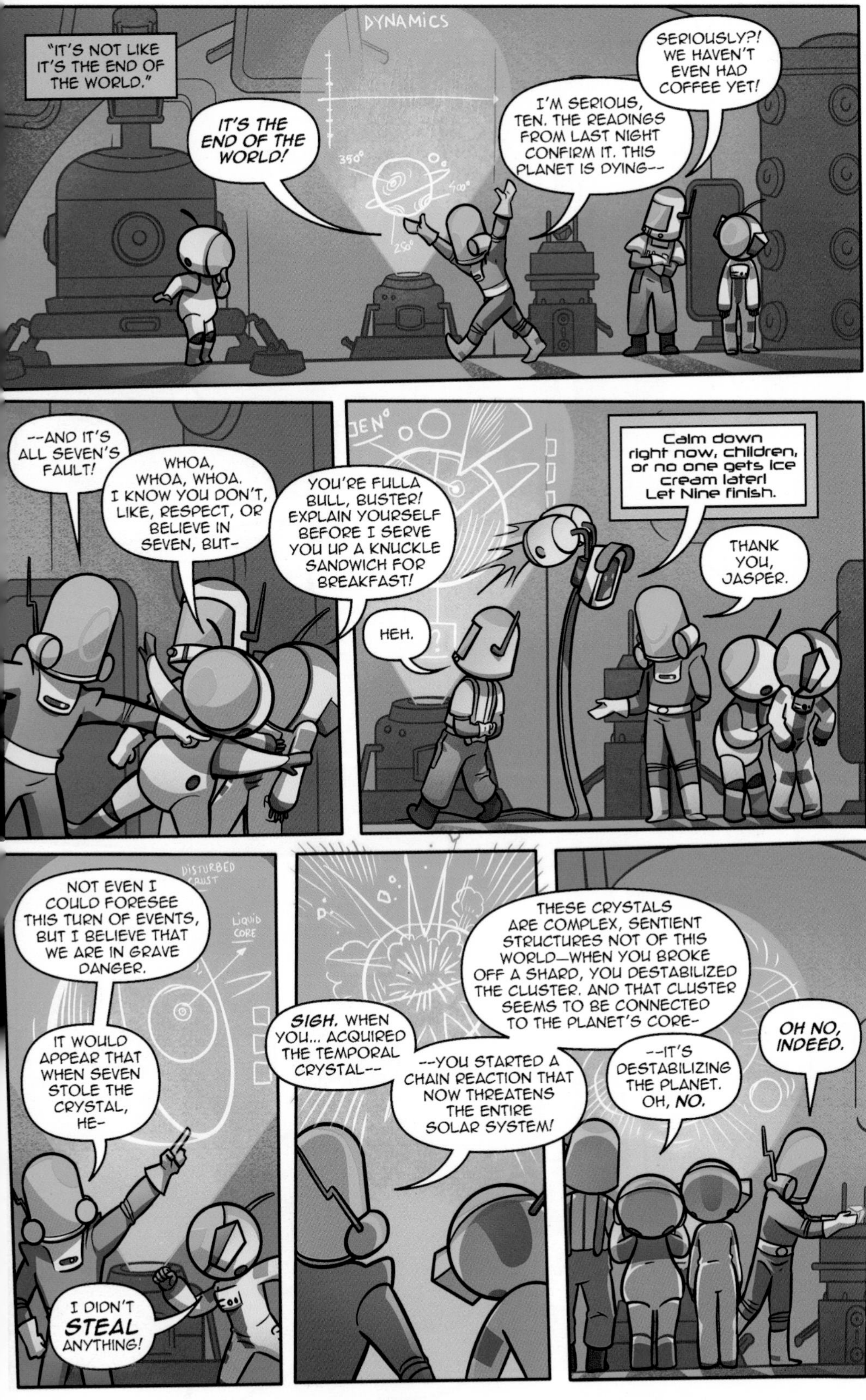
DYNAMICS
"IT'S NOT LIKE IT'S THE END OF THE WORLD."
IT'S THE END OF THE WORLD!
I'M SERIOUS, TEN. THE READINGS FROM LAST NIGHT CONFIRM IT. THIS PLANET IS DYING--
SERIOUSLY?! WE HAVEN'T EVEN HAD COFFEE YET!
--AND IT'S ALL SEVEN'S FAULT!
WHOA, WHOA, WHOA. I KNOW YOU DON'T, LIKE, RESPECT, OR BELIEVE IN SEVEN, BUT-
YOU'RE FULLA BULL, BUSTER! EXPLAIN YOURSELF BEFORE I SERVE YOU UP A KNUCKLE SANDWICH FOR BREAKFAST!
HEH.
Calm down right now, children, or no one gets ice cream later! Let Nine finish.
THANK YOU, JASPER.
DISTURBED CRUST
LIQUID CORE
NOT EVEN I COULD FORESEE THIS TURN OF EVENTS, BUT I BELIEVE THAT WE ARE IN GRAVE DANGER.
IT WOULD APPEAR THAT WHEN SEVEN STOLE THE CRYSTAL, HE-
I DIDN'T STEAL ANYTHING!
SIGH. WHEN YOU... ACQUIRED THE TEMPORAL CRYSTAL--
--YOU STARTED A CHAIN REACTION THAT NOW THREATENS THE ENTIRE SOLAR SYSTEM!
THESE CRYSTALS ARE COMPLEX, SENTIENT STRUCTURES NOT OF THIS WORLD—WHEN YOU BROKE OFF A SHARD, YOU DESTABILIZED THE CLUSTER. AND THAT CLUSTER SEEMS TO BE CONNECTED TO THE PLANET'S CORE-
--IT'S DESTABILIZING THE PLANET. OH, NO.
OH NO, INDEED.

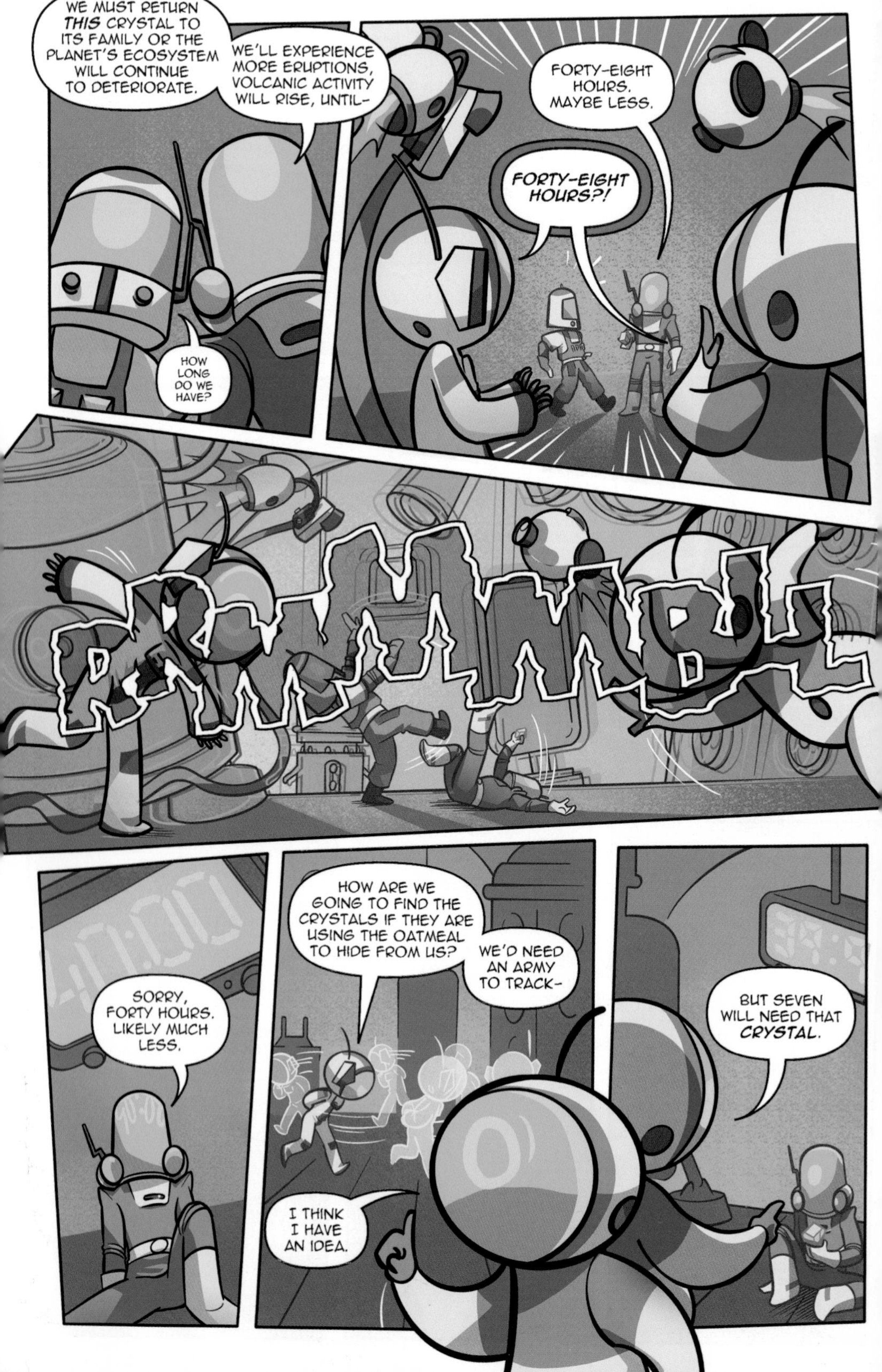
WE MUST RETURN THIS CRYSTAL TO ITS FAMILY OR THE PLANET'S ECOSYSTEM WILL CONTINUE TO DETERIORATE.
WE'LL EXPERIENCE MORE ERUPTIONS, VOLCANIC ACTIVITY WILL RISE, UNTIL-
HOW LONG DO WE HAVE?
FORTY-EIGHT HOURS. MAYBE LESS.
FORTY-EIGHT HOURS?!
SORRY, FORTY HOURS. LIKELY MUCH LESS.
HOW ARE WE GOING TO FIND THE CRYSTALS IF THEY ARE USING THE OATMEAL TO HIDE FROM US?
WE'D NEED AN ARMY TO TRACK-
I THINK I HAVE AN IDEA.
BUT SEVEN WILL NEED THAT CRYSTAL.

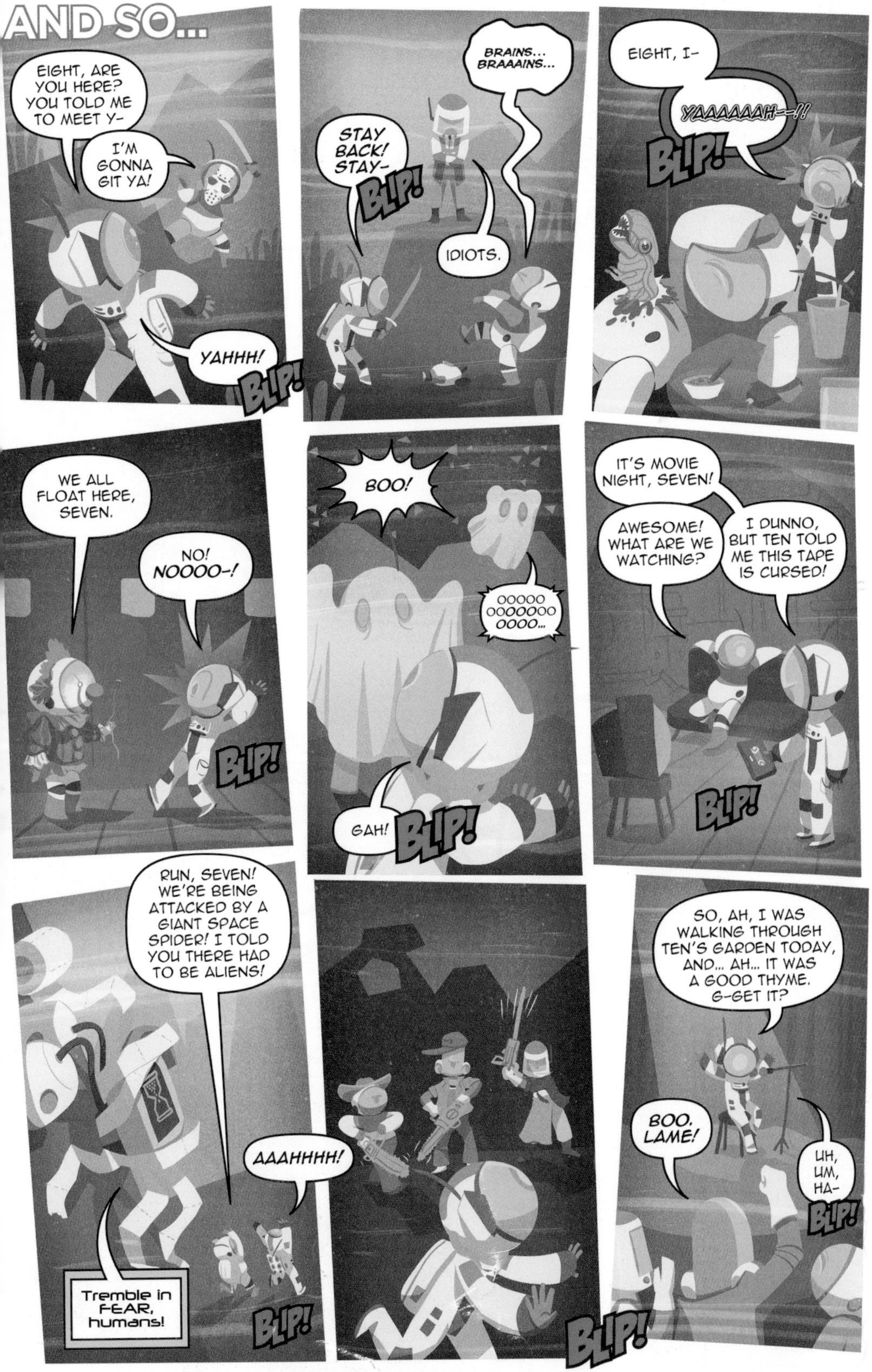
AND SO...
EIGHT, ARE YOU HERE? YOU TOLD ME TO MEET Y-
I'M GONNA GIT YA!
YAHHH!
BLIP!
BRAINS... BRAAAINS...
STAY BACK! STAY-
BLIP!
IDIOTS.
EIGHT, I-
YAAAAAAH--!!
BLIP!
WE ALL FLOAT HERE, SEVEN.
NO! NOOOO-!
BLIP!
BOO!
OOOOO OOOOOOO OOOO...
GAH!
BLIP!
IT'S MOVIE NIGHT, SEVEN!
AWESOME! WHAT ARE WE WATCHING?
I DUNNO, BUT TEN TOLD ME THIS TAPE IS CURSED!
BLIP!
RUN, SEVEN! WE'RE BEING ATTACKED BY A GIANT SPACE SPIDER! I TOLD YOU THERE HAD TO BE ALIENS!
AAAHHHH!
Tremble in FEAR, humans!
BLIP!
BLIP!
SO, AH, I WAS WALKING THROUGH TEN'S GARDEN TODAY, AND... AH... IT WAS A GOOD THYME. G-GET IT?
BOO. LAME!
UH, UM, HA-
BLIP!

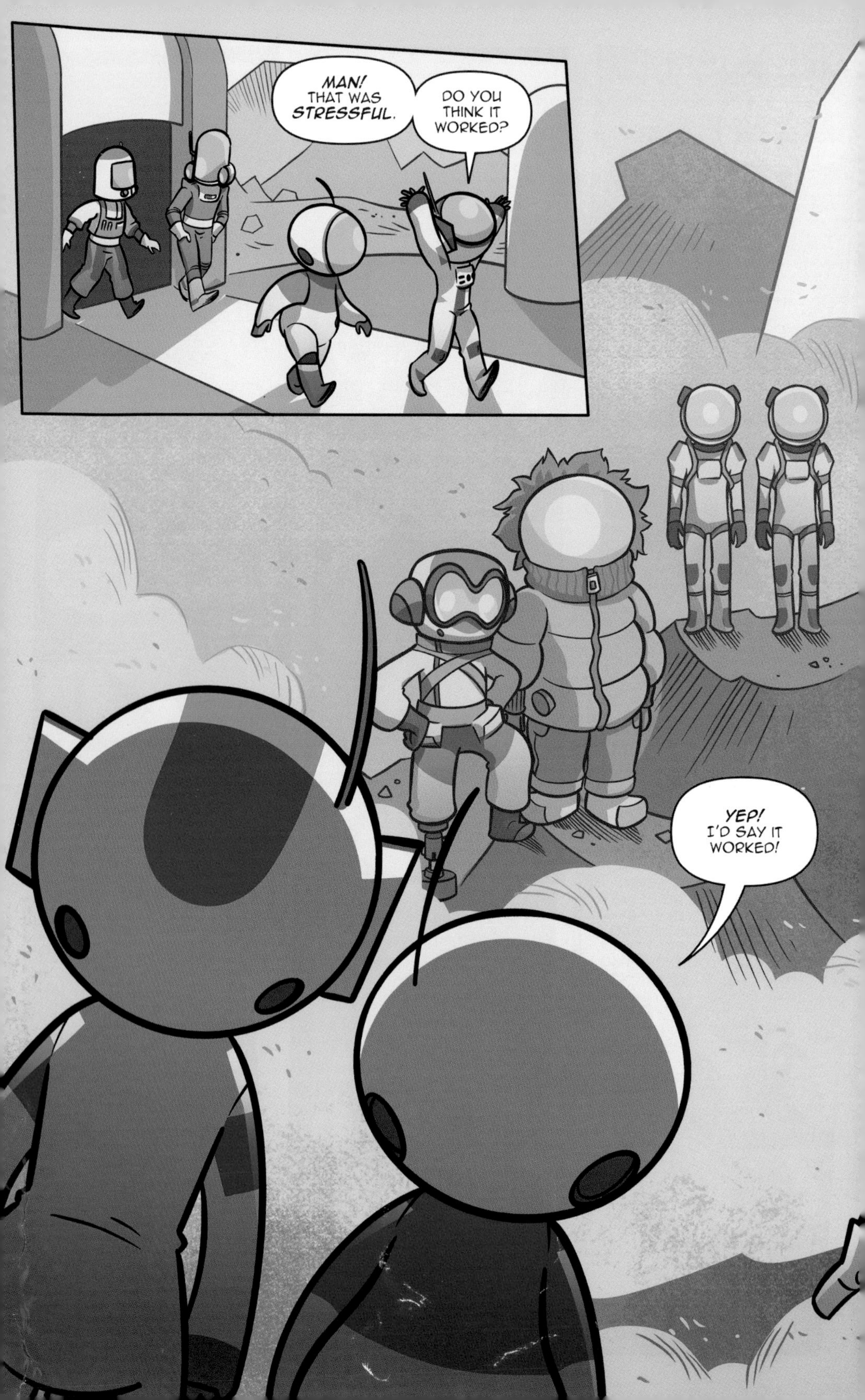
MAN! THAT WAS STRESSFUL.
DO YOU THINK IT WORKED?
YEP! I'D SAY IT WORKED!

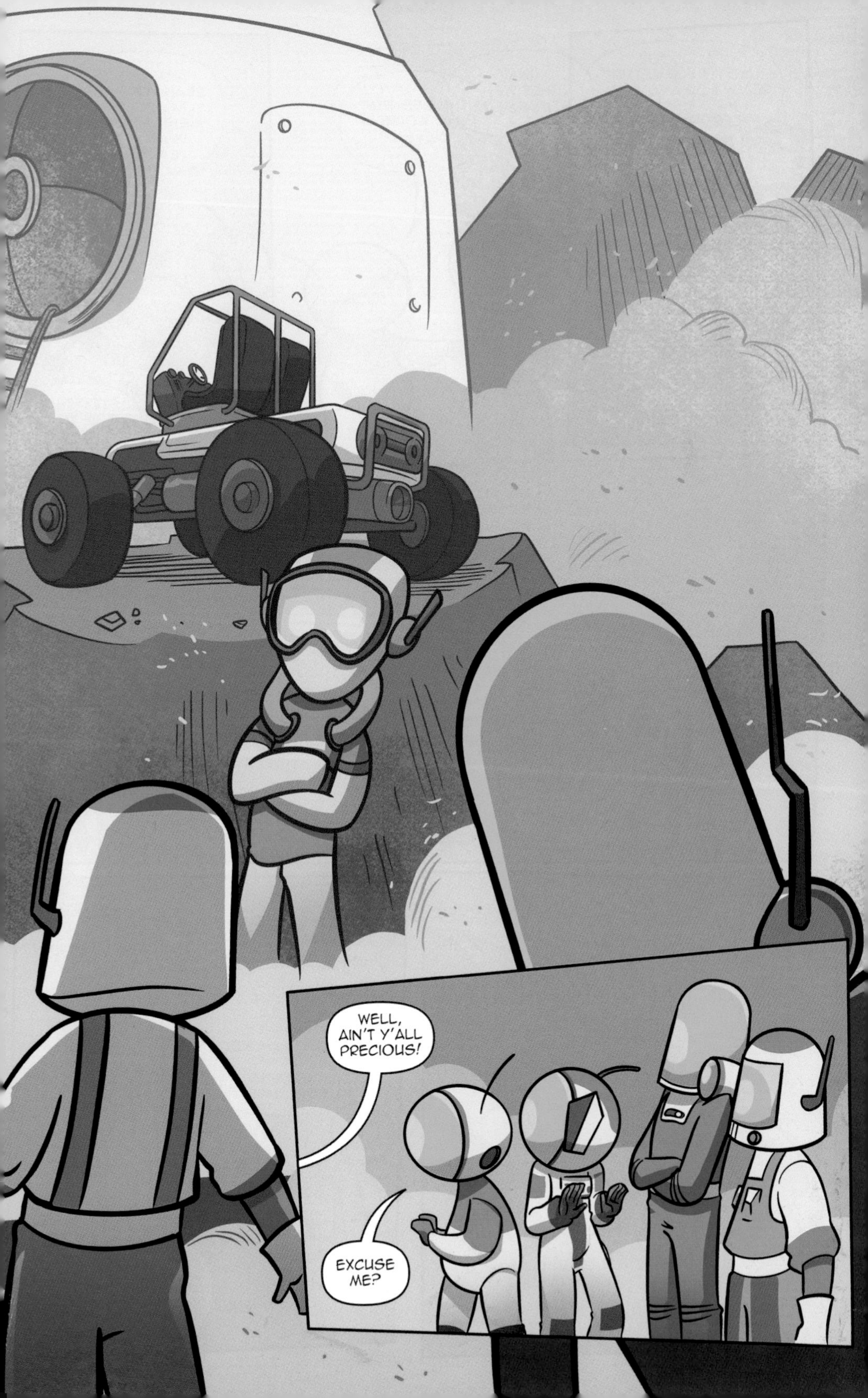
WELL, AIN'T Y'ALL PRECIOUS!
EXCUSE ME?

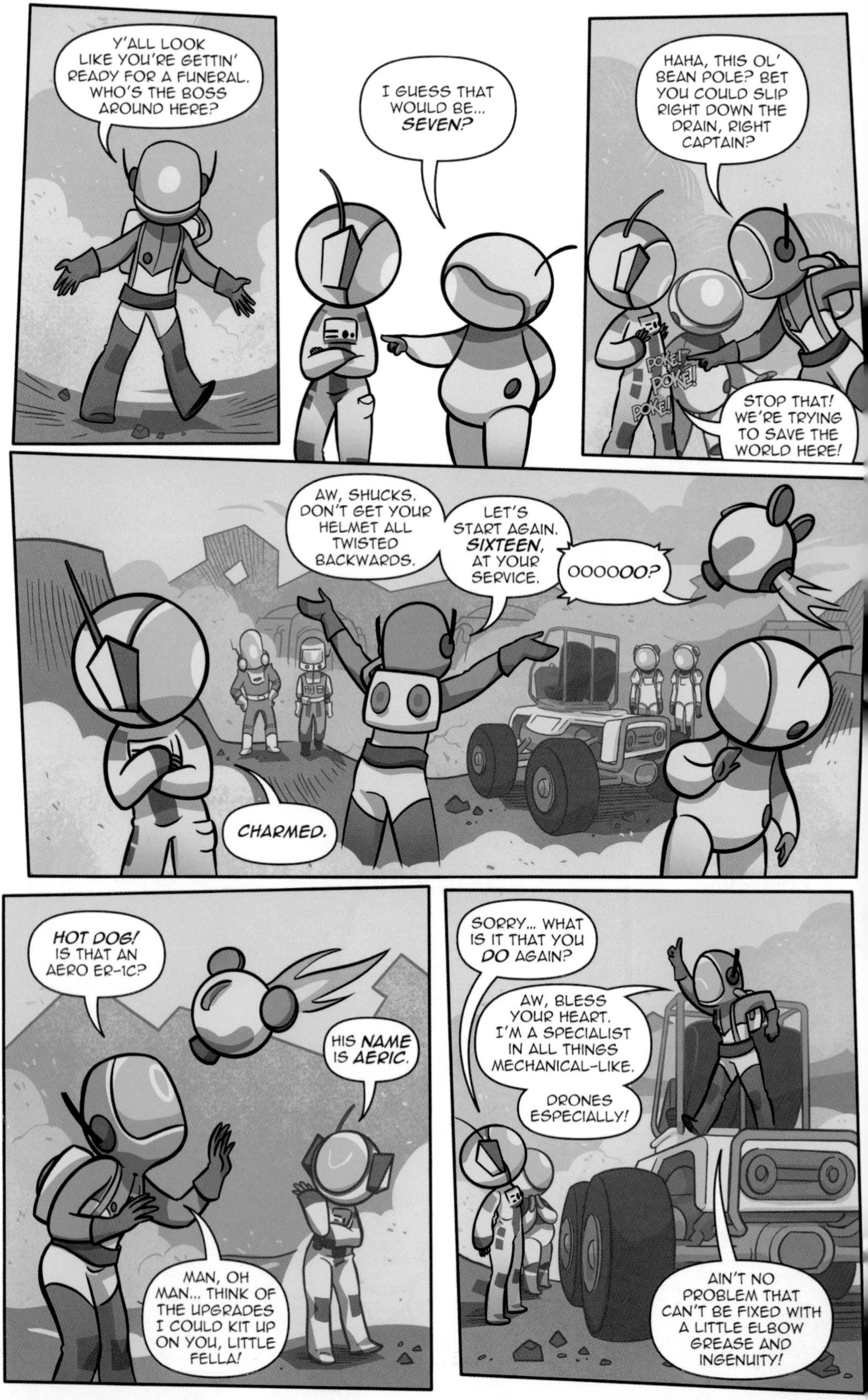
Y'ALL LOOK LIKE YOU'RE GETTIN' READY FOR A FUNERAL. WHO'S THE BOSS AROUND HERE?
I GUESS THAT WOULD BE... SEVEN?
HAHA, THIS OL' BEAN POLE? BET YOU COULD SLIP RIGHT DOWN THE DRAIN, RIGHT CAPTAIN?
POKE! POKE! POKE!
STOP THAT! WE'RE TRYING TO SAVE THE WORLD HERE!
AW, SHUCKS. DON'T GET YOUR HELMET ALL TWISTED BACKWARDS.
LET'S START AGAIN. SIXTEEN, AT YOUR SERVICE.
OOOOOO?
CHARMED.
HOT DOG! IS THAT AN AERO ER-1C?
HIS NAME IS AERIC.
MAN, OH MAN... THINK OF THE UPGRADES I COULD KIT UP ON YOU, LITTLE FELLA!
SORRY... WHAT IS IT THAT YOU DO AGAIN?
AW, BLESS YOUR HEART. I'M A SPECIALIST IN ALL THINGS MECHANICAL-LIKE.
DRONES ESPECIALLY!
AIN'T NO PROBLEM THAT CAN'T BE FIXED WITH A LITTLE ELBOW GREASE AND INGENUITY!

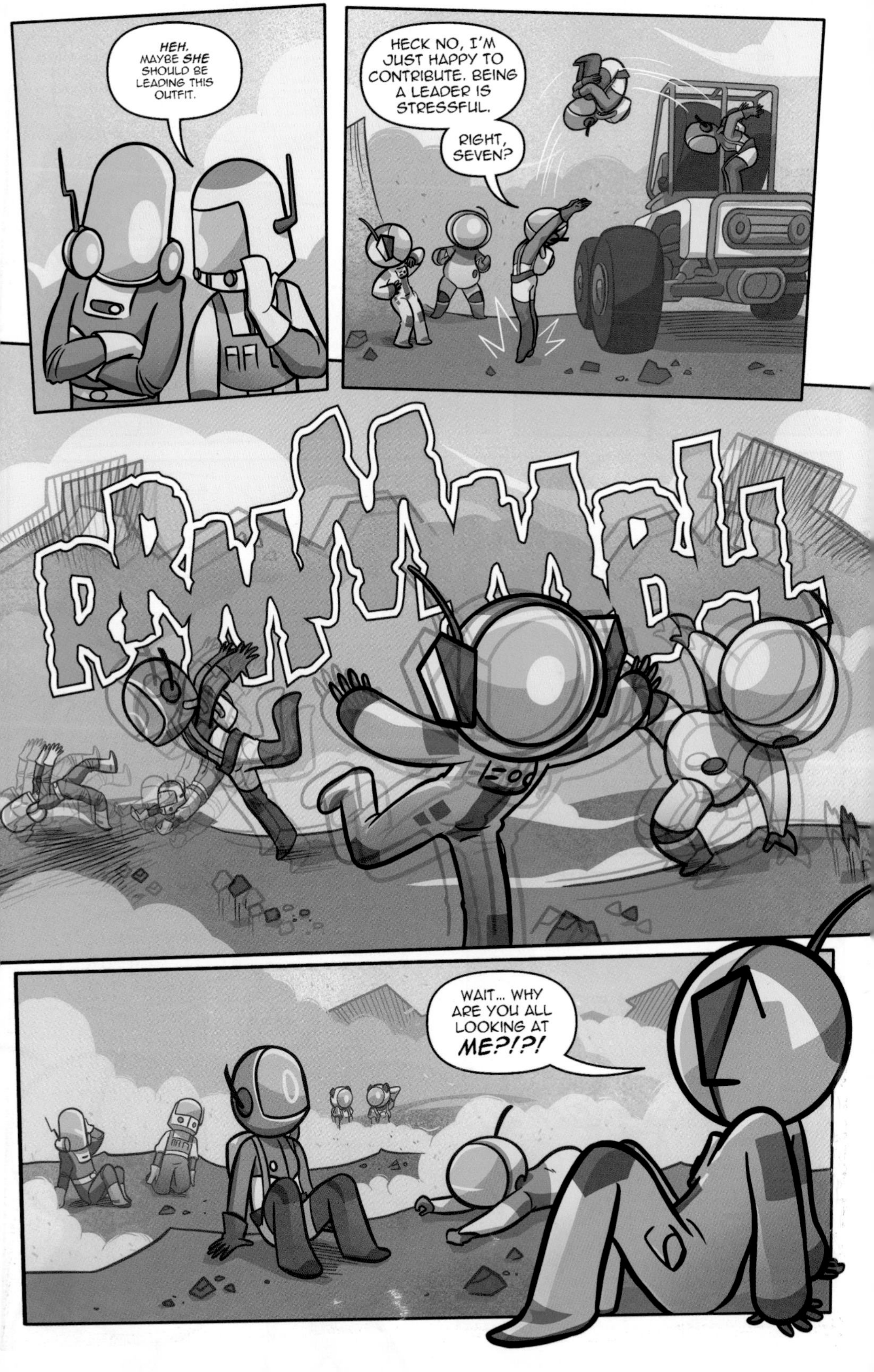
HEH. MAYBE SHE SHOULD BE LEADING THIS OUTFIT.
HECK NO, I'M JUST HAPPY TO CONTRIBUTE. BEING A LEADER IS STRESSFUL.
RIGHT, SEVEN?
WAIT... WHY ARE YOU ALL LOOKING AT ME?!?!

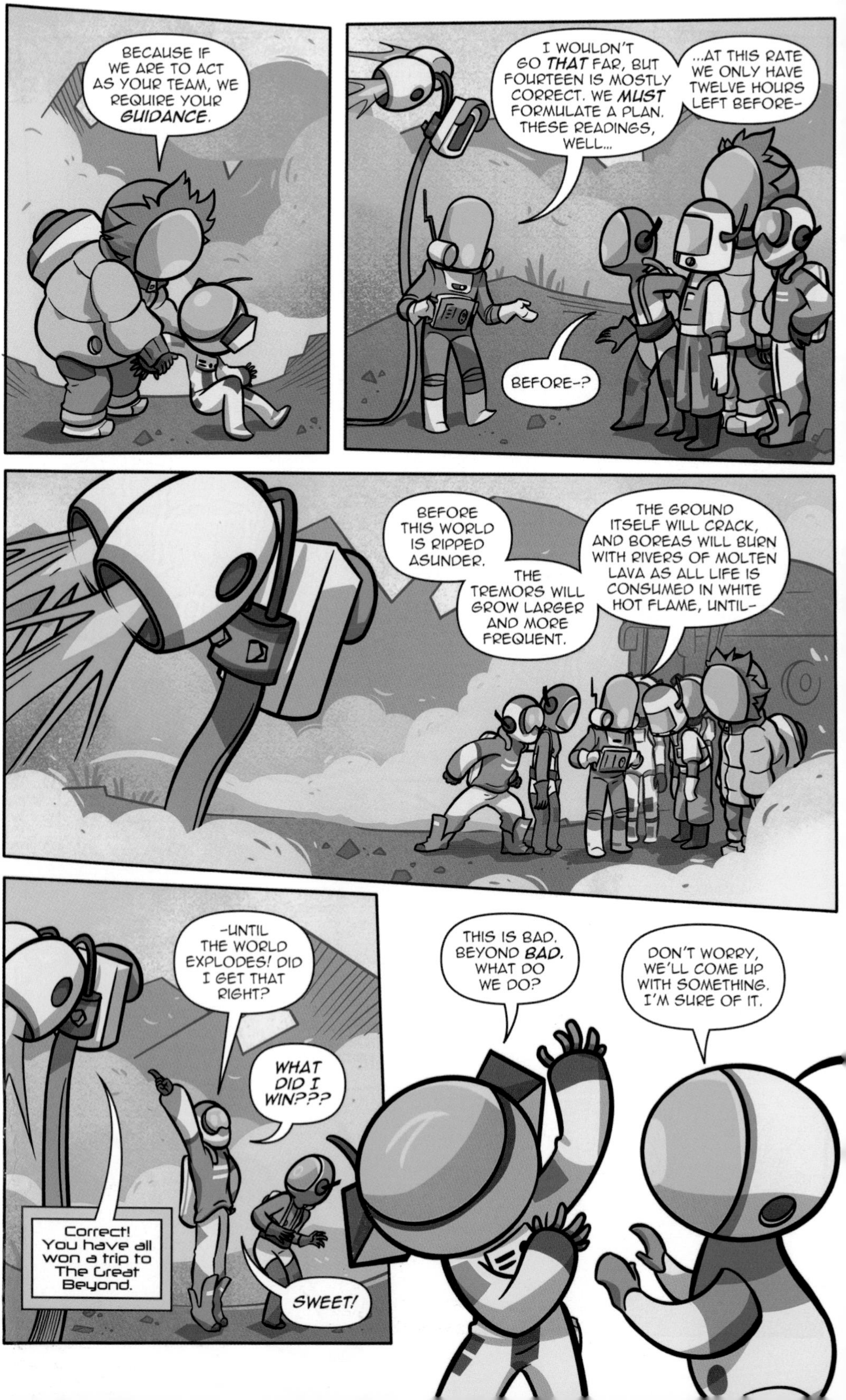
BECAUSE IF WE ARE TO ACT AS YOUR TEAM, WE REQUIRE YOUR GUIDANCE.
I WOULDN'T GO THAT FAR, BUT FOURTEEN IS MOSTLY CORRECT. WE MUST FORMULATE A PLAN. THESE READINGS, WELL...
...AT THIS RATE WE ONLY HAVE TWELVE HOURS LEFT BEFORE-
BEFORE-?
BEFORE THIS WORLD IS RIPPED ASUNDER.
THE TREMORS WILL GROW LARGER AND MORE FREQUENT.
THE GROUND ITSELF WILL CRACK, AND BOREAS WILL BURN WITH RIVERS OF MOLTEN LAVA AS ALL LIFE IS CONSUMED IN WHITE HOT FLAME, UNTIL-
-UNTIL THE WORLD EXPLODES! DID I GET THAT RIGHT?
Correct! You have all won a trip to The Great Beyond.
WHAT DID I WIN???
SWEET!
THIS IS BAD. BEYOND BAD. WHAT DO WE DO?
DON'T WORRY, WE'LL COME UP WITH SOMETHING. I'M SURE OF IT.

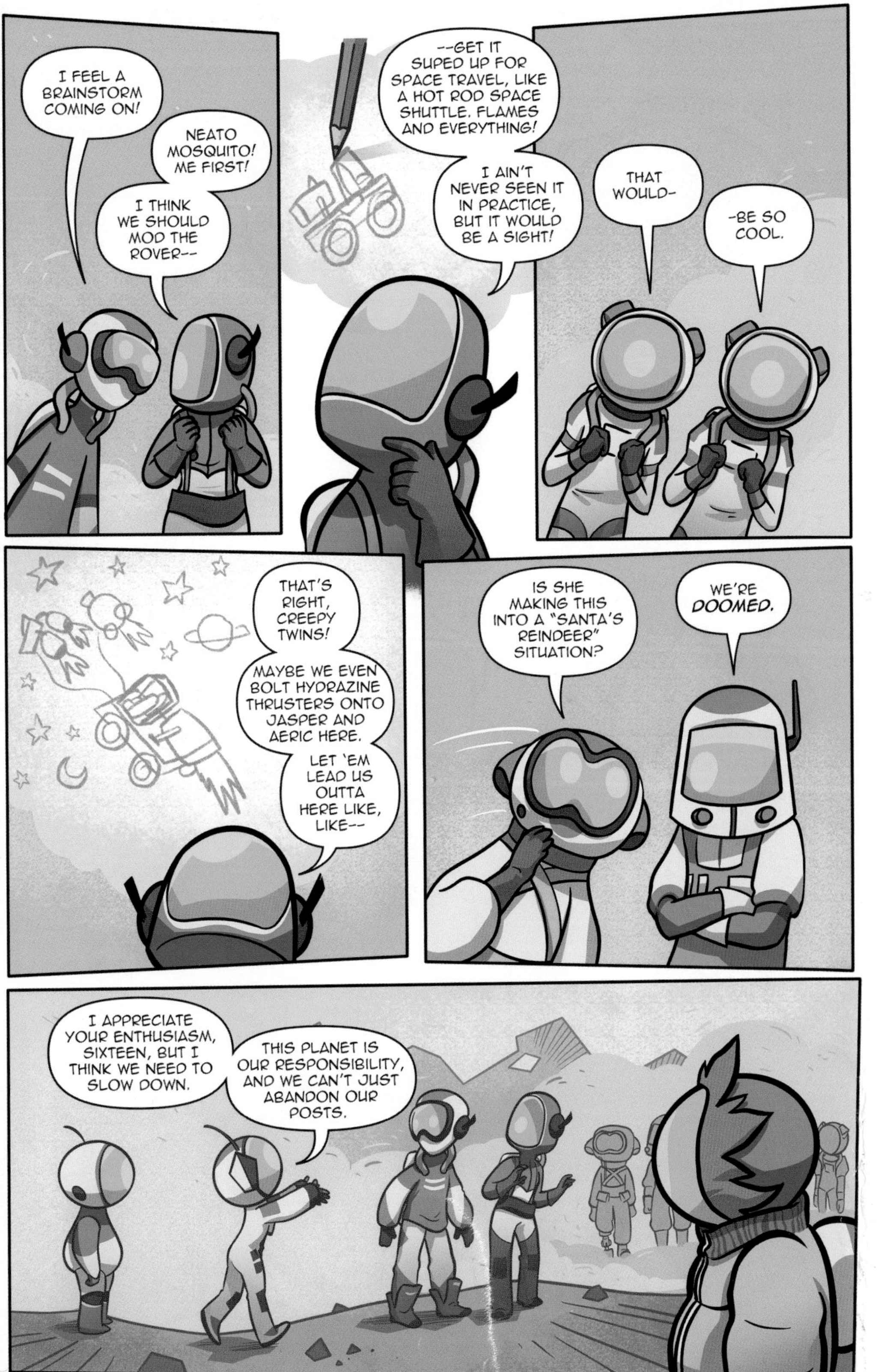
I FEEL A BRAINSTORM COMING ON!
NEATO MOSQUITO! ME FIRST!
I THINK WE SHOULD MOD THE ROVER--
--GET IT SUPED UP FOR SPACE TRAVEL, LIKE A HOT ROD SPACE SHUTTLE. FLAMES AND EVERYTHING!
I AIN'T NEVER SEEN IT IN PRACTICE, BUT IT WOULD BE A SIGHT!
THAT WOULD-
-BE SO COOL.
THAT'S RIGHT, CREEPY TWINS!
MAYBE WE EVEN BOLT HYDRAZINE THRUSTERS ONTO JASPER AND AERIC HERE.
LET 'EM LEAD US OUTTA HERE LIKE, LIKE--
IS SHE MAKING THIS INTO A "SANTA'S REINDEER" SITUATION?
WE'RE *DOOMED.*
I APPRECIATE YOUR ENTHUSIASM, SIXTEEN, BUT I THINK WE NEED TO SLOW DOWN.
THIS PLANET IS OUR RESPONSIBILITY, AND WE CAN'T JUST ABANDON OUR POSTS.

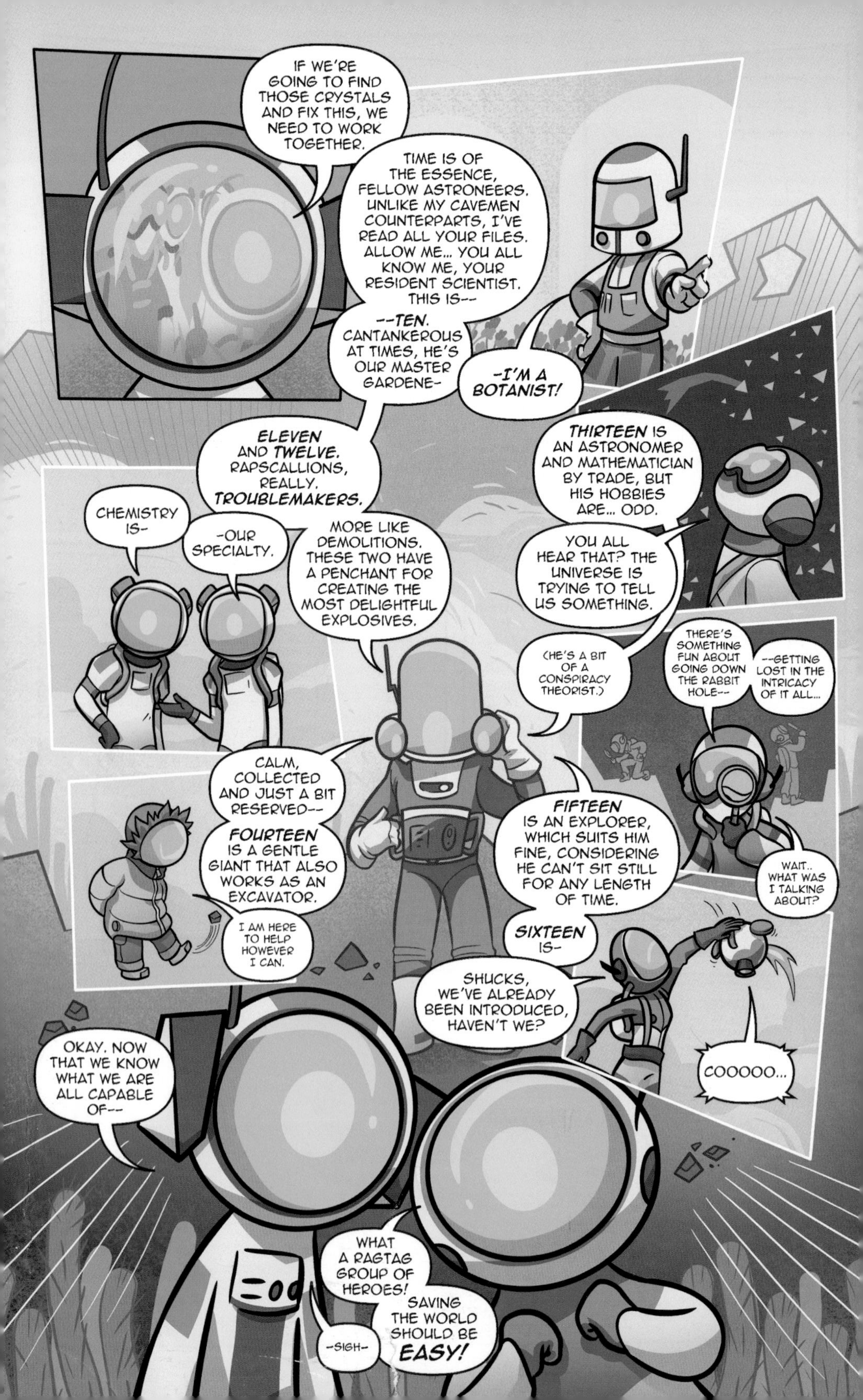
IF WE'RE GOING TO FIND THOSE CRYSTALS AND FIX THIS, WE NEED TO WORK TOGETHER.
TIME IS OF THE ESSENCE, FELLOW ASTRONEERS. UNLIKE MY CAVEMEN COUNTERPARTS, I'VE READ ALL YOUR FILES. ALLOW ME... YOU ALL KNOW ME, YOUR RESIDENT SCIENTIST. THIS IS--
--TEN. CANTANKEROUS AT TIMES, HE'S OUR MASTER GARDENE-
-I'M A BOTANIST!
ELEVEN AND TWELVE. RAPSCALLIONS, REALLY. TROUBLEMAKERS.
CHEMISTRY IS-
-OUR SPECIALTY.
MORE LIKE DEMOLITIONS. THESE TWO HAVE A PENCHANT FOR CREATING THE MOST DELIGHTFUL EXPLOSIVES.
THIRTEEN IS AN ASTRONOMER AND MATHEMATICIAN BY TRADE, BUT HIS HOBBIES ARE... ODD.
YOU ALL HEAR THAT? THE UNIVERSE IS TRYING TO TELL US SOMETHING.
(HE'S A BIT OF A CONSPIRACY THEORIST.)
THERE'S SOMETHING FUN ABOUT GOING DOWN THE RABBIT HOLE--
--GETTING LOST IN THE INTRICACY OF IT ALL...
WAIT.. WHAT WAS I TALKING ABOUT?
CALM, COLLECTED AND JUST A BIT RESERVED--
FOURTEEN IS A GENTLE GIANT THAT ALSO WORKS AS AN EXCAVATOR.
I AM HERE TO HELP HOWEVER I CAN.
FIFTEEN IS AN EXPLORER, WHICH SUITS HIM FINE, CONSIDERING HE CAN'T SIT STILL FOR ANY LENGTH OF TIME.
SIXTEEN IS-
SHUCKS, WE'VE ALREADY BEEN INTRODUCED, HAVEN'T WE?
COOOOO...
OKAY. NOW THAT WE KNOW WHAT WE ARE ALL CAPABLE OF--
WHAT A RAGTAG GROUP OF HEROES!
SAVING THE WORLD SHOULD BE EASY!
-SIGH-

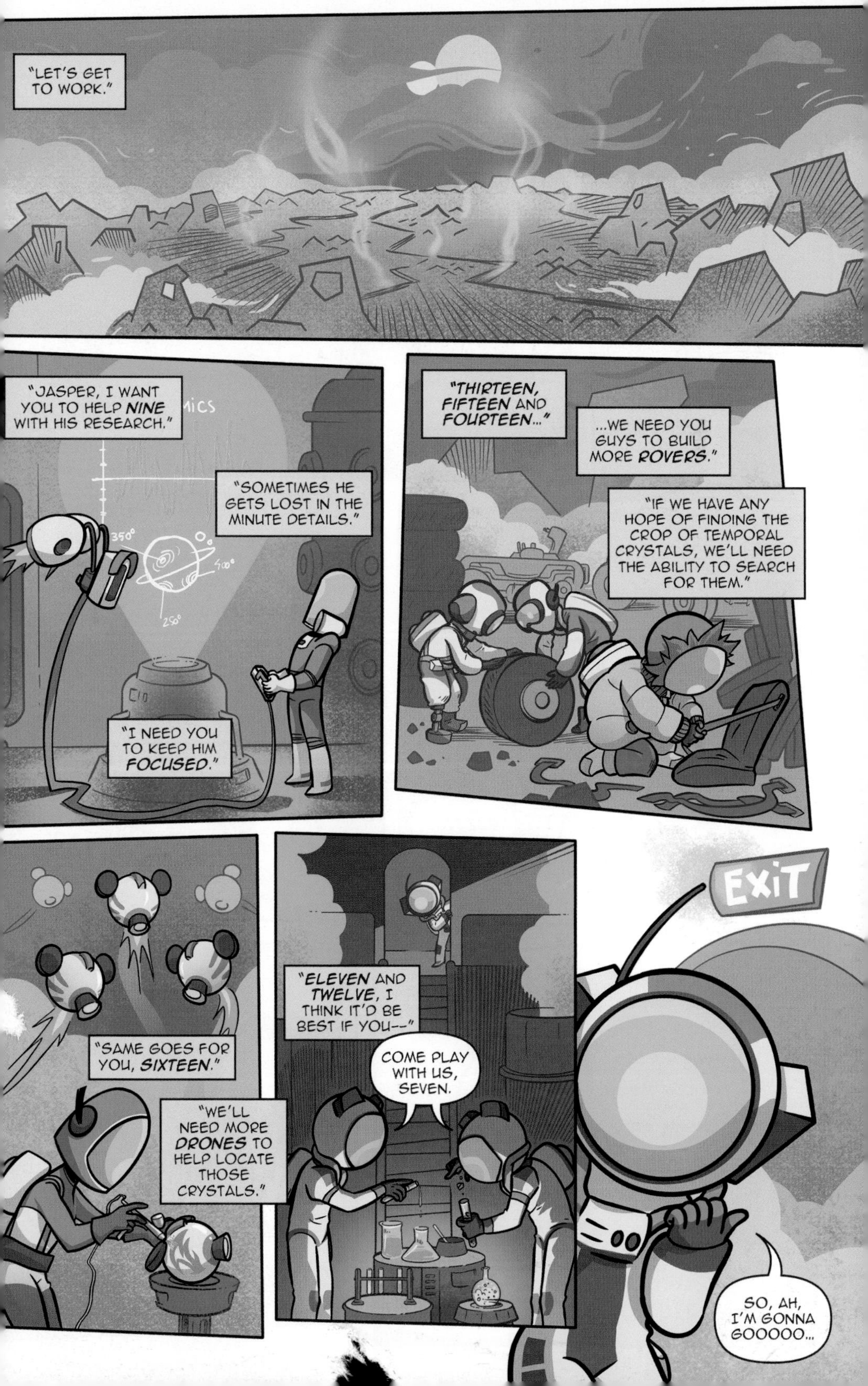
"LET'S GET TO WORK."
"JASPER, I WANT YOU TO HELP NINE WITH HIS RESEARCH."
"SOMETIMES HE GETS LOST IN THE MINUTE DETAILS."
"I NEED YOU TO KEEP HIM FOCUSED."
"THIRTEEN, FIFTEEN AND FOURTEEN..."
...WE NEED YOU GUYS TO BUILD MORE ROVERS."
"IF WE HAVE ANY HOPE OF FINDING THE CROP OF TEMPORAL CRYSTALS, WE'LL NEED THE ABILITY TO SEARCH FOR THEM."
"SAME GOES FOR YOU, SIXTEEN."
"WE'LL NEED MORE DRONES TO HELP LOCATE THOSE CRYSTALS."
"ELEVEN AND TWELVE, I THINK IT'D BE BEST IF YOU--"
COME PLAY WITH US, SEVEN.
EXIT
SO, AH, I'M GONNA GOOOOO...

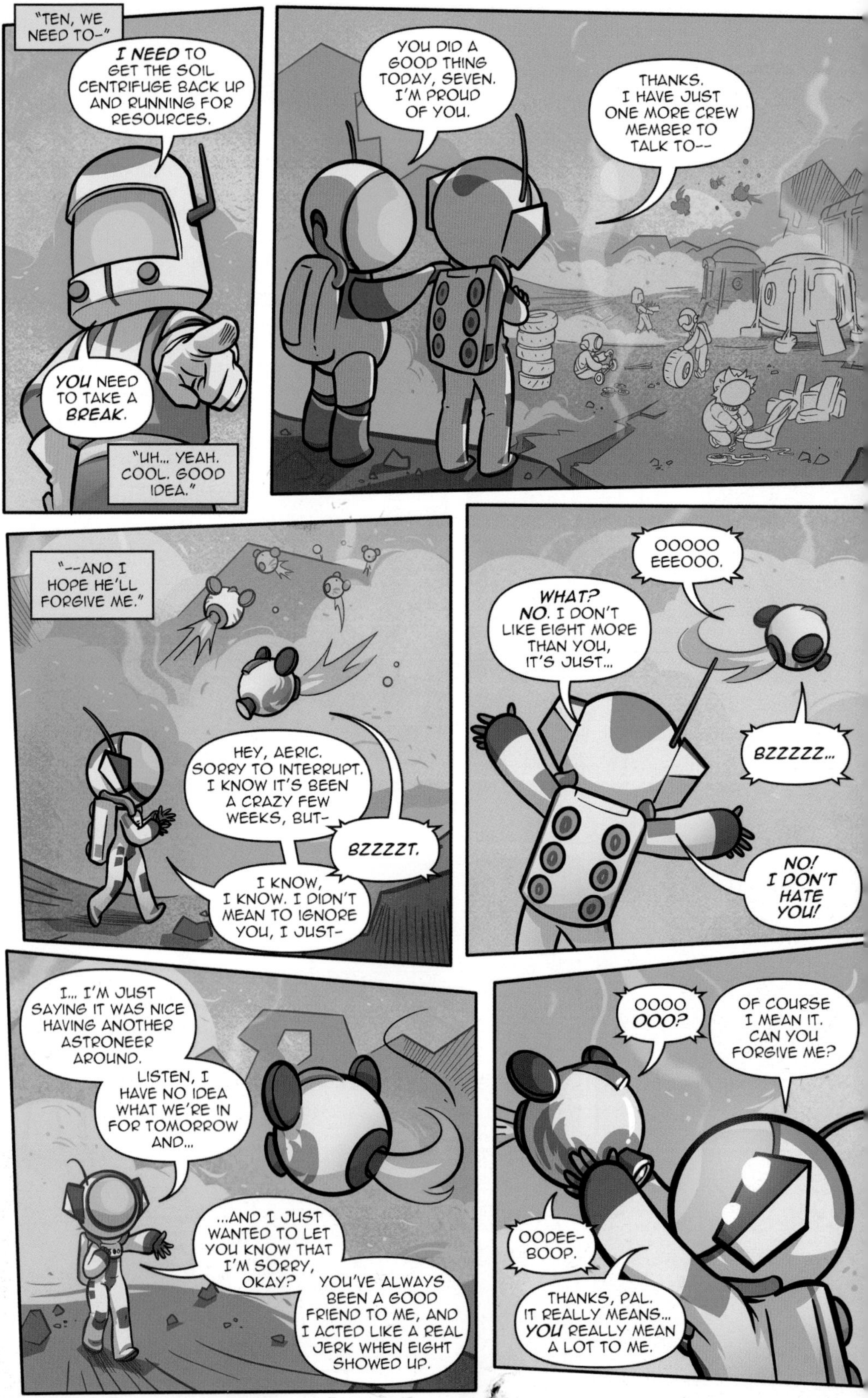
"TEN, WE NEED TO-"
I NEED TO GET THE SOIL CENTRIFUGE BACK UP AND RUNNING FOR RESOURCES.
YOU NEED TO TAKE A BREAK.
"UH... YEAH. COOL. GOOD IDEA."
YOU DID A GOOD THING TODAY, SEVEN. I'M PROUD OF YOU.
THANKS. I HAVE JUST ONE MORE CREW MEMBER TO TALK TO--
"--AND I HOPE HE'LL FORGIVE ME."
HEY, AERIC. SORRY TO INTERRUPT. I KNOW IT'S BEEN A CRAZY FEW WEEKS, BUT-
BZZZZT.
I KNOW, I KNOW. I DIDN'T MEAN TO IGNORE YOU, I JUST-
OOOOO EEEOOO.
WHAT? NO. I DON'T LIKE EIGHT MORE THAN YOU, IT'S JUST...
BZZZZZ...
NO! I DON'T HATE YOU!
I... I'M JUST SAYING IT WAS NICE HAVING ANOTHER ASTRONEER AROUND.
LISTEN, I HAVE NO IDEA WHAT WE'RE IN FOR TOMORROW AND...
...AND I JUST WANTED TO LET YOU KNOW THAT I'M SORRY, OKAY?
YOU'VE ALWAYS BEEN A GOOD FRIEND TO ME, AND I ACTED LIKE A REAL JERK WHEN EIGHT SHOWED UP.
OOOO OOO?
OF COURSE I MEAN IT. CAN YOU FORGIVE ME?
OODEE-BOOP.
THANKS, PAL. IT REALLY MEANS... YOU REALLY MEAN A LOT TO ME.

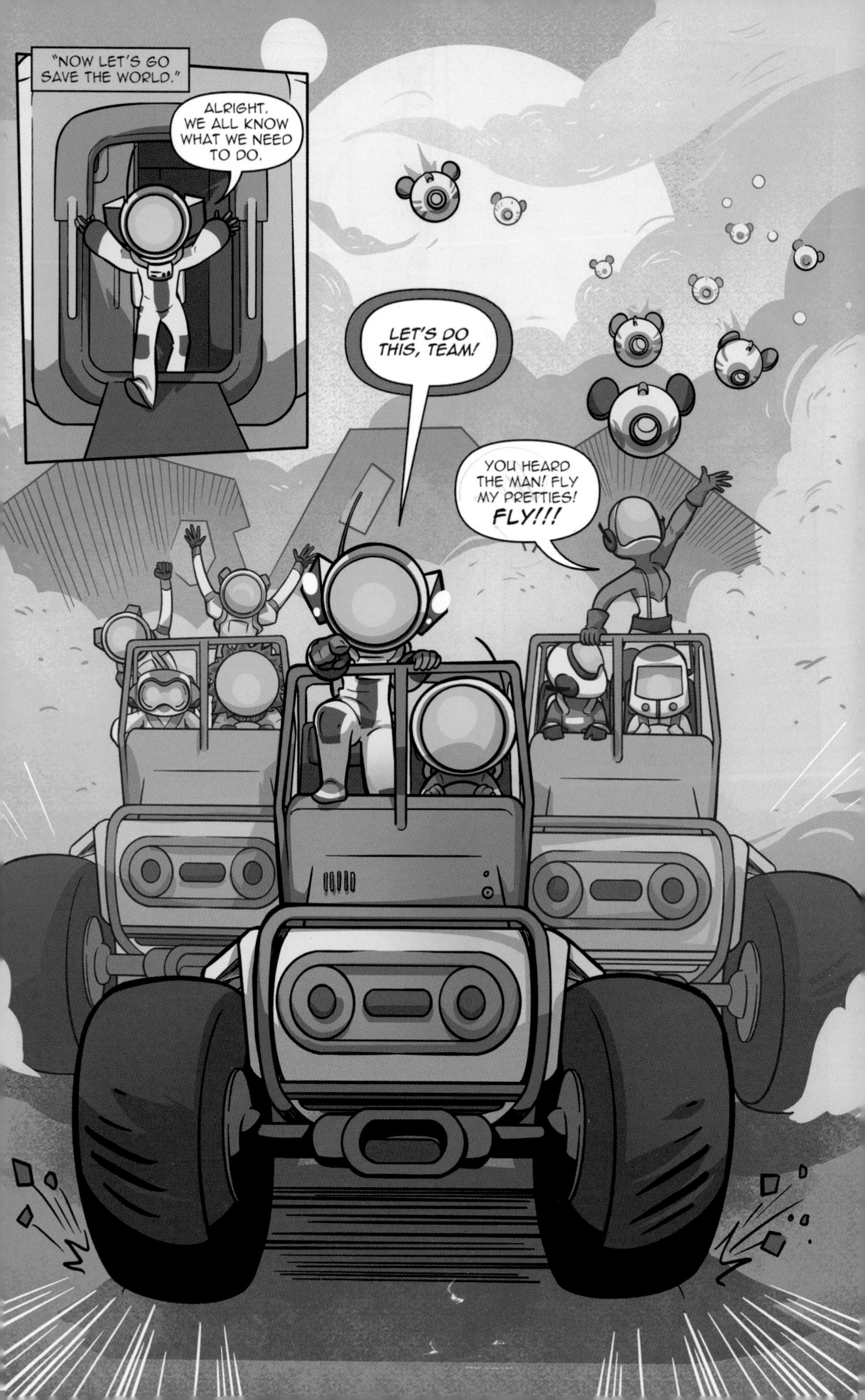
"NOW LET'S GO SAVE THE WORLD."
ALRIGHT. WE ALL KNOW WHAT WE NEED TO DO.
LET'S DO THIS, TEAM!
YOU HEARD THE MAN! FLY MY PRETTIES! FLY!!!

WOW. SIXTEEN WASN'T LYING ABOUT SUPING UP THE DRONES.

YEP! WITH THE EXTRA BOOSTERS, THEY'LL BE ABLE TO FLY AHEAD AND SCAN THE AREA.

HOPEFULLY BY TRIANGULATING THEIR READINGS, THEY'LL PICK UP SOMETHING THAT'LL HELP NINE FIND THOSE CRYSTALS.

ALRIGHT, GUYS. SHOW 'EM WHAT YOU CAN DO. MANEUVER ZETA!

LOOK AT 'EM GO!

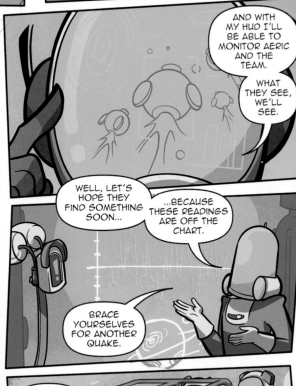

AND WITH MY HUD I'LL BE ABLE TO MONITOR AERIC AND THE TEAM.

WHAT THEY SEE, WE'LL SEE.

WELL, LET'S HOPE THEY FIND SOMETHING SOON...

...BECAUSE THESE READINGS ARE OFF THE CHART.

BRACE YOURSELVES FOR ANOTHER QUAKE.

WHAT DID HE SAY?

I CAN'T HEAR ANYTHING OVER THE ENGINES.

HE SAID THAT ANOTHER QUAKE--

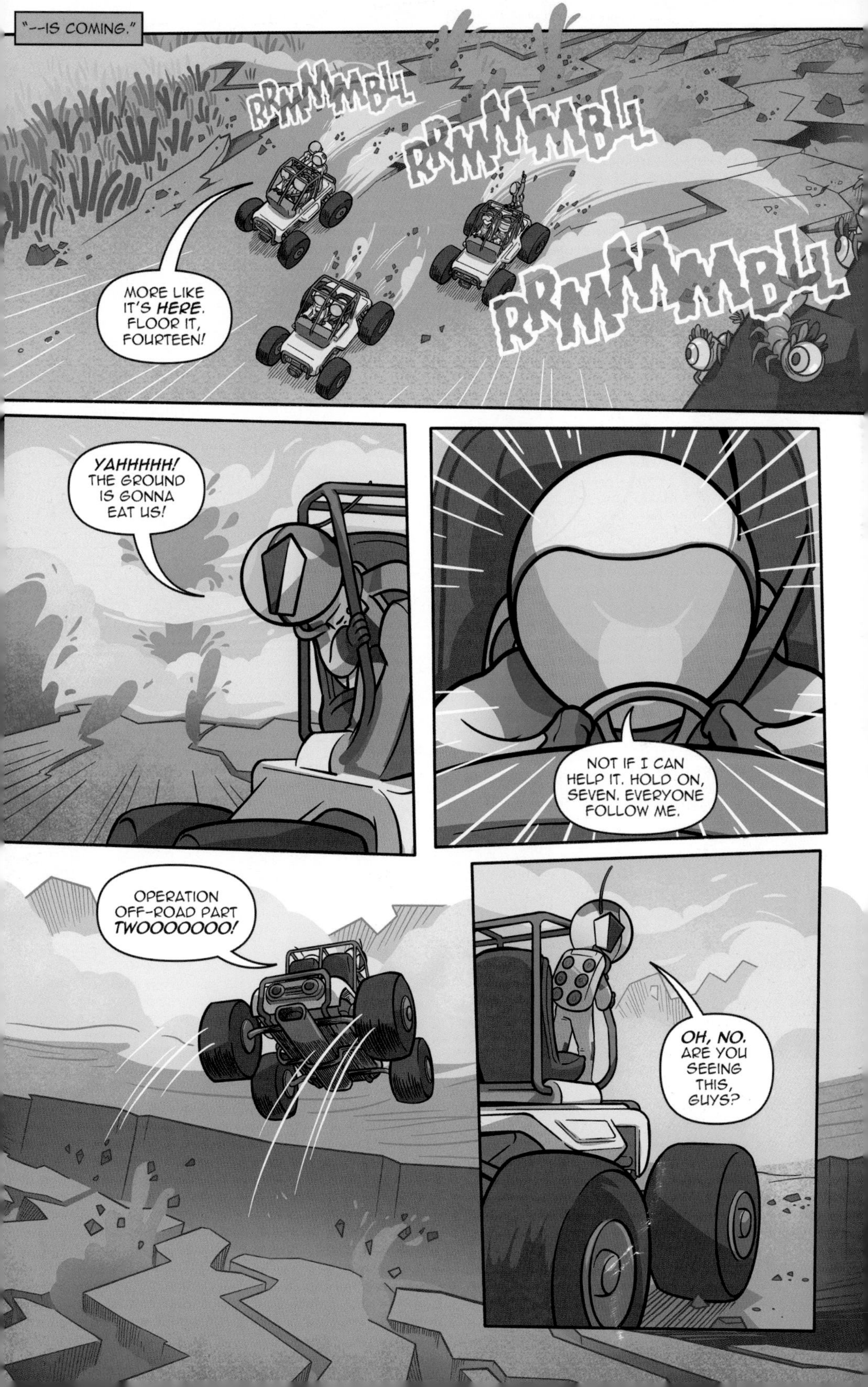
"--IS COMING."
RRMMMBLL
RRMMMBLL
MORE LIKE IT'S HERE. FLOOR IT, FOURTEEN!
RRMMMBLL
YAHHHHH! THE GROUND IS GONNA EAT US!
NOT IF I CAN HELP IT. HOLD ON, SEVEN. EVERYONE FOLLOW ME.
OPERATION OFF-ROAD PART TWOOOOOOO!
OH, NO. ARE YOU SEEING THIS, GUYS?

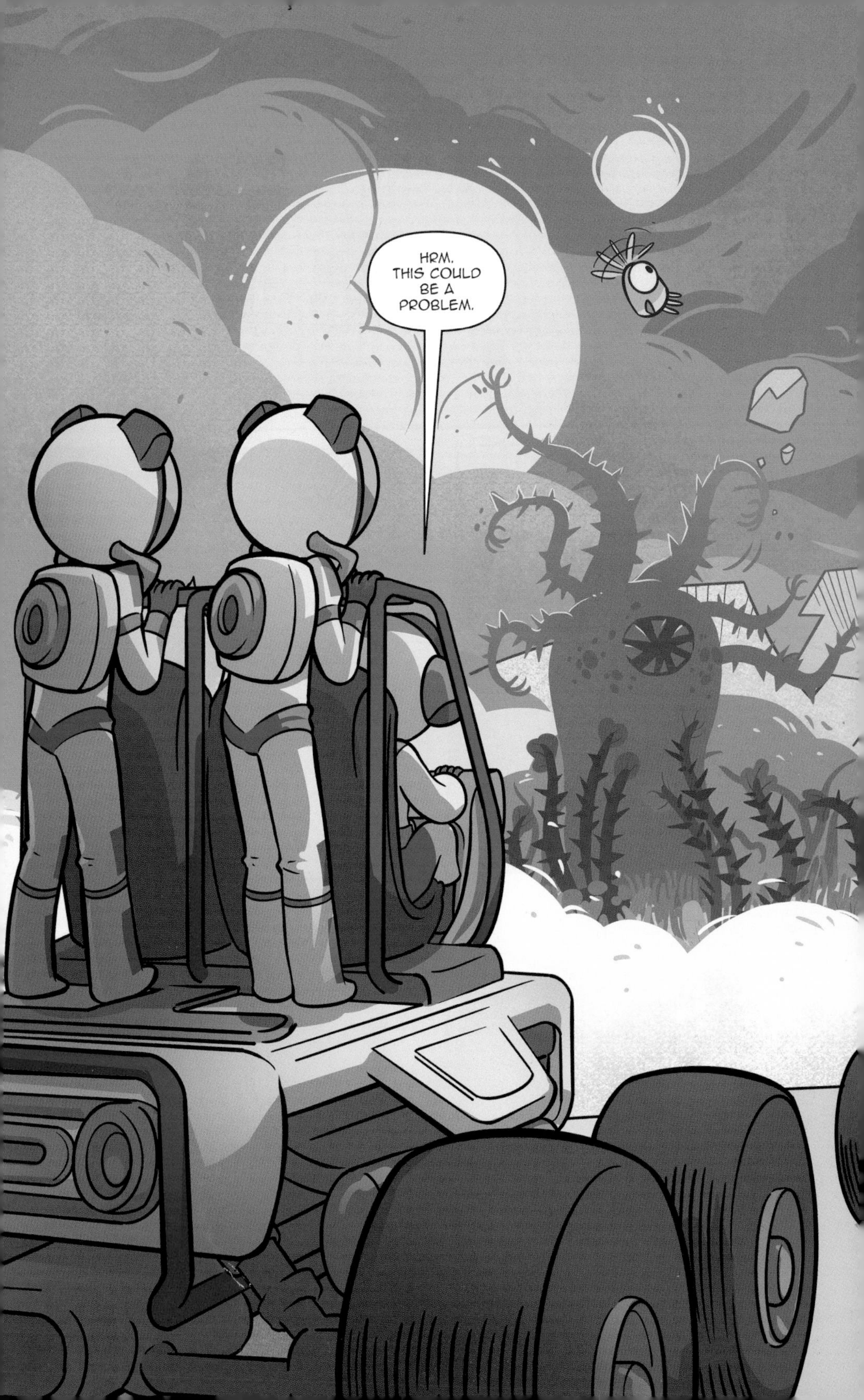
HRM. THIS COULD BE A PROBLEM.

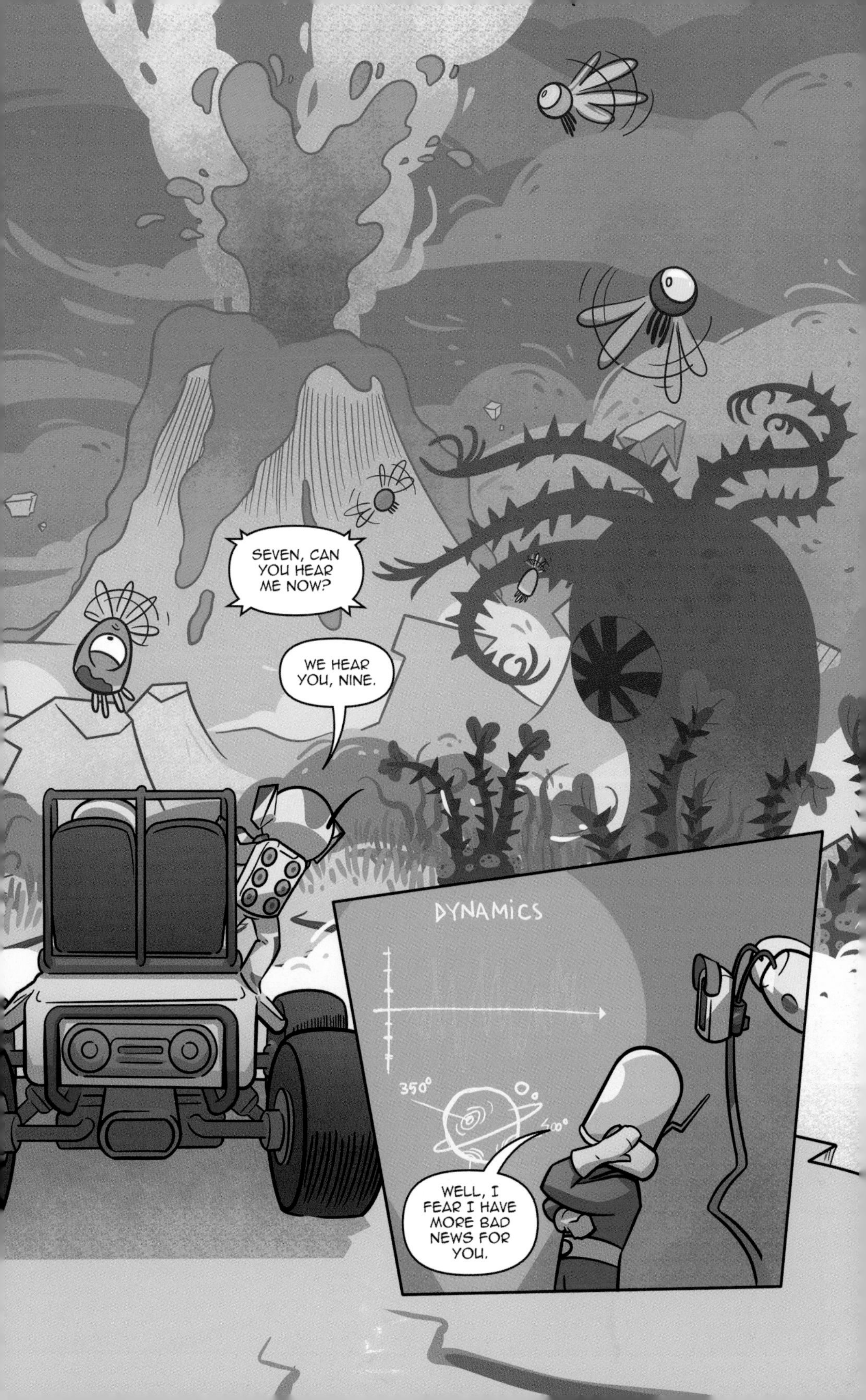
SEVEN, CAN YOU HEAR ME NOW?
WE HEAR YOU, NINE.
DYNAMICS
350°
0°
400°
WELL, I FEAR I HAVE MORE BAD NEWS FOR YOU.

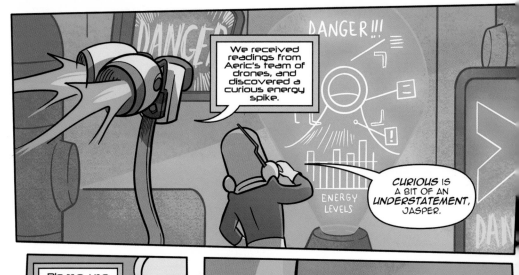

DANGER!!!
We received readings from Aeric's team of drones, and discovered a curious energy spike.
CURIOUS IS A BIT OF AN UNDERSTATEMENT, JASPER.
ENERGY LEVELS
Please, use your human words then.
THEY ARE ALL HUMAN WORDS, JASPER, I -SIGH- NEVERMIND.
AS JASPER WAS FAILING TO DESCRIBE, WE FOUND AN ANOMALOUS ENERGY READING.
I'VE NEVER SEEN ANYTHING LIKE IT...
...WELL, UNTIL I BEGAN STUDYING YOUR CRYSTAL. THE READINGS ARE SIMILAR, BUT AMPLIFIED.
I BELIEVE THAT THE CRYSTALS HAVE BEEN TELEPORTING; USING YOUR "OATMEAL" TO SEARCH FOR YOUR CRYSTAL--
--THEIR LOST BROTHER.
SEISMIC ACTIVITY
AND WE'VE DISCOVERED THE LOCATION OF YOUR CRYSTAL'S "FAMILY."
WHAT? THAT DOESN'T SOUND LIKE BAD NEWS AT ALL.

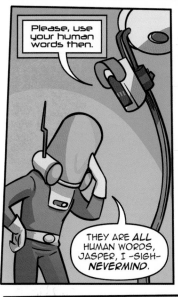

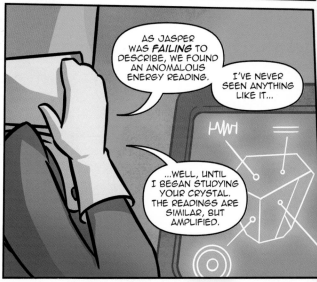

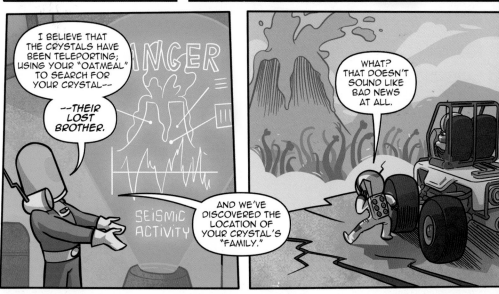

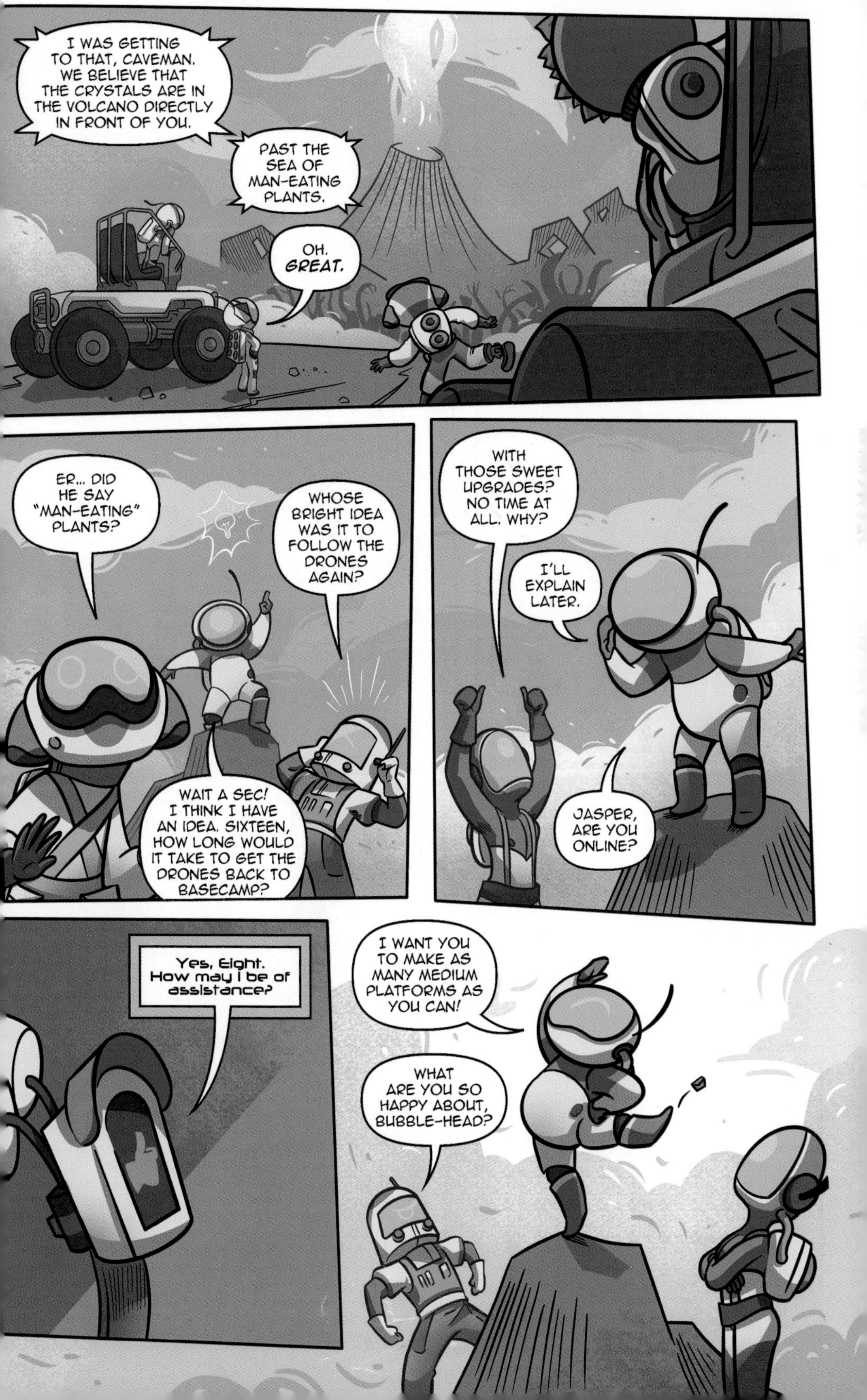
I WAS GETTING TO THAT, CAVEMAN. WE BELIEVE THAT THE CRYSTALS ARE IN THE VOLCANO DIRECTLY IN FRONT OF YOU.
PAST THE SEA OF MAN-EATING PLANTS.
OH. GREAT.
ER... DID HE SAY "MAN-EATING" PLANTS?
WHOSE BRIGHT IDEA WAS IT TO FOLLOW THE DRONES AGAIN?
WAIT A SEC! I THINK I HAVE AN IDEA. SIXTEEN, HOW LONG WOULD IT TAKE TO GET THE DRONES BACK TO BASECAMP?
WITH THOSE SWEET UPGRADES? NO TIME AT ALL. WHY?
I'LL EXPLAIN LATER.
JASPER, ARE YOU ONLINE?
Yes, Eight. How may I be of assistance?
I WANT YOU TO MAKE AS MANY MEDIUM PLATFORMS AS YOU CAN!
WHAT ARE YOU SO HAPPY ABOUT, BUBBLE-HEAD?

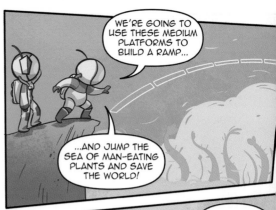

WE'RE GOING TO USE THESE MEDIUM PLATFORMS TO BUILD A RAMP...

...AND JUMP THE SEA OF MAN-EATING PLANTS AND SAVE THE WORLD!

TWENTY MINUTES LATER.

SO, AH, WHAT ARE WE DOING EXACTLY?

IT'S SIMPLE!

THAT'S YOUR PLAN?!

WHAT? IT'S A GREAT IDEA!

IT *COULD* WORK, BUT IF OUR CALCULATIONS ARE OFF, WELL...

YOU'RE CORRECT, THIRTEEN. WHICH IS WHY I'VE BEEN RUNNING SIMULATIONS HERE IN THE LAB.

I'VE GOTTEN US UP TO A 72% RATE OF SUCCESS. I'M SENDING YOU ALL BLUEPRINTS NOW.

SEE, THERE'S ONLY A 5% CHANCE THIS WILL END HORRIBLY!

MATH REALLY ISN'T YOUR THING, IS IT KID?

EIGHT IS RIGHT. THE ROVERS ARE TOO HEAVY FOR THE DRONES TO CARRY AND WE'RE OUT OF OPTIONS. THIS IS THE BEST PLAN WE'VE GOT.

WE'RE ASTRONEERS-- WE CAN DO THIS! *TOGETHER!*

YEAH!

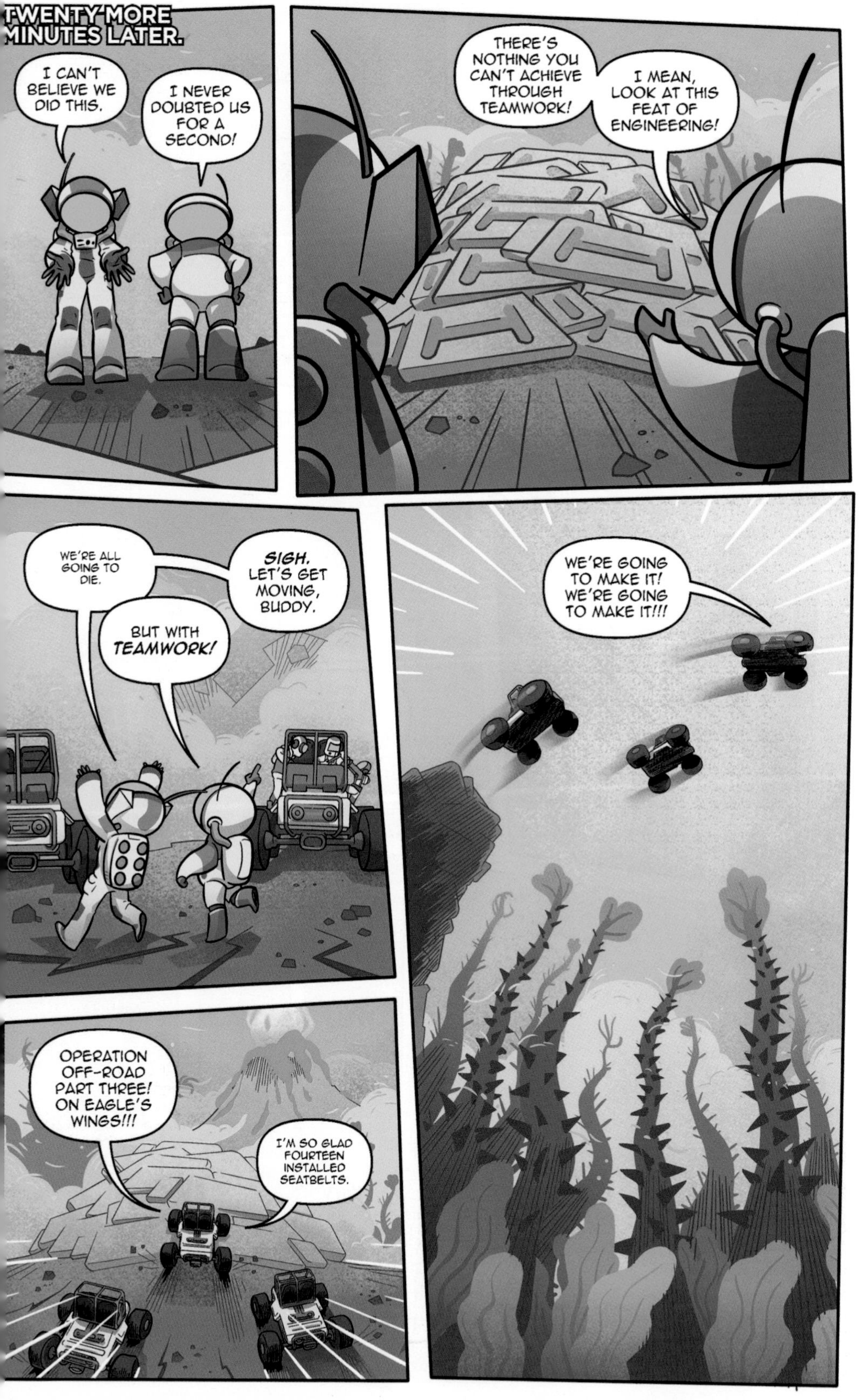
TWENTY MORE MINUTES LATER.
I CAN'T BELIEVE WE DID THIS.
I NEVER DOUBTED US FOR A SECOND!
THERE'S NOTHING YOU CAN'T ACHIEVE THROUGH TEAMWORK!
I MEAN, LOOK AT THIS FEAT OF ENGINEERING!
WE'RE ALL GOING TO DIE.
SIGH. LET'S GET MOVING, BUDDY.
BUT WITH TEAMWORK!
OPERATION OFF-ROAD PART THREE! ON EAGLE'S WINGS!!!
I'M SO GLAD FOURTEEN INSTALLED SEATBELTS.
WE'RE GOING TO MAKE IT! WE'RE GOING TO MAKE IT!!!

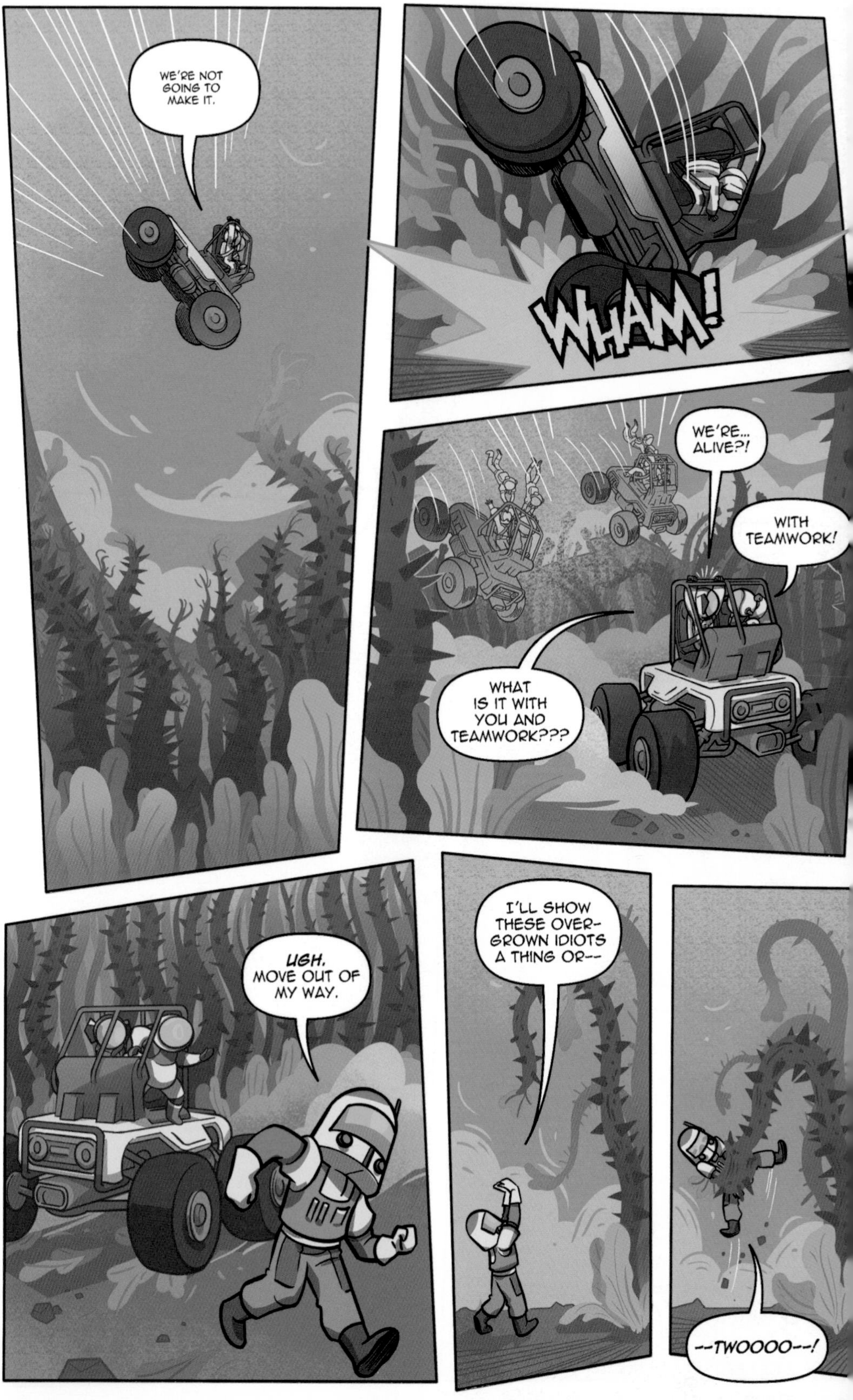
WE'RE NOT GOING TO MAKE IT.
WHAM!
WE'RE... ALIVE?!
WITH TEAMWORK!
WHAT IS IT WITH YOU AND TEAMWORK???
UGH. MOVE OUT OF MY WAY.
I'LL SHOW THESE OVER-GROWN IDIOTS A THING OR--
--TWOOOO--!

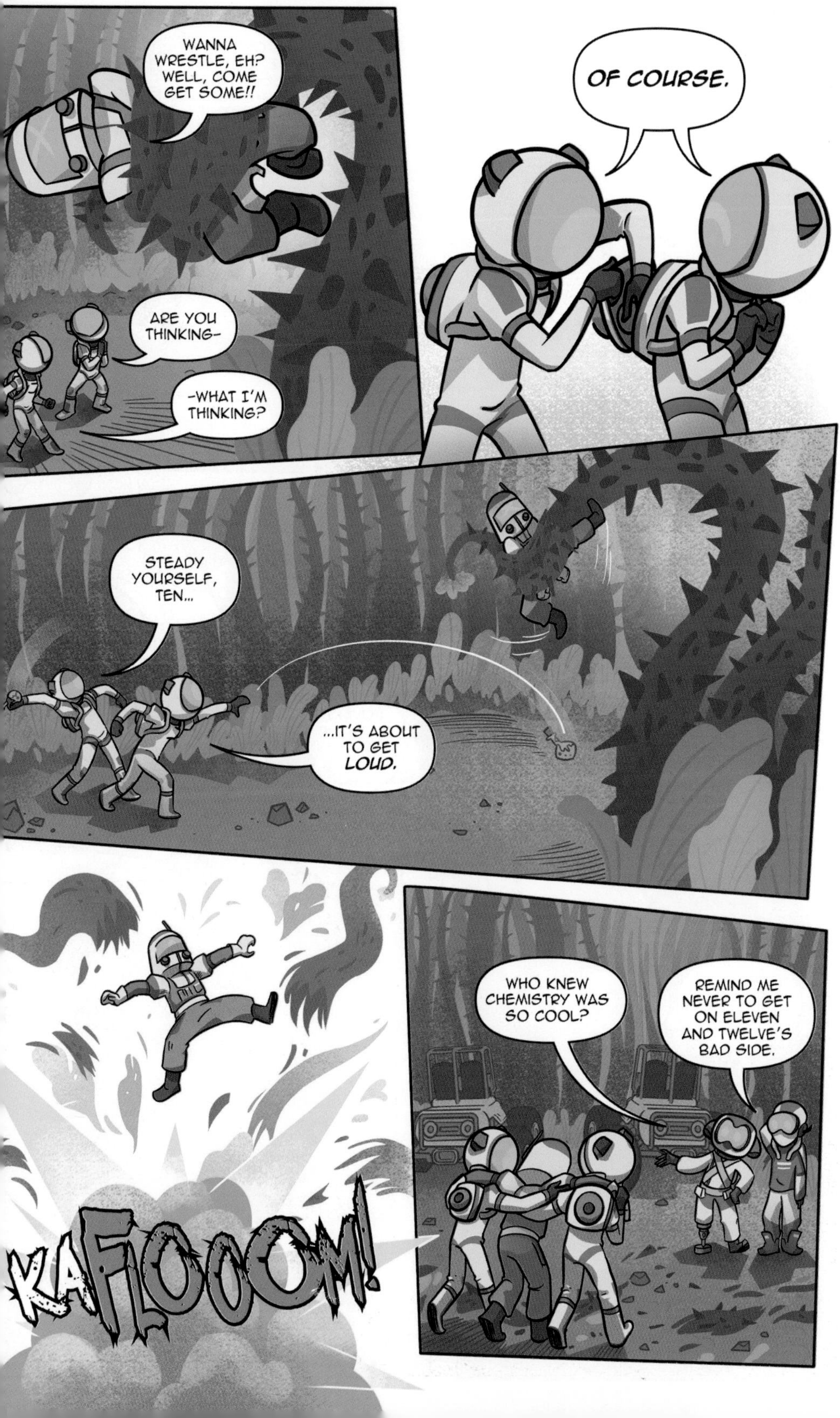
WANNA WRESTLE, EH? WELL, COME GET SOME!!
ARE YOU THINKING-
-WHAT I'M THINKING?
OF COURSE.
STEADY YOURSELF, TEN...
...IT'S ABOUT TO GET LOUD.
KAFLOOOM!
WHO KNEW CHEMISTRY WAS SO COOL?
REMIND ME NEVER TO GET ON ELEVEN AND TWELVE'S BAD SIDE.

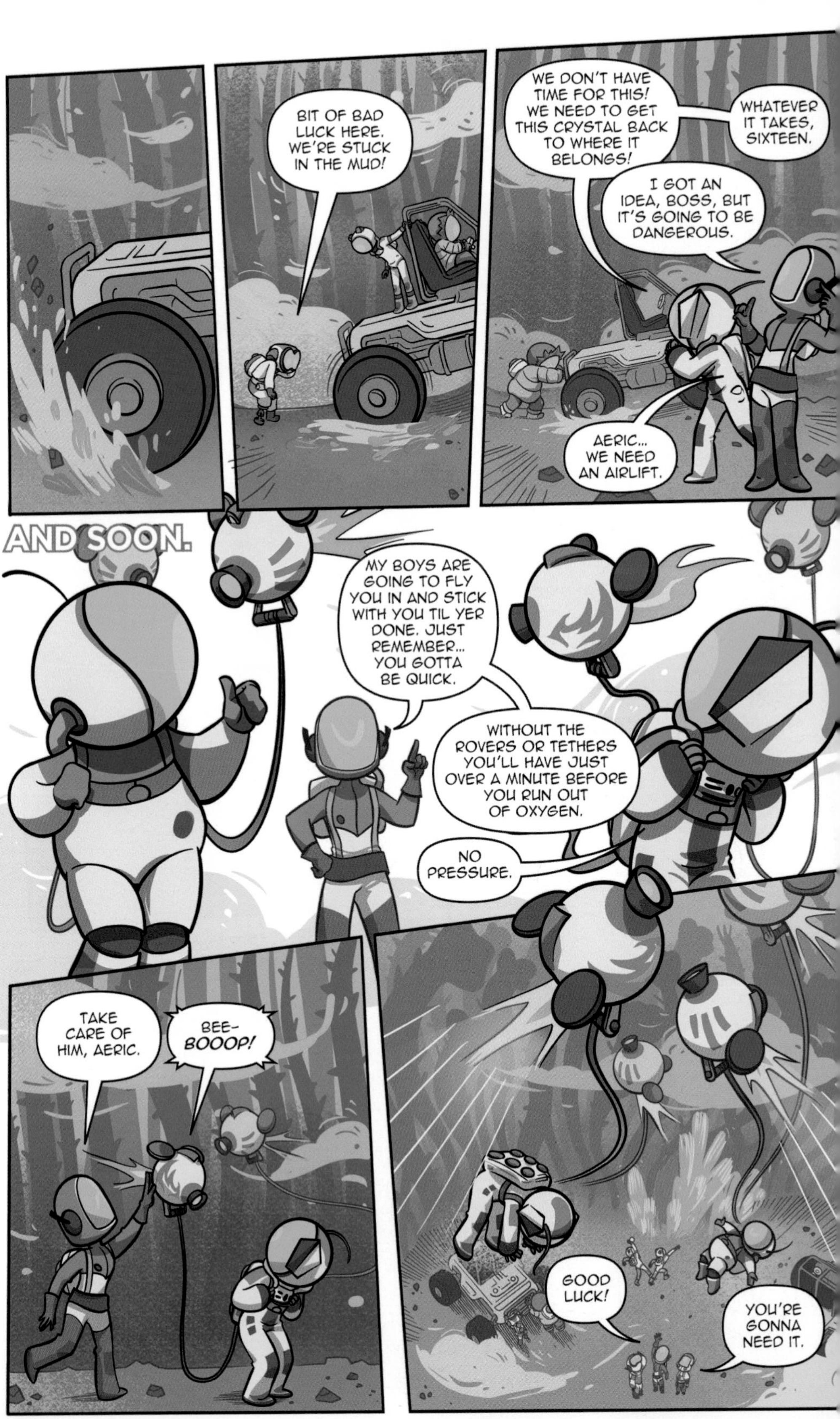
BIT OF BAD LUCK HERE. WE'RE STUCK IN THE MUD!
WE DON'T HAVE TIME FOR THIS! WE NEED TO GET THIS CRYSTAL BACK TO WHERE IT BELONGS!
WHATEVER IT TAKES, SIXTEEN.
I GOT AN IDEA, BOSS, BUT IT'S GOING TO BE DANGEROUS.
AERIC... WE NEED AN AIRLIFT.
AND SOON.
MY BOYS ARE GOING TO FLY YOU IN AND STICK WITH YOU TIL YER DONE. JUST REMEMBER... YOU GOTTA BE QUICK.
WITHOUT THE ROVERS OR TETHERS YOU'LL HAVE JUST OVER A MINUTE BEFORE YOU RUN OUT OF OXYGEN.
NO PRESSURE.
TAKE CARE OF HIM, AERIC.
BEE-BOOOP!
GOOD LUCK!
YOU'RE GONNA NEED IT.

WOOO HOO! THIS IS THE COOLEST THING I'VE EVER DONE!
I THINK I'M GOING TO BE SICK IN MY HELMET.
C'MON, SEVEN! WHEN ARE WE EVER GOING TO GET A CHANCE TO DO ANY-THING THIS CRAZY AGAIN?
LIVE IN THE MOMENT!
IF WE DON'T REUNITE OUR CRYSTAL WITH ITS FAMILY WE WON'T BE LIVING AT ALL!
WELL, IF THIS IS OUR LAST ADVENTURE, LET'S MAKE IT ONE FOR THE HISTORY BOOKS!
I'M GETTING ANOTHER ENERGY SPIKE, SEVEN... MUCH LARGER THAN THE LAST.
I FEAR THIS MAY TRIGGER ANOTHER QUAKE. YOU MUST HURRY!
WHERE TO, NINE?
I'M UPLOADING GEOGRAPHICAL MAPPING FROM WITHIN THE VOLCANO TO YOUR DRONES NOW.
DO YOU SEE THAT OPENING ON THE LEFT?
YEP! YOU HEARD THE MAN--INTO THE BREACH!
WA-HOOO!

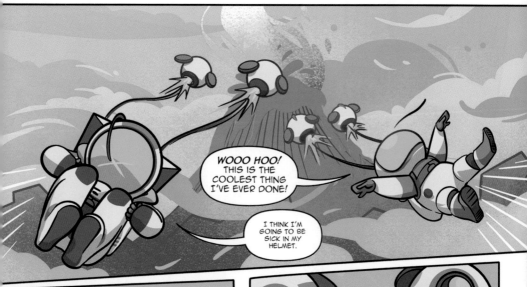

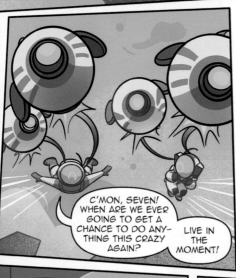

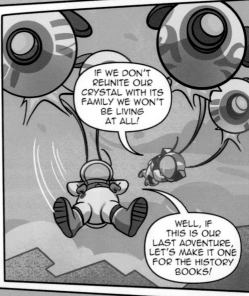

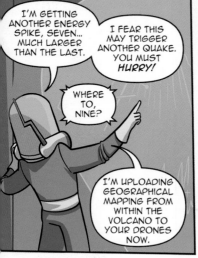

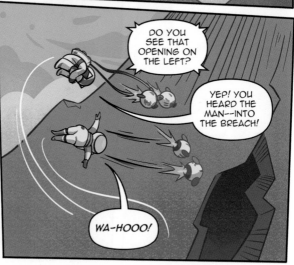

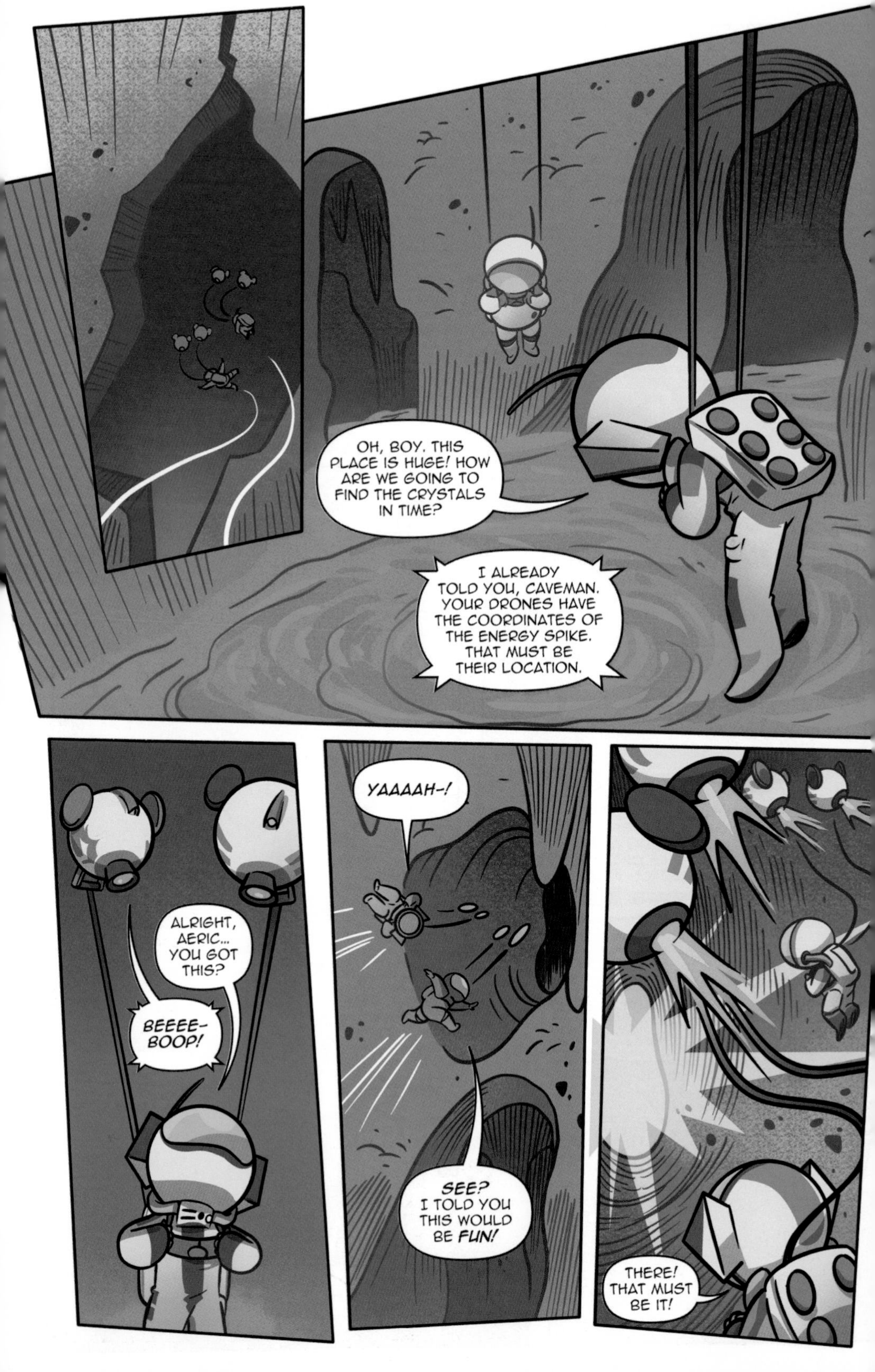
OH, BOY. THIS PLACE IS HUGE! HOW ARE WE GOING TO FIND THE CRYSTALS IN TIME?
I ALREADY TOLD YOU, CAVEMAN. YOUR DRONES HAVE THE COORDINATES OF THE ENERGY SPIKE. THAT MUST BE THEIR LOCATION.
ALRIGHT, AERIC... YOU GOT THIS?
BEEEE-BOOP!
YAAAAH-!
SEE? I TOLD YOU THIS WOULD BE FUN!
THERE! THAT MUST BE IT!

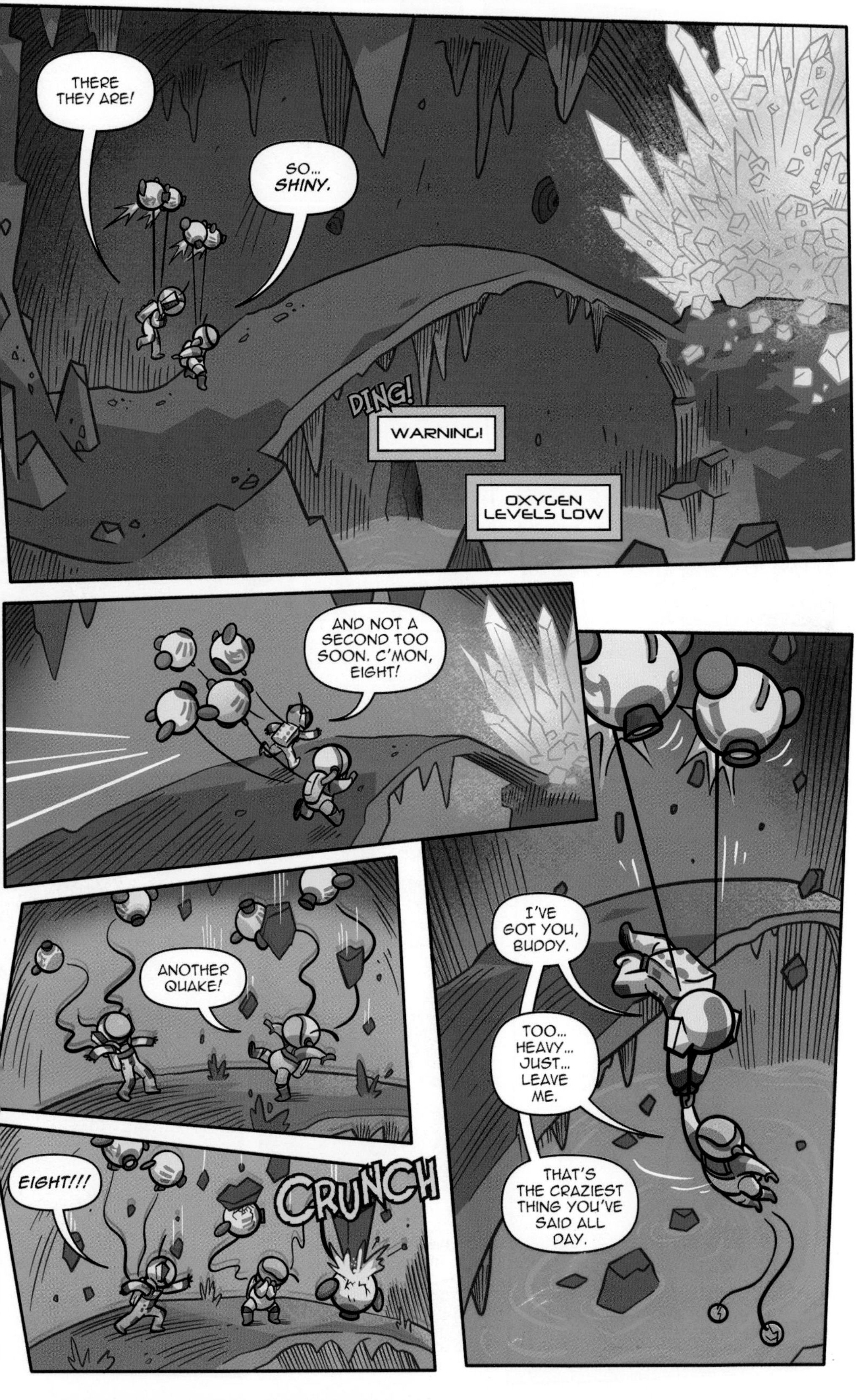
THERE THEY ARE!
SO... SHINY.
DING!
WARNING!
OXYGEN LEVELS LOW
AND NOT A SECOND TOO SOON. C'MON, EIGHT!
ANOTHER QUAKE!
EIGHT!!!
CRUNCH
I'VE GOT YOU, BUDDY.
TOO... HEAVY... JUST... LEAVE ME.
THAT'S THE CRAZIEST THING YOU'VE SAID ALL DAY.

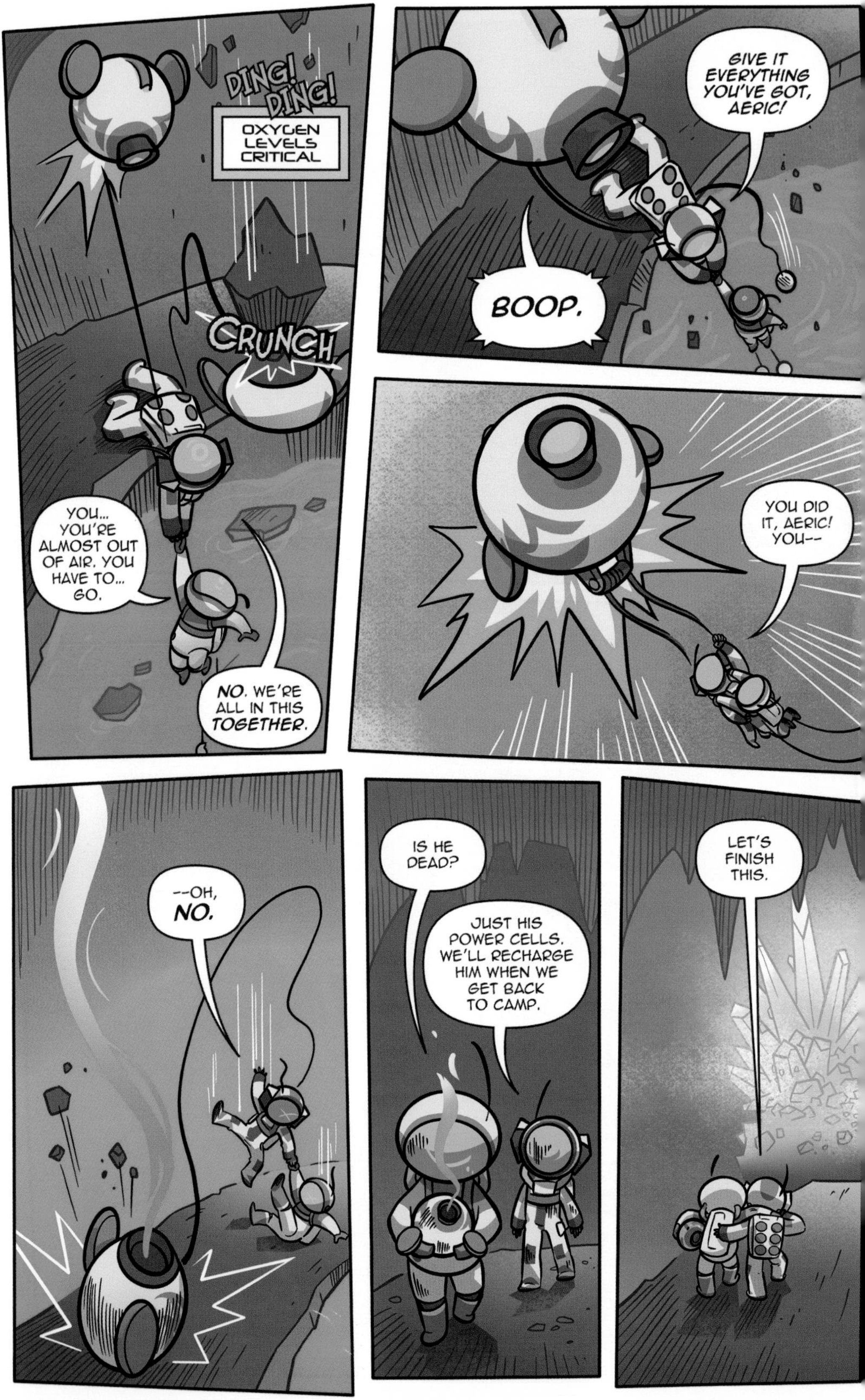
DING! DING!
OXYGEN LEVELS CRITICAL
CRUNCH
YOU... YOU'RE ALMOST OUT OF AIR. YOU HAVE TO... GO.
NO. WE'RE ALL IN THIS TOGETHER.
GIVE IT EVERYTHING YOU'VE GOT, AERIC!
BOOP.
YOU DID IT, AERIC! YOU--
--OH, NO.
IS HE DEAD?
JUST HIS POWER CELLS. WE'LL RECHARGE HIM WHEN WE GET BACK TO CAMP.
LET'S FINISH THIS.

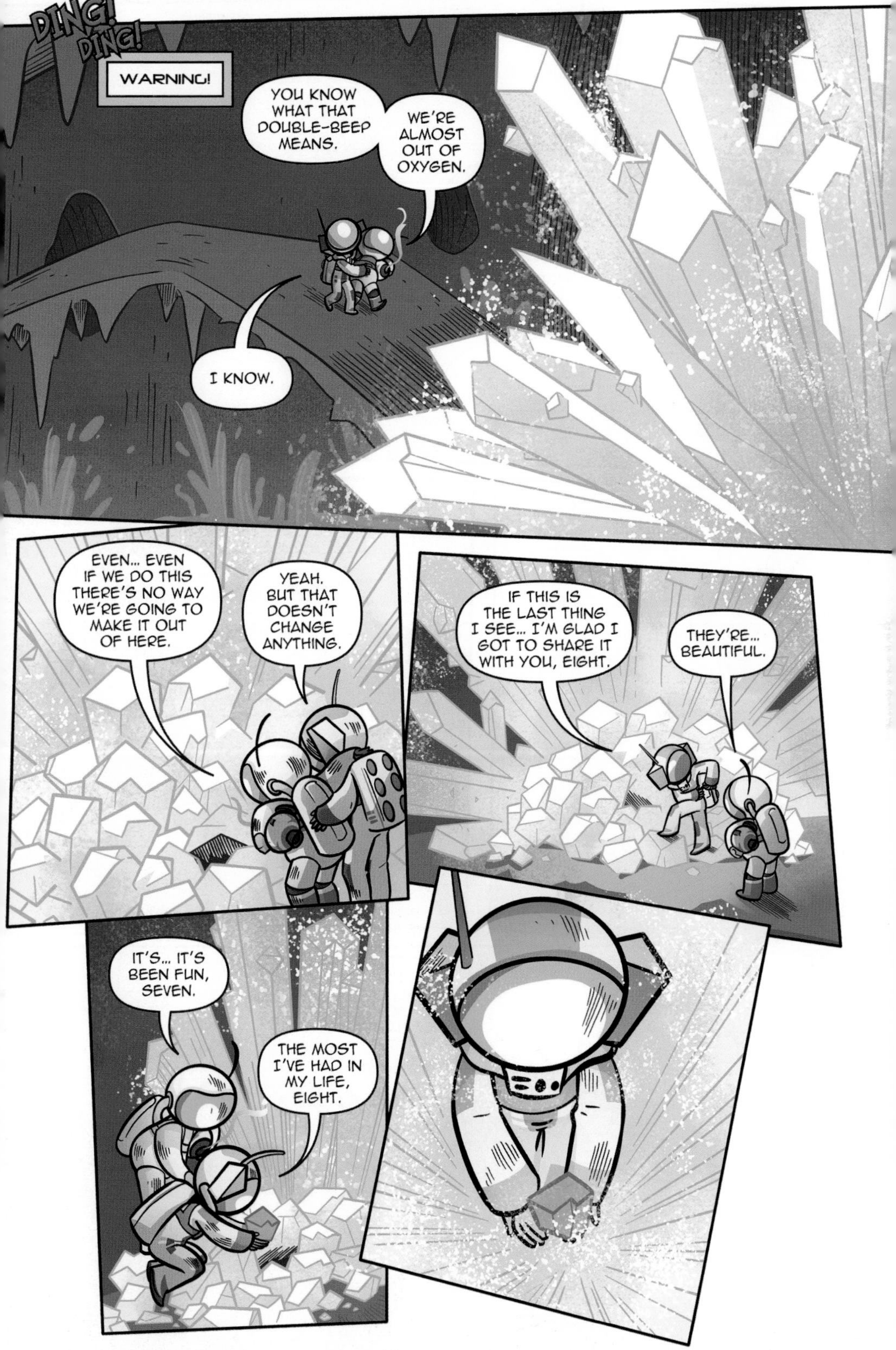
DING! DING!
WARNING!
YOU KNOW WHAT THAT DOUBLE-BEEP MEANS.
WE'RE ALMOST OUT OF OXYGEN.
I KNOW.
EVEN... EVEN IF WE DO THIS THERE'S NO WAY WE'RE GOING TO MAKE IT OUT OF HERE.
YEAH. BUT THAT DOESN'T CHANGE ANYTHING.
IF THIS IS THE LAST THING I SEE... I'M GLAD I GOT TO SHARE IT WITH YOU, EIGHT.
THEY'RE... BEAUTIFUL.
IT'S... IT'S BEEN FUN, SEVEN.
THE MOST I'VE HAD IN MY LIFE, EIGHT.

"I DIDN'T KNOW THEM AS WELL AS SOME OF YOU, AND FOR THAT I HAVE REGRET."

AND WHILE I DIDN'T GET THE CHANCE TO CALL THEM FRIENDS, I KNOW THAT THEY ARE *HEROES*.

SEVEN AND EIGHT SAVED THE WORLD, NO, THE *UNIVERSE*.

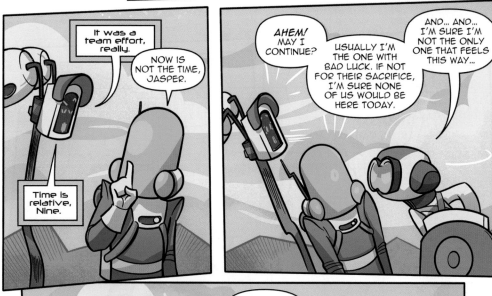

It was a team effort, really.

NOW IS NOT THE TIME, JASPER.

Time is relative, Nine.

AHEM! MAY I CONTINUE?

USUALLY I'M THE ONE WITH BAD LUCK. IF NOT FOR THEIR SACRIFICE, I'M SURE NONE OF US WOULD BE HERE TODAY.

AND... AND... I'M SURE I'M NOT THE ONLY ONE THAT FEELS THIS WAY...

...BUT... I'D SWITCH PLACES WITH THEM IN A HEARTBEAT. THEY... THEY...

IT'S ALL RIGHT, THIRTEEN.

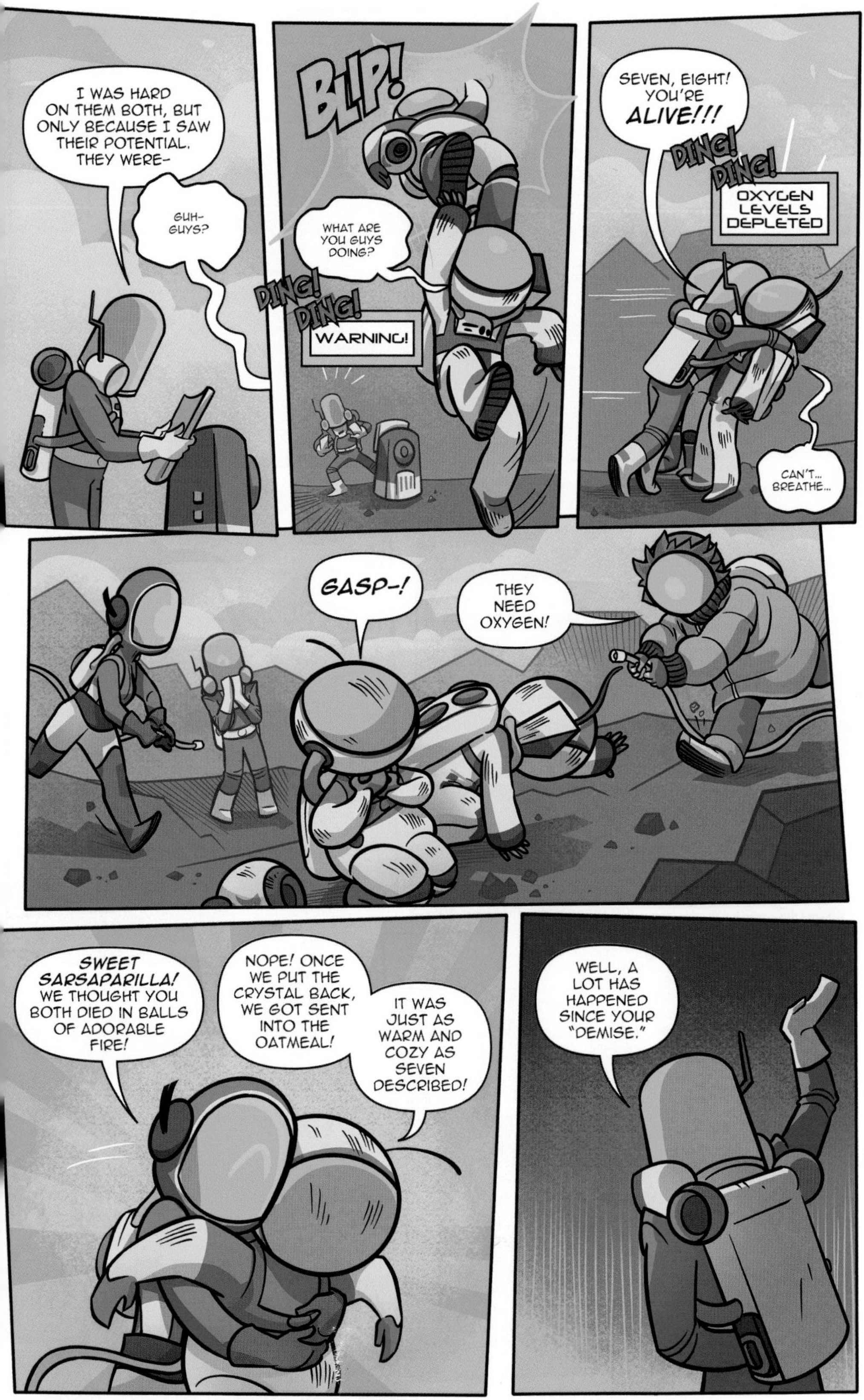
I WAS HARD ON THEM BOTH, BUT ONLY BECAUSE I SAW THEIR POTENTIAL. THEY WERE-
GUH-GUYS?
BLIP!
WHAT ARE YOU GUYS DOING?
DING! DING!
WARNING!
SEVEN, EIGHT! YOU'RE ALIVE!!!
DING! DING!
OXYGEN LEVELS DEPLETED
CAN'T... BREATHE...
GASP-!
THEY NEED OXYGEN!
SWEET SARSAPARILLA! WE THOUGHT YOU BOTH DIED IN BALLS OF ADORABLE FIRE!
NOPE! ONCE WE PUT THE CRYSTAL BACK, WE GOT SENT INTO THE OATMEAL!
IT WAS JUST AS WARM AND COZY AS SEVEN DESCRIBED!
WELL, A LOT HAS HAPPENED SINCE YOUR "DEMISE."

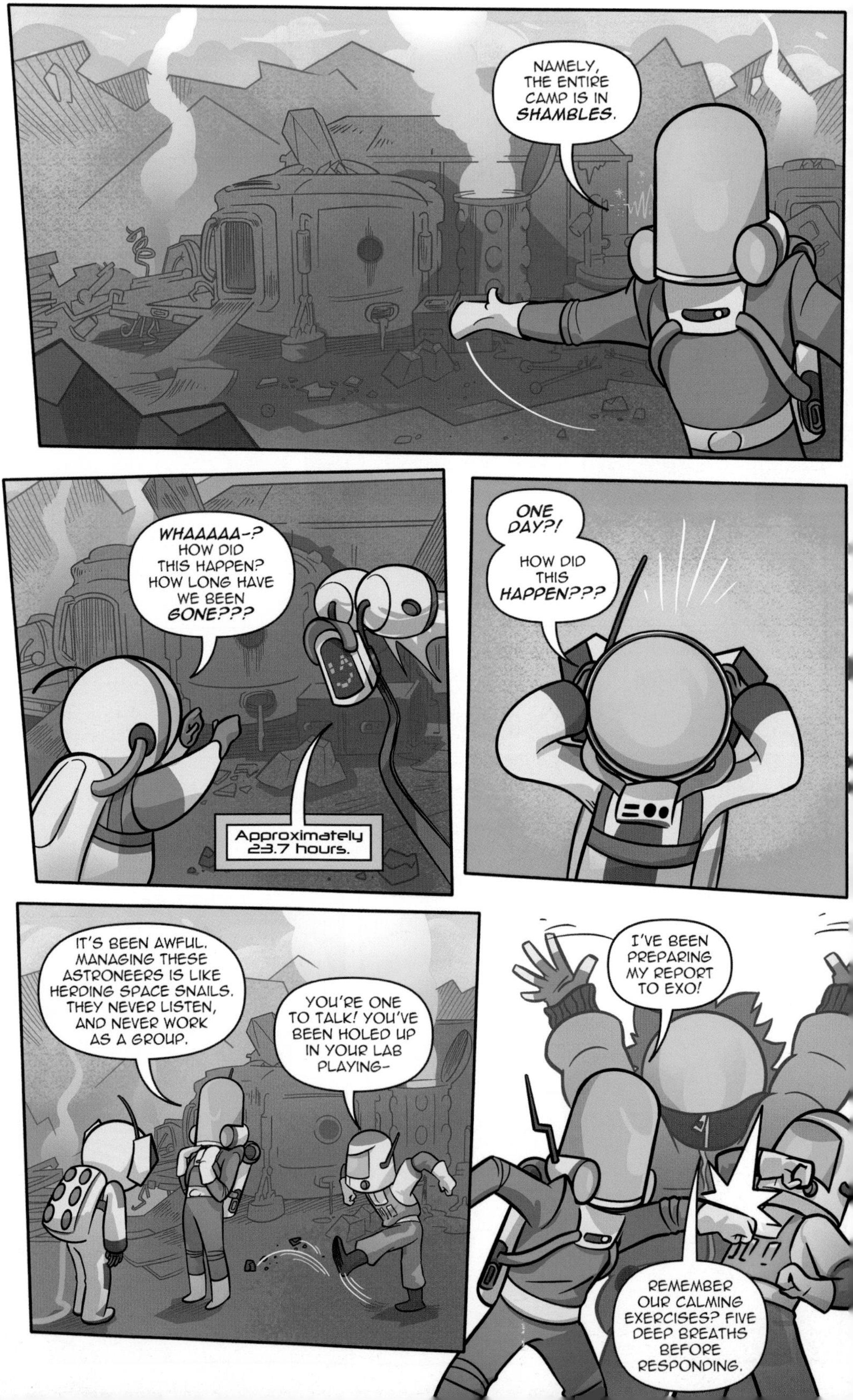
NAMELY, THE ENTIRE CAMP IS IN SHAMBLES.
WHAAAAA-? HOW DID THIS HAPPEN? HOW LONG HAVE WE BEEN GONE???
Approximately 23.7 hours.
ONE DAY?!
HOW DID THIS HAPPEN???
IT'S BEEN AWFUL. MANAGING THESE ASTRONEERS IS LIKE HERDING SPACE SNAILS. THEY NEVER LISTEN, AND NEVER WORK AS A GROUP.
YOU'RE ONE TO TALK! YOU'VE BEEN HOLED UP IN YOUR LAB PLAYING-
I'VE BEEN PREPARING MY REPORT TO EXO!
REMEMBER OUR CALMING EXERCISES? FIVE DEEP BREATHS BEFORE RESPONDING.

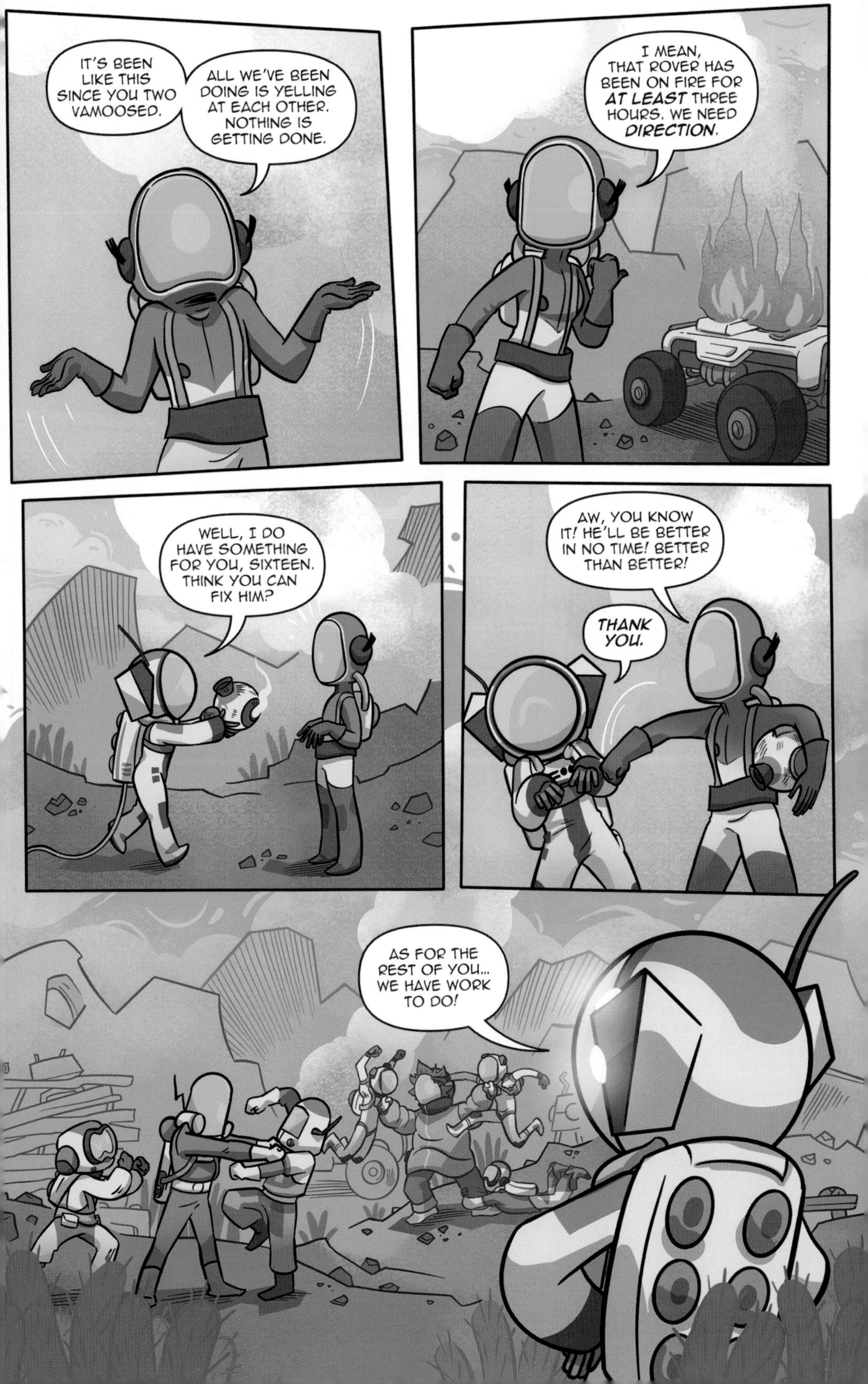
IT'S BEEN LIKE THIS SINCE YOU TWO VAMOOSED.
ALL WE'VE BEEN DOING IS YELLING AT EACH OTHER. NOTHING IS GETTING DONE.
I MEAN, THAT ROVER HAS BEEN ON FIRE FOR AT LEAST THREE HOURS. WE NEED DIRECTION.
WELL, I DO HAVE SOMETHING FOR YOU, SIXTEEN. THINK YOU CAN FIX HIM?
AW, YOU KNOW IT! HE'LL BE BETTER IN NO TIME! BETTER THAN BETTER!
THANK YOU.
AS FOR THE REST OF YOU... WE HAVE WORK TO DO!

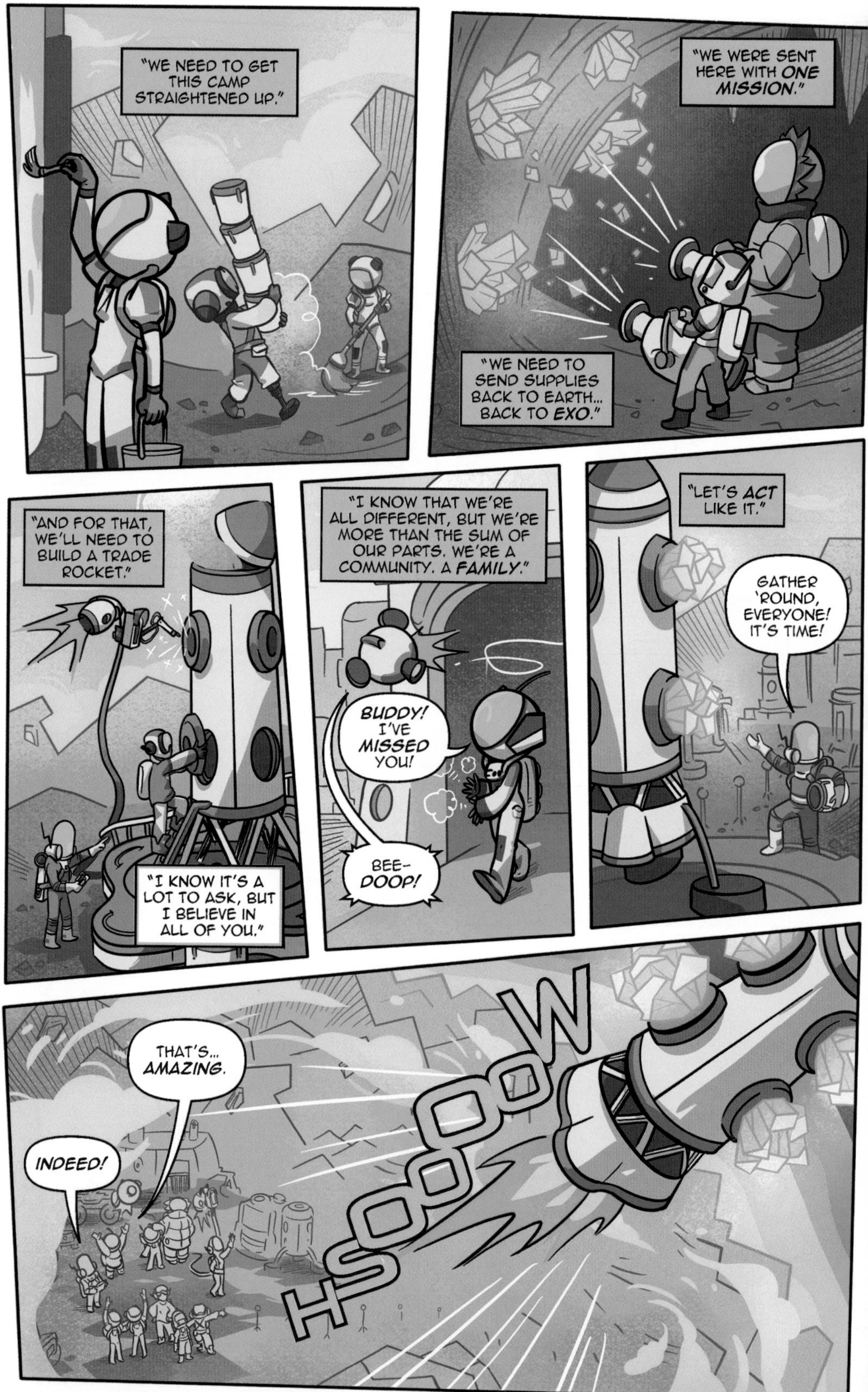
"WE NEED TO GET THIS CAMP STRAIGHTENED UP."
"WE WERE SENT HERE WITH *ONE MISSION*."
"WE NEED TO SEND SUPPLIES BACK TO EARTH... BACK TO *EXO*."
"AND FOR THAT, WE'LL NEED TO BUILD A TRADE ROCKET."
"I KNOW IT'S A LOT TO ASK, BUT I BELIEVE IN ALL OF YOU."
"I KNOW THAT WE'RE ALL DIFFERENT, BUT WE'RE MORE THAN THE SUM OF OUR PARTS. WE'RE A COMMUNITY. A *FAMILY*."
BUDDY! I'VE *MISSED* YOU!
BEE-*DOOP!*
"LET'S *ACT* LIKE IT."
GATHER 'ROUND, EVERYONE! IT'S TIME!
THAT'S... *AMAZING*.
INDEED!
HSOOOOOW

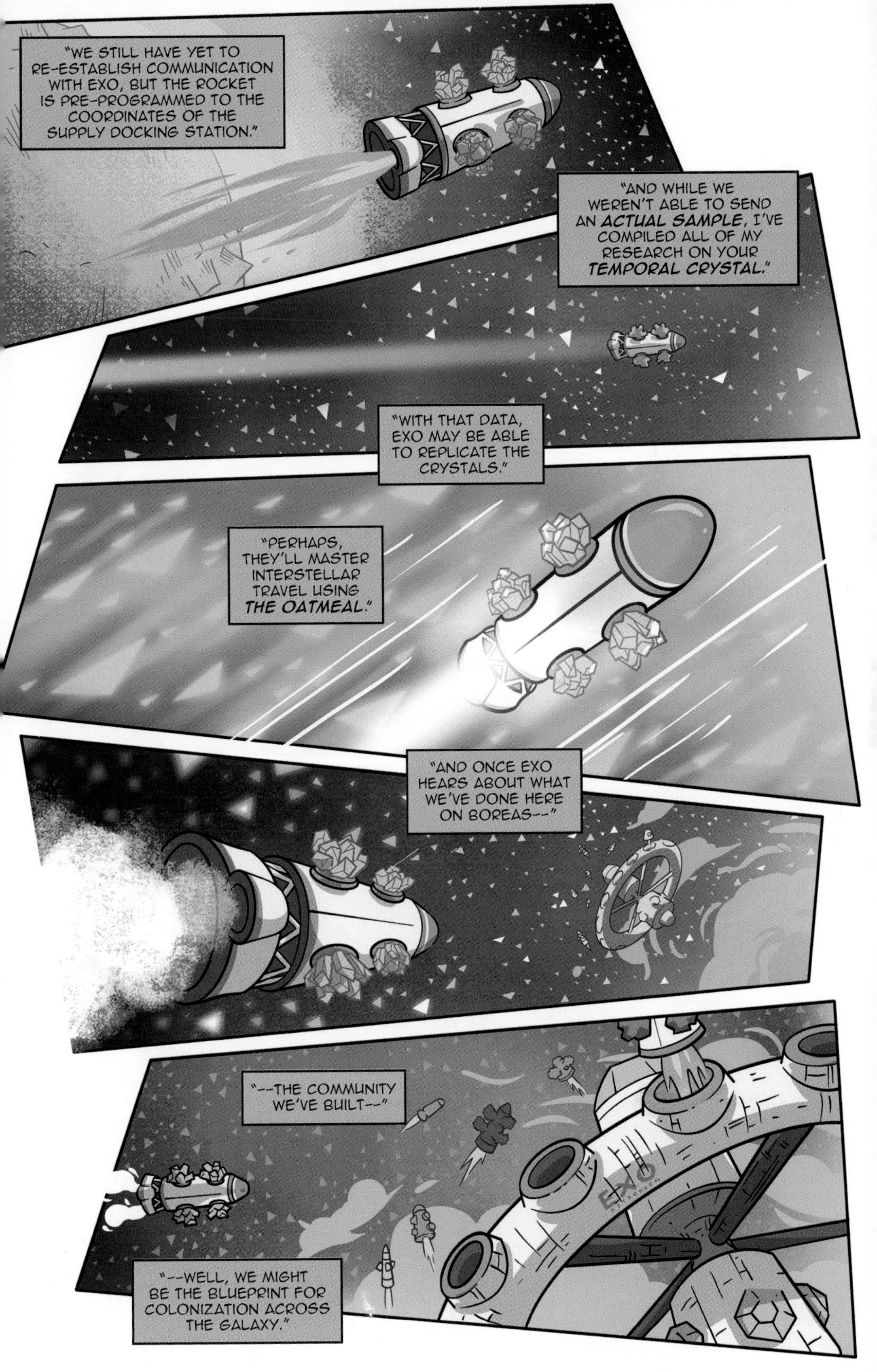
"WE STILL HAVE YET TO RE-ESTABLISH COMMUNICATION WITH EXO, BUT THE ROCKET IS PRE-PROGRAMMED TO THE COORDINATES OF THE SUPPLY DOCKING STATION."
"AND WHILE WE WEREN'T ABLE TO SEND AN *ACTUAL SAMPLE*, I'VE COMPILED ALL OF MY RESEARCH ON YOUR *TEMPORAL CRYSTAL*."
"WITH THAT DATA, EXO MAY BE ABLE TO REPLICATE THE CRYSTALS."
"PERHAPS, THEY'LL MASTER INTERSTELLAR TRAVEL USING *THE OATMEAL*."
"AND ONCE EXO HEARS ABOUT WHAT WE'VE DONE HERE ON BOREAS--"
"--THE COMMUNITY WE'VE BUILT--"
EXO
"--WELL, WE MIGHT BE THE BLUEPRINT FOR COLONIZATION ACROSS THE GALAXY."

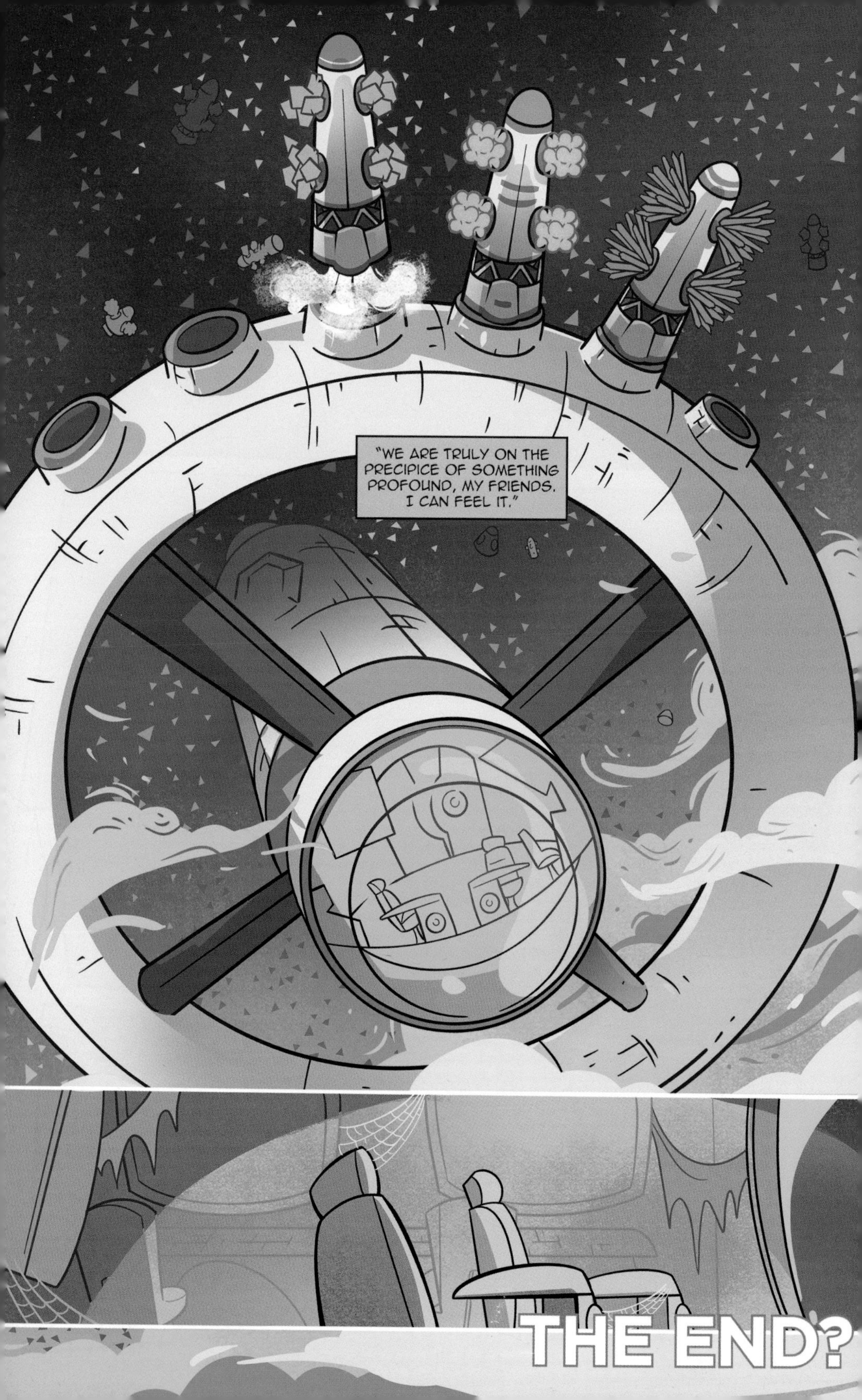
"WE ARE TRULY ON THE PRECIPICE OF SOMETHING PROFOUND, MY FRIENDS. I CAN FEEL IT."
THE END?

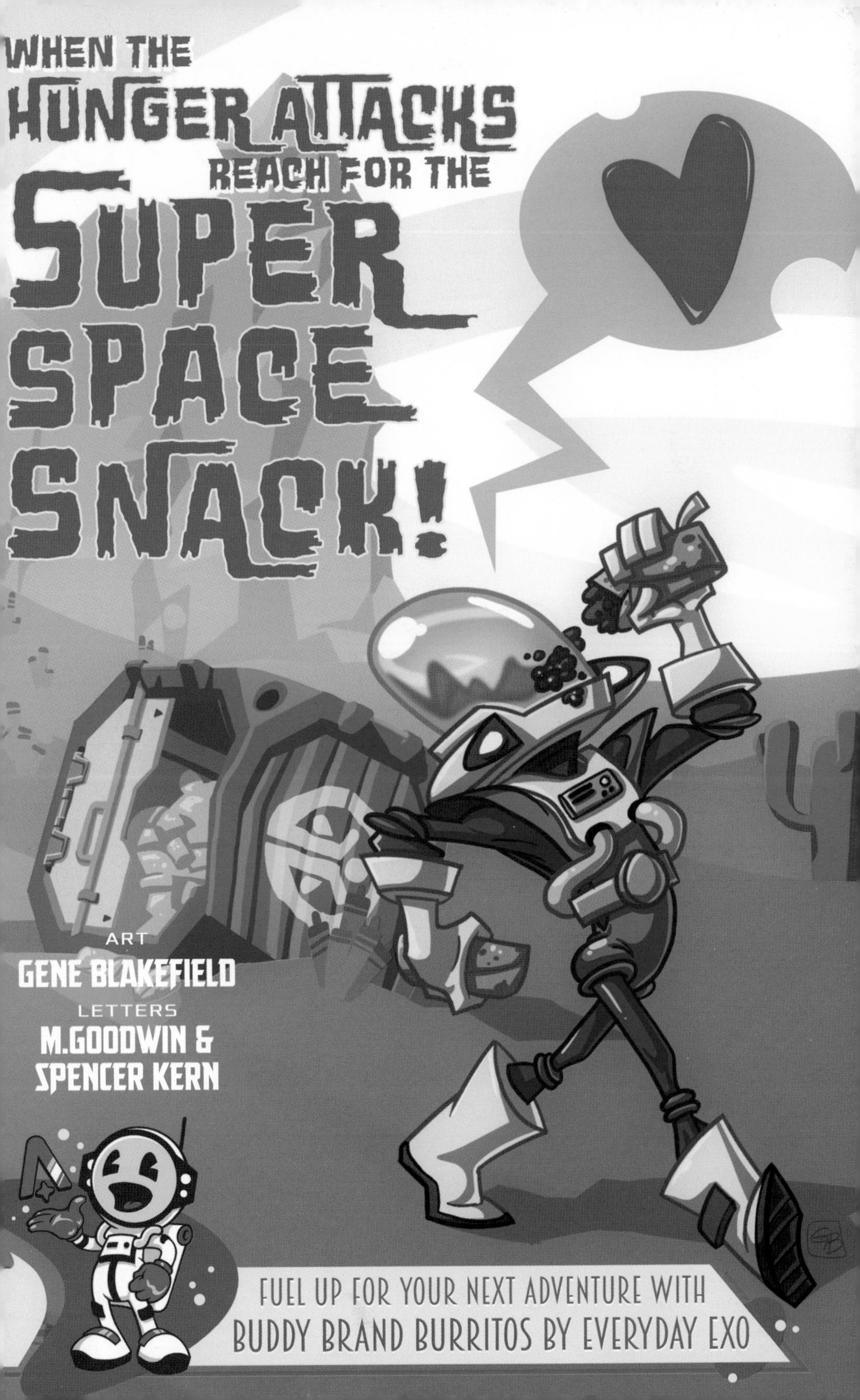
WHEN THE
HUNGER ATTACKS
REACH FOR THE
SUPER
SPACE
SNACK!
ART
GENE BLAKEFIELD
LETTERS
M.GOODWIN &
SPENCER KERN
FUEL UP FOR YOUR NEXT ADVENTURE WITH
BUDDY BRAND BURRITOS BY EVERYDAY EXO

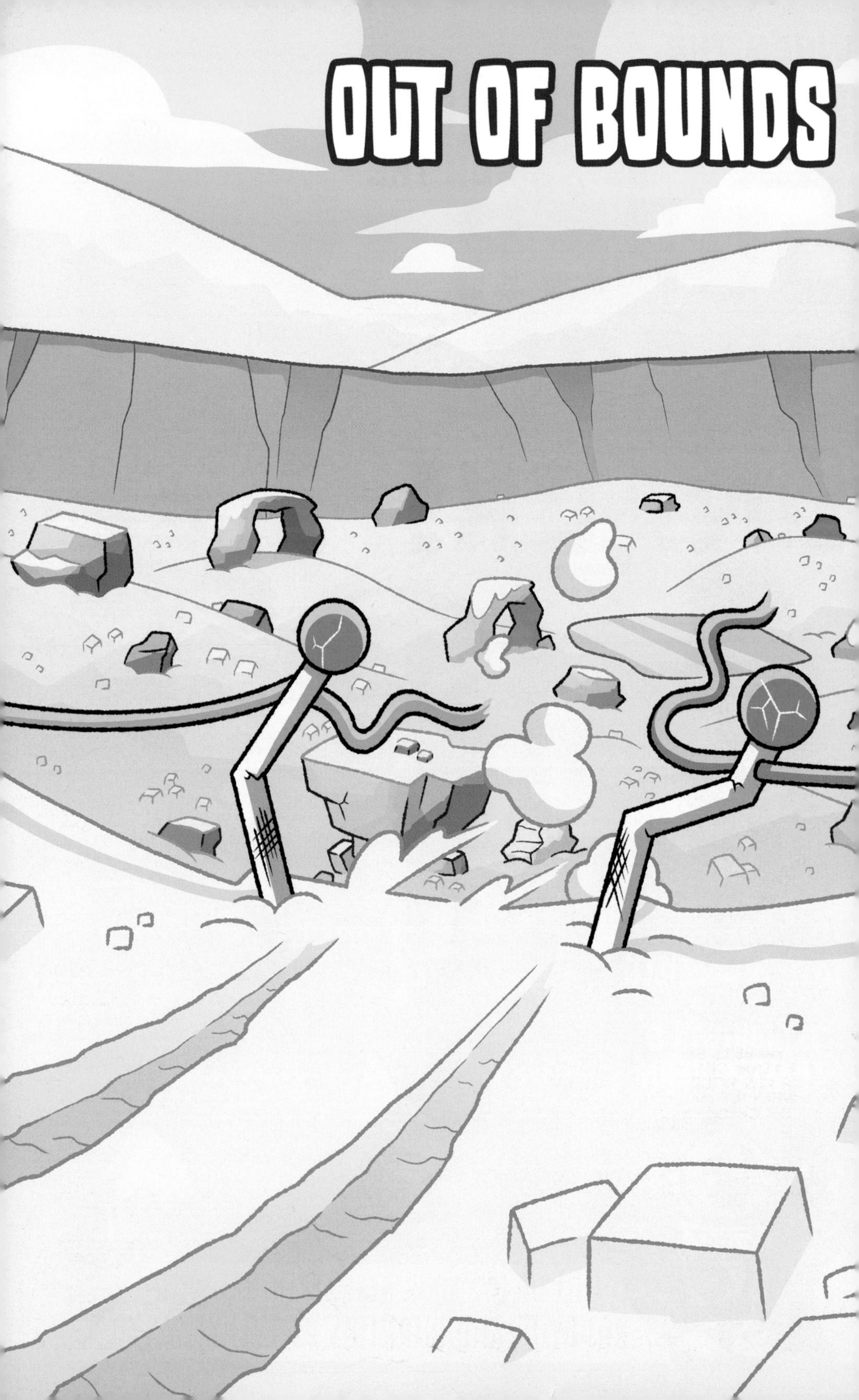
OUT OF BOUNDS

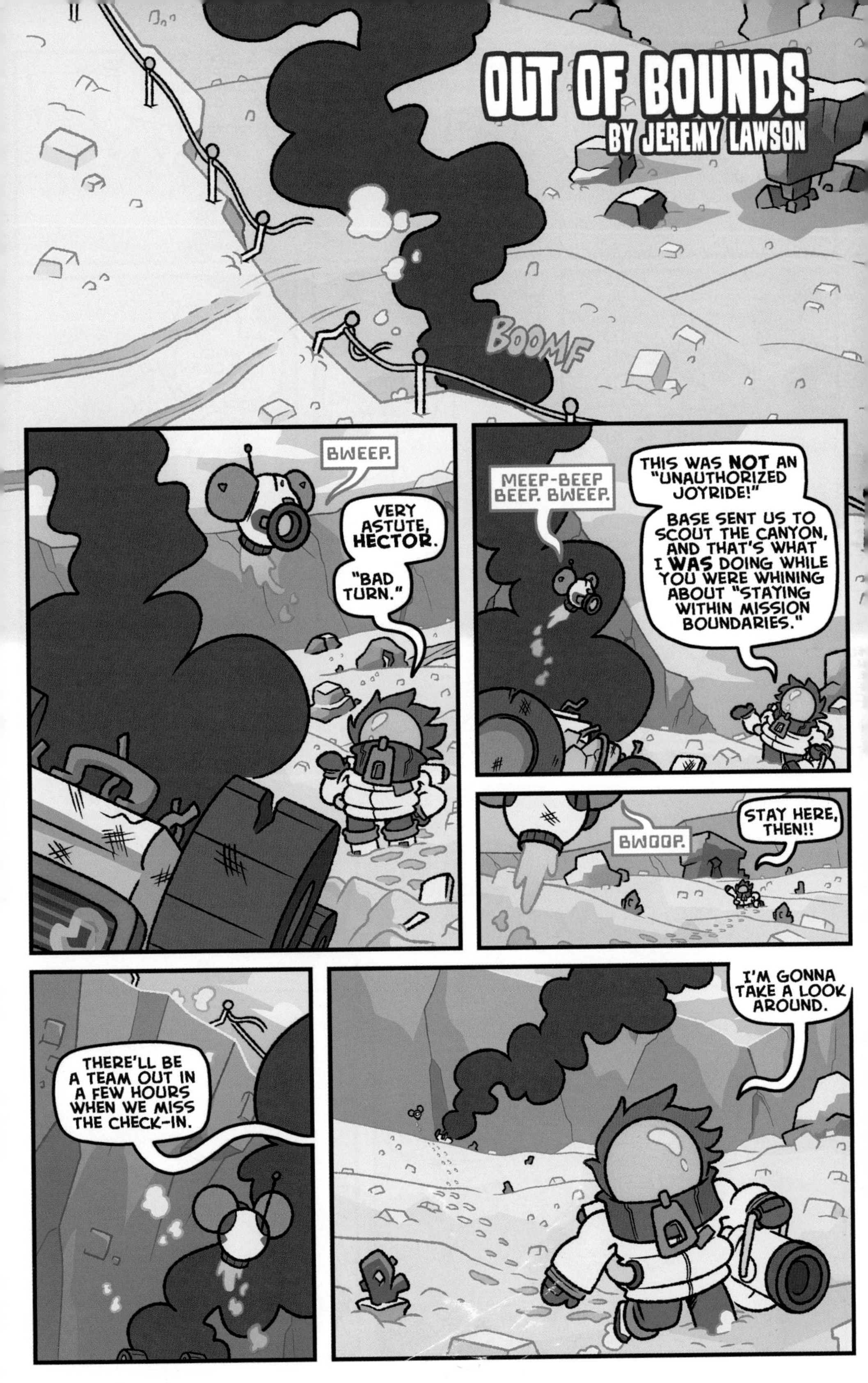
OUT OF BOUNDS
BY JEREMY LAWSON
BOOMF
BWEEP.
VERY ASTUTE, HECTOR.
"BAD TURN."
MEEP-BEEP BEEP. BWEEP.
THIS WAS NOT AN "UNAUTHORIZED JOYRIDE!"
BASE SENT US TO SCOUT THE CANYON, AND THAT'S WHAT I WAS DOING WHILE YOU WERE WHINING ABOUT "STAYING WITHIN MISSION BOUNDARIES."
BWOOP.
STAY HERE, THEN!!
THERE'LL BE A TEAM OUT IN A FEW HOURS WHEN WE MISS THE CHECK-IN.
I'M GONNA TAKE A LOOK AROUND.

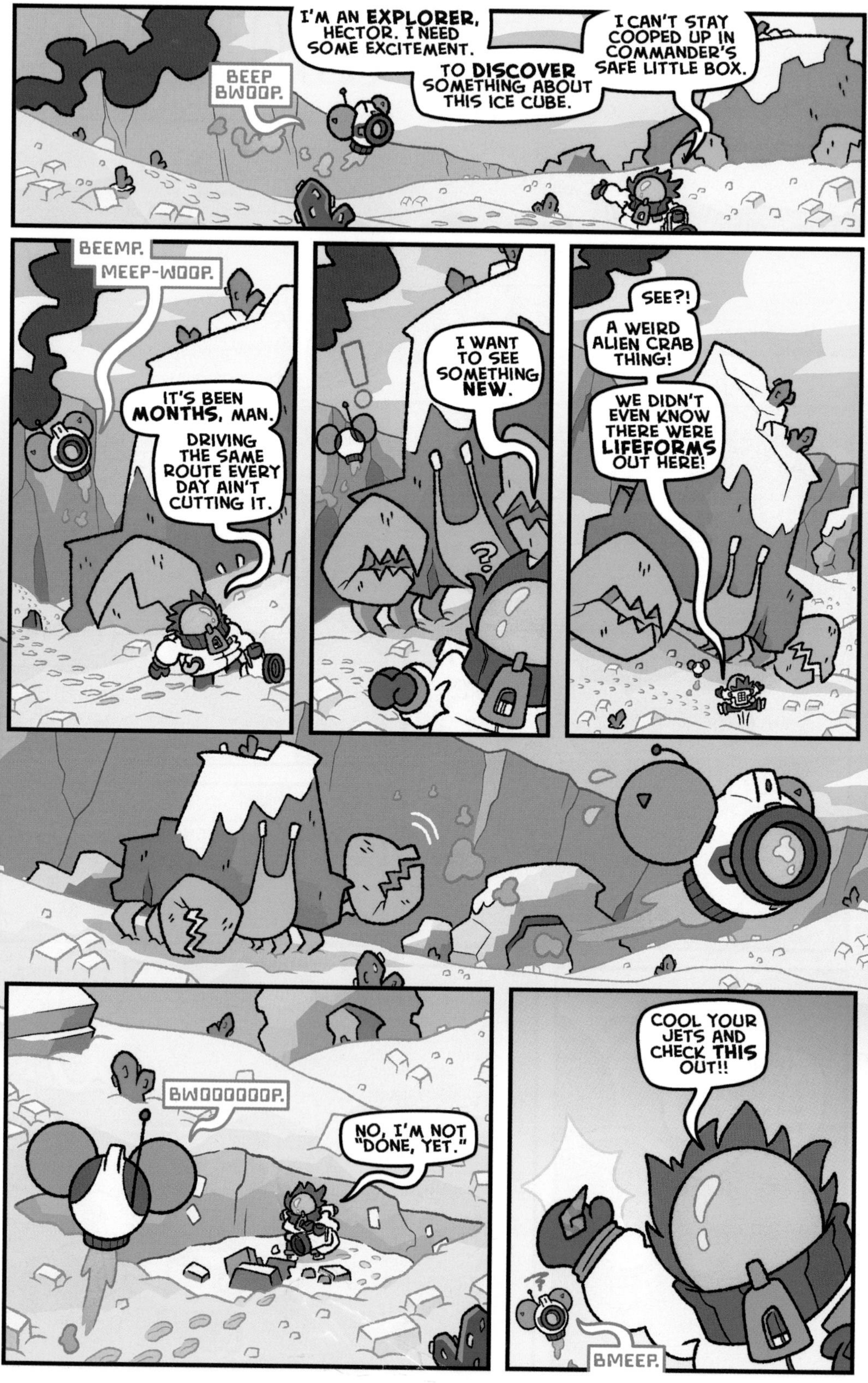
BEEP BWOOP.
I'M AN EXPLORER, HECTOR. I NEED SOME EXCITEMENT.
TO DISCOVER SOMETHING ABOUT THIS ICE CUBE.
I CAN'T STAY COOPED UP IN COMMANDER'S SAFE LITTLE BOX.
BEEMP.
MEEP-WOOP.
IT'S BEEN MONTHS, MAN.
DRIVING THE SAME ROUTE EVERY DAY AIN'T CUTTING IT.
I WANT TO SEE SOMETHING NEW.
SEE?!
A WEIRD ALIEN CRAB THING!
WE DIDN'T EVEN KNOW THERE WERE LIFEFORMS OUT HERE!
BWOOOOOOP.
NO, I'M NOT "DONE, YET."
COOL YOUR JETS AND CHECK THIS OUT!!
BMEEP.

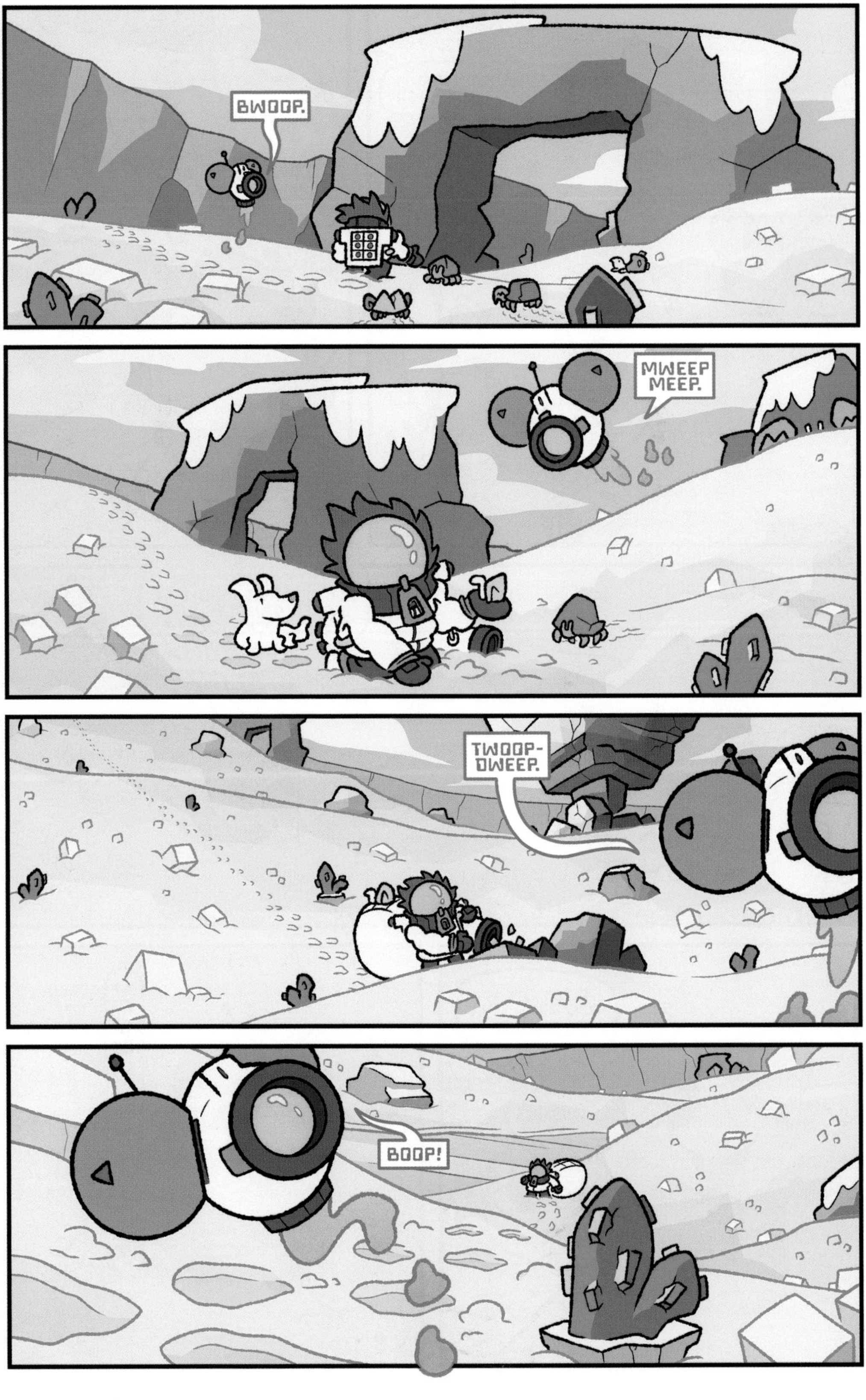
BWOOP.
MWEEP MEEP.
TWOOP-DWEEP.
BOOP!

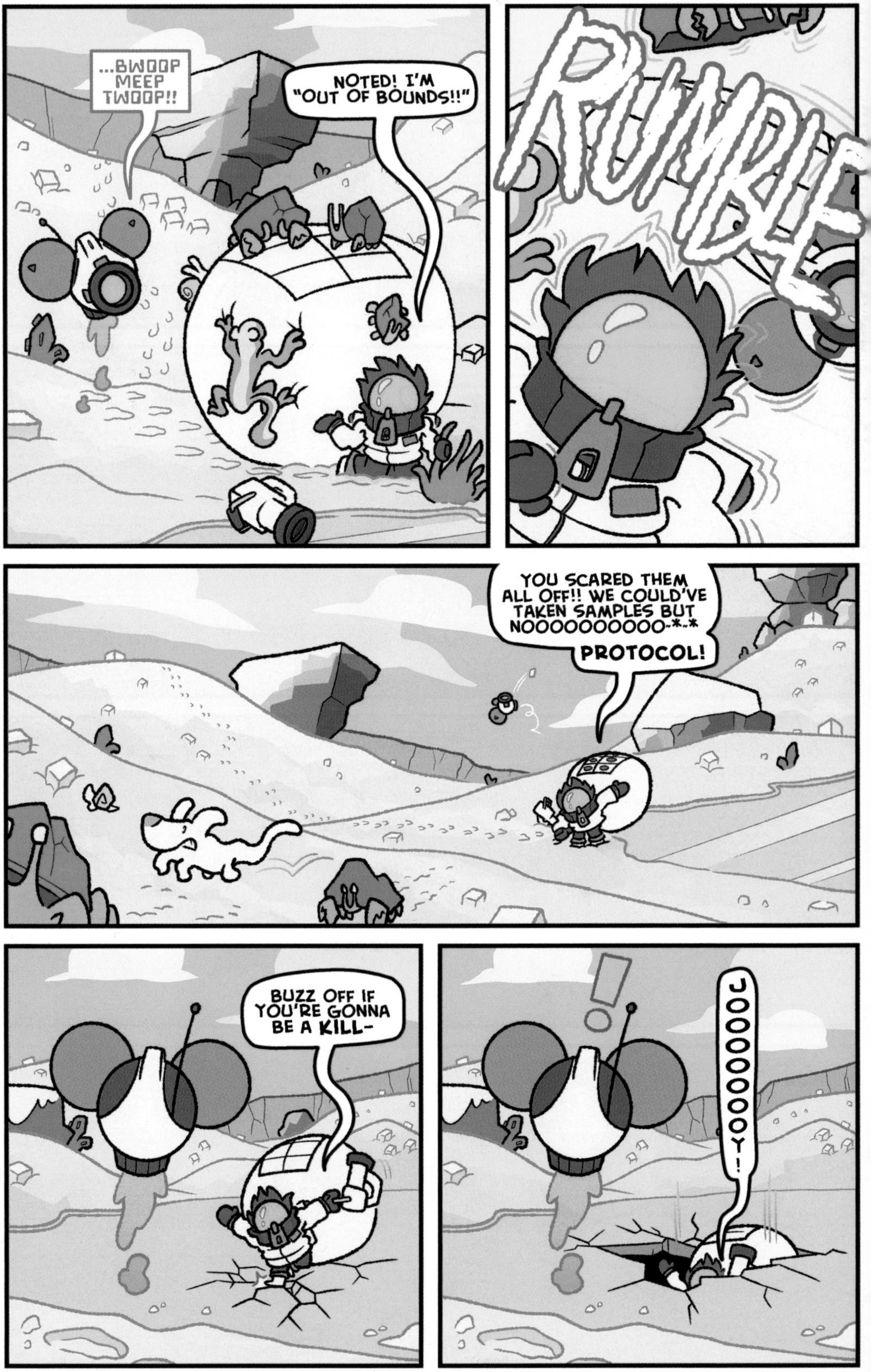
...BWOOP MEEP TWOOP!!
NOTED! I'M "OUT OF BOUNDS!!"
RUMBLE
YOU SCARED THEM ALL OFF!! WE COULD'VE TAKEN SAMPLES BUT NOOOOOOOOOO~*~*
PROTOCOL!
BUZZ OFF IF YOU'RE GONNA BE A KILL-
!
JOOOOOOOOY!

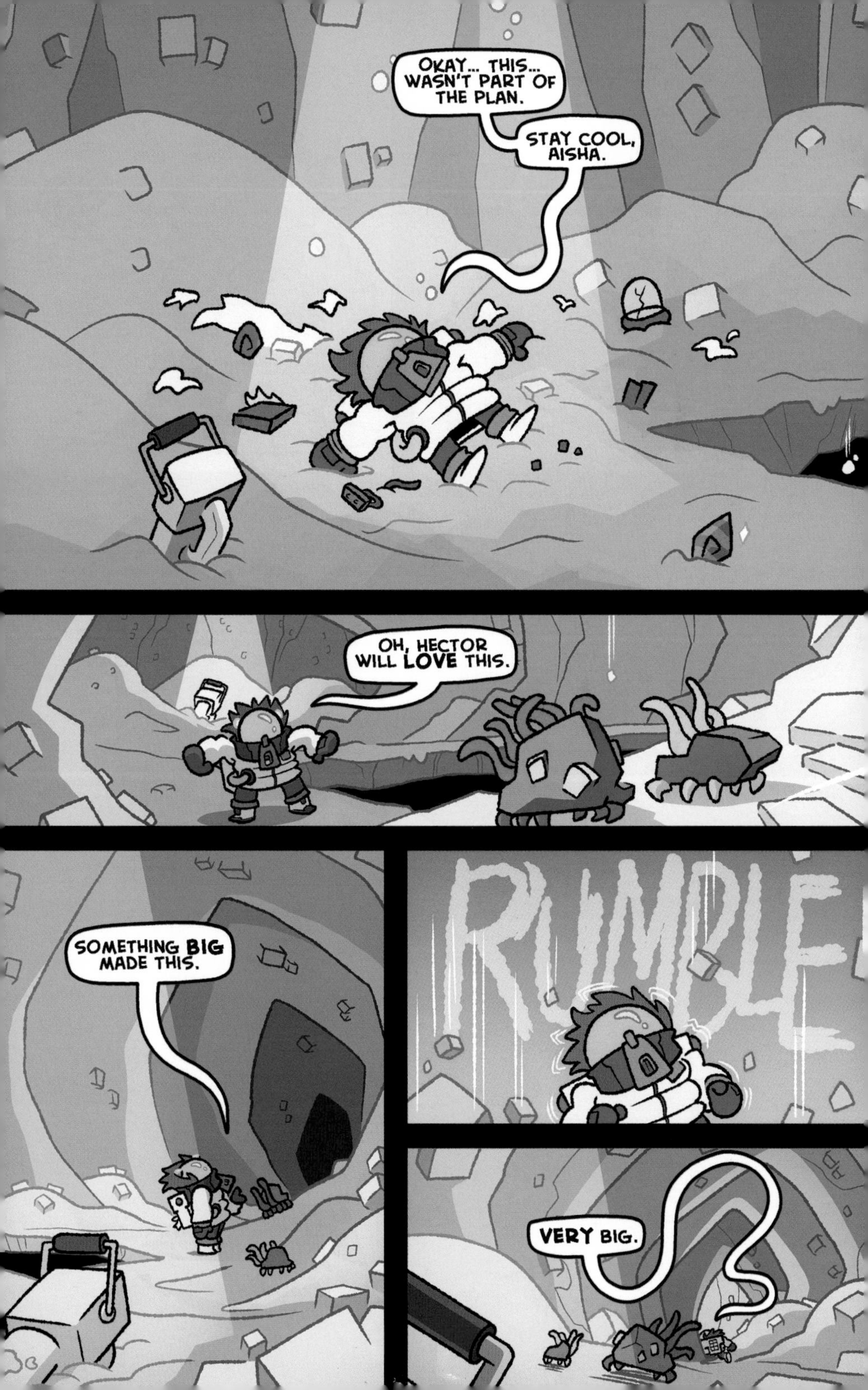
OKAY... THIS... WASN'T PART OF THE PLAN.
STAY COOL, AISHA.
OH, HECTOR WILL LOVE THIS.
SOMETHING BIG MADE THIS.
RUMBLE
VERY BIG.

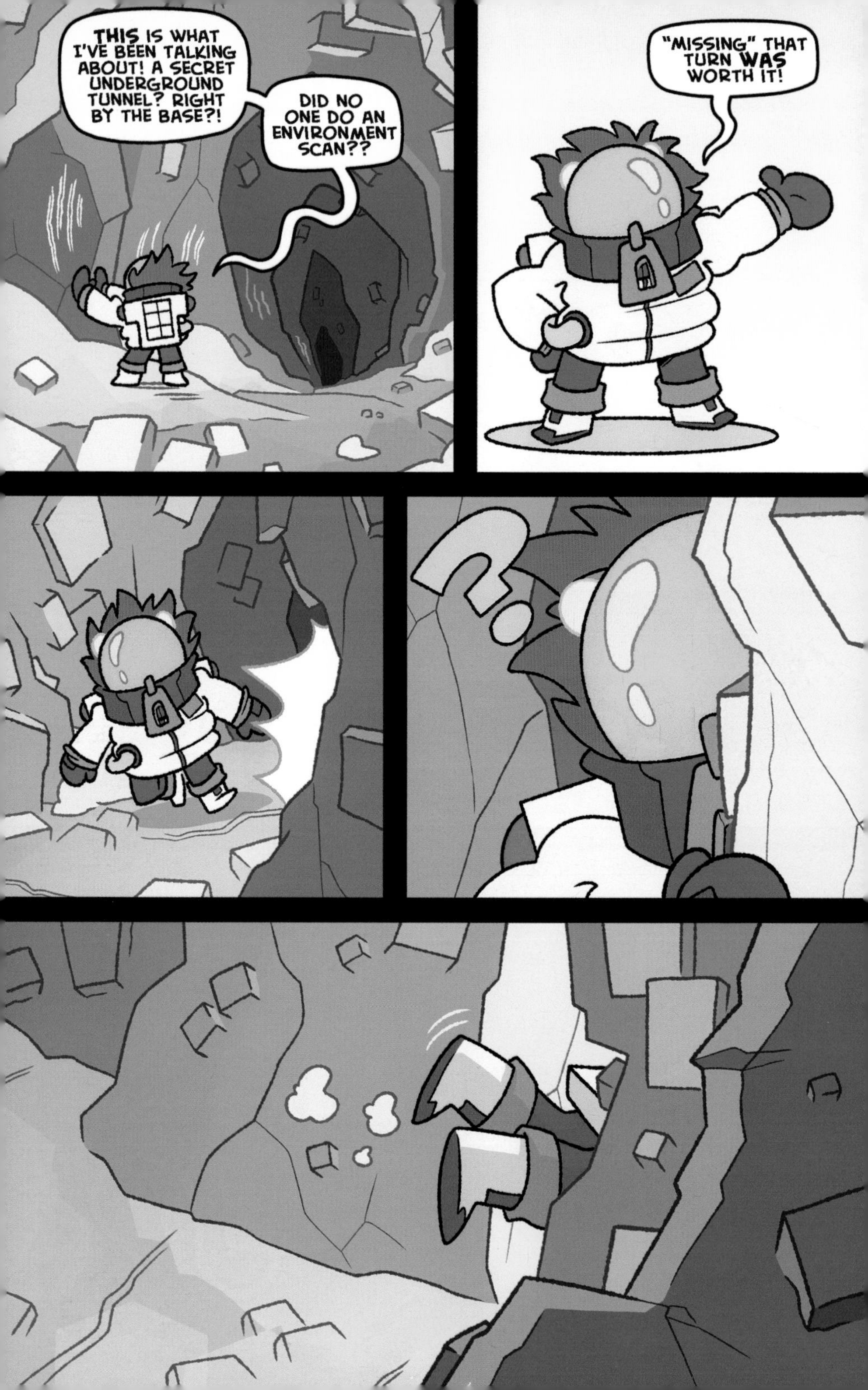
THIS IS WHAT I'VE BEEN TALKING ABOUT! A SECRET UNDERGROUND TUNNEL? RIGHT BY THE BASE?!
DID NO ONE DO AN ENVIRONMENT SCAN??
"MISSING" THAT TURN WAS WORTH IT!

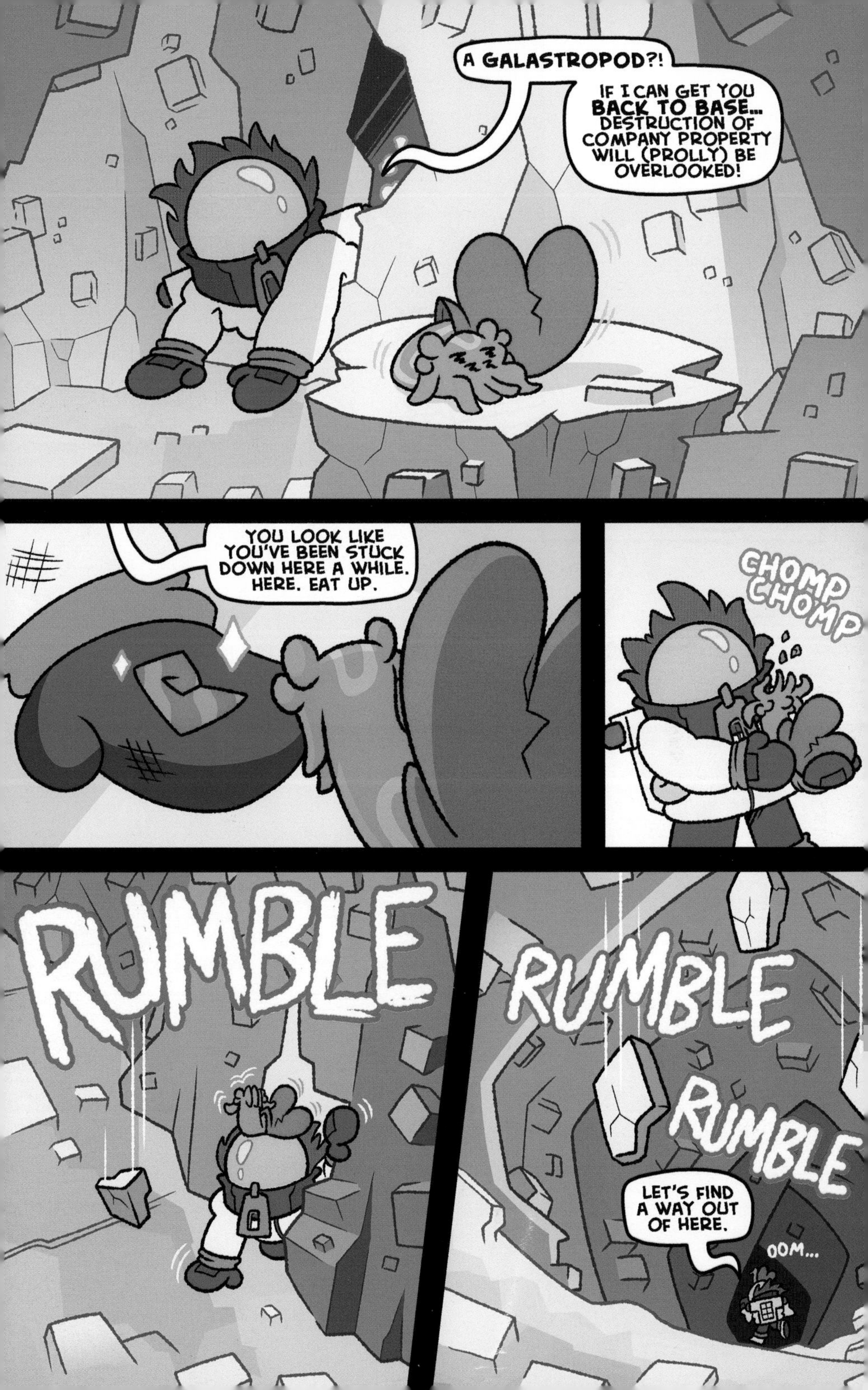
A GALASTROPOD?!
IF I CAN GET YOU BACK TO BASE... DESTRUCTION OF COMPANY PROPERTY WILL (PROLLY) BE OVERLOOKED!
YOU LOOK LIKE YOU'VE BEEN STUCK DOWN HERE A WHILE. HERE. EAT UP.
CHOMP CHOMP
RUMBLE
RUMBLE
RUMBLE
LET'S FIND A WAY OUT OF HERE.
OOM...

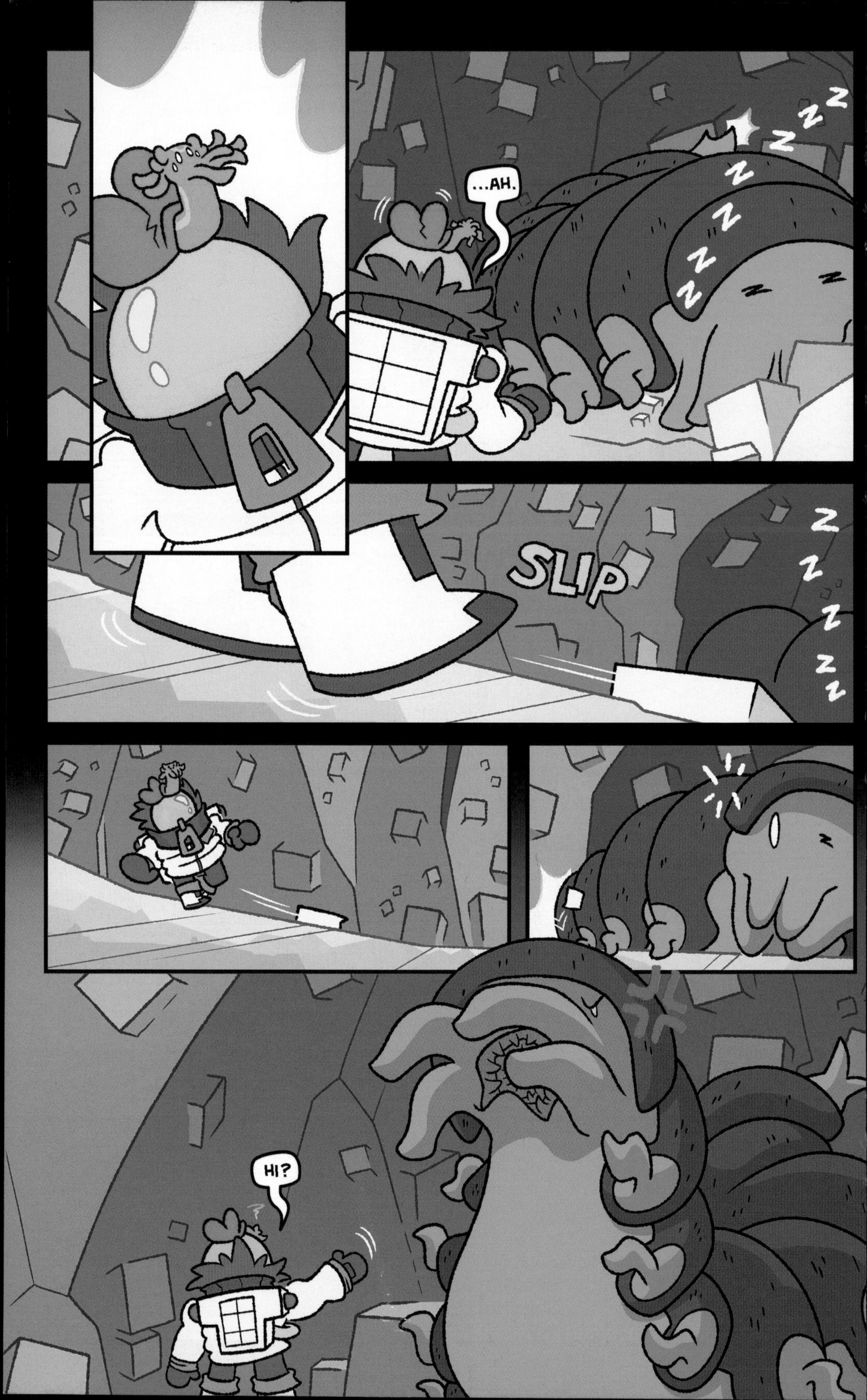
...AH.
ZZZZZZZZZ
SLIP
ZZZZZ
HI?

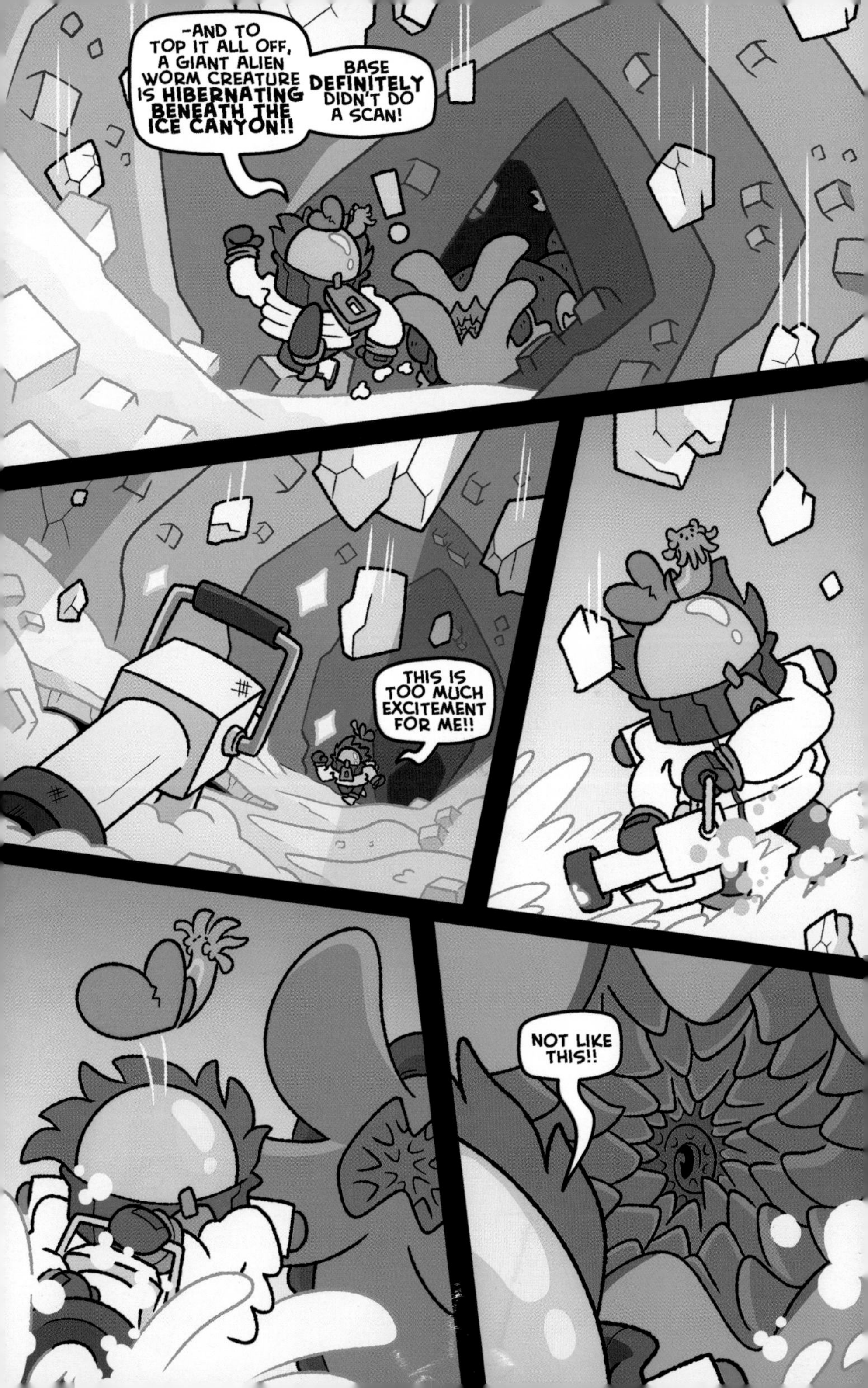
-AND TO TOP IT ALL OFF, A GIANT ALIEN WORM CREATURE IS HIBERNATING BENEATH THE ICE CANYON!!
BASE DEFINITELY DIDN'T DO A SCAN!
!
THIS IS TOO MUCH EXCITEMENT FOR ME!!
NOT LIKE THIS!!

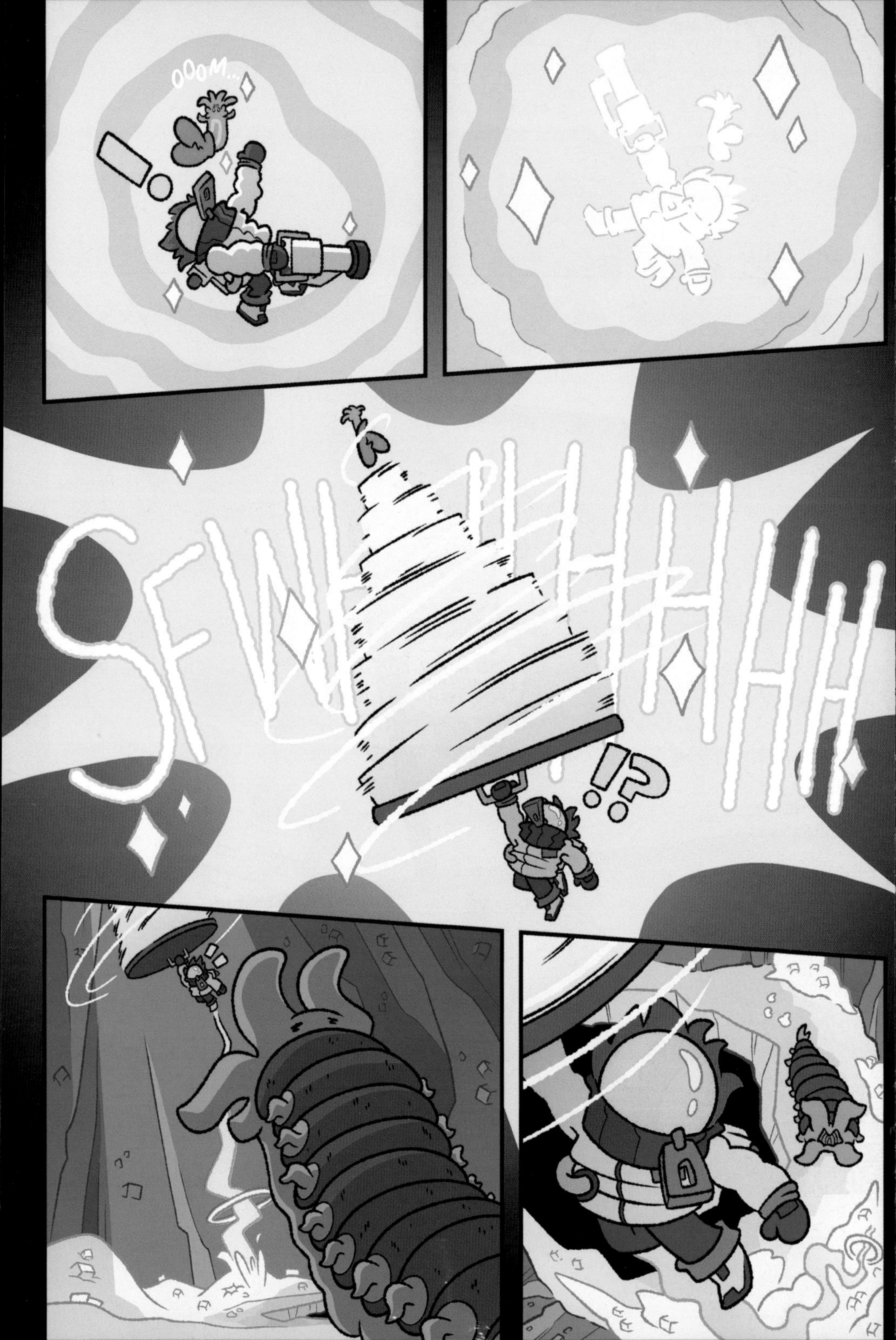
OOOM...
SFWHHHHHHH!!
!?

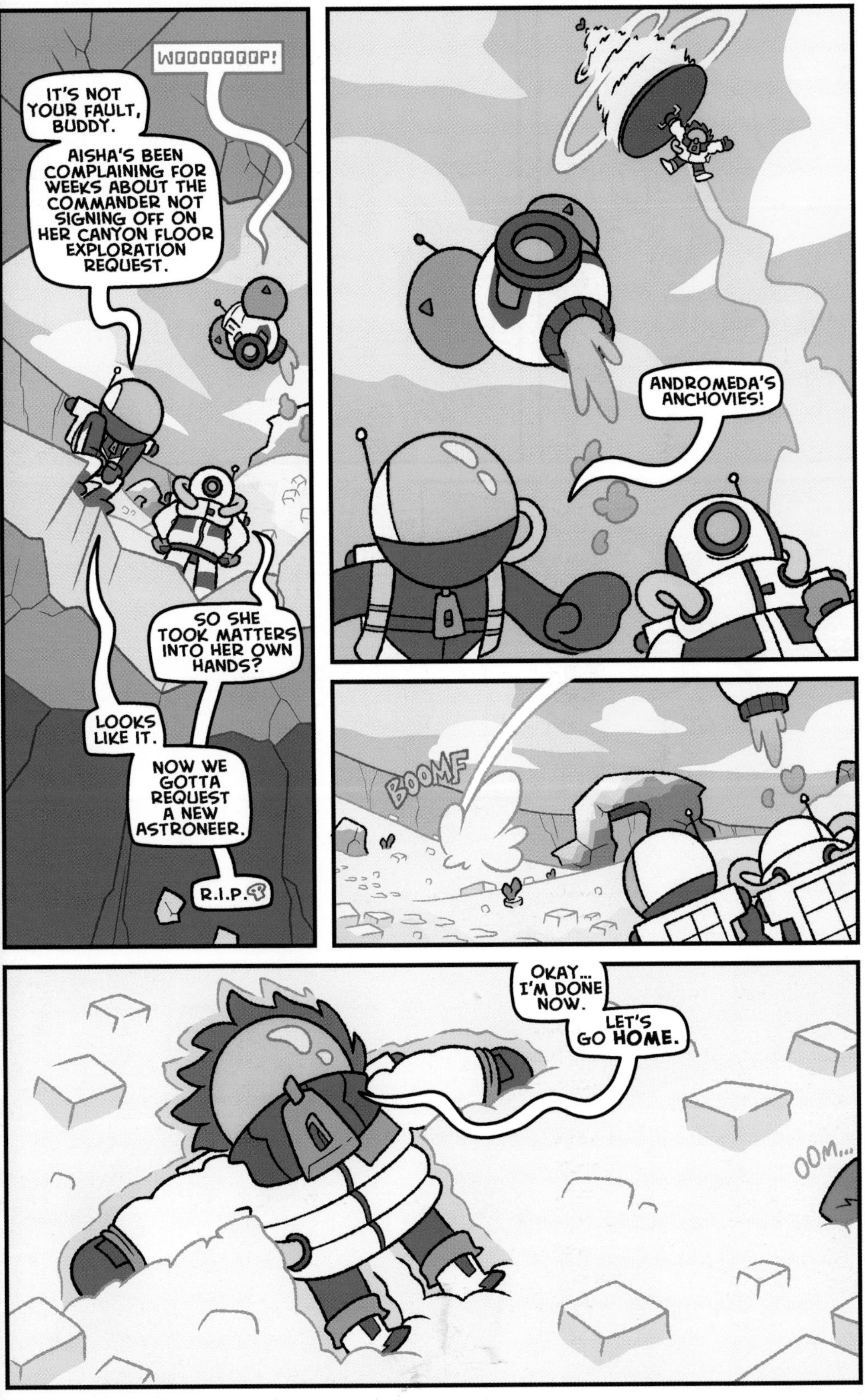
WOOOOOOOP!
IT'S NOT YOUR FAULT, BUDDY.
AISHA'S BEEN COMPLAINING FOR WEEKS ABOUT THE COMMANDER NOT SIGNING OFF ON HER CANYON FLOOR EXPLORATION REQUEST.
SO SHE TOOK MATTERS INTO HER OWN HANDS?
LOOKS LIKE IT.
NOW WE GOTTA REQUEST A NEW ASTRONEER.
R.I.P.
ANDROMEDA'S ANCHOVIES!
BOOMF
OKAY... I'M DONE NOW.
LET'S GO HOME.
OOM...

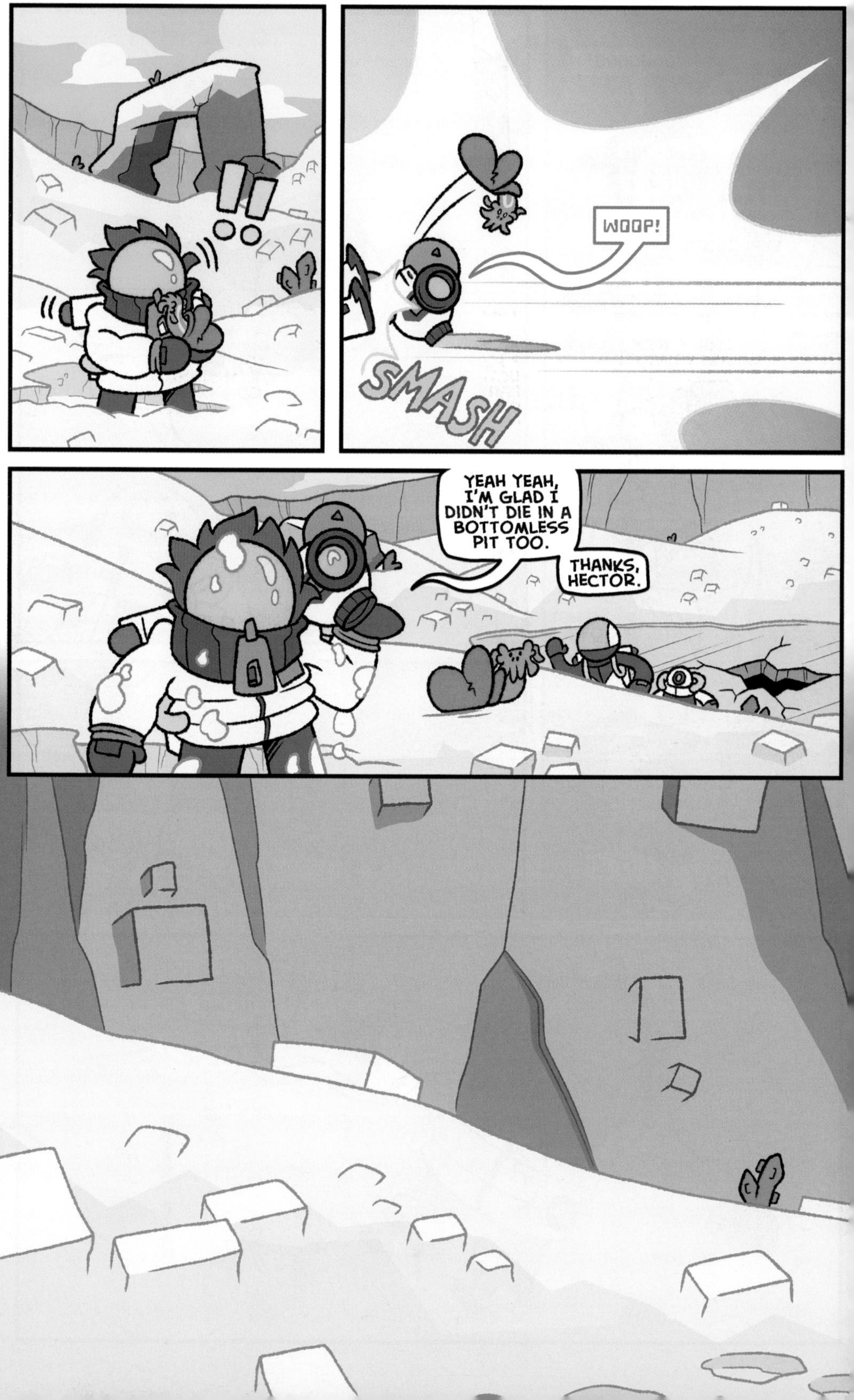
!!
WOOP!
SMASH
YEAH YEAH, I'M GLAD I DIDN'T DIE IN A BOTTOMLESS PIT TOO.
THANKS, HECTOR.

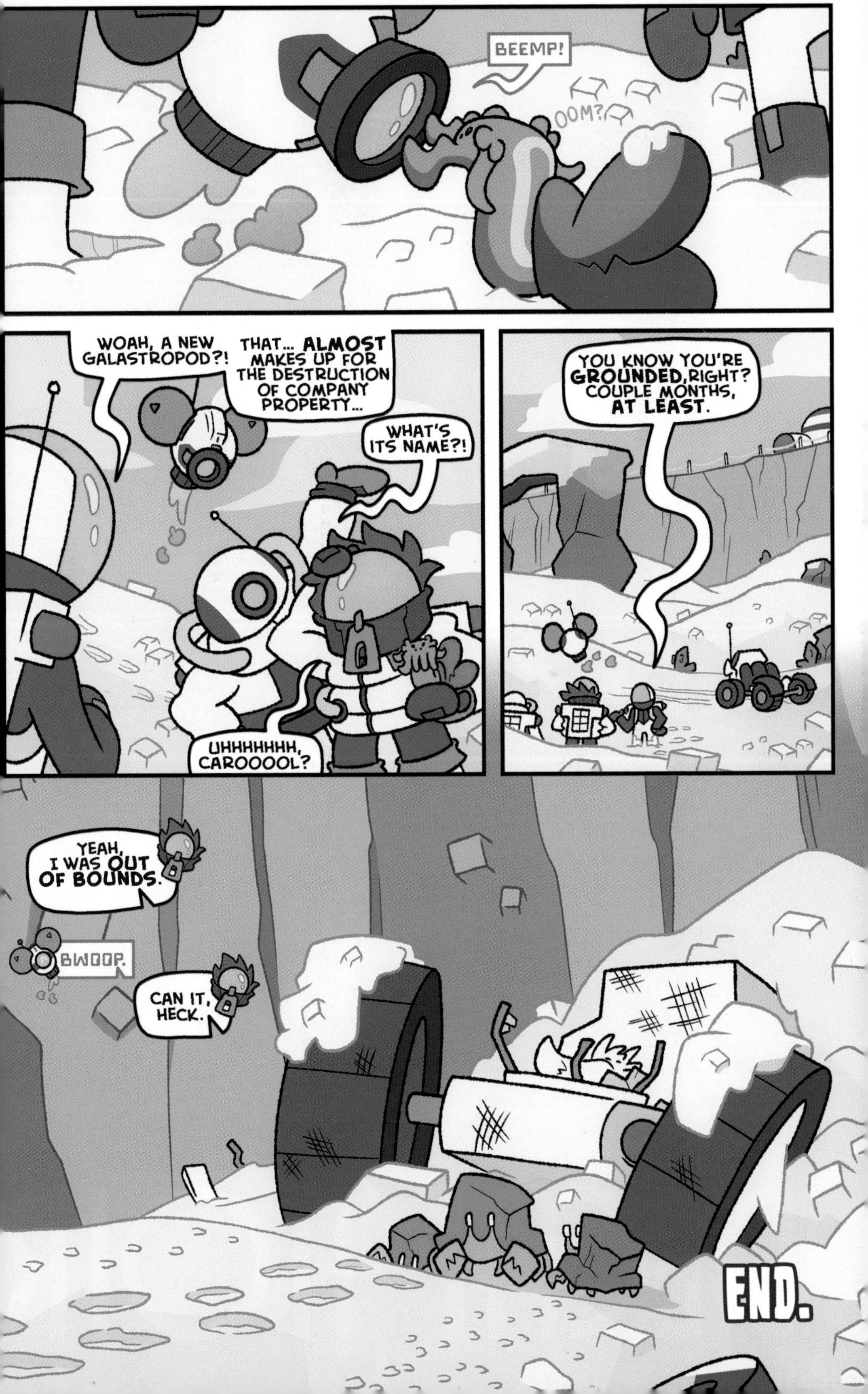
BEEMP!
OOM?
WOAH, A NEW GALASTROPOD?!
THAT... **ALMOST** MAKES UP FOR THE DESTRUCTION OF COMPANY PROPERTY...
WHAT'S ITS NAME?!
UHHHHHHH, CAROOOOL?
YOU KNOW YOU'RE **GROUNDED**, RIGHT? COUPLE MONTHS, **AT LEAST**.
YEAH, I WAS **OUT OF BOUNDS**.
BWOOP.
CAN IT, HECK.
END.

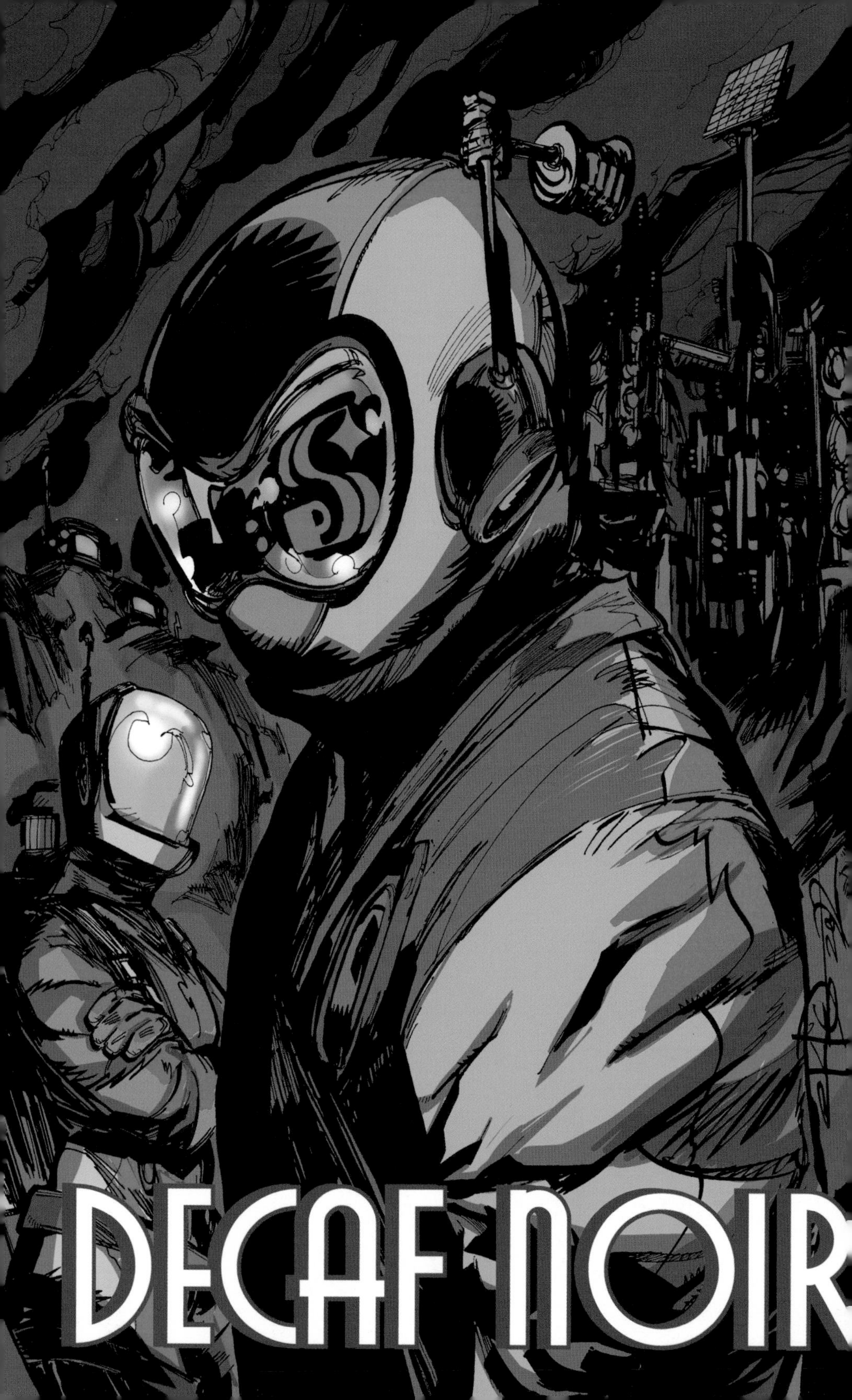
DECAF NOIR

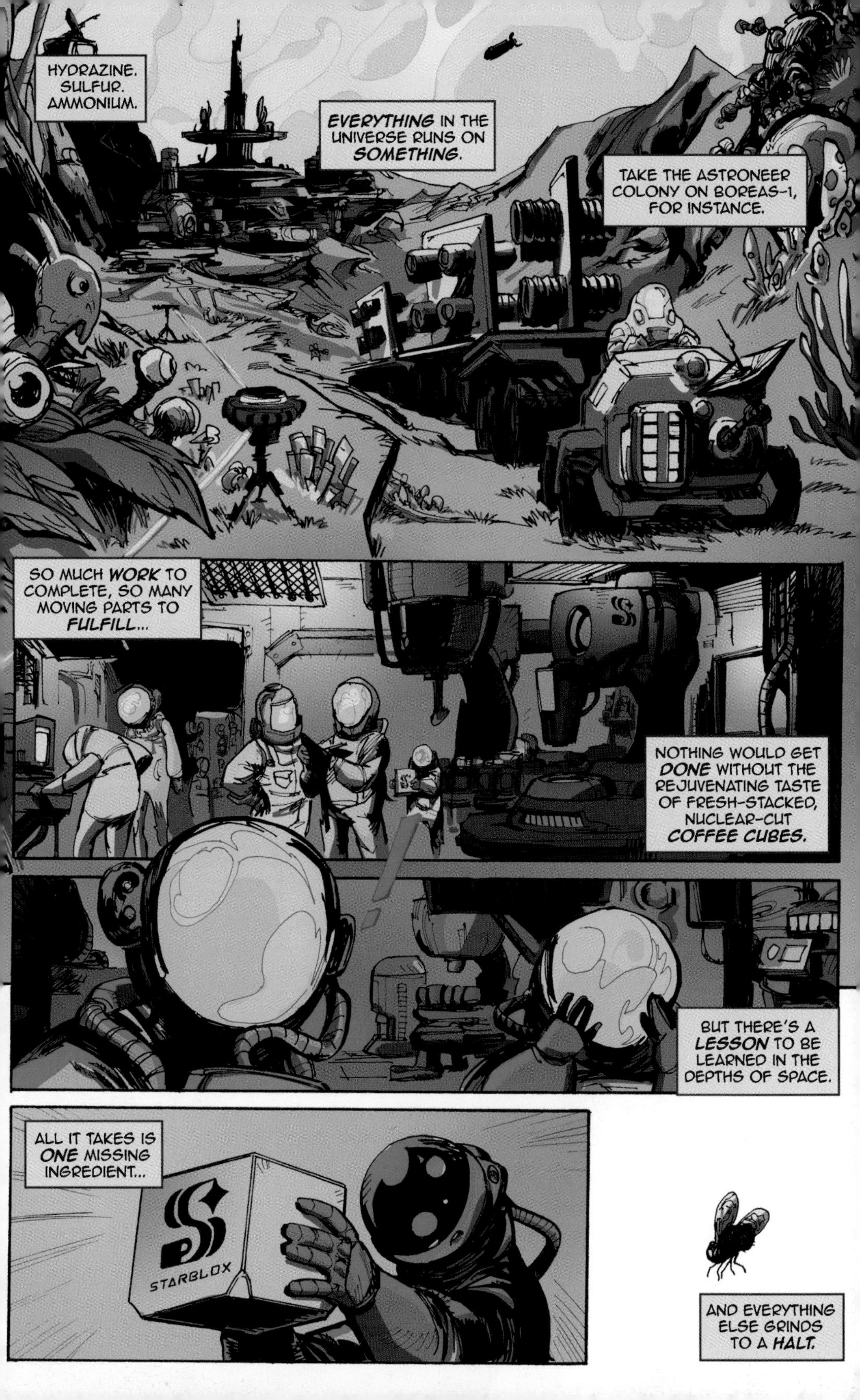
HYDRAZINE. SULFUR. AMMONIUM.
EVERYTHING IN THE UNIVERSE RUNS ON SOMETHING.
TAKE THE ASTRONEER COLONY ON BOREAS-1, FOR INSTANCE.
SO MUCH WORK TO COMPLETE, SO MANY MOVING PARTS TO FULFILL...
NOTHING WOULD GET DONE WITHOUT THE REJUVENATING TASTE OF FRESH-STACKED, NUCLEAR-CUT COFFEE CUBES.
BUT THERE'S A LESSON TO BE LEARNED IN THE DEPTHS OF SPACE.
ALL IT TAKES IS ONE MISSING INGREDIENT...
STARBLOX
AND EVERYTHING ELSE GRINDS TO A HALT.

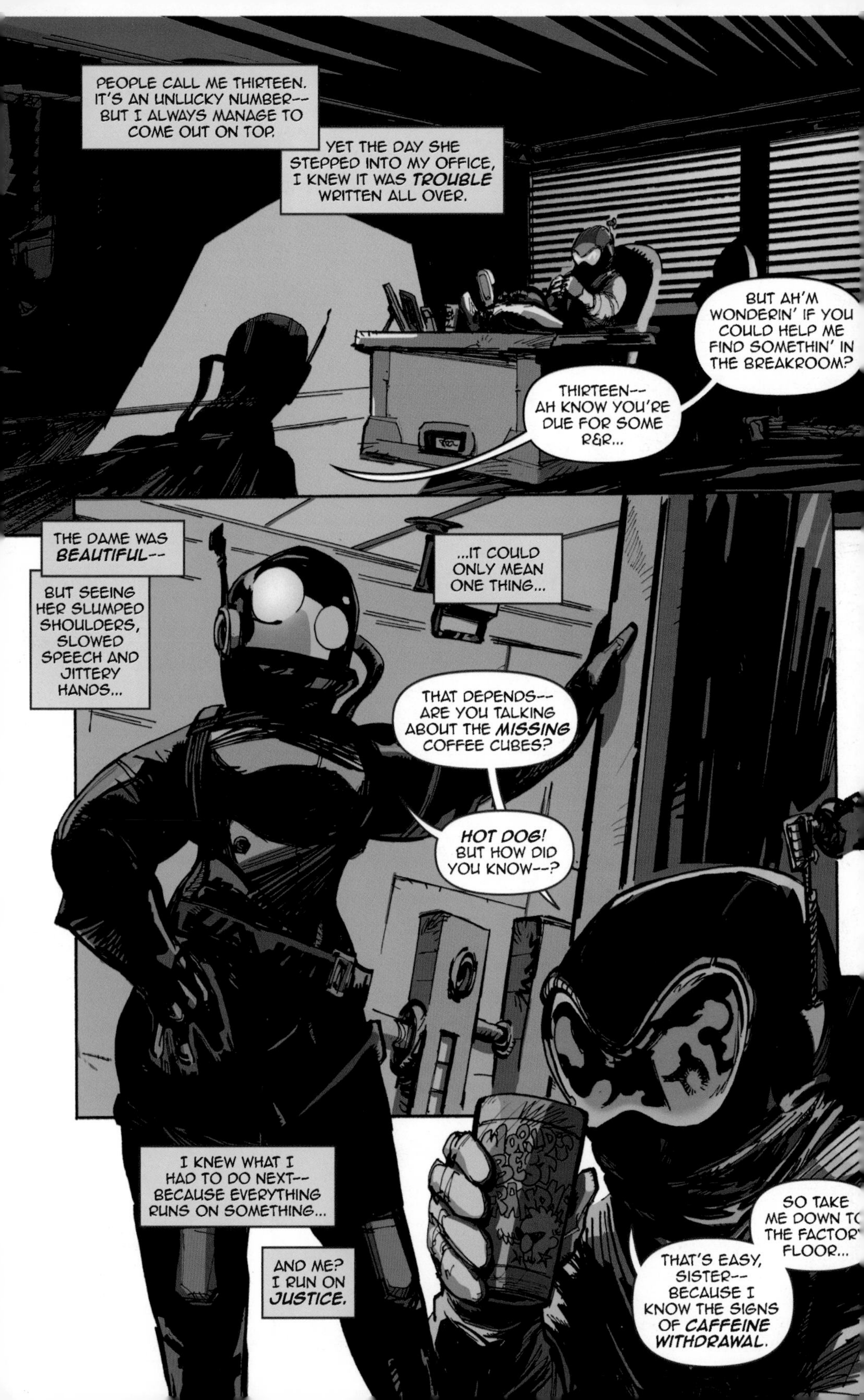
PEOPLE CALL ME THIRTEEN. IT'S AN UNLUCKY NUMBER-- BUT I ALWAYS MANAGE TO COME OUT ON TOP.
YET THE DAY SHE STEPPED INTO MY OFFICE, I KNEW IT WAS *TROUBLE* WRITTEN ALL OVER.
THIRTEEN-- AH KNOW YOU'RE DUE FOR SOME R&R...
BUT AH'M WONDERIN' IF YOU COULD HELP ME FIND SOMETHIN' IN THE BREAKROOM?
THE DAME WAS *BEAUTIFUL*--
BUT SEEING HER SLUMPED SHOULDERS, SLOWED SPEECH AND JITTERY HANDS...
...IT COULD ONLY MEAN ONE THING...
THAT DEPENDS-- ARE YOU TALKING ABOUT THE *MISSING* COFFEE CUBES?
HOT DOG! BUT HOW DID YOU KNOW--?
I KNEW WHAT I HAD TO DO NEXT-- BECAUSE EVERYTHING RUNS ON SOMETHING...
AND ME? I RUN ON *JUSTICE.*
THAT'S EASY, SISTER-- BECAUSE I KNOW THE SIGNS OF *CAFFEINE WITHDRAWAL.*
SO TAKE ME DOWN TO THE FACTORY FLOOR...

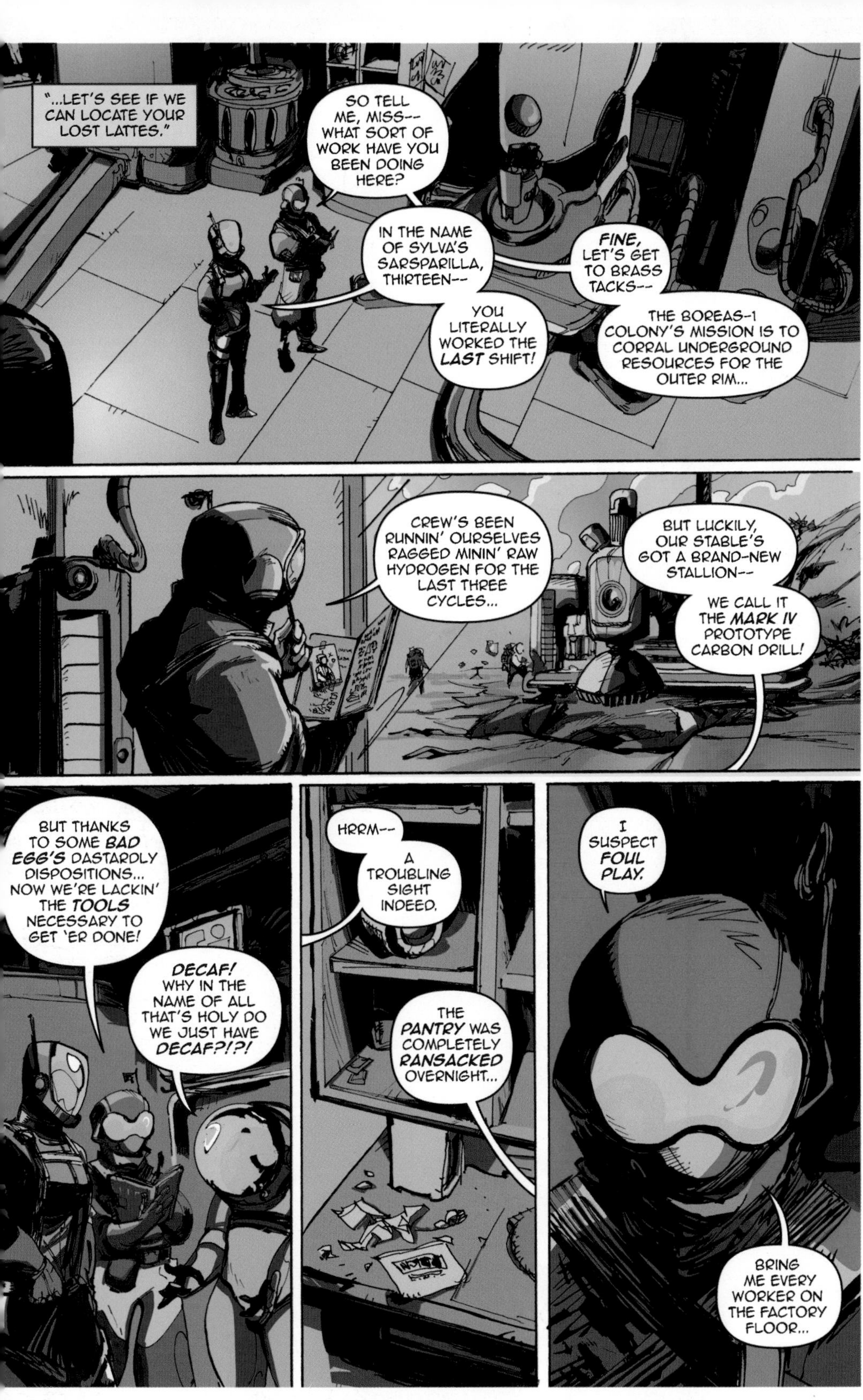
"...LET'S SEE IF WE CAN LOCATE YOUR LOST LATTES."
SO TELL ME, MISS-- WHAT SORT OF WORK HAVE YOU BEEN DOING HERE?
IN THE NAME OF SYLVA'S SARSPARILLA, THIRTEEN--
YOU LITERALLY WORKED THE LAST SHIFT!
FINE, LET'S GET TO BRASS TACKS--
THE BOREAS-1 COLONY'S MISSION IS TO CORRAL UNDERGROUND RESOURCES FOR THE OUTER RIM...
CREW'S BEEN RUNNIN' OURSELVES RAGGED MININ' RAW HYDROGEN FOR THE LAST THREE CYCLES...
BUT LUCKILY, OUR STABLE'S GOT A BRAND-NEW STALLION--
WE CALL IT THE MARK IV PROTOTYPE CARBON DRILL!
BUT THANKS TO SOME BAD EGG'S DASTARDLY DISPOSITIONS... NOW WE'RE LACKIN' THE TOOLS NECESSARY TO GET 'ER DONE!
DECAF! WHY IN THE NAME OF ALL THAT'S HOLY DO WE JUST HAVE DECAF?!?!
HRRM--
A TROUBLING SIGHT INDEED.
THE PANTRY WAS COMPLETELY RANSACKED OVERNIGHT...
I SUSPECT FOUL PLAY.
BRING ME EVERY WORKER ON THE FACTORY FLOOR...

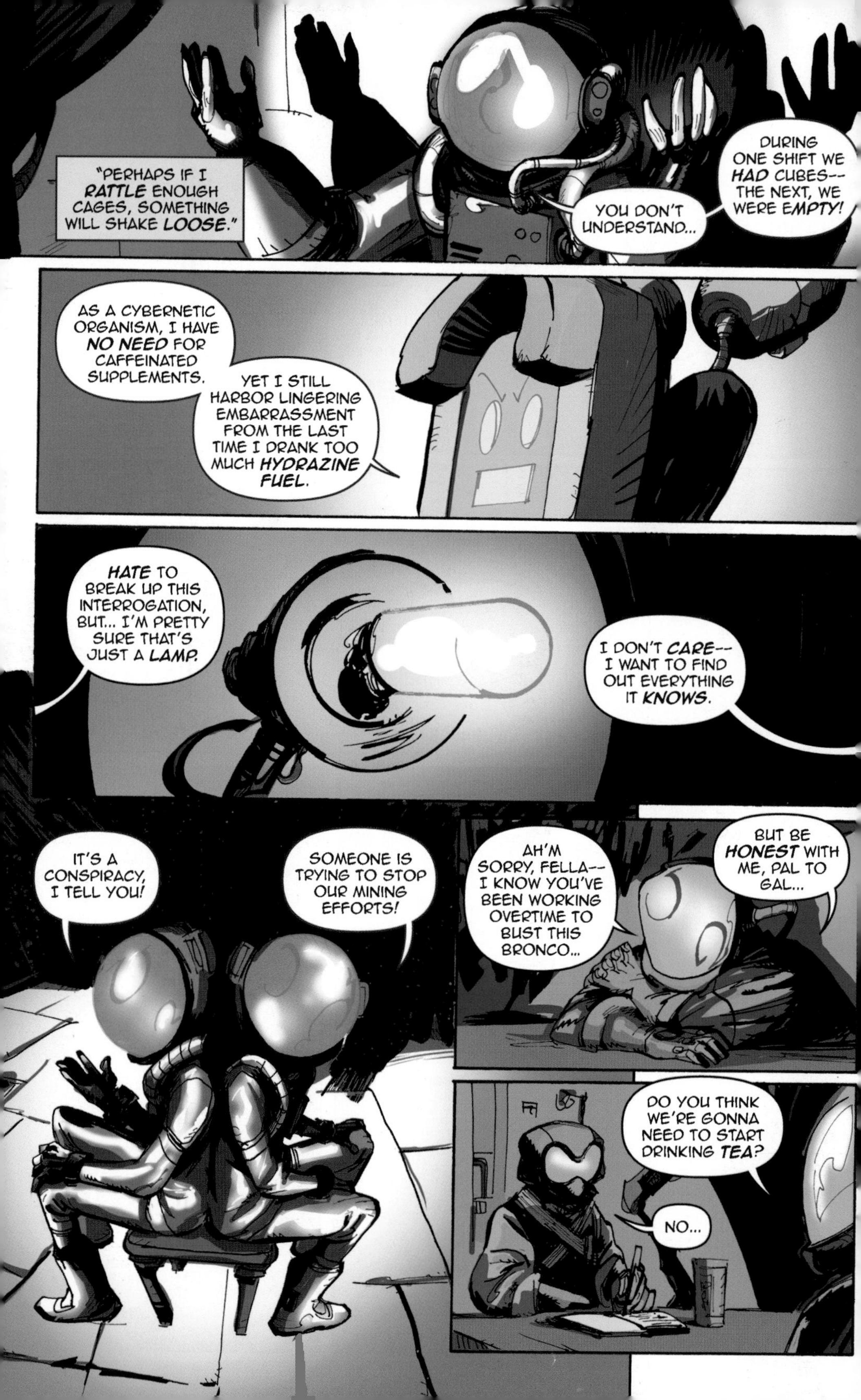
"PERHAPS IF I RATTLE ENOUGH CAGES, SOMETHING WILL SHAKE LOOSE."
YOU DON'T UNDERSTAND...
DURING ONE SHIFT WE HAD CUBES-- THE NEXT, WE WERE EMPTY!
AS A CYBERNETIC ORGANISM, I HAVE NO NEED FOR CAFFEINATED SUPPLEMENTS.
YET I STILL HARBOR LINGERING EMBARRASSMENT FROM THE LAST TIME I DRANK TOO MUCH HYDRAZINE FUEL.
HATE TO BREAK UP THIS INTERROGATION, BUT... I'M PRETTY SURE THAT'S JUST A LAMP.
I DON'T CARE-- I WANT TO FIND OUT EVERYTHING IT KNOWS.
IT'S A CONSPIRACY, I TELL YOU!
SOMEONE IS TRYING TO STOP OUR MINING EFFORTS!
AH'M SORRY, FELLA-- I KNOW YOU'VE BEEN WORKING OVERTIME TO BUST THIS BRONCO...
BUT BE HONEST WITH ME, PAL TO GAL...
DO YOU THINK WE'RE GONNA NEED TO START DRINKING TEA?
NO...

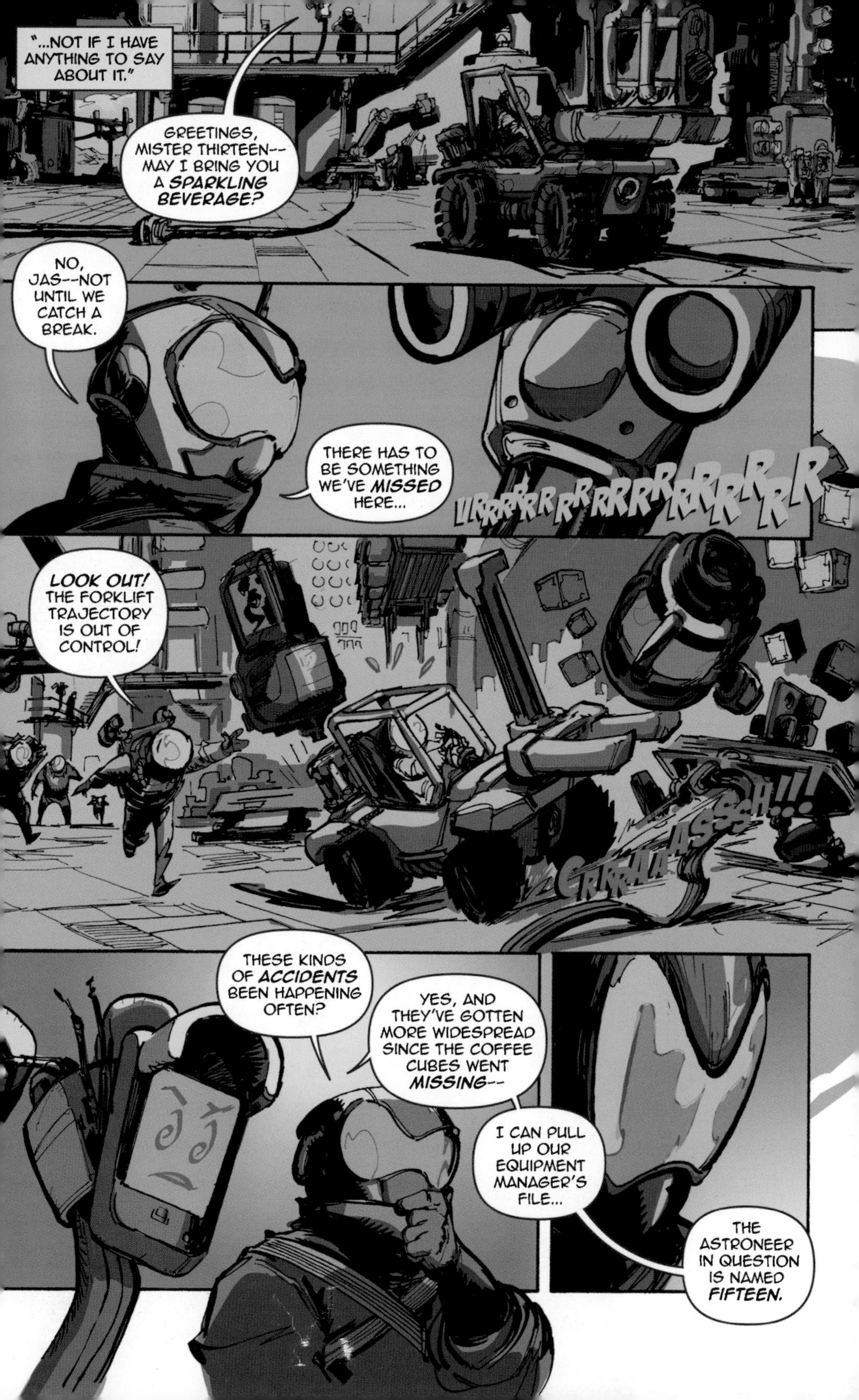
"...NOT IF I HAVE ANYTHING TO SAY ABOUT IT."
GREETINGS, MISTER THIRTEEN-- MAY I BRING YOU A SPARKLING BEVERAGE?
NO, JAS--NOT UNTIL WE CATCH A BREAK.
THERE HAS TO BE SOMETHING WE'VE MISSED HERE...
URRRRRRRRRRRRRRRRR
LOOK OUT! THE FORKLIFT TRAJECTORY IS OUT OF CONTROL!
CRRRAAASSSH!!!
THESE KINDS OF ACCIDENTS BEEN HAPPENING OFTEN?
YES, AND THEY'VE GOTTEN MORE WIDESPREAD SINCE THE COFFEE CUBES WENT MISSING--
I CAN PULL UP OUR EQUIPMENT MANAGER'S FILE...
THE ASTRONEER IN QUESTION IS NAMED FIFTEEN.

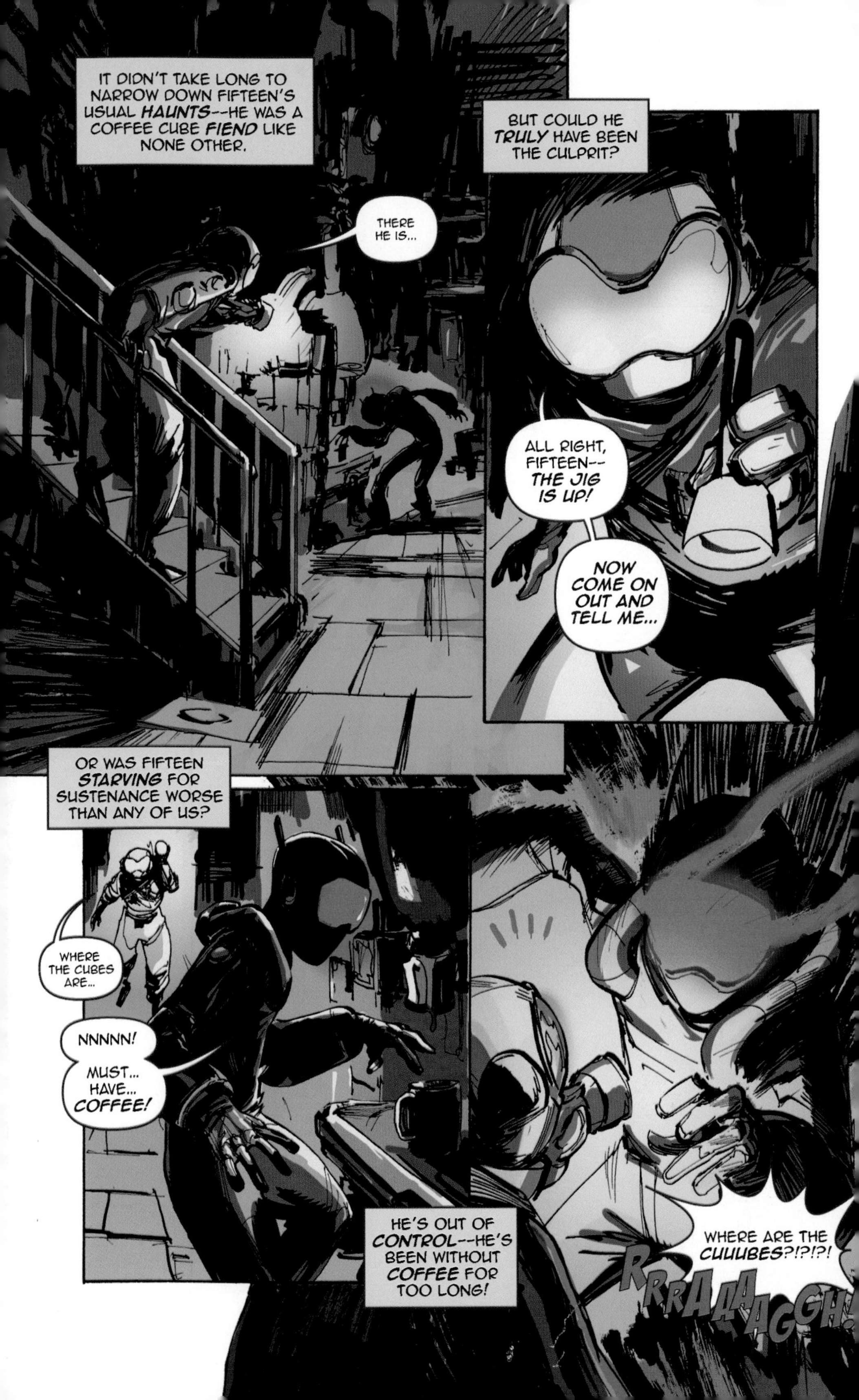
IT DIDN'T TAKE LONG TO NARROW DOWN FIFTEEN'S USUAL HAUNTS--HE WAS A COFFEE CUBE FIEND LIKE NONE OTHER.
THERE HE IS...
BUT COULD HE TRULY HAVE BEEN THE CULPRIT?
ALL RIGHT, FIFTEEN-- THE JIG IS UP!
NOW COME ON OUT AND TELL ME...
OR WAS FIFTEEN STARVING FOR SUSTENANCE WORSE THAN ANY OF US?
WHERE THE CUBES ARE...
NNNNN!
MUST... HAVE... COFFEE!
HE'S OUT OF CONTROL--HE'S BEEN WITHOUT COFFEE FOR TOO LONG!
WHERE ARE THE CUUUBES?!?!?!
RRRAAAAGGH!

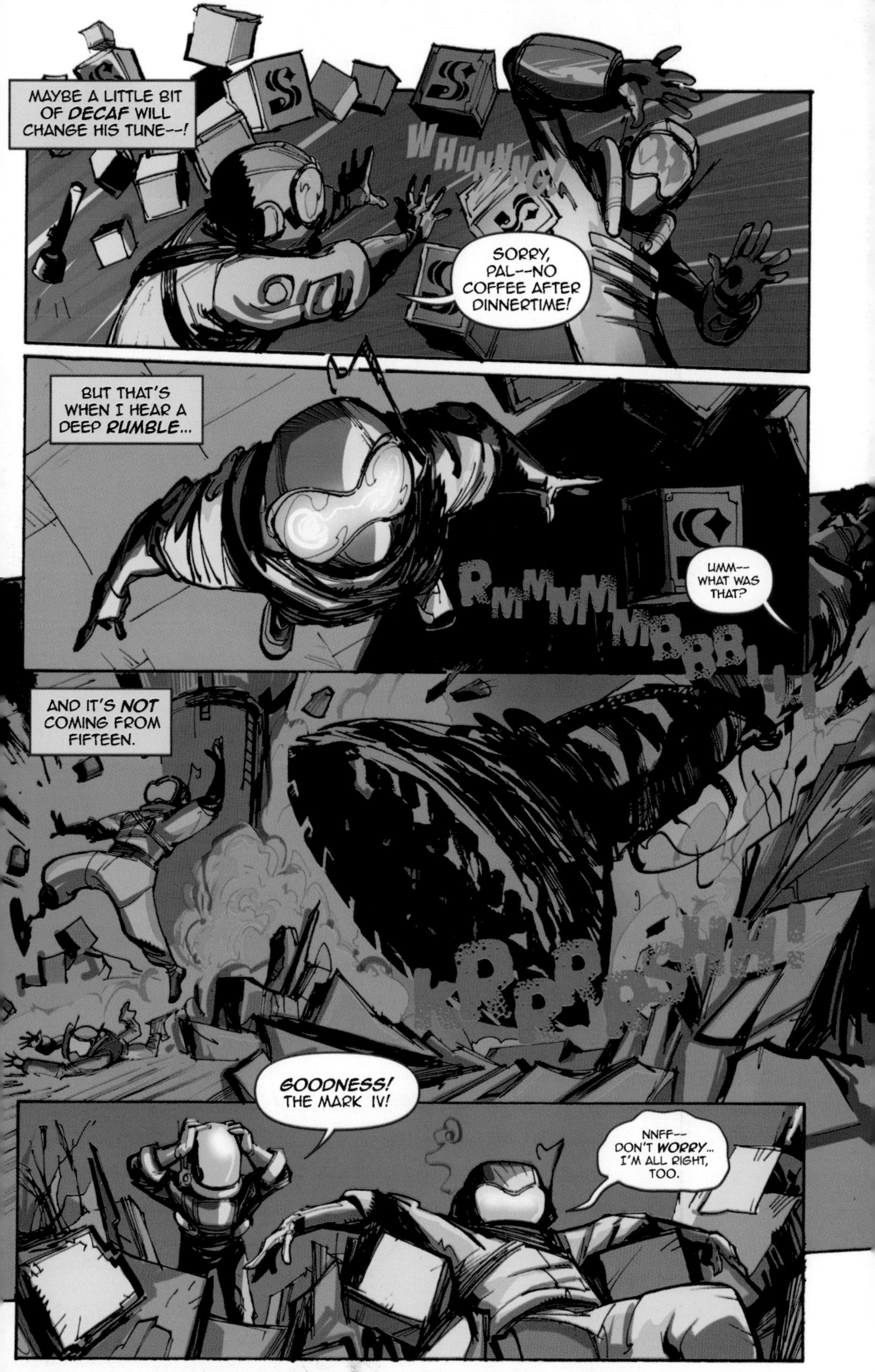
MAYBE A LITTLE BIT OF DECAF WILL CHANGE HIS TUNE--!
WHUNNNG!
SORRY, PAL--NO COFFEE AFTER DINNERTIME!
BUT THAT'S WHEN I HEAR A DEEP RUMBLE...
UMM-- WHAT WAS THAT?
RMMMMMMBBBLLL
AND IT'S NOT COMING FROM FIFTEEN.
KRRRRSHH!
GOODNESS! THE MARK IV!
NNFF-- DON'T WORRY... I'M ALL RIGHT, TOO.

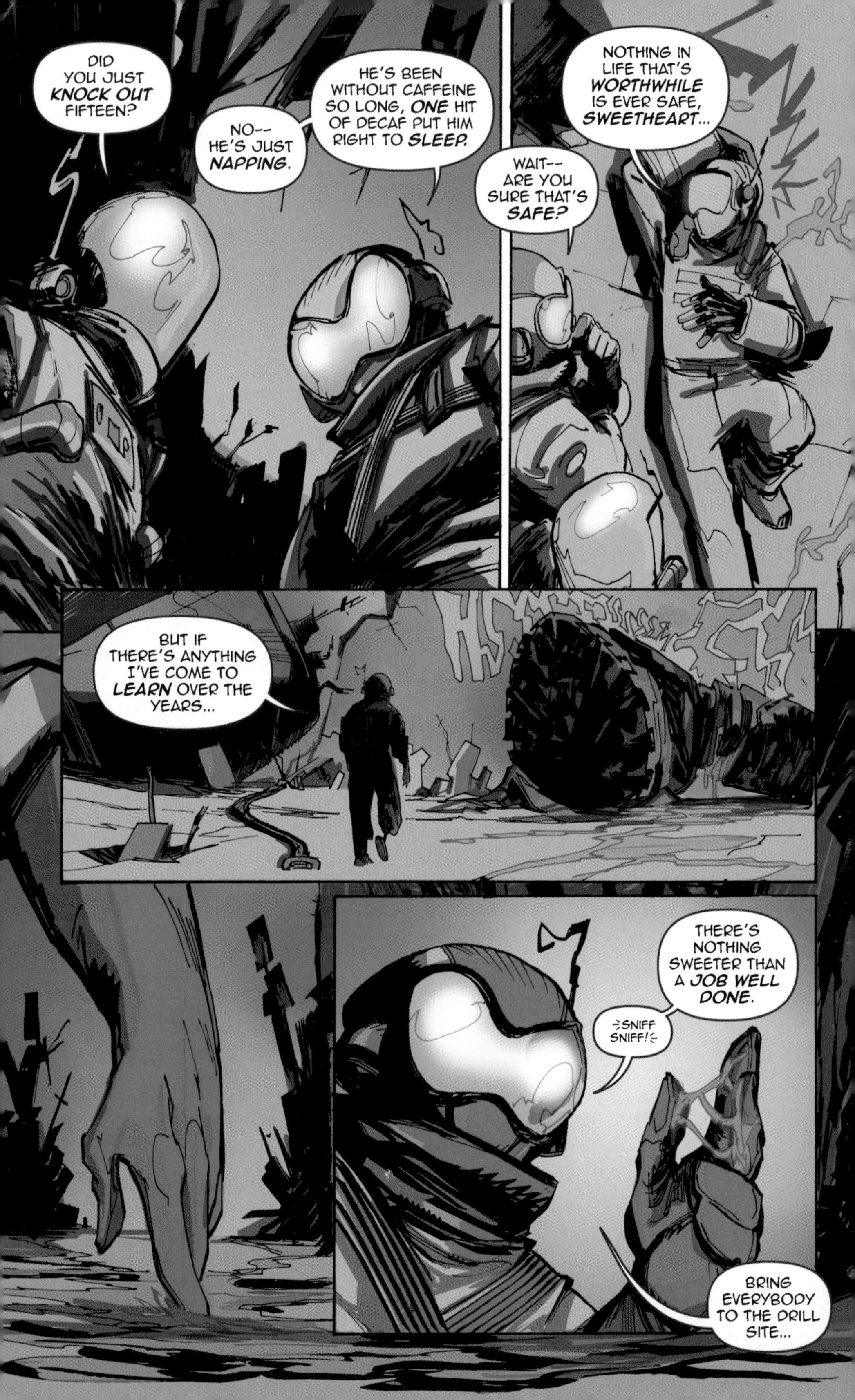
DID YOU JUST KNOCK OUT FIFTEEN?
NO-- HE'S JUST NAPPING.
HE'S BEEN WITHOUT CAFFEINE SO LONG, ONE HIT OF DECAF PUT HIM RIGHT TO SLEEP.
WAIT-- ARE YOU SURE THAT'S SAFE?
NOTHING IN LIFE THAT'S WORTHWHILE IS EVER SAFE, SWEETHEART...
BUT IF THERE'S ANYTHING I'VE COME TO LEARN OVER THE YEARS...
THERE'S NOTHING SWEETER THAN A JOB WELL DONE.
SNIFF SNIFF!
BRING EVERYBODY TO THE DRILL SITE...

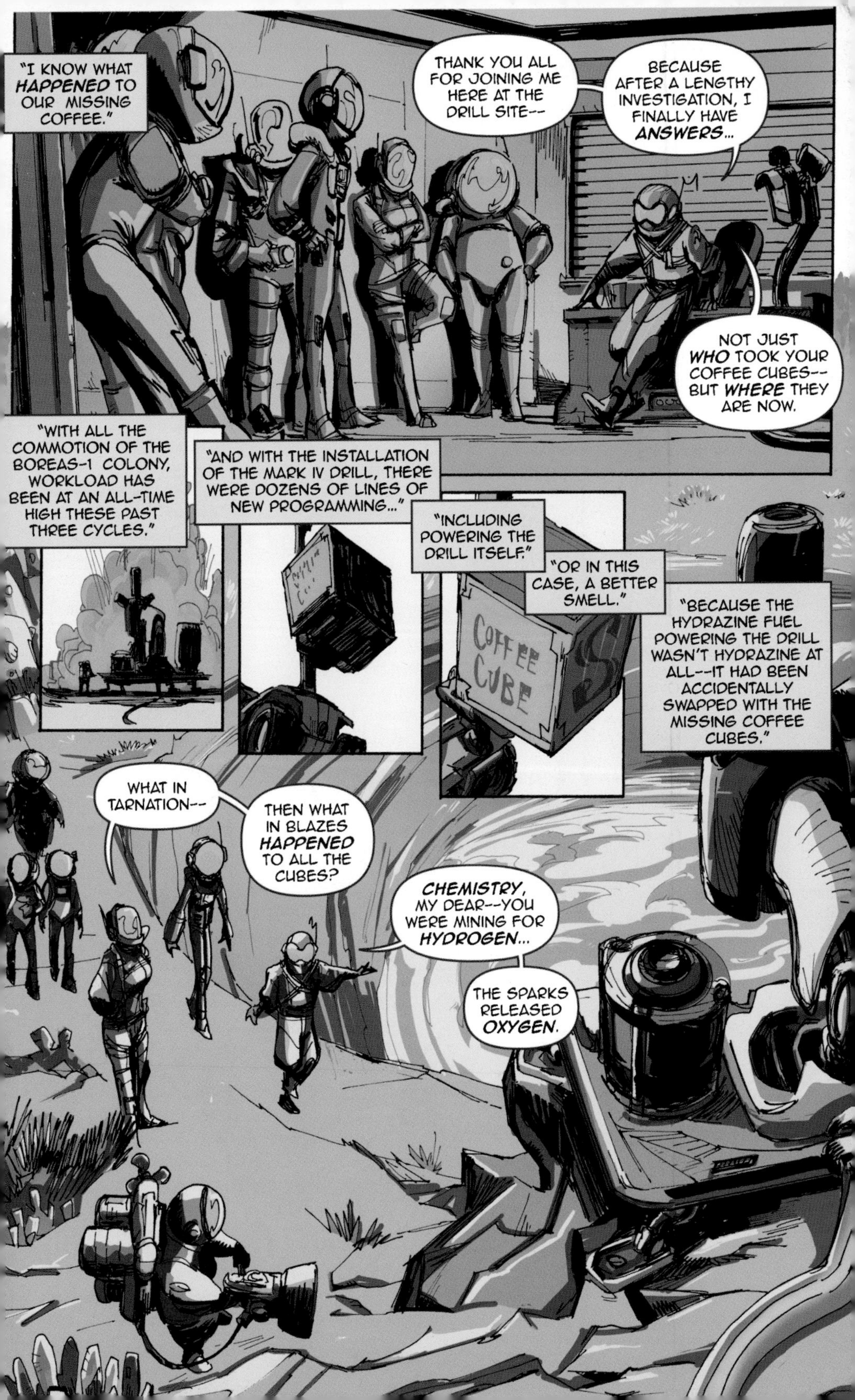
"I KNOW WHAT HAPPENED TO OUR MISSING COFFEE."
THANK YOU ALL FOR JOINING ME HERE AT THE DRILL SITE--
BECAUSE AFTER A LENGTHY INVESTIGATION, I FINALLY HAVE ANSWERS...
NOT JUST WHO TOOK YOUR COFFEE CUBES--BUT WHERE THEY ARE NOW.
"WITH ALL THE COMMOTION OF THE BOREAS-1 COLONY, WORKLOAD HAS BEEN AT AN ALL-TIME HIGH THESE PAST THREE CYCLES."
"AND WITH THE INSTALLATION OF THE MARK IV DRILL, THERE WERE DOZENS OF LINES OF NEW PROGRAMMING..."
"INCLUDING POWERING THE DRILL ITSELF."
"OR IN THIS CASE, A BETTER SMELL."
COFFEE CUBE
"BECAUSE THE HYDRAZINE FUEL POWERING THE DRILL WASN'T HYDRAZINE AT ALL--IT HAD BEEN ACCIDENTALLY SWAPPED WITH THE MISSING COFFEE CUBES."
WHAT IN TARNATION--
THEN WHAT IN BLAZES HAPPENED TO ALL THE CUBES?
CHEMISTRY, MY DEAR--YOU WERE MINING FOR HYDROGEN...
THE SPARKS RELEASED OXYGEN.

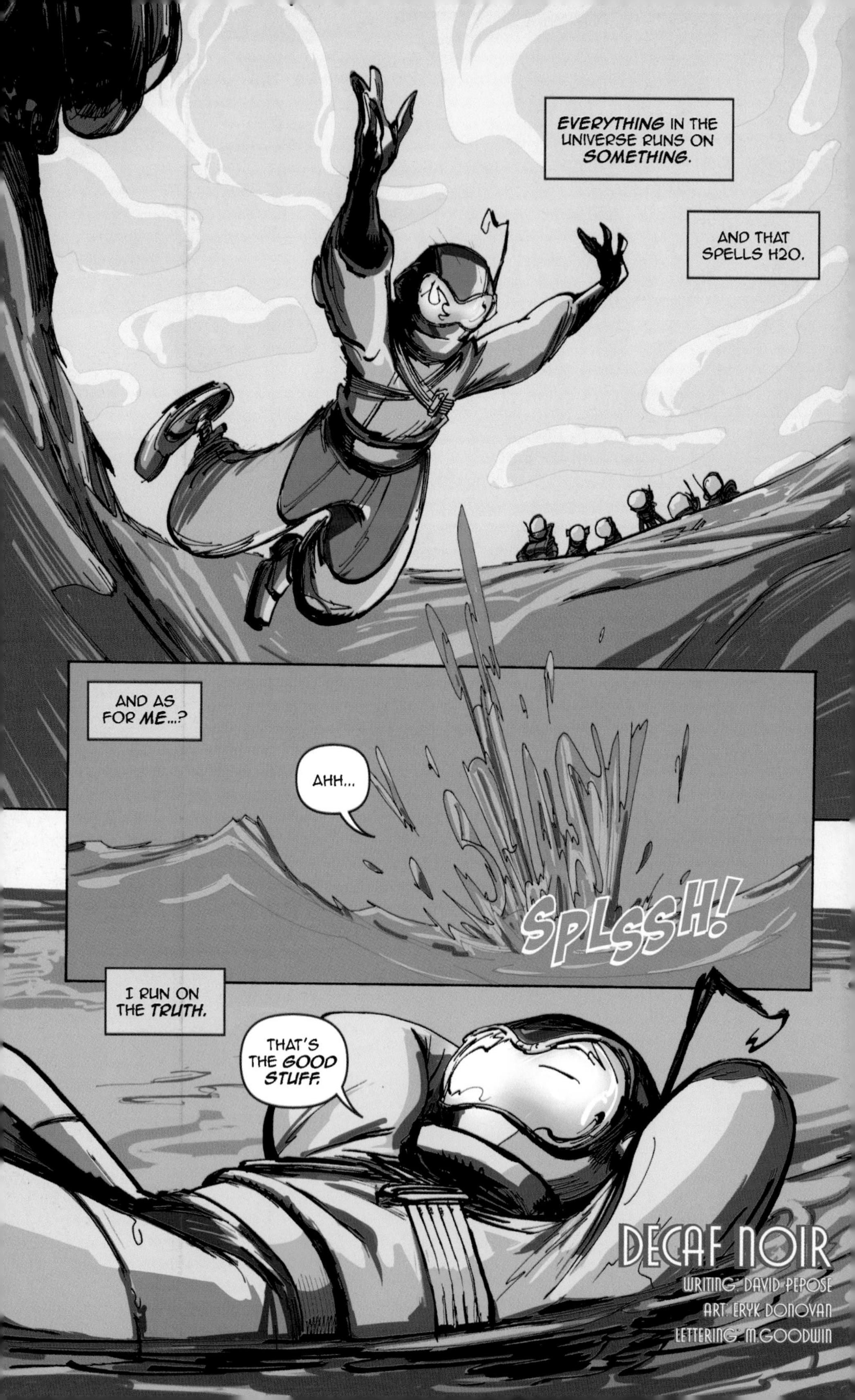
EVERYTHING IN THE UNIVERSE RUNS ON SOMETHING.
AND THAT SPELLS H2O.
AND AS FOR ME...?
AHH...
SPLSSH!
I RUN ON THE TRUTH.
THAT'S THE GOOD STUFF.
DECAF NOIR
WRITING: DAVID PEPOSE
ART: ERYK DONOVAN
LETTERING: M.GOODWIN

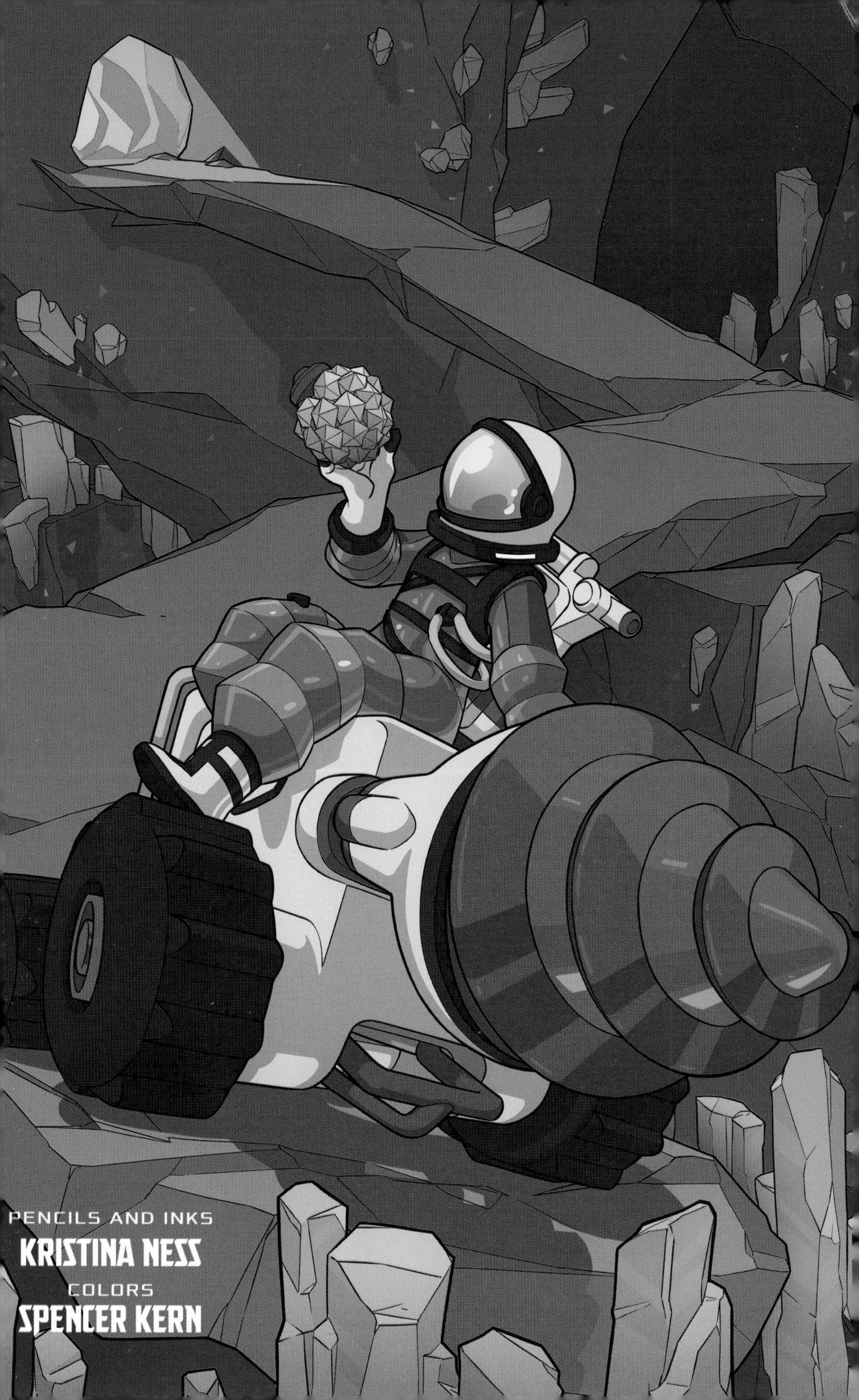

PENCILS AND INKS
KRISTINA NESS
COLORS
SPENCER KERN

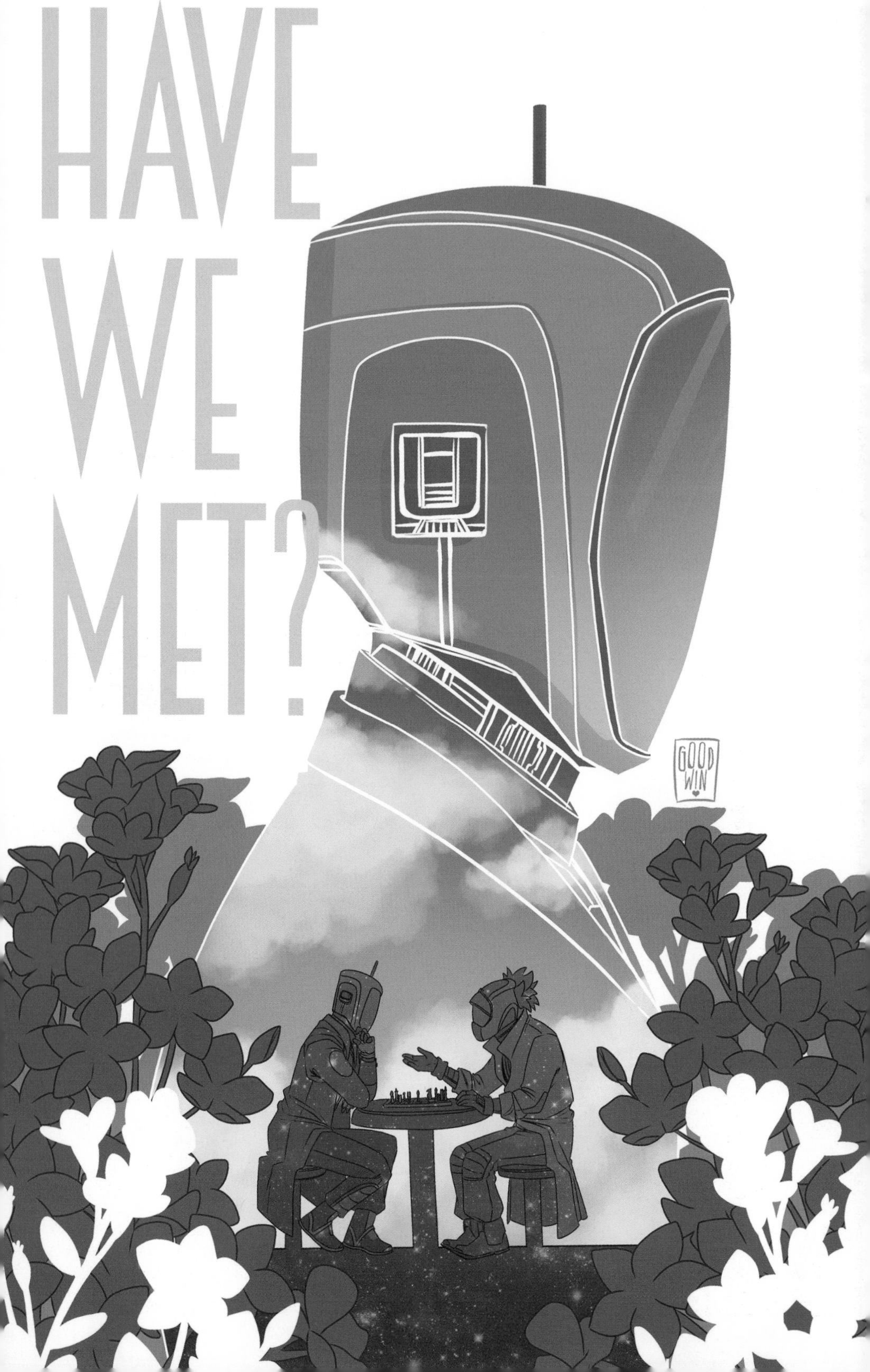
HAVE
WE
MET?
GOOD
WIN

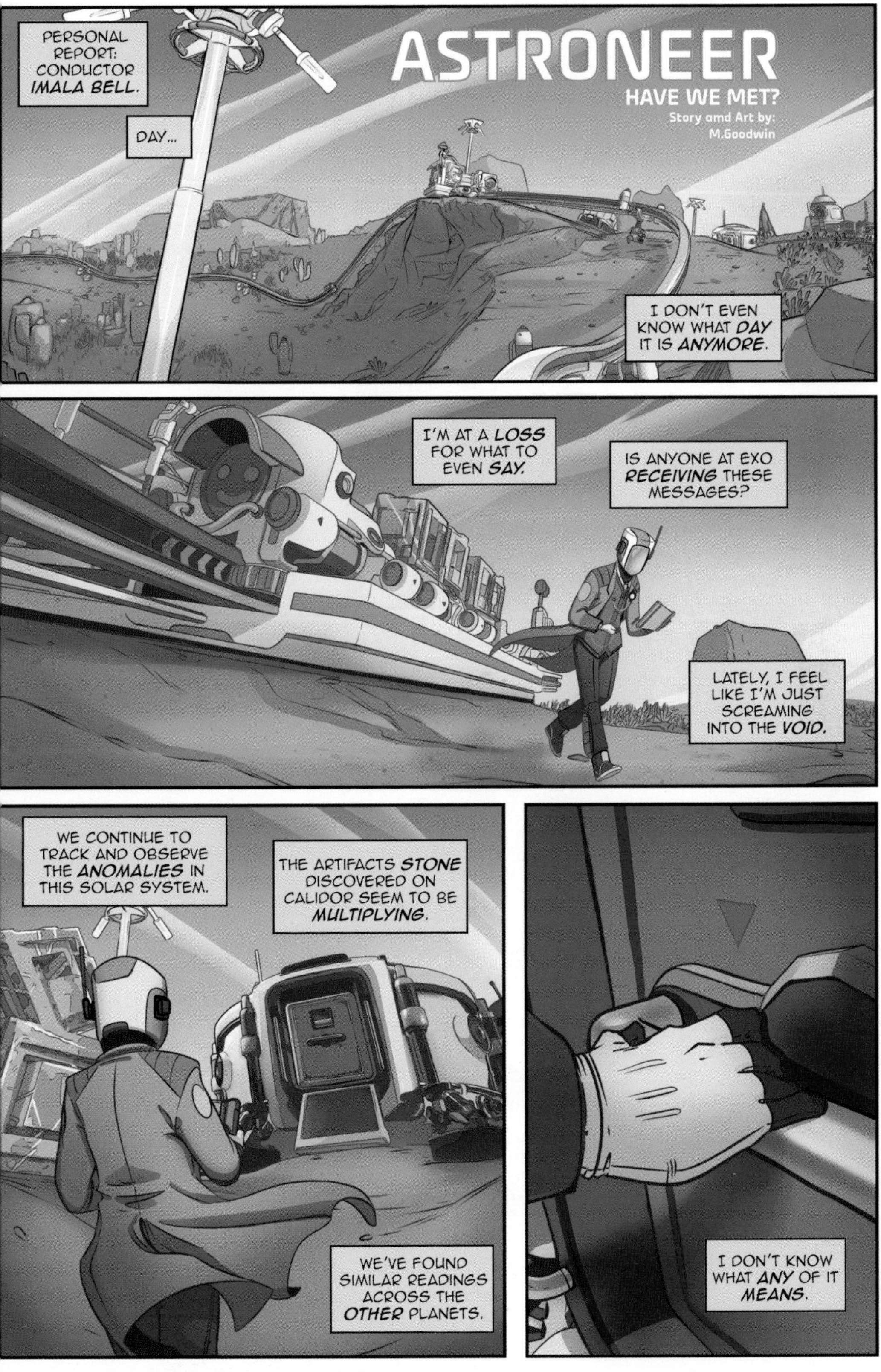
PERSONAL REPORT: CONDUCTOR IMALA BELL.
ASTRONEER
HAVE WE MET?
Story amd Art by: M.Goodwin
DAY...
I DON'T EVEN KNOW WHAT DAY IT IS ANYMORE.
I'M AT A LOSS FOR WHAT TO EVEN SAY.
IS ANYONE AT EXO RECEIVING THESE MESSAGES?
LATELY, I FEEL LIKE I'M JUST SCREAMING INTO THE VOID.
WE CONTINUE TO TRACK AND OBSERVE THE ANOMALIES IN THIS SOLAR SYSTEM.
THE ARTIFACTS STONE DISCOVERED ON CALIDOR SEEM TO BE MULTIPLYING.
WE'VE FOUND SIMILAR READINGS ACROSS THE OTHER PLANETS.
I DON'T KNOW WHAT ANY OF IT MEANS.

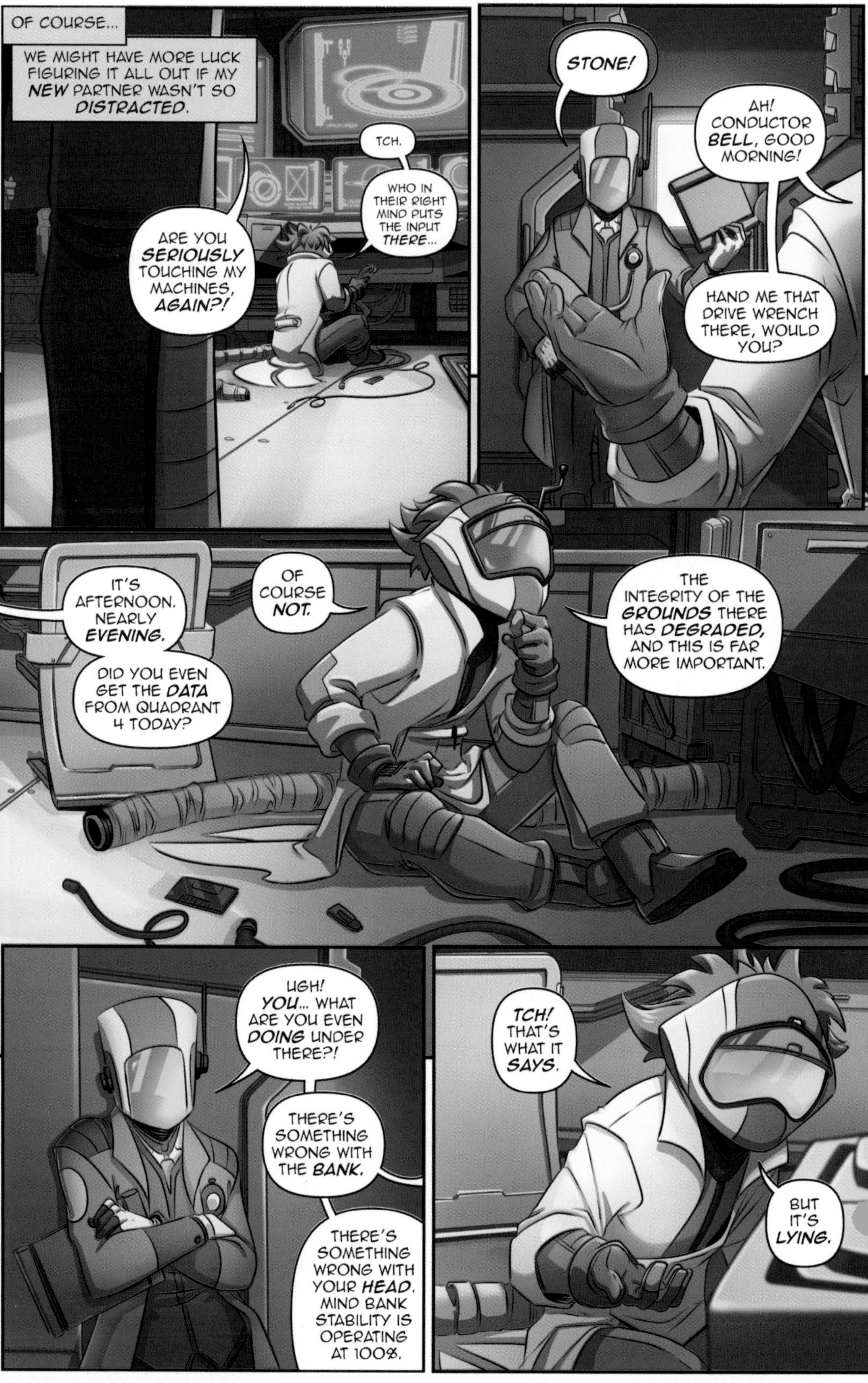
OF COURSE...
WE MIGHT HAVE MORE LUCK FIGURING IT ALL OUT IF MY NEW PARTNER WASN'T SO DISTRACTED.
TCH.
WHO IN THEIR RIGHT MIND PUTS THE INPUT THERE...
ARE YOU SERIOUSLY TOUCHING MY MACHINES, AGAIN?!
STONE!
AH! CONDUCTOR BELL, GOOD MORNING!
HAND ME THAT DRIVE WRENCH THERE, WOULD YOU?
IT'S AFTERNOON. NEARLY EVENING.
DID YOU EVEN GET THE DATA FROM QUADRANT 4 TODAY?
OF COURSE NOT.
THE INTEGRITY OF THE GROUNDS THERE HAS DEGRADED, AND THIS IS FAR MORE IMPORTANT.
UGH! YOU... WHAT ARE YOU EVEN DOING UNDER THERE?!
THERE'S SOMETHING WRONG WITH THE BANK.
THERE'S SOMETHING WRONG WITH YOUR HEAD. MIND BANK STABILITY IS OPERATING AT 100%.
TCH! THAT'S WHAT IT SAYS.
BUT IT'S LYING.

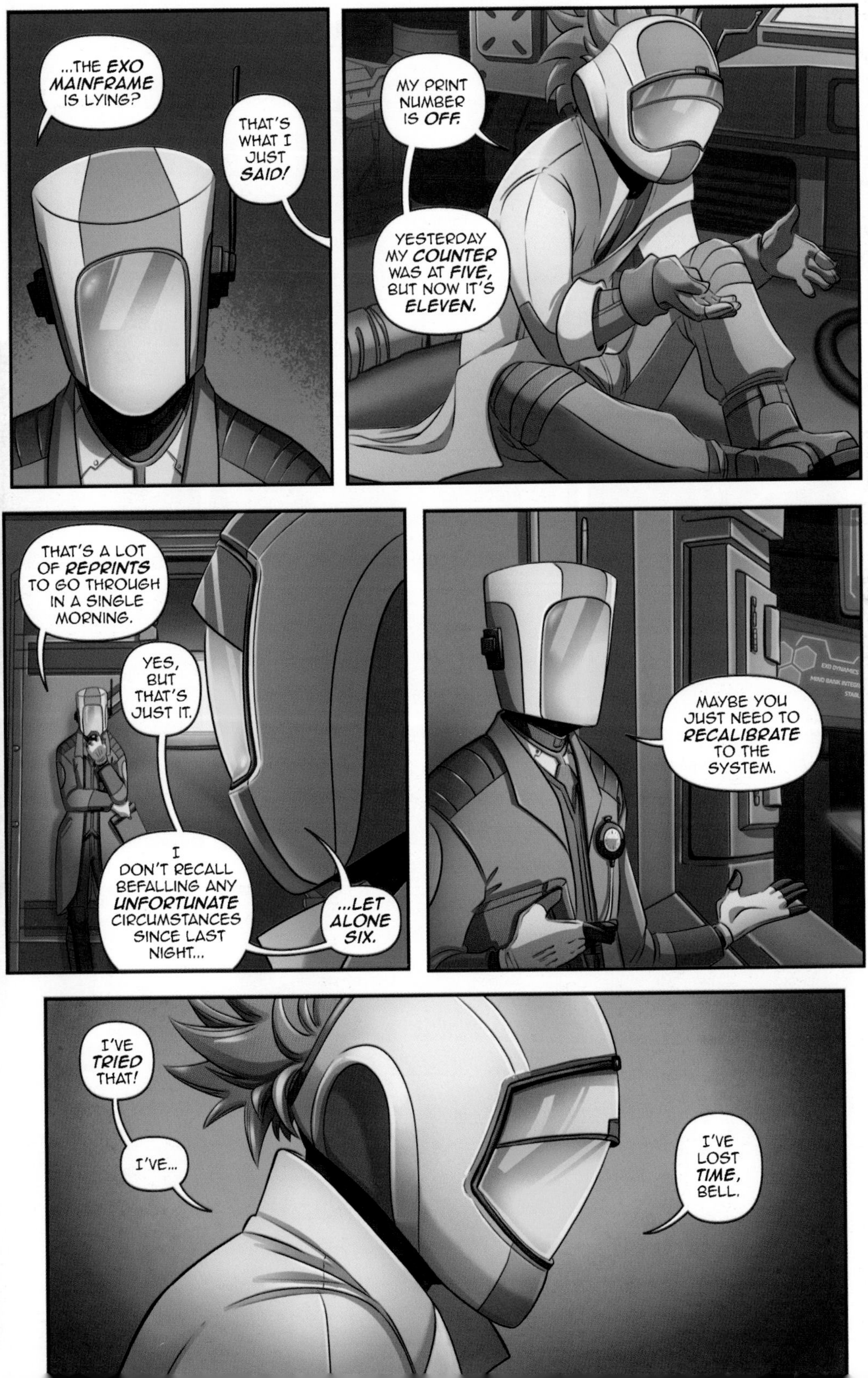
...THE EXO MAINFRAME IS LYING?
THAT'S WHAT I JUST SAID!
MY PRINT NUMBER IS OFF.
YESTERDAY MY COUNTER WAS AT FIVE, BUT NOW IT'S ELEVEN.
THAT'S A LOT OF REPRINTS TO GO THROUGH IN A SINGLE MORNING.
YES, BUT THAT'S JUST IT.
I DON'T RECALL BEFALLING ANY UNFORTUNATE CIRCUMSTANCES SINCE LAST NIGHT...
...LET ALONE SIX.
MAYBE YOU JUST NEED TO RECALIBRATE TO THE SYSTEM.
I'VE TRIED THAT!
I'VE...
I'VE LOST TIME, BELL.

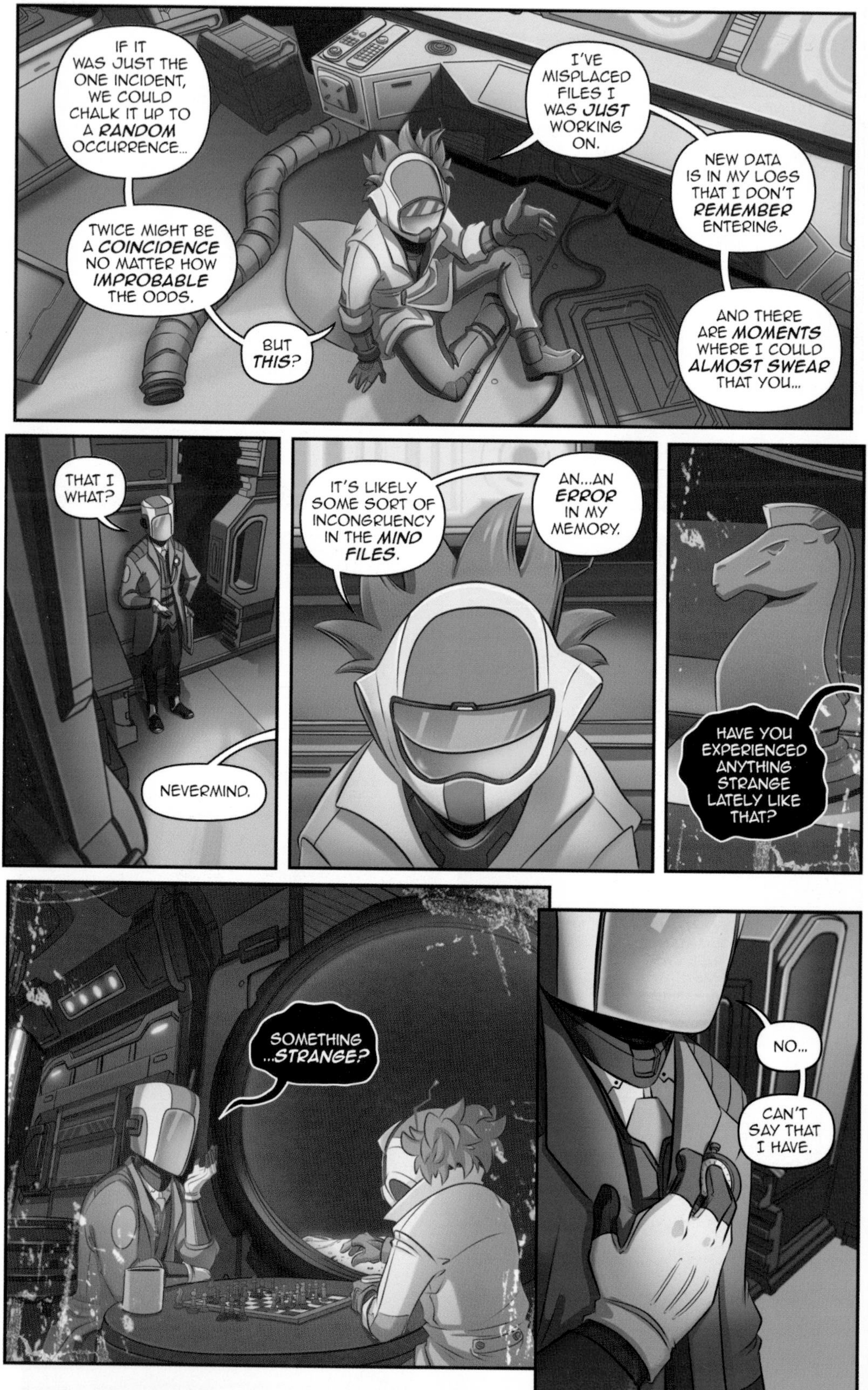
IF IT WAS JUST THE ONE INCIDENT, WE COULD CHALK IT UP TO A RANDOM OCCURRENCE...
TWICE MIGHT BE A COINCIDENCE NO MATTER HOW IMPROBABLE THE ODDS.
BUT THIS?
I'VE MISPLACED FILES I WAS JUST WORKING ON.
NEW DATA IS IN MY LOGS THAT I DON'T REMEMBER ENTERING.
AND THERE ARE MOMENTS WHERE I COULD ALMOST SWEAR THAT YOU...
THAT I WHAT?
NEVERMIND.
IT'S LIKELY SOME SORT OF INCONGRUENCY IN THE MIND FILES.
AN...AN ERROR IN MY MEMORY.
HAVE YOU EXPERIENCED ANYTHING STRANGE LATELY LIKE THAT?
SOMETHING ...STRANGE?
NO...
CAN'T SAY THAT I HAVE.

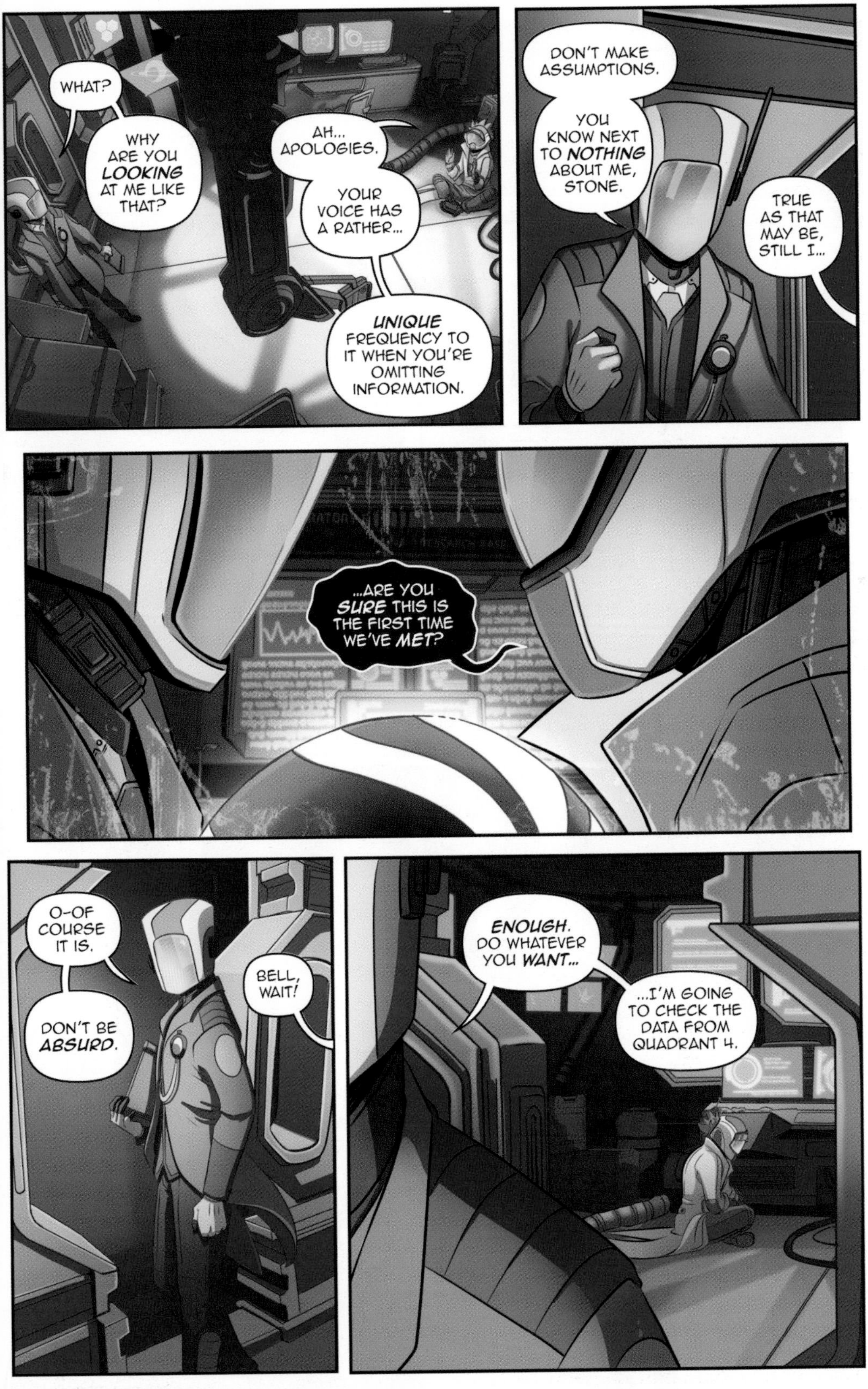
WHAT?
WHY ARE YOU LOOKING AT ME LIKE THAT?
AH... APOLOGIES.
YOUR VOICE HAS A RATHER...
UNIQUE FREQUENCY TO IT WHEN YOU'RE OMITTING INFORMATION.
DON'T MAKE ASSUMPTIONS.
YOU KNOW NEXT TO NOTHING ABOUT ME, STONE.
TRUE AS THAT MAY BE, STILL I...
...ARE YOU SURE THIS IS THE FIRST TIME WE'VE MET?
O-OF COURSE IT IS.
DON'T BE ABSURD.
BELL, WAIT!
ENOUGH. DO WHATEVER YOU WANT...
...I'M GOING TO CHECK THE DATA FROM QUADRANT 4.

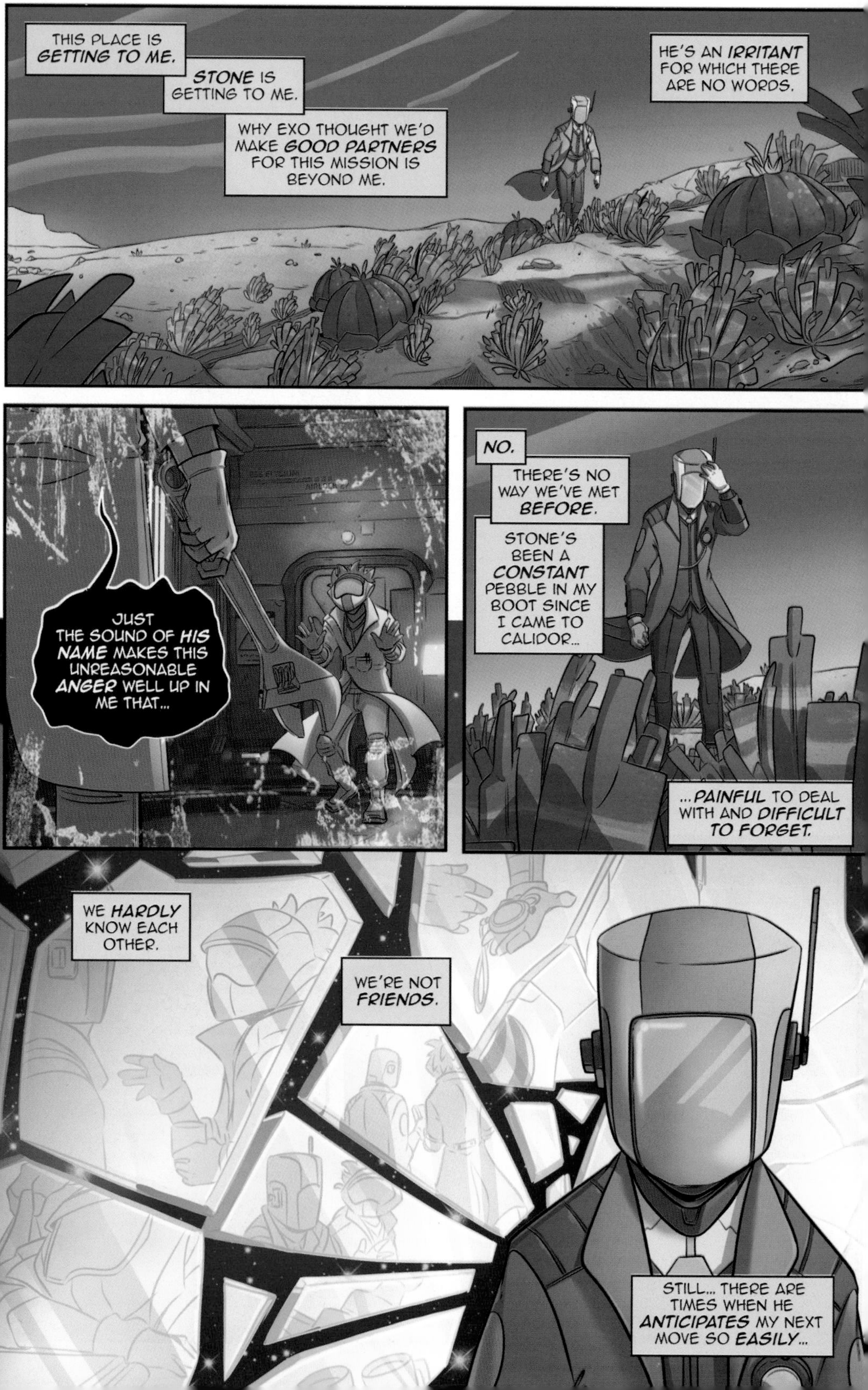
THIS PLACE IS GETTING TO ME.
STONE IS GETTING TO ME.
WHY EXO THOUGHT WE'D MAKE GOOD PARTNERS FOR THIS MISSION IS BEYOND ME.
HE'S AN IRRITANT FOR WHICH THERE ARE NO WORDS.
JUST THE SOUND OF HIS NAME MAKES THIS UNREASONABLE ANGER WELL UP IN ME THAT...
NO.
THERE'S NO WAY WE'VE MET BEFORE.
STONE'S BEEN A CONSTANT PEBBLE IN MY BOOT SINCE I CAME TO CALIDOR...
...PAINFUL TO DEAL WITH AND DIFFICULT TO FORGET.
WE HARDLY KNOW EACH OTHER.
WE'RE NOT FRIENDS.
STILL... THERE ARE TIMES WHEN HE ANTICIPATES MY NEXT MOVE SO EASILY...

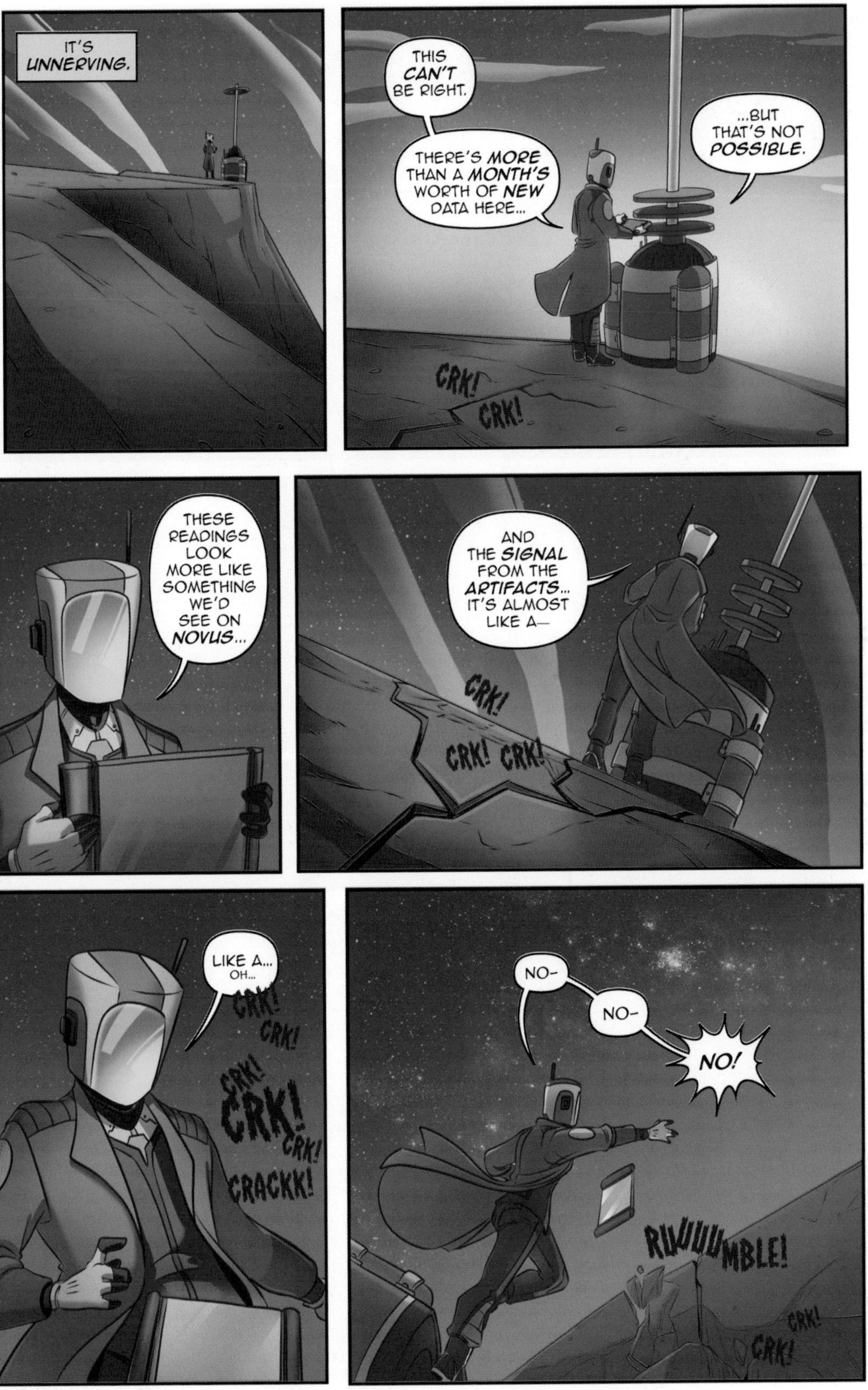
IT'S UNNERVING.
THIS CAN'T BE RIGHT.
THERE'S MORE THAN A MONTH'S WORTH OF NEW DATA HERE...
...BUT THAT'S NOT POSSIBLE.
CRK! CRK!
THESE READINGS LOOK MORE LIKE SOMETHING WE'D SEE ON NOVUS...
AND THE SIGNAL FROM THE ARTIFACTS... IT'S ALMOST LIKE A—
CRK!
CRK! CRK!
LIKE A... OH...
CRK! CRK! CRK! CRK! CRK!
CRACKK!
NO-
NO-
NO!
RUUUUMBLE!
CRK! CRK!

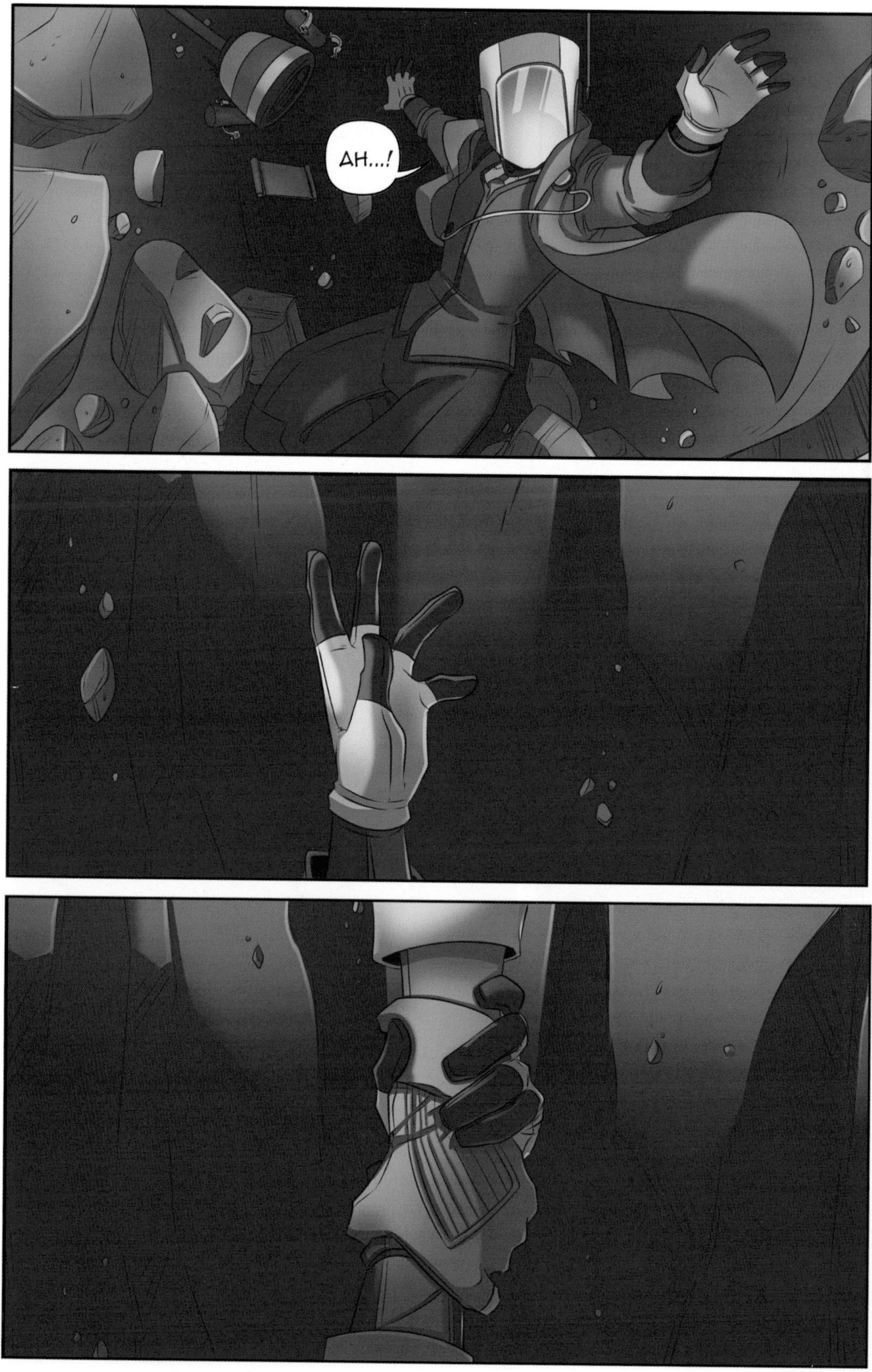
AH...!

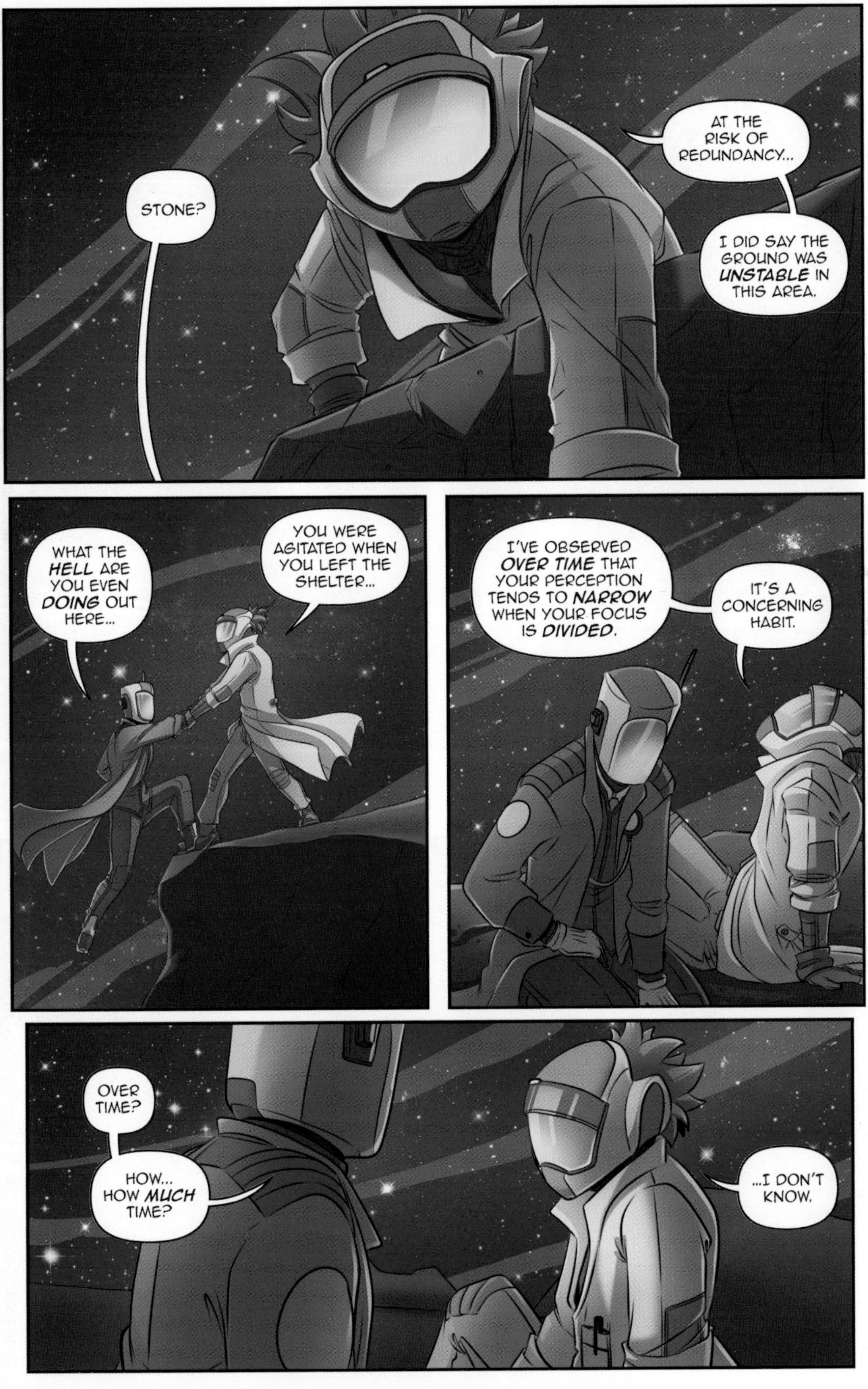
STONE?
AT THE RISK OF REDUNDANCY...
I DID SAY THE GROUND WAS **UNSTABLE** IN THIS AREA.
WHAT THE **HELL** ARE YOU EVEN **DOING** OUT HERE...
YOU WERE AGITATED WHEN YOU LEFT THE SHELTER...
I'VE OBSERVED **OVER TIME** THAT YOUR PERCEPTION TENDS TO **NARROW** WHEN YOUR FOCUS IS **DIVIDED**.
IT'S A CONCERNING HABIT.
OVER TIME?
HOW... HOW **MUCH** TIME?
...I DON'T KNOW.

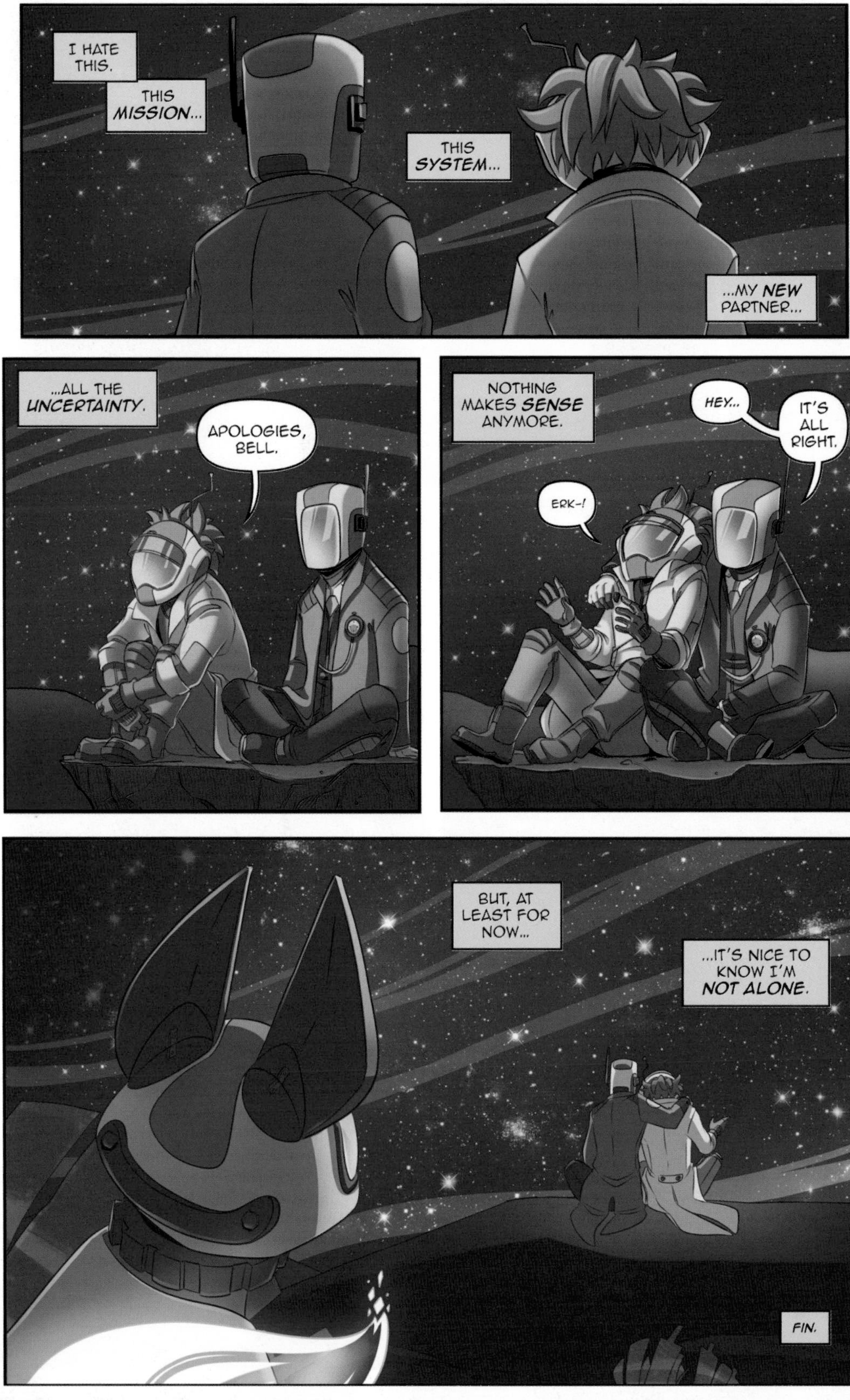
I HATE THIS.
THIS MISSION...
THIS SYSTEM...
...MY NEW PARTNER...
...ALL THE UNCERTAINTY.
APOLOGIES, BELL.
NOTHING MAKES SENSE ANYMORE.
HEY...
IT'S ALL RIGHT.
ERK-!
BUT, AT LEAST FOR NOW...
...IT'S NICE TO KNOW I'M NOT ALONE.
FIN.

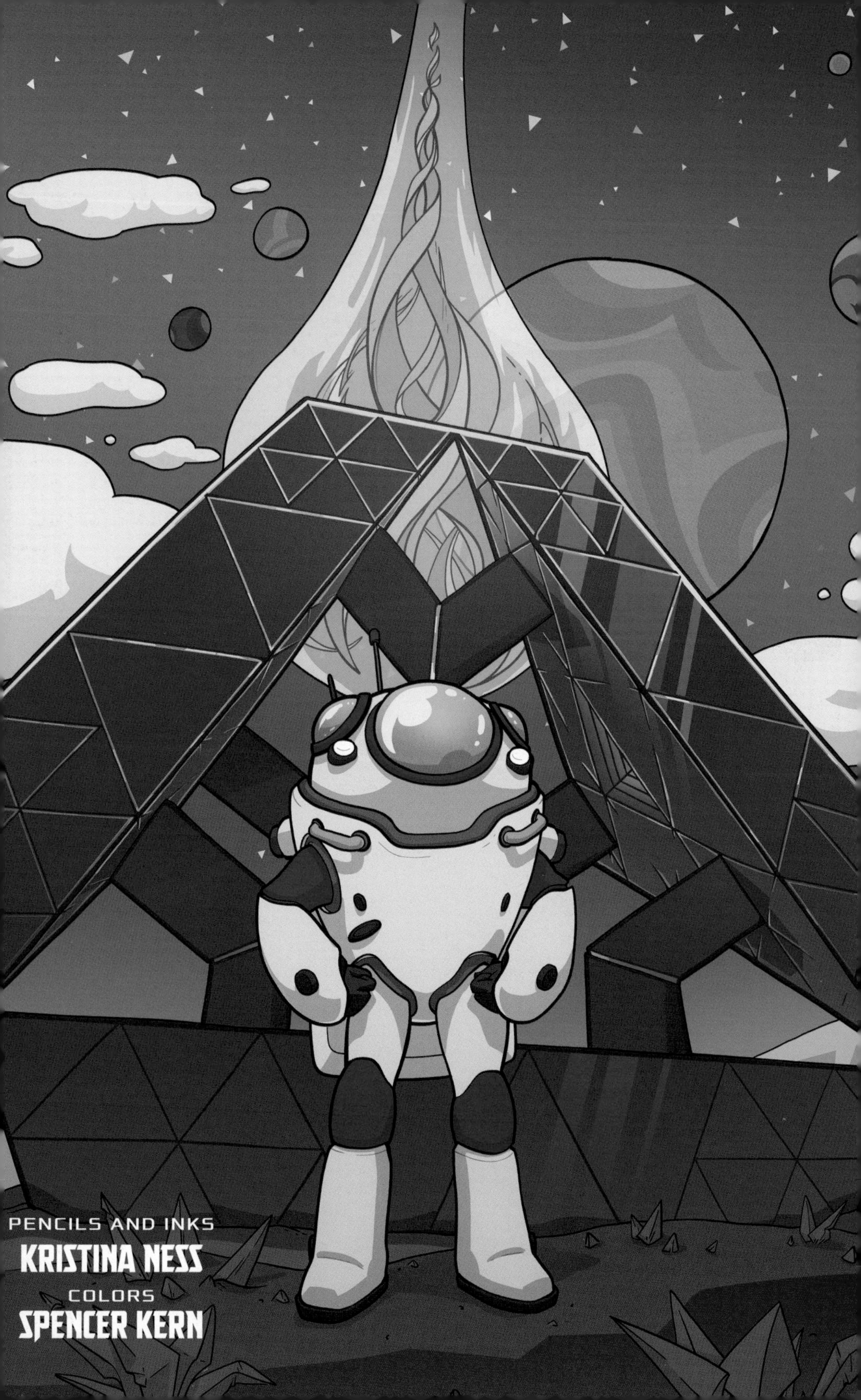
PENCILS AND INKS
KRISTINA NESS
COLORS
SPENCER KERN

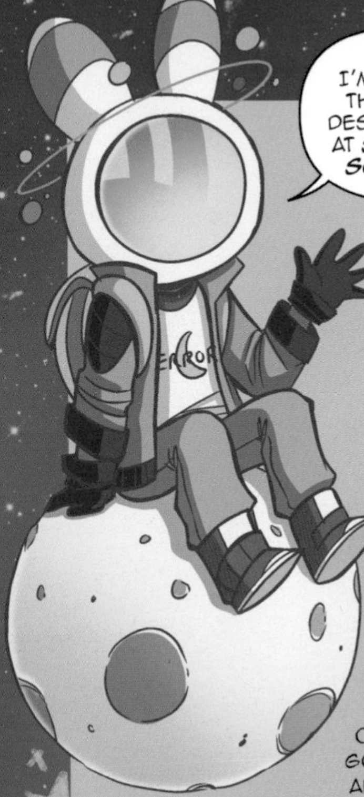
HELLO! I'M M.GOODWIN, THE NARRATIVE DESIGN DIRECTOR AT SYSTEM ERA SOFTWORKS.
THANK YOU SO MUCH FOR READING AND SUPPORTING OUR BOOK!
THIS WAS TRULY A LABOR OF LOVE AND A PROJECT WE HOPE ALL FANS OF ASTRONEER WILL ENJOY.

ABOUT THE BOOK

HERE AT *SYSTEM ERA*, WE'RE PASSIONATE ABOUT INSPIRING DREAMS OF A BRIGHT FUTURE, BUT BACK WHEN I STARTED WORK ON THIS BOOK IN 2020... THAT WAS A DIFFICULT STORY TO IMAGINE. IT WAS SOMETHING THAT *DAVE DWONCH* AND I DISCUSSED OFTEN WHEN WE WERE LAYING DOWN THE FOUNDATIONS FOR *COUNTDOWN* AND THE *BOREAS SYSTEM CREW.* INDIVIDUALLY, ASTRONEERS CAN DO AMAZING THINGS, BUT IT'S THROUGH THEIR STRONG BONDS OF FRIENDSHIP AND COMMUNITY TOWARDS A SHARED GOAL THAT REALLY SET THE STARS WITHIN THEIR REACH AND MAKE THE DARK TIMES EASIER TO GET THROUGH.

TO QUOTE ONE OF OUR FOUNDERS, BRENDAN WILSON: PEOPLE CAN LOOK UP AT THE STARS AND THINK "NONE OF THIS MATTERS, WE'RE DOOMED TO DESTROY OURSELVES" OR, THEY CAN LOOK UP AND THINK "WE COULD HAVE A FUTURE OUT THERE, AND I WANT TO HELP REALIZE IT." THE UNIVERSE IN ASTRONEER IS NOT A UTOPIA, BUT ONE IN WHICH THERE ARE PEOPLE WHO NOT ONLY BELIEVE IN A POSITIVE FUTURE, BUT WHO ARE WORKING *TOGETHER* TO MAKE IT HAPPEN.

THIS BOOK CERTAINLY WOULDN'T HAVE HAPPENED WITHOUT THE AMAZING WORK OF DAVE DWONCH, DAVID PEPOSE, XENIA PAMFIL, JEREMY LAWSON, AND ERYK DONOVAN; THE SUPPORT WE'VE RECEIVED FROM OUR PARTNERS AT TITAN COMICS, JAKE, CALUM, AND DUNCAN; OUR EVO AGENTS, KIRSTI AND TREVOR; AND OF COURSE: THE SUPPORT OF EVERYONE AT THE STUDIO, OUR ASTRONEER COMMUNITY (HI, FRIENDS!), AND OUR WONDERFUL READERS...LIKE *YOU*!

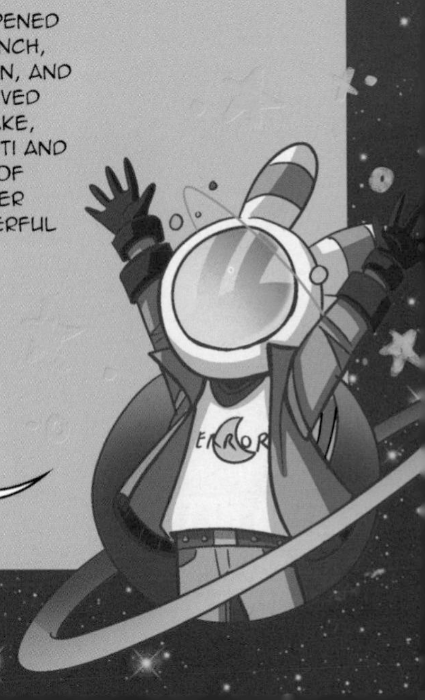
WE HOPE YOU'VE ENJOYED THE STORIES WITHIN ASTRONEER: COUNTDOWN AND THAT YOU'LL JOIN US AGAIN IN THE ASTRONEER UNIVERSE AS WE CONTINUE INTO THE FUTURE.
ALL HAIL, LORD ZEBRA!

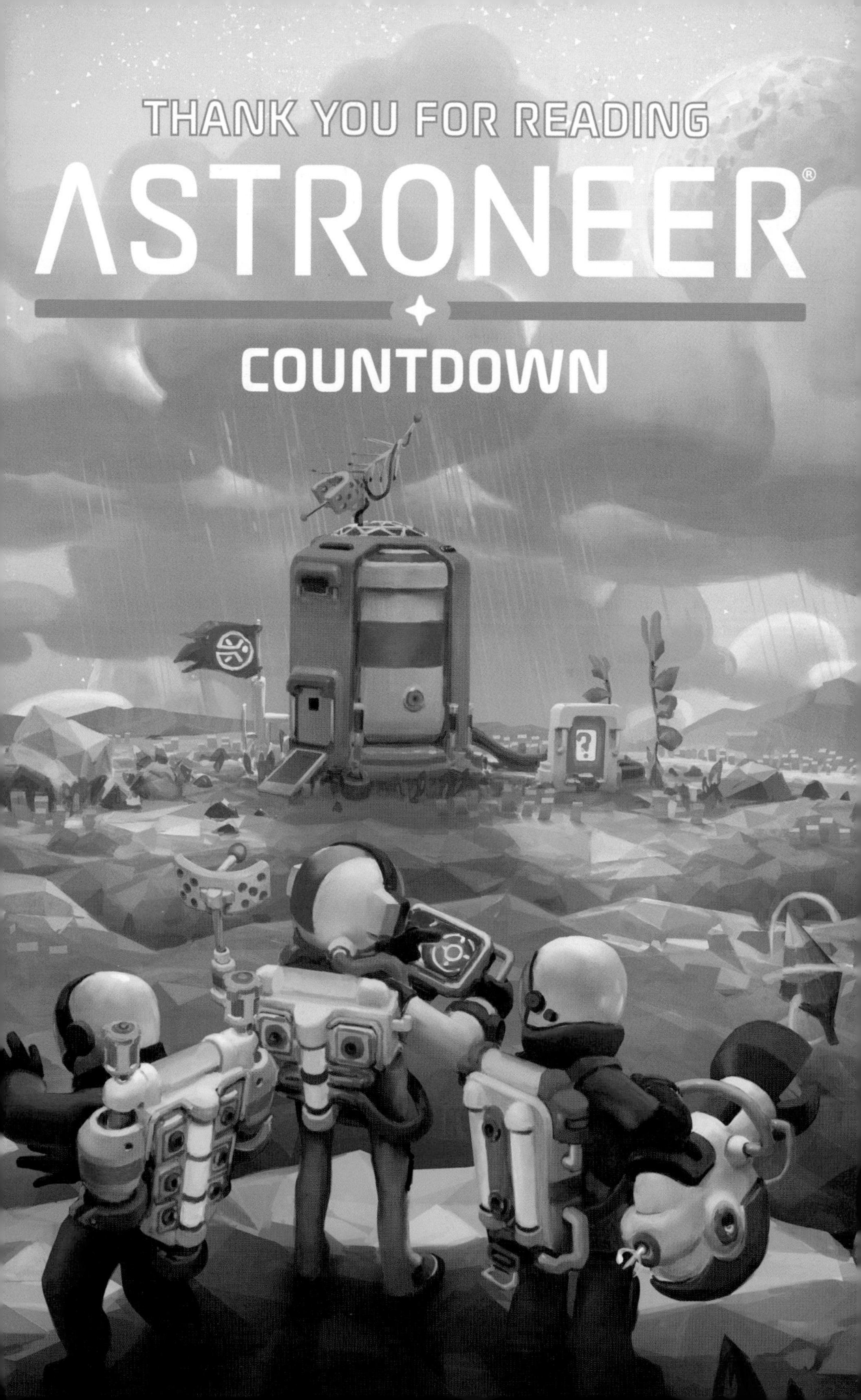
THANK YOU FOR READING
ASTRONEER®
COUNTDOWN

NEXT LEVEL
GRAPHIC NOVELS

DARK SOULS: THE COMPLETE COLLECTION

LIFE IS STRANGE VOL.6 SETTLING DUST

BLOODBORNE VOL. 5 LADY OF THE LANTERNS

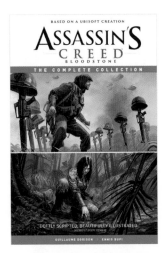

HORIZON ZERO DAWN VOL.2 LIBERATION

ASSASSIN'S CREED: BLOODSTONE COLLECTION

SEA OF THIEVES ORIGINS: CHAMPION OF SOULS

FOR THE
GAMER IN YOU!

WATCHDOGS

SEA OF THIEVES ORIGINS

LITTLE NIGHTMARES

**WOLFENSTEIN:
THE DEEP**

**THE EVIL WITHIN VOL.2
THE INTERLUDE**

**DISHONORED:
THE WYRMWOOD DECEIT**

CREATOR BIOS

DAVE DWONCH has been a writer and artist producing comics for over a decade. In 2010 he founded Action Lab Entertainment and as Creative Director, helped produce several of their titles including the Eisner nominated series Princeless, for which he served as Editor. He has penned several titles, most notably Vamplets for Scholastic, Cyrus Perkins and the Haunted Taxi Cab, CBR's Top 100 series Double Jumpers, and the coming-of-age-horror/dramedy, SPORES: Prom of the Dead. He's currently working on Jenny Zero for Dark Horse. Dave lives in Los Angeles with his very supportive wife and three loving cats.

XENIA PANFIL studied fine arts at the Arts University in Iasi, Romania before getting the opportunity to attend the Manchester Metropolitan University in the UK for computer graphics. Her comic credits include the Princeless spin-off, Raven the Pirate Princess from Action Lab, Rainbow Brite from Dynamite Comics, and Mishka and the Sea Devil, which she also wrote. She has also adapted folk tales like Povestea Porcului by Ion Creanga in short comic form for children's publications. Xenia works as an art teacher, creating comic curriculums for children in Romania and rarely sleeps.

A former crime reporter turned comic book professional, **DAVID PEPOSE** is the Ringo Award-nominated writer of Savage Avengers, Spencer&Locke, Scout's Honor, The O.Z, Going to the Chapel, and more. In addition to developing properties for comics, TV, and film, he has also worked for CBS, Netflix, and Universal Studios. Raised in St. Louis, David currently resides in sunny Los Angeles, where he lives with his understanding partner, their rambunctious terrier, and at least six deadlines. Follow him on Twitter @peposed

ERYK DONOVAN is a comic author & illustrator known for his expressive ink work, approachable characters, and thematic compositions. His work first debuted in 2014 with Boom! Studio's GLAAD Award Nominated series MEMETIC, alongside writer James Tynion IV. Eryk's work can be seen in various publications, including the surreal afterlife erotic action/romance series HEAVY with Vault Comics, the critically acclaimed APOCALYPTIC Trilogy for Boom! Studios, CONSTANTINE: The Hellblazer & GOTHAM CITY GARAGE for DC Comics, QUANTUM TEENS ARE GO for Black Mask, and the Eisner and Harvey nominated IN THE DARK: Anthology for IDW publishing, amongst others. He currently resides in Portland, OR.

JEREMY LAWSON is a cartoonist from Texas currently hangin' in Denver, Colorado. He spends most of his time drawing cute sword boys and monsters, tinkering with retro gaming handhelds, and playing with his miniature dachshund, Hector. His current book is *Imp King*, a queer comedy adventure about friendship and booty. He's down for chatting on social media (but don't be creepy) or via email at jeremy@impkingcomics.com twitter (@friendship sage) | instagram (@friendshipsage)

M. GOODWIN is an award-winning story and sequential arts professional working in comics, narrative design, education, and IP development. Previously, they worked for Retro Studios, Playful Studios, and Trendy Entertainment in story development for games, Ocean Park Hong Kong on Theme Park Design, as a professor of sequential art both in the U.S and in Hong Kong, and their 2016 top 100 comic series Tomboy is currently optioned for television. M is now the Narrative Design Director and Transmedia Manager at System Era Softworks and survives mostly on coffee and horror films.